Recipe
for Love

Katie FFORDE

Recipe for Love

CENTURY · LONDON

Published by Century in 2012

2 4 6 8 10 9 7 5 3 1

Copyright © Katie Fforde Ltd 2012

First published in Great Britain in 2012 by Century
Random House, 20 Vauxhall Bridge Road
London SW1V 2SA

www.randomhouse.co.uk

Addresses for companies within The Random House Group Limited can be found at:
www.randomhouse.co.uk/offices.htm

The Random House Group Limited Reg. No. 954009

A CIP catalogue record for this book
is available from the British Library

ISBN 9781846056529

The Random House Group Limited supports The Forest Stewardship Council
(FSC®), the leading international forest certification organisation. Our books
carrying the FSC label are printed on FSC® certified paper. FSC is the only forest
certification scheme endorsed by the leading environmental organisations,
including Greenpeace. Our paper procurement policy can be found at
www.randomhouse.co.uk/environment

Typeset in Palatino by Palimpsest Book Production Limited,
Falkirk, Stirlingshire

Printed and bound by CPI Group (UK) Ltd, Croydon CR0 4YY

To Frank Fforde and Heidi Cawley with
much love and gratitude.
Also to Téo Fforde just because he's there.

Acknowledgements

Writers are like snowballs, they go through life picking up bits of knowledge – often without knowing they're doing it. But there are several people who I know made real contributions to this book. In no particular order:

Elizabether Garret for Cliff Cottage which really helped to prevent deadline panic.

Judy Astley and Kate Lace, who helped Cliff Cottage with the deadline assistance.

Edd Kimber @theboywhobakes who was jolly helpful about cookery competitions.

Liz Godsell for telling me about cheese.

Heidi Cawley for telling me about delis, for making her own pancetta and for taking me shopping, also for learning about cupcakes with me.

Frank Fforde who helped with professional kitchen advice and for telling me you can make a quick custard with white chocolate.

Helen Child Villiers – Chepstow Cupcakes – who taught me how to make them and mocked my efforts

Molly Haynes, who, when I appealed on Twitter for a canapé recipe, responded with something truly delicious.

Karin Cawley, for producing bread pudding so delicious I had to put it in the book. She also produced Heidi, which was even more clever.

As always my wonderful husband and research assistant, Desmond Fforde, who continues to put up with me.

And not forgetting Briony Fforde who keeps me in order and makes me laugh. Nothing runs smoothly without laughter.

Recipe
for Love

Chapter One

Zoe Harper lay on the bank in the sun with her eyes closed, listening to a lark high above her. Nearer her ear she could hear the crackling of the grass and the buzzing of insects. The weather had been changeable recently in typical British-weather fashion, but today it was a perfect early summer's day.

Warned that Sat Nav didn't work in the area she'd allowed far too much getting-lost time and arrived far too early at the venue. She'd wondered if she was in the right place as the huge old mansion seemed to be undergoing some fairly major restoration, going by large sections of scaffolding and several contractors' vans parked in the drive. Fenella Gainsborough, heavily pregnant, confirmed that she was, and, obviously not ready for her guests yet, had thrust a map into Zoe's hands and sent her out for a walk. Zoe, relieved that she had reached her destination, was happy to leave her car and explore on foot. As none of the other contestants had arrived yet – they were not expected till the early evening – she'd set off alone.

Now she tried to relax but in spite of the sun on her eyelids she was finding it hard. Her walk from Somerby House had used up some of her nervous energy but she was still full of adrenalin. Excited about the impending cookery competition she'd been so thrilled to win a place on, she was also a bundle of nerves. It didn't help that it was also being filmed, prior to being televised later in the year. Zoe consoled herself with the thought that at least it wasn't going out live. She still couldn't quite believe she'd made it through the rigorous selection process. She'd only entered on the insistence of her mother and her best friend, Jenny, but now, here she was in a field in the middle of nowhere feeling as if she was about to go to her execution. She sighed and stretched. She'd do better to breathe deeply and try and doze.

Just as the peace of the English meadow was finally beginning to work its magic she heard a car in the lane below her and was suddenly fully awake.

The car went past and then stopped. It had obviously reached the gate blocking the lane. Zoe had reached it herself about half an hour ago and had decided against climbing over it. A large notice saying 'Trespassers keep out' had helped her in her decision.

Zoe waited and then heard the car reverse throatily. It would have to reverse all the way back down the lane unless it was small, and it didn't sound small. It stopped and she heard the gear change. Just as she realised what it intended, she sat up and started down the bank. There was a ditch, hidden by long grasses. She wouldn't have found it herself if she hadn't nearly stumbled into it.

Too late. By the time she had reached the lane, brushing bits of vegetation off her jeans, the car's back wheel was hovering over the ditch. The front end was nearly in the ditch on the other side of the lane. The driver got out of the car and slammed the door.

'Bloody stupid place to put a ditch,' he growled.

He was a fairly impressive figure. Tall and broad with dark hair, he had the air of a person who was not accustomed to being thwarted by civil engineering.

Zoe wanted to laugh but managed to shrug instead. 'A

2

fairly usual place I'd have thought, by the side of the road, draining the water away.'

The man glared at her. 'Don't try and baffle me with logic. What am I going to do?'

It was probably a rhetorical question but Zoe, who was very literal-minded, said, 'Call the AA, RAC, something like that?'

He scowled. 'Do I look like the sort of man who's a member of the AA?'

Zoe considered. She hadn't thought there was a typical look to a member of a roadside rescue service but as she studied him more closely she noticed his curly, slightly too long hair was actually a very dark red. He had green eyes and curving mouth and a large, slightly hooked nose. She couldn't decide if he was very handsome or really quite ugly, but she did have to admit he was extremely sexy. He looked like the kind of man who assumed he'd never break down.

'What am I do to?' he said, again rhetorically.

He triggered the devil in Zoe. She knew he was expecting her not to answer, or just to offer to go for help, but she decided to tease him. She felt slightly light-headed.

'Well, there're quite a lot of branches by the gate. Maybe we could pile them up under the wheel and you could reverse enough to turn.' In spite of her desire to provoke him, it was a genuine suggestion.

'You are a practical little thing, aren't you?' he said, making it seem as if it was bad to be practical, but he set off down the lane in the direction she'd pointed and then called imperiously over his shoulder. 'Come on. I'll need you.'

Infuriated at his manner – 'little thing'? – yet pleased to be doing something active so her nerves about the upcoming competition could be worked off, Zoe followed

3

him. But as she went she chided herself; this could get her into serious trouble.

She'd worked out who he was by now – who else would be so close to Somerby who wasn't going there? And this man – arrogant and argumentative – had to be one of the judges. He could never be a mere contestant in a cookery competition. And as she knew the other judges by sight from their television appearances, this could only be Gideon Irving. He was a well-known name in the world of food, as a critic, food writer and entrepreneur. His writing style was acerbic and often cruel, but he loved to discover new chefs and had brought a lot of young talent to the notice of the restaurant-going public.

She hadn't been exactly rude but she had leant a bit in that direction. She wouldn't win the competition now. And wouldn't being alone with one of the judges – however innocently – be against the rules? Why oh why hadn't she just stayed lying in the grass, listening to the larks? She ran to catch him up.

They found some biggish logs as well as the branches. Some clearing had been done nearby, most of the tree trunks had been removed but quite a lot remained.

'I'll take some of the larger bits of timber and you bring what you can carry,' he said.

She nodded and began gathering up the bits of birch, fir and beech that lay about.

'If this doesn't work,' she said, finding it hard to keep up with him even though his arms were full of logs, 'we could go to the house and ask them to send a tractor or something.'

'We could,' Gideon Irving agreed, 'but we'll try this first.' He didn't quite smile at her but the speculative look he shot her indicated he liked what he saw.

Zoe wasn't her own biggest fan but her short, curly

brown hair, small frame, pale skin and freckles hadn't given her any complexes. She knew she could scrub up fairly well, only today she wasn't scrubbed up at all. She was wearing her jeans, plimmies and a striped Breton top. She never wore much make-up but currently wasn't wearing any. She had blue eyes and dark lashes, and knew her size made her look younger than twenty-seven.

'OK.'

Together they piled the wood into the ditch, building a platform for the overhanging wheel. They didn't speak much but Zoe was enjoying herself. She liked problem-solving and when she spotted some stones that had fallen out of a wall, went to get them.

Her thanks was a glance and a grunt but somehow she felt rewarded. He did have amazing eyes. She felt a flutter of excitement.

'The question is, do we have to do this all over again in the other ditch?' he asked.

'Yes,' she said. She had been considering this while she worked. 'But now we've got the stones it won't take so long.'

Zoe was filthy and fairly sweaty by the time they'd finished. He'd long since thrown off his jacket and his white T-shirt was covered in mud.

'Can you drive?' he demanded.

'Yes.'

'Follow simple instructions?'

'Yes.' Yet again, Zoe decided not to take offence. It was easier to just get in the car. Really, she wanted to laugh but sensed that would not be a good move. Men really didn't like being laughed at when they were in trouble with their cars. She was no expert on men, but even she knew that.

The car smelt slightly of rather delicious cologne and

leather upholstery. It had a dashboard which took a moment to understand.

He loomed over her as he spoke through the open window. 'You accelerate – gently – and we'll see what happens.'

Some moments and a fair amount of mud later, he came back to the window and scowled at her.

She smiled back sympathetically. 'I can still walk back to the house and get help.' Zoe looked up at him. He was sweating too now and a lock of hair was caught on his forehead.

He shook his head. 'I'll walk back if it comes to that.' He paused, inspecting her, his gaze inscrutable. 'Try reversing.'

It took quite a lot of backing and edging forward and ditch-filling but at last the car was turned round. Zoe felt she'd run a marathon. She got out and found she was trembling although she'd only been driving.

'Well done,' he said, and then smiled. She felt as if she'd just won Gold in the hundred metres.

'Like a lift back to the house?' He was still smiling.

'Oh . . . yes,' she said, unsure if her legs were shaking because of what she'd just been through or something else.

'So get in then,' he said when she didn't move.

Somehow she made her body function and got in the car. Now the sharp smell of man overlaid the cologne and the leather. Zoe moistened her dry lips and looked firmly out of the passenger window. Being so close to him seemed almost too much although she wasn't entirely sure why. He had a very unsettling effect on her. She wasn't sure whether she liked it or not.

At the bottom of the long drive, he stopped the car. 'Are you a contestant?'

She nodded. 'Are you a judge?' she asked although she knew the answer.

He nodded. 'Better get out here then,' he said.

'Yup.' She paused. 'Maybe we'd better pretend we haven't met before.'

'If you like,' he said, 'but it won't make any difference to how I judge you.'

'Oh.' She blushed. 'Not that I thought it would. I just wanted to help.'

'And you did.' He almost smiled. 'But it won't make you win.'

'I'll get out now,' said Zoe.

'And I'll have a drive around the lanes.'

Zoe walked up the hill to the house, her legs stiff after their exertion. Somerby was a big house, but not imposing It was as friendly-looking as its owner had seemed on first meeting.

Brushing off flecks of mud and grass, she knocked on the front door and waited a little while for Fenella to answer. When she did, she didn't seem very pleased to see her. Several dogs streamed out of the door and on to the grass in front of the house.

'Oh! You're back already!'

'I'm afraid so,' said Zoe. 'You said four o'clock before you wanted to see me again. And it's four o'clock now.'

Fenella sighed and brushed her hair back from her face. 'I would really like it to go on being two o'clock for a lot longer.'

Zoe laughed. 'One of those days?'

Fenella nodded. 'However hard you try to plan and prepare and make lists, some days just go wrong anyway.'

Zoe hovered on the doorstep. 'Has anything in particular gone wrong?'

'No, just nothing has gone particularly right.' She sighed again. 'It's because Rupert – that's my husband – is away.'

'Bad timing!'

'Yes! And I've got the judges' tea to do and my careful plans for there to be a cake have gone wrong. I haven't even got time to buy one now.'

'Oh.'

Fenella held the door wider. 'Do come in. None of this is your problem. I'm sure soggy digestive biscuits are just what snobby foody people like with their afternoon tea.'

'Absolutely!' Zoe agreed diplomatically.

'We're hoping to have a "restaurant with rooms" type thing in the barn. We might need the snobby foody people on our side.' She paused for breath and looked at Zoe properly. 'What happened to you? You look like you've been mud-wrestling!'

'I know. I have. Well, sort of.'

Possibly sensing Zoe didn't want to go into details Fenella went on, 'Let me show you to your room so you can get cleaned up. Of course you know you have to share, but at least you're in the grounds. Dogs!'

The small pack came lolloping into the house and Fenella led Zoe through the back and out across the court-yard to the converted cowshed where Zoe and another contestant were to be billeted. Not all of them could be accommodated at Somerby: some were in local B and Bs. The cowshed was charming and had a wood-burning stove, a little cooker, a dinky sofa and a double bed. A single bed had been squeezed in, presumably for the sake of the contestants. 'You're here first,' said Fenella, 'so you get the double bed!'

'Fab! But a shower first, I think.'

Fenella said, 'It's through there. Do you mind if I don't show you? I've got this bloody tea to sort out.'

Zoe sensed that Fenella didn't usually swear about small things – she must be really panicking. 'Look,' she said, 'why don't I shower and change and then come and make you some scones or something? What time are they coming?'

Fenella looked at her watch. 'In three-quarters of an hour. No time to make anything.' She sighed. 'A girlfriend from the village was coming up with a cake. I had it all organised but one of her children is ill and she can't leave him.'

'I'll just wash my hands and come. Scones don't take that long.'

Fenella made a face that was intended to be firm and denying but ended up pleading. 'I couldn't ask you to do that!'

'You didn't and I'd rather be active. It was only when I got here – the first time – that I realised how absolutely terrified I am of this whole competition thing.' She meant it: she'd always hated exams but at least exams didn't involve television cameras. 'I'll be better if I'm doing something.'

'So I'd be doing you a favour letting you help?'

Zoe chuckled. 'Sort of. Although I suppose I'd better find something clean to put on.'

'I'll lend you one of Rupert's shirts. I've been living in them. They'll cover you better than operating theatre scrubs.'

After dumping her rucksack Zoe followed Fenella back to the main house. She noted a few ladders leaning up against random walls and that quite a bit of work still needed to be done on some of the outhouses, but it was all very picturesque. Somerby itself would be a beautiful backdrop to the competition and it was a very photogenic time of year.

'This is probably horribly against the rules,' said Fenella after she'd found flour, butter and eggs for Zoe. 'We'd better not tell anyone. I mean if the judges found out that they were eating your scones and they were delicious—'

'Which they will be. Baking is my speciality.'

'—it would look like we were trying to give you an advantage or something.'

Zoe nodded. 'I agree. I just won't let anyone see me.'

Fenella suddenly looked doubtful again. 'Are you sure you want to do this?'

'Oh yes! Doing something practical is so much better than sitting around chewing my nails.' Or helping stranded motorists, however attractive, she thought. 'I know what I'm doing in a kitchen with a bit of flour and a half-decent oven.'

The scones were too hot to fill with jam and cream so they were in separate bowls on the laden tray. Fenella had wanted to do this but Zoe – her knowledge of pregnancy sketchy – felt she knew enough to insist carrying heavy trays up flights of stairs wasn't a good idea. She'd carry them up and then retreat to the kitchen and let Fenella face the judges. That way she should avoid being seen.

She was just setting things out before going back down for extra hot water when she heard voices and knew she was about to get caught.

She had a moment of panic but then she calmed down. Unless it was Gideon Irving she'd be fine. She wouldn't make eye contact, she'd whisk out of the room before anyone took in what she looked like.

As the voices got nearer she realised it wouldn't be quite that simple.

'Got stuck in a bloody ditch,' said a gravelly voice she knew quite well now. 'Luckily a passing rambler helped me out.'

She turned her head away and carried on putting out plates, setting cups on their saucers on the little table in the window. She was swathed in white poplin, courtesy of Rupert, and doubted if she would be recognised. People didn't recognise others if they didn't expect to see then.

'Yes,' Gideon went on, 'she was only a slip of a thing but could drive a car and heft logs like a weightlifter.'

Zoe felt herself blush at the back-handed compliment. She doubted Gideon would say that to her face.

'So who was she again?' The other male judge, an amiable chef who went into housewives' kitchens and taught them how to make gravy, moved towards the table.

'Just someone on a walk. I don't see the point of walking myself, if you don't need to get anywhere.'

Thankfully, Fenella then appeared and said, 'Help yourselves to tea, gentlemen.'

Zoe scuttled away, muttering, 'I'll just get some hot water.'

Zoe had had a Saturday job in a café for years and was quite happy dealing with customers. What she wasn't so happy about was trying not to be seen. She didn't do subterfuge and now she had two secrets – both because she couldn't help being helpful. Her mother had said she'd been born with a helpful gene. It was a virtue really, but just now it seemed like a vice.

Just as Zoe was about to return with the hot water, Fenella reappeared. 'Oh thank you,' she said. 'Would you mind taking it up? I don't think anyone noticed you, did they?'

She was about to say that Gideon might but then remembered Fenella wasn't to know that she and Gideon had

11

already met – and Fenella *was* pregnant. She didn't have a choice. She took the jug. 'I'll be back.'

'Now what do you have to do, Fen?' she asked when she got back again. (Fenella had insisted Zoe call her Fen, saying no one called her Fenella unless they were cross with her.) Luckily Gideon and the other judge had been too deep in conversation to notice her. She was enjoying herself. She knew the nerves she'd been keeping at bay would come flooding back the moment she returned to her room. This had been just the distraction she'd needed.

Fenella sighed. 'Oh, nothing much at all. Put some spuds into the Aga for supper. You're all going to the pub to eat and the judges and telly people are eating here. Then there's the official meeting afterwards? Or before.' She frowned. 'Honestly, the production company is dreadfully bossy. I gave them some names of lovely local taxi drivers but no, they had to get people down from London to do it. Mad!'

She pushed a lock of hair back from her forehead, making Zoe long to lend her a hair slide. 'Anyway, I'm now cooking for the scary judges and the local pub, who is quite used to doing this, is cooking for you lot.'

'Why?'

'It's Rupert's fault. He told the TV people it's easier to cook for six than twelve, but it's become more than six with all the producers and things.' She paused. 'And he should be back to help with it. The stew's done already. I just have to do the veg really.' She leant against the kitchen table. 'You can imagine how nerve-racking it is, cooking for famous chefs and a food critic.'

'I can imagine it only too well, considering that's what this competition is all about.' Zoe thought Fenella looked really tired and, seeing her put her hand on her stomach, wondered if she was all right. 'Supposing Rupert isn't back in time?'

'I'm sure he will be.' She didn't sound very sure.

Zoe made a decision. Fenella – whom she'd liked from the start – needed her. 'I'll prep the potatoes for you. What veg are you having?'

'Things out of the garden: baby broad beans, some cabbage – and some asparagus from down the road. It's all local stuff.'

'Are you doing a starter?'

'Soup. Rupert has made it all as easy as possible.'

'So, do you want me to help?'

Fen chewed her lip and sighed. She fiddled with a pen out of a pot on the kitchen table. Indecision was written all over her. 'Only if Rupert doesn't turn up. You do have to be at your dinner. I've seen your schedule. It's for briefing, getting to know each other, vital stuff.' She paused. 'But if Rupert isn't here it would be wonderful if you could just help in the beginning.' Fenella smiled. 'The minibus isn't collecting you until eight. My dinner is at seven thirty.'

'So in theory I could get the stuff upstairs for you and then dash down in time to get on the bus.'

Fenella nodded. 'When we've got the dining room restored we'll have a dumb waiter for me to put things on but as it's not such a nice room we haven't done it yet.'

'Well, I don't mind being the dumb waiter.'

Fenella gave a half-smile and lowered herself into a chair. 'I know I shouldn't say yes,' she said, 'but I can't seem to help myself.' She put on a fierce expression. 'And I know perfectly well you're putting off thinking about the competition by rushing round being helpful.'

Zoe sat down next to her. 'I know.'

'I wouldn't normally beat myself up about accepting help but if you're breaking some rule or other you could ruin your chances of winning it. You might even be thrown out before you start!'

'But we don't know it's against any rule, and no one will notice, I'm sure. I got away with it at the tea, didn't I?' She giggled. 'I could wear an apron and a little mob cap, as disguise.'

'Don't joke about it!' said Fenella. 'I happen to have those very items! We did an Edwardian Tea last year and we all dressed up as maids.'

Zoe laughed. 'I'll do the spuds now and clean the other veg and then I suppose I'd better settle in over the road.'

'Your room-mate is there. She came while you were upstairs.'

'Oh, what's she like?'

'Very glam. I hope you put your bag on the double bed!'

Chapter Two

When Zoe got back to the cowshed she found it occupied
by a very lovely blonde woman of about her own age
who looked more like a model than a cook. Apart from
the age, Zoe couldn't discern any other similarities
between them. The other girl was tall, with long straight
subtly highlighted hair, a lot of make-up including false
eyelashes, a tiny skirt and a strappy top, although it wasn't
all that warm. Her shoes, kicked off now because she was
lying on the double bed, were high strappy sandals.

Zoe smiled, determined that the superficial differences
between the two of them shouldn't mean that they
couldn't co-habit happily.

'Hi! I'm Zoe,' she said.

'Cher,' said the model-alike. 'I hope you don't mind me
having the double bed. I can't sleep in single beds.'

'Oh? But you're so thin, it can't be that they're not big
enough.'

Cher had a silver laugh, a little too high-pitched for
Zoe's taste. 'No! Not that, but I need to spread out. It's
having such long legs.'

'You're not expecting me to be sorry for you because
you've got long legs, surely?'

'No,' said Cher sharply, 'but I do expect you to let me
have the double bed.'

Zoe blinked at Cher's sudden change of tone but
decided against having an argument along the lines of 'I

was here first' as they weren't schoolgirls and if they had to share it would be better if they at least got on superficially. She could see she'd have to pick her battles with Cher and this was one she didn't feel was worth a fight.

'OK.' She went to her rucksack, dumped unceremoniously on the single bed. She opened it and began taking out her things. There wasn't very much and she didn't usually bother to unpack, but some deeply hidden territorial instinct made her want to spread her spoor.

The wardrobe was full of Cher's clothes. Tiny skirts, a couple of pairs of shorts (in case of a heat wave, obviously) and some skinny jeans. Many pairs of strappy sandals and handbags littered the floor of the cupboard.

Zoe hung up her one dress, a couple of pairs of jeans and some shirts and tops, then she took out her wash bag. 'I must have a shower and wash my hair.' She went into the bathroom, hoping her room-mate hadn't used all the towels.

She was just drying her hair with her fingers, her normal method, when Cher, who was lying on the bed watching, said, 'I've got a hair dryer if you want to borrow it.'

Zoe turned round. 'Thanks, but I never bother to dry it. It doesn't take long if I just scrunch it.'

Cher got up. 'You'd look much better if you blow-dried it. Quite different. I'll do it for you if you like.'

'It's OK, thanks. I decided years ago not to have a style that depended on electrical appliances, in case I don't have access to them.'

Cher shrugged as if Zoe were mad. 'I did hairdressing for a bit,' she said.

Zoe tried to decide if she liked her or not. She seemed like a WAG, only interested in her looks and people thinking she was pretty. But the offer to help with her hair had been kind. Maybe she just couldn't bear to see

Zoe's hair all tousled and unkempt, which might mean she was a control freak.

'So what made you enter the competition?' asked Zoe, deciding it was time to find out something about her room-mate.

'Oh, I want to be on television. I really want to be famous and I think if I can get seen, I'll get other offers.'

Zoe looked at her in surprise. 'Don't you like cooking?'

Cher shrugged. 'Not much.'

'But you passed the audition?'

'Oh yes. I'm good, I just don't enjoy it that much. I don't like getting my fingers mucky.' She paused and looked at Zoe as if somehow connecting her with the word mucky. 'At least put on a bit of make-up and a dress. I don't want to be associated with a munter.'

Zoe could hardly believe her ears, and had to bite back a retort, remembering her resolve to try and get on with Cher. She pulled on her dress, grudgingly admitting to herself that Cher, although unbelievably rude, could be right: it might be a good idea for first impressions. She looked at her watch. It was now nearly seven o'clock and she wanted an excuse to leave so she could help Fenella. She might have started being helpful to work off her nerves but now she was enjoying feeling part of it. 'I might go for a wander. It's very pretty round here.'

As Zoe had predicted, Cher didn't suggest coming with her. 'I don't do walking. Wrong sort of shoes.'

Zoe glanced at Cher's feet. 'I'm surprised you can cook in those. How do you cope with all the standing?' She couldn't quite imagine Cher in the sort of clogs a lot of cooks wore; her own pair were in her rucksack. She hadn't noticed any in the wardrobe amongst all the heels. Nor could she imagine Cher in check trousers. But then again Zoe didn't wear those either.

'I wear trainers to cook in. Not that I do a lot of it.'

That made Zoe even more curious. 'But how did you get into a cookery competition if you don't do much cooking?'

Cher got up from the bed and flicked her hair behind her shoulder. 'I just make sure that what I do do is very good.' She gave Zoe a smile. 'I intend to win, you know.' She went to the mirror and inspected herself closely. 'I always achieve what I set out to do – get a job, get a man, whatever. This time I'm going to be famous, which means I *have* to win the competition.'

Cher's dedication was scary. 'So why a cookery competition if you don't like it? Why not – I don't know – *The X Factor*, or *Britain's Next Top Model?*'

'I thought of them, of course, but there'll be far less competition if I do cookery.'

'What on earth makes you think that? There could be some really great cooks in this! Me for a start!'

'It's not all about the cooking. I've seen how contestants flirt with the judges.' She regarded Zoe with something resembling pity. 'I told you, I can cook well if I put my mind to it. I might not be the best cook here, but I will be the prettiest, the sexiest, so I'll win. Although you look loads better now than you did before, don't think you're in with a chance.'

Zoe regarded her. After what Cher had said before, her bluntness was no longer a surprise. 'That's me told!' she said with forced cheerfulness.

'So why did you enter?' Cher asked, turning away from the mirror, having obviously decided you couldn't perfect perfection.

'Oh, I want to win too. I want the money to set up a little deli or bistro or something where I can cook the food I love. What do you want to do with the money?'

'The money's not remotely important. My father's really rich. I just want the fame and the opportunities that'll bring me.'

'Well, may the best cook win,' said Zoe, her flippant manner disguising her ever-increasing determination to beat this woman at the competition even if it killed her. And not just because she wanted the double bed.

'So did you give up a good job and a lovely boyfriend to come on this?' asked Cher. 'I do a bit of events management, by the way, although Daddy gives me an allowance I can just about live off.'

'I had an OK job in an estate agent's, but someone was promoted over me even though I'd been there for ages so I didn't mind giving it up.' She was still slightly sore about the whole episode but she wasn't one for regrets and anyway, she really did want to run her own business.

'And the boyfriend? I can see you going out with the same boy from school before settling down and having kids.' She yawned. 'So not for me!'

'Not me either,' said Zoe, infuriated by this assumption although still determined not to show it. 'I decided a while ago not to pin my chance of happiness on a man. If someone wonderful comes along and sweeps me off my feet, I guess I'd go along with it, but they'd have to be really special.'

Zoe thought back to her rather uneventful relationship history: a short list of very nice, decent young men. She'd been fond of them all but there hadn't been one she had felt she really couldn't live without. A picture of Gideon all mud-splattered and sweaty sprang into her mind at this point but she dismissed it as quickly as it had appeared.

Cher was nodding. 'Respec', sista! I feel that way myself. No point in signing one's life away for someone who turns out to be a no-hoper.' She walked over to the little fridge. 'I've got a bottle of wine. Fancy a glass?'

'No thanks. I'll keep my head clear for tomorrow. I'll have that walk now.' Zoe suddenly felt she needed some air. She also wanted to check on Fenella.

As she walked over to the house she chuckled to herself. Cher was extraordinary but there was no point in being indignant at her wild pronouncements and steely determination to win. She and Cher had to share a room together, which would be impossible if she got upset and made trouble.

Slightly apprehensive about being seen by the crew and judges, Zoe was relieved to spot a large man in the kitchen, which meant Fenella wasn't on her own. The large man – rather to her surprise – gave her a bear hug and kissed her fondly.

'Thank you so much for helping my pregnant wife!' he said. 'For that you deserve rubies, coffers of gold but failing those, what about a glass of red? Or would you rather have a gin?'

'Rupert! said Fenella, looking far less stressed than when Zoe had last seen her. 'Zoe – you look lovely by the way – this, as you've probably gathered, is my husband, Rupert.'

'Hello, Rupert,' said Zoe, accepting the glass of wine he handed her and feeling a bit of a hypocrite for refusing Cher's offer with such a priggish excuse.

'Do sit down. Because you helped earlier there's no great rush and anyway, Rupert will do it.'

Zoe pulled out a chair and looked around the kitchen properly; there didn't seem to have been time before. She decided it was perfect. Huge, with an Aga the size of a car, an old dresser, a sofa, a refectory table long enough for a small school and a stone-flagged floor. There were pictures on the walls, a large bookcase full of an assortment of what looked like cookery, gardening, flower and bird books, and a lot of clutter. It felt like a proper home.

'I'd love a kitchen like this,' she said.

'I'd like it better if it didn't have a money pit to go with it,' said Rupert, having just tasted the stew and tossed the teaspoon into the sink. 'Although, of course, we do love the house too.'

'Why wouldn't you? It's wonderful!'

'It is,' agreed Fenella, 'but it's so expensive to renovate and keep up. We keep having to think up ways of earning money from it, which is why we were so thrilled to get this cookery competition gig.'

'We nearly didn't,' said Rupert, 'as we've got a wedding right in the middle of the competition.'

'Rupert! I don't think you were supposed to say that. It's a surprise. I mean, all the tasks are a surprise – the contestants aren't to be told about them till the night before.'

Zoe chuckled. 'Well, I won't tell anyone.'

'Fortunately, the wedding planner for it is a mate of ours, Sarah, and she managed to convince the couple that the enormous amount of money they'll be saving by having you lot do the catering was well worth a bit of inconvenience.' Rupert, apparently deciding he had a bit of spare time, had joined the two women at the table.

'Darling, it won't be inconvenient – we've made sure of that.'

'The food is a bit of a risk,' said Rupert. 'But it often is at weddings.'

'Not at Somerby,' said Fenella primly.

Rupert laughed and Zoe basked in the warmth of the easy banter between them. How wonderful to be secure in the knowledge that you loved and were loved in return.

When Zoe got up to go, Fenella said, 'Now do help yourself to anything from here you might need. Milk, for example. There is some in your fridge, but if you run out you can come back and get some. And there are packets of biscuits in this box here. Rupert brought in fresh supplies.'

'I wouldn't want to take anything you might have plans for.'

'Don't worry,' said Rupert. 'We have specially designated biscuits for clients. I'm not allowed near them.'

Zoe hurried back to the room and brushed her teeth so no one would smell red wine on her breath.

'Where have you been?' asked Cher curiously.

'Oh, just round and about,' said Zoe through the toothpaste, feeling unaccountably guilty.

'Well, if you don't hurry we'll miss the bus.'

A couple of hours later they were back from the pub, being ushered up the stairs to the committee room at Somerby by a slightly harried Rupert. 'Here we are!' he said, opening the door to a big room with a huge table in it. He paused as they all filed in. 'The judges are still eating I'm afraid but some of the production team are here to talk to you. I must go and serve the pud.' He left the room as fast as he decently could.

Zoe and the others sat at the chairs arranged round the table.

'Good evening, everyone!' A good-looking blonde woman with a very faint American accent, hair like Marilyn Monroe and eyes like sapphires walked into the room. The steel beneath her beauty shone through. 'My name is Miranda Marlyn. You probably all know I'm the head of the production company that is making this programme. And we are all sure that it will be a huge success – for us and for you.' She paused. 'It's going to be very intense.

As you probably know by now you'll be doing a challenge roughly every two or three days.' The tension in the room went up a notch as her gaze slid over every contestant, making Zoe, at least, feel she'd already been judged – and she hadn't won.

'We would expect you to be preparing on the other days but there will be a break somewhere in the middle. Anyway, Mike will go into more detail. I hope you've all had a chance to get to know each other during the meal. The thing to remember is that although you are competing, a lot of the tasks will involve teamwork. There'll be marks for leading a team and being a team player as well as for excellent cooking.'

Another steely stare. By now almost everyone (except Cher) was looking twitchy. Zoe enjoyed teamwork but always thought of herself as a second in command rather than a leader. Would she have the force of personality required to make a plan and get her team to follow it?

'Now I'm going to pass you over to Mike.'

Everyone clapped as she sat down.

'Hi, guys,' said Mike, who, after their pub meal, seemed like an old friend, helpful and unthreatening. 'Now, unlike some cookery competitions, you haven't yet met your judges . . .'

'We knew that,' whispered Cher, emboldened by several glasses of wine over dinner.

'. . . because the auditions were done by other people.'

'For God's sake! We were there! We know the bloody judges were too "busy"' – Cher made the movement with her fingers to indicate inverted commas – 'to turn up!' Her *sotto voce* was getting less *sotto* by the minute.

Mike's tone was consoling. 'But you are going to meet them tomorrow, and I'm sure you're all very excited about that.'

'I'm wetting myself with joy,' said Cher, no longer bothering to keep her voice down.

Fortunately for Zoe's embarrassment threshold, the rest of Mike's talk gave Cher no excuse to mutter and Zoe listened with half an ear. The rest of her thoughts lingered on the other contestants, some of whom she'd spoken to in the pub, and others just observed from a distance.

There was the wild young man with a shock of hair that stood almost upright. She'd chatted to him and found out his name was Shadrach. He was passionate about food and seemed to suit his name. Then there was motherly Muriel who had escaped her family with glee, describing herself as 'only a good home cook' but who looked to Zoe like strong competition.

Previously, Cher had sashayed her way round to where two young men sat, legs apart, feet tapping, the testosterone almost visible as if it were steam coming off sweating horses. They – Zoe knew them to be Dwaine and Daniel – practically had 'Competition' tattooed on their foreheads. Cher had done a lot of hair-flicking and lip-moistening and had allowed both of them a peek down her cleavage. That was apparently her version of team-building. And it could work, Zoe thought. But supposing they both fell in love with her? There could be a horribly noisy scrap, with blood on the carpet. Now, in her seat at the front row, Cher sent messages saying 'look at me' with her eyes, hands and hair.

Sitting just behind Zoe and Cher there was a rather serious girl whom Zoe hadn't spoken to yet. She could be a potential winner. She was shy, with mousy hair held back by an unbecoming slide but she had a determination that was evident even from a distance. She was Becca. Next to her were two older-looking men, one of whom

24

was called Bill, and Shona, who'd informed Zoe over dinner that she was a 'bag of nerves'.

'OK, people,' said Miranda Marlyn, standing up again, 'that's all you'll hear from me until the end of the competition. As Mike says, tomorrow you'll meet the judges and find out what your first task is. I should warn you all, though, that our judges will make Lord Sugar look like a teddy bear. It's a very tough business and you need to be equally tough to succeed.' She swept out, a young man with a clipboard, who was obviously her right-hand-man, in tow.

Everyone was now milling round, chatting, sizing up the opposition, as if they finally realised the competition was about to start. There were an awful lot of people to take in, thought Zoe, but with ten contestants and several people from the television company, there was bound to be.

Someone came up behind Zoe. 'Well, that was all pretty much as expected, don't you think? I'm Alan, by the way. We didn't get a chance to speak over dinner.'

Alan was medium height with thick greying hair with a hint of a tan. He seemed faintly familiar and she wondered if they'd actually met or if he was an actor or something.

'Zoe.' She put her hand into his outstretched one. 'Do I know you from somewhere? Television, perhaps?'

He inclined his head. 'It's possible. I was a jobbing actor for years, but not recently. Cooking is what I'm into now. Hence the competition.'

'So what do you hope to get from it?' Zoe was always curious about people but having asked her question wondered if she'd been a bit abrupt and so confessed her own motives. 'I'm in it for the money myself but my room-mate, Cher – over there? The beautiful blonde wowing those young men? – she's looking for fame.' She paused. 'What about you?'

Alan didn't seem to mind her asking. 'I suppose I want them both: fame *and* fortune. I fancy a riverside pub, with food. You know the sort of thing: boats moored up outside, summer food, chilled white wine, beautiful young people with platinum credit cards, who come because it's the new hot place to go.' He laughed. 'But I also want families. Somewhere granny and all the kids have a good meal in relaxed surroundings.'

Zoe smiled back at him. 'It sounds as if you've written the brochure already.'

'I admit I am being a little bit previous, but that's what I'll do if I win the competition. You?'

'I fancy a little deli with pre-cooked meals so people have the convenience of a takeaway but with really good food.'

'Oh! Lovely idea. You should get to know Gideon Irving. He's a big importer of olive oil, olives, stuff like that. You'd need that if you had a deli.'

'Oh? I thought he was a food writer.'

'He is, but he's also part of a big co-operative that sources delicatessen-type foods from all over the world. The food writing is a sort of hobby – although it is his passion.'

'How do you know all this?' Zoe was gripped.

'A cousin of mine was on some committee or other with him. Apparently he had to be bullied into being a judge.'

'Really?'

Alan nodded. 'Yes! According to my cousin he said he didn't want to eat a lot of grim recipes handed down from grannies who'd learned to cook during rationing in the War.'

'Goodness! Was your cousin actually present when he said this?' It could easily be just a rumour.

'Yup. He told the committee about how he'd been forced

26

to say yes.' He frowned slightly. 'He does sound appall-ingly arrogant.'

'He does,' Zoe agreed. She knew this much herself.

'And he can be a bit bad-tempered. Doesn't suffer fools.'

She'd picked up this much too. 'Oh.'

Alan nodded wisely. 'So better go carefully with him. Your friend Cher might find she's up against a man she can't charm.'

Zoe laughed. 'Yes, but you know what men are like – always susceptible to a leggy blonde.'

'Not all men.' Alan was giving her a look that could have just been friendly but might be significant.

Zoe thought about him. He was nice but a little old for her. Then her mind flicked to Gideon Irving. He wasn't much younger than Alan and yet she'd definitely found him attractive. Just as well she'd been warned. Although had she been told anything she didn't know? Not really, apart from about the food empire.

Gradually everyone dispersed, some to local B and Bs, and the rest to converted outbuildings.

Back in their room, Cher took so long in the bathroom that Zoe had to resort to brushing her teeth by her bed and spitting down a handy drain outside. But in the morning, after Zoe had silently condemned her as a selfish cow, Cher had chatted in a friendly way and lent Zoe a hair product that definitely helped her curls look more meant and less randomly natural. She was a tricky one, Zoe decided, as Cher stood behind her, looking into the mirror at Zoe and adjusting a last curl so every hair was perfect.

The meeting with the judges was to be held in the large marquee in the field just by the house. They found the others inside swapping notes about accommodation and wondering what the judges would be like. Almost everyone was nervous. The night before had been like a party. Now, in the marquee, slightly chilly in the early morning, it felt like a competition.

'It's like when the school hall turned into an exam room, isn't it?' Zoe whispered to Cher as they found their name badges.

Cher regarded her questioningly. 'Is it? I didn't take exams much.'

Zoe, who considered herself a fairly calm person, couldn't help being impressed by Cher's coolness. She could have been going to the movies, judging by how she behaved.

'Come on,' said Cher. 'Let's go to the front row. We won't get noticed if we sit at the back.'

Zoe, feeling there was plenty of time to be noticed, meekly followed her.

As they sat, waiting for the judges, Zoe's stomach churned with nerves and excitement. She'd already met one of them but of course she couldn't admit this to anyone. She wondered if he'd acknowledge her at all. Cher, poised and beautiful, seemingly oblivious to the tension around her, checked her French manicure for flaws, but didn't find any.

Mike came out to address them. He stood in front of a table that was obviously designed for the judges. Zoe's nerves increased. This was it; it was all about to begin in earnest. Cher was still unmoved. She also had French-manicured toenails, Zoe noticed. Zoe, whose sang-froid had long deserted her, found her hand creeping up to fiddle with her hair. Cher, obviously spotting this from the corner of her eye, shot out her own hand and held Zoe's down. No one was messing with her creation, even if she wasn't wearing it.

'OK, guys. This next bit isn't going to be televised but just a few words about that part of it.' He went on about sound and lighting guys as well as camera operators. 'You'll get used to the cameras very soon, which is good, but do please be careful not to swear. You're going to meet the judges now, and then we'll film the whole thing.'

Zoe glanced at the camera crew milling about with their equipment and clipboards. They were like a team of ants. She'd almost forgotten the television part of it all, she'd been focusing so hard on the competition, on cooking as well as she could.

'Big hand for the judges, guys . . .' finished Mike.

Everyone clapped obediently.

The first to step forward was the kindly television chef, Fred Acaster, who talked people through basic recipes with a gentleness which made the world love him. He was a little older than he'd appeared on the box but still looked friendly.

Cher, Zoe noticed, sat up a little straighter and paid him her full attention. It could have been some sort of magic ray that she projected towards him. He noticed her and smiled. Zoe couldn't quite work out what she'd done but suddenly she was shining at him without really moving. It was impressive!

The second judge was a woman, Anna Fortune. She ran a cookery school and was known to be terrifying. She'd been on a television show when a team of professional chefs had a 'back to school' experience with her and she'd been savage. Definitely the one to impress. But Cher didn't bother to connect with her.

And then came Gideon Irving. Her memory of him was when he was muddy, dishevelled and sweaty. Now his hair was still untidy but it was clean as was the T-shirt under his linen jacket. Armed with her inside information that he had not wanted to be a judge, Zoe felt his sultry grumpiness was in some way explained.

Beside her, Cher positively glowed. Zoe saw Gideon glance at her but what he thought she couldn't tell.

She had felt at once that it was the woman, Anna Fortune, who would cut through the contestants in swathes, but Cher was focused on the men. It made sense in a way. There were two men to only one woman and if you could get both of those on side, you were bound to go through. Zoe felt uncharacteristically daunted. It was one thing to cook well at home, or in the small café where she'd had her Saturday job. To do it in such an (albeit modest) public space was hard enough; to do it with a camera pointing at you was worse again.

After introducing themselves Anna Fortune dived straight in. 'Right, the first task. It's been arranged for you to take over two restaurants. You'll be put into teams and run one each. We'll appoint roles for each of you. Listen out for your names . . .'

'You can tell she runs a school, can't you?' said Cher, once again slightly too loudly for Zoe's peace of mind.

Zoe sighed. It was going to be a long meeting.

Chapter Three

·❦·

Zoe found herself in a team with one of the lads – Dwaine – Muriel the older woman, Alan the ex-actor and Cher. Bill, Shona, Shadrach, Becca and Daniel were in a restaurant on the other side of the village.

Gideon Irving was in charge of who did what in Zoe's team. Anna had gone with the others and a car was on standby to ferry the judges between the two. After taking the keys from the owner (who had hovered nervously for a few minutes until Gideon had reassured him his restaurant was in good hands and he wouldn't let anyone burn it down), he stared at them all for a few agonising moments and then said, 'OK. Dwaine, you're the chef. Muriel – sous; Alan – commis; Zoe – KP; and Cher, front of house. Are you clear of your roles?'

'I show people to their seats and bring them menus?' said Cher.

Gideon nodded. 'You also liaise with the kitchen, organise the waiting staff – the owner has kindly allowed us to use a couple of his regular members of staff – and smooth over any difficulties.'

'Easy,' she said, her voice so full of innuendo Zoe was quite embarrassed.

'Zoe? You're clear what you have to do as a KP?'

Zoe gave him a look as evil as she dared, which wasn't very. 'Washing up. I get it.'

'You'll probably have to do a bit more than that and

although it seems a menial task there is plenty of opportunity to shine.' He paused. 'We'll be observing you from time to time as well as looking at the footage that's been taken during the day. Nothing you do will go unnoticed – good or bad.' He gave Cher a glance that made her giggle alluringly, infuriating Zoe.

When he'd made sure everyone knew what they were doing he turned to go. He glanced at Zoe and winked as he passed. She blushed, hoping no one else had noticed.

The restaurant, not unsurprisingly, was near to Somerby and served good basic bistro-style food. Reading the menu, Zoe saw that it did asparagus wrapped in parma ham that came with a poached egg. She knew this shouldn't pose a problem to anyone, let alone someone in a cookery competition, but was very relieved she wouldn't be expected to produce them. Of all the things that were supposed to be easy, poached eggs were definitely the hardest.

Dwaine was thrilled to be the chef although he looked at the menu disparagingly. According to him – and he liked to share his feelings – as there were no foams, veloutés or deep-fried soft-shelled crabs in tempura batter, there was no challenge in it at all.

'Oh, for fuck's sake! I can't believe I'm supposed to cook fucking Chicken Kiev!' He went on effing and blinding at the simple pub-grub dishes which were popular and reasonably priced until he realised that his expletive-per-minute rate was possibly record-breaking and that the faces watching him were not impressed. It was as well the cameras weren't rolling yet. 'I'm a chef,' he said, by way of explanation. 'I don't expect to serve up prepared food.'

'There's a restaurant with an open kitchen near me that pre-prepares a lot of stuff,' said Alan. 'Otherwise it would be bloody hours before you got fed.'

Dwaine grunted. 'And what about the equipment? Where's the rotisserie? The sous vide? The water bath? I'm not used to this!'

'You'll *get* used to it,' said Zoe. 'A chef with your high standards will be able to manage, I'm sure.' She was checking out the dishwasher, glad that her work in the café had trained her well.

Once assured that her most useful tool was present and functioning, she took a look at what else there was there – or not there.

Apart from two massive cookers, there was a Bamix liquidiser, a toaster, a blow torch, the separate sink for hand washing, a sign on the wall about the coded cutting boards and also, worryingly, a glass cupboard in which hung some lethal-looking knives and choppers. She wondered if this was locked. Given the nature of their chef for the day, she hoped it was.

Dwaine was convinced he had been chosen because of his ability. This could have been true – his audition might have been brilliant – but none of the others knew and there was already muttering in the ranks.

Everyone had been issued with chef's whites and hats but Dwaine had brought his own trousers with huge checks, and instead of a chef's hat, he wore a bandanna in the manner of Marco Pierre White. Then he got out his knives. So much for the locked cupboard, thought Zoe as she and Muriel exchanged a look.

Dwaine unrolled the case revealing knives big enough to cut down small trees. He released one from its protective sheath.

'Look at this bad boy!' he said, making a few terrifying

passes with it. 'Samurai sharp, this is. Cut a silk scarf easy as anything—'

'Oh, put it away, do,' said Muriel. 'You'll hurt someone, possibly yourself, and then you won't be able to cook at all.' Her motherly reaction had the right effect and Dwaine stopped showing off for a few minutes.

There was a moment of uneasy calm and then they heard 'start rolling' and their first task in the competition began. Zoe felt a lot would have to be edited out if the earlier torrent of foul language was anything to go by, but that wasn't her problem. Having sorted out where the dirty dishes would be put and where they went once they were clean, she was chopping onions. It seemed a good idea to keep herself occupied while she was waiting for something to wash.

Gideon Irving came into the kitchen. He surveyed it like a lion selecting a wildebeest. Zoe, who should have been beneath his notice as the modern version of a scullery maid, was his first victim. He pushed her aside from her chopping and picked up her board.

'Where's the cloth? Without a cloth under your board it'll slip around! Put one there now!'

'But you're not a chef,' said Zoe, finding a cloth and spreading it under her board. She could sense the watchful eye of a camera trained on them both.

'That doesn't mean I haven't spent a lot of time in professional kitchens,' he said. 'Now, let me check your technique.'

Zoe had been happy chopping onions. They were making her eyes water but she was coping. She picked up her knife and started on a new one.

'To start with, you need a bigger knife,' he said. He selected one from the knife rack. 'That's better, it's got a bit of weight to it.' He tested the blade with his thumb

34

and then produced a steel. He gave it several passes before he was satisfied.

She picked up the knife and made to cut off the root. 'No!' said Gideon. 'Leave the root on, or it'll bleed and make you cry more. Now slice it in half.' He nudged her out of the way and took hold of the onion and held it. 'This way, if the knife slips you won't cut yourself. Either use the bridge' – he placed his fingers over the onion – 'or the claw.' He shifted his position. 'See? Show me.'

Zoe, feeling thoroughly undermined, and on camera too, made a few tentative cuts.

'Better,' said Gideon, less aggressive now he was teaching her. 'Try it like this . . .'

Two minutes later, Zoe was chopping onions like a pro. Gideon might have been brusque but he was a good teacher.

Gideon and the camera had gone to where Alan was putting eggs on to boil but Dwaine was looking at her pityingly. 'I can't believe you entered a competition like this without knowing how to chop onions.'

'Oh shut up,' said Zoe calmly. 'I passed the audition, same as you did.'

'Yes but really—'

'Leave her alone!' said Muriel. 'She's doing fine. And what about you? Are you ready?'

Gideon, having swooped in like a trouble-shooting eagle and given nearly everybody some advice, left them to get on with it. It was only the contestants and a camera team.

'Ok.' Cher came in with a slip of paper. 'There are some people in, and they want like, something really quick?'

'Can't they read the menu?' growled Dwaine, determined to play the grumpy chef.

'Yeah, but what can they have that is quick?' insisted Cher.

There was silence while everyone looked at the menu.

Nothing seemed really quick. Even the cassoulet that just needed heating up would take a few minutes to assemble.

'What about a sandwich?' suggested Muriel.

'They want something hot,' said Cher.

'Toasted sandwich?' suggested Zoe. 'I spotted some of those bag things.'

'Good idea,' said Muriel. 'Pop the toaster on, Alan.'

'Just who is in charge here?' roared Dwaine. 'Toasted sandwiches are not on the bloody menu!'

'What's the quickest thing then?' asked Cher impatiently.

'I don't know but I don't serve bloody sandwiches!' sulked Dwaine.

'They don't take long, and in the real world, if they go away happy they're more likely to come back,' Muriel was standing firm.

'But sandwiches are not on the menu!' repeated Dwaine. 'They can't have something that's not on the menu just because it's quick!'

'But how long does it take to make a sandwich?' said Zoe, who felt they could have had them melting away in the toaster by now.

'About ten seconds if people don't waste time arguing about it,' said Muriel.

'I'm with Dwaine,' said Cher. 'I don't think they should be allowed to go off piste like this. How long does it take to make risotto?'

Zoe exchanged glances with Muriel. 'I'll go and ask what they'd like,' said Zoe. 'Risotto takes ages.'

Muriel nodded. 'And don't forget, you two, this is a competition. And the customer is always right. What will the judges think if we let customers go away without being served? It's up to us to give them what they need.'

'I'm not here to making fucking sandwiches!' Sensing

36

Cher's back-up, Dwaine took the brakes off his language as the sound boom swung round.

'We'll do it then,' said Zoe. 'Muriel's right. People come here for a hot snack, we have a kitchen, we'll give them one! Go out there and tell them, please Cher!'

Cher folded her arms and shook her golden head.

Things were getting out of hand. This was their first task and already they were at each other's throats. So much for teamwork. Zoe sighed, pulled off her chef's hat, which she'd been dying to get rid of, and went into the restaurant.

The family – parents and two young teenagers – stood there, looking bleak. She smiled broadly at them.

'Hello! So sorry you've been kept waiting. We could do you toasted sandwiches quite quickly. Why don't you sit down. Can I get you drinks? Coffee? Tea, hot chocolate?'

The family relaxed and made themselves comfortable at a table. Zoe went behind the bar to suss out the coffee machine and was relieved to find all she needed. Rashly, she opened a couple of packets of crisps, tipped them into a bowl and put them on the table. Then she went back into the kitchen.

'OK, people. Let's get to work!'

Chapter Four

❧

It was nine o'clock, and the contestants were huddled together in one of the barns at Somerby, shell shocked and drinking wine. A makeshift bar had been set up for them, almost as if the powers that be sensed they would need it after the gruelling day they'd had. There were six of them: the other three remaining contestants, who were staying in the village, had already gone back home to bed.

Of course everyone knew someone would be eliminated. It was a competition; one person would be leaving after each task. But because both groups had found the task so hard, they had somehow forgotten this aspect. And Dwaine had gone, just like that.

Zoe thought her group had been a disaster. She and Muriel had ended up doing most of the work. Dwaine had spent far too long building towers of food, hunched over plates, placing little bits of God-knew-what on top of worrying brown smears until the whole lot was stone cold and was then sent back.

And his food didn't taste of much either. It turned out that he had learnt all his cooking from television programmes but didn't ever taste anything. According to him, if it looked right it was right and that was his undoing. He refused to compromise. And despite everything he had remained confident to the end.

Anna Fortune had come in halfway through service. She had observed the kitchen, which Muriel and Zoe had turned into a factory for omelette (served with chips and salad), and gone out again with an audible sniff.

After a couple of seconds exchanging horrified glances, Zoe and Muriel carried on with their plan. Alan had made salads, Muriel the omelettes and Zoe had been the gofer, running between the kitchen and the restaurant making sure everyone was happy. Cher had polished glasses and served wine. Dwaine had sulked.

Just at the end of service, Zoe observed a dark figure slink out, like a wolf. It was Gideon. It was odd, they decided as they gave the kitchen a final wipe down, that after the initial nervousness, having the camera crew observing their every move hadn't felt as if they were being watched. But a judge was like a presence from on high, taking note of every move.

'Poor Dwaine, he was totally out of his depth,' said Zoe, now passing the bottle of wine to Alan on her left.

'He wasn't a team player, though, was he?' said Alan.

'No,' agreed Muriel vehemently.

'He was the weakest link, he had to go,' said Cher.

Muriel and Zoe exchanged glances. Cher had been a fairly weak link herself and yet she was still here. Zoe wondered if Muriel was also wondering if it was Cher's good looks that saved her this time, and if they always would.

'Any clue what the next challenge will be?' asked Bill, an ex-builder in his sixties, who'd been on the other team.

'I hope it's something individual,' said Becca, the one who Zoe had immediately identified as major competition, although she didn't say much. 'I'm better on my own.'

'I reckon you did really well today,' said Bill. 'Cooked up a storm, she did.'

'Will we always be in the same teams, do you think?' asked Zoe, thinking she'd swap kindly Bill for Cher any day of the week.

Cher was great at looking as if she was doing something if the camera was on her or if there was a judge present, but she didn't do much in between.

'Oh, I think they'll mix us up for team challenges,' said Muriel. She yawned. 'I think I'll go to bed. I don't have the stamina I once had.'

'Me too,' agreed Bill. 'I'll walk you back. You're in one of the stables, aren't you? Me, I'm in the pigsty.'

Everyone agreed they were tired and the party broke up. Cher and Zoe walked back towards their converted cowshed. 'If we're put into pairs I want to be with you,' said Cher briskly. Had she been more friendly, Zoe might have been flattered, but she suspected an ulterior motive. Her instincts weren't wrong. 'I feel we look good together. You set me off nicely, being short and dark.'

'So you think you look better – taller and blonder – if you're next to me?' Zoe wanted confirmation her suspicions were right.

'Yup. Don't be offended. You're not bad looking, but you're just not . . .' She paused. 'You're just not as good looking as I am.'

'Right,' said Zoe, feeling suddenly that the less they had to do with each other, the better. 'I think I'll go up to the house to get some milk for tea in the morning. We seem to have run out.'

'Oh good. See you later.'

'And do try to be out of the bathroom by the time I get back.'

The Somerby kitchen was empty and in a state. The remains of a large dinner party was on the table and every working surface had saucepans, greasy roasting tins and dirty glasses on it. The sink was full of more pans, soaking. Zoe, who thought her legs wouldn't function very much longer, went to the fridge, trying to ignore the mess. And then she thought of Fenella, heavily pregnant, who had probably gone to bed without tidying up for very good reasons. She wouldn't want to see all this in the morning.

'I must give up being so bloody helpful!' she said aloud as she started clearing the table and loading the dishwasher. 'I should just get the milk and go back to my bed, and get a good night's sleep before tomorrow's challenge.'

But she didn't listen. She seemed to be on autopilot; having spent all day clearing up, she couldn't stop now.

She was putting the last things in, cramming the dishwasher as full as she could, when she heard a voice behind her.

'What are you doing here?'

She turned, hoping it was Rupert but knowing perfectly well it wasn't.

'I could ask you the same question!' she said, remembering too late she should try and stay on his good side.

'I left my notes here and I need them for tomorrow. We're still upstairs discussing things.' Gideon gestured towards a briefcase on a chair. 'You?'

'I was getting milk for tea tomorrow morning. Fen said we should do that.'

'And Fen keeps milk in the dishwasher, does she?'

Probably because she was tired, Zoe found herself smiling. 'Of course, doesn't everyone?'

Gideon, who, now she looked at him properly, seemed tired too – the whole day had been fraught and even though the judges had had an easier time of it they obviously took their roles seriously – allowed his mouth to quirk a little in return. 'I was here when Fen went to bed. You've tidied up this lot, haven't you?'

Zoe couldn't think if she was allowed to help Fenella or not. 'I might have . . .'

Gideon nodded. 'You've been brainwashed during the day. You can't see washing-up without having to do it.'

Her forehead wrinkled a little. 'I think maybe that's right.' She looked under the sink and found some tablets and put the dishwasher on. 'OK, milk.'

'It might seem a mad idea but I suggest you look in the fridge.'

Zoe ignored this, but as she turned back to the room, a plastic bottle in her hand, she saw Gideon yawning. He stretched out his arms to their full extent and groaned. It made Zoe think of a bear – albeit a very sexy one. He smiled sleepily. 'You know, I have a sudden desire for hot chocolate. How much milk is there in the fridge?'

Zoe looked back into it. 'Masses.' Then she heard herself say, 'Shall I make you some?' She really shouldn't keep offering to do things for people all the time. He'd probably think she was trying to suck up to him, which would never do.

He saved her from herself. He shook his head. 'You sit down. I'm an expert.'

'At hot chocolate? But you're a food critic and entrepreneur!' He'd never manage without real chocolate from Mexico and possibly cream.

'That doesn't mean I can't make fabulous cocoa, does it? Sit!'

Zoe pulled out a chair and sat, telling herself he wasn't talking to her as if she was a dog but just insisting she took the weight off her feet, which she did need to do. And if he could make cocoa, then good for him.

The cocoa did take a bit more in the way of creaming, whisking and reheating than Zoe would have thought necessary but when he put a steaming, foaming mug in front of her the aroma was heavenly.

'Biscuits,' he said firmly.

'In that box,' Zoe said, pointing. 'Fen said they are for clients' use only. That's me, if not you.'

Gideon rummaged in the box and brought a packet of digestives back with him. 'There are others if you'd rather but I think these are best with hot chocolate.'

Zoe giggled.

'What's funny?' he demanded.

His outrage made her laugh even more. 'I'm sorry. It's just so . . . I don't know, cheffy of you – although I know you're not a chef – to have a special biscuit to go with hot chocolate.'

He gave her a look which could have been a warning. 'I think, given that you've entered a cookery competition, you should take it all a bit more seriously.'

But Zoe was past being warned. 'I may have entered a cookery competition but that doesn't mean I have to be a pretentious prat!' She paused. 'Does it?'

'Taking your art seriously doesn't mean you're pretentious.' He pulled out another chair and sat down, cupping his hands around his own mug of cocoa.

'Except in your case!' She sent him a glance, challenging him.

'Don't flash your eyes at me. I'm the expert here! You're the lowly contestant.'

Zoe took a sip of the hot chocolate and sighed. 'I must admit, you may have made a great deal of fuss and even more mess, but this is heavenly.'

'I'm flattered.'

'Oh don't be. My opinion counts for nothing. I am only a "lowly contestant", after all.'

He laughed properly now. 'Not one that seems intent on charming the judges, that's for sure. The girl who did your front of house in the challenge today certainly knew which side her bread was buttered.'

'Glad to hear it. It's a cookery competition.'

He shook his head gently. 'That's not really funny, you know.'

'I know. But I am taking the competition seriously. And if I don't win because I don't flirt with the judges, that's OK. I want to win on my own merits.'

He looked at her steadily and said, 'I don't know much about your merits – yet – but you're not doing a bad job at flirting with the judges.'

Zoe was horrified. 'You don't think I was flirting, do you? I was just joking around!'

'Then that's all right then. I absolve you of flirting.'

Although, she thought, perhaps she had flirted a little bit? Gideon had that effect on her and secretly she'd rather enjoyed it. He was much less formidable in the cosy Somerby kitchen. But she had to be careful.

'Good! I want to win this fair and square.'

'That's very admirable.' He paused. 'So why do you want to win?'

She was quite glad they were on safer ground.

She considered. 'I want to win because I love food and I love cooking. I gave up a job I'd had for a while and I really want the prize.' She sent him a rueful look. 'I'm not totally focused on money or anything, but I want to set up a deli. The cash would help.'

'Fair enough.'

He was looking at her rather too intently so she decided to ask him a question. 'So what about you? Do you have any long-held ambitions? Or are you a complete success?'

He laughed. 'Far from it! And yes, I do have long-held ambitions.'

'Which are?'

'I feel like a Miss World contestant when I say this but I really want to do something to help education about

44

food. Jamie Oliver has done so much but I'd like to join that fight.' He was stirring the remains of his cocoa as he spoke, a look of concentration on his face. It was clearly something he felt passionate about.

'So why don't you? It's nothing to be ashamed of, after all.'

'I haven't really found the right platform. It needs to be big, but I'll do it. One day.'

'I think that's a terrific ambition. Much better than just wanting to open a deli.' Zoe was rather pleased he had ideals. It made her like him even more.

'We can't all change the world and good delis are wonderful.'

Zoe nodded. 'Don't start me on them. I have so many ideas . . .' Suddenly she yawned.

'Hey, you'd better go to bed. You need to sleep. You've got a competition to win.'

'I suddenly feel terribly guilty.'

'Why?' Gideon was bemused.

'Telling you my ambitions. It might make you favour me.'

He laughed. 'I promise you, I'm incorruptible. You'll probably get your deli one day even if you don't win.'

'Maybe. Anyway . . .' She hesitated, reluctant to leave although she knew she should.

'I think if you're really determined, you will get what you want.' He seemed to think her hesitation was lack of self-belief.

'Perhaps you're right.' She felt strangely free to say what she thought with Gideon: she felt more comfortable with him than she usually did with men nearer her own age with more similar backgrounds. There was something about the kitchen too that invited intimacy.

Maybe he felt the same because instead of going back

45

upstairs (surely people would be wondering what had happened to him?) he said, 'So what's it like, staying on the premises?'

'It's only been one night but Fen and Rupert are very hospitable. It's why I cleared up for them – they've been so lovely to me.'

'I might blag myself a bed here then.'

'Why? Isn't your hotel comfortable?'

'I'm sure it is. I'm just allergic to them. I spend too much time away and would much rather stay in someone's house.'

Zoe thought of Fenella, who already had far too much to do. 'Well, I don't think you should.'

He was surprised. 'Why on earth not?'

'It's nothing to do with me, of course, but Fen's pregnant. You staying here would make much more work for her.'

'Would it?'

'Of course! She'd have to make proper breakfast, make sure your room was tidy – all sorts of things she probably could do without.'

He studied her more closely. 'You're very protective of her.'

'No – well, maybe I am. But I feel sorry for her having all these people around her when she's just about to pop.'

He considered. 'OK, if I promise not to demand – or even accept – any special attention, even breakfast, clean up after myself and don't come in late and drunk, can I ask if there's a spare bed they could put me into? The television company would be paying them, after all.'

Zoe made a face. 'Of course, it's none of my business—'

'None at all.'

'But if you stick to those terms and conditions—'

'Ooh, formal,' he teased.

'You can ask if you can stay.'

Gideon got up and took Zoe's empty mug. 'I'll say I have permission from their tame Rottweiler.'

'Oh please don't.' Zoe was suddenly serious. 'They'd be mortified, if not seriously annoyed. I don't want that.'

'OK, it'll stay our secret.'

Zoe got up and collected the milk. Gideon strode towards her. 'Goodnight.' He looked as if he might kiss her cheek, as he would if they had met socially, in the normal way.

Zoe looked up at him and tried to think of something smart to say to end the conversation but nothing came to her, so, clutching the milk, she turned and left.

Much to her relief, Cher was asleep when she got back. She didn't have to endure questions as to whether she'd had to milk the cow because it had taken her so long to get back with it. By morning she'd have thought up a good excuse. Cher was a very suspicious character. It was like living with the Spanish Inquisition even if you hadn't done anything wrong. After all, there was nothing in the rules to say she couldn't share hot chocolate with one of the judges. Or was there?

Chapter Five

CR3KR

'There's no yoghurt, no berries and no bread,' said Cher, staring into the fridge the next morning.

'Oh,' said Zoe, not knowing what other comment she could make. 'I could go and get some bread, I suppose.'

'Considering you were so long getting the milk last night you could have knocked up a loaf.'

Zoe sighed. Cher had a point. None of her excuses for being so long with the milk had seemed to wash with her, which was hardly surprising, really.

'So as you know the way,' said Cher, 'you'd better trot along and pick some up.'

Once again stifling an angry retort, Zoe left the cowshed abruptly. Honestly, she was appalling! The cottage felt cramped with Cher's personality all over it and Zoe was glad to leave it – and she felt drawn to Somerby, for all sorts of reasons. She crossed the courtyard and let herself into the kitchen by the back door.

Fenella was already there. She had her own questions. 'You tidied the kitchen last night, didn't you?'

'Sorry, I just—'

'Oh, for goodness sake!' Fenella came over and put her arms round Zoe. 'I wasn't telling you off! I just couldn't face it and nor could Rupes. He said he'd do it this morning but I came down early.' She rubbed the side of her stomach. 'I'm not sleeping that well, and it was like the elves had been in the night! It was all gleaming.'

'Well, I felt so sorry for you. You've got so much on as well as being pregnant.'

'You're a sweetheart. I really hope you win.' Fenella opened a large bread bin and took out a loaf. 'Is this what you came for? The others get their bread and milk delivered by the cleaners but as you're so near the house, I'm supposed to do it,' Fenella explained apologetically. 'But since I've got so huge I don't seem to get round to it.'

'I don't mind collecting it and it looks lovely.'

'We have a super bakery. Our guests just love their bread.'

Zoe thought of another guest they might have and nearly warned Fenella so she could have an excuse ready if she needed to. Then she realised she mustn't say anything or Fenella would wonder how on earth she knew about Gideon wanting to move out of his hotel.

They chatted for a few moments about this and that when Fenella said, 'I was just wondering about one thing though. Did you have hot chocolate before you went back with the milk?'

Zoe thought quickly. 'Yes – yes I did. I hope that's all right?'

'Of course it's all right! Whatever you like! Goodness, if the elves come in the night, you don't grudge them a bit of drinking chocolate.'

'That's OK then. I'd better take this bread before Cher starts eating her own arm. Not that there's a lot there to eat.'

Fenella chuckled. 'She'll never balloon up to a size ten, will she?'

Zoe shook her head. 'Nope.' She picked up the loaf. 'Bye!'

'Bye then!' called Fenella. 'And you don't need to tell me why there were two mugs on the drainer.'

Quite obviously Fenella wanted her to tell her very much but Zoe just shrugged. 'Elves! You know what they're like!' And she whisked away before Fenella could ask any more questions.

But she liked the fact that Gideon had washed the mugs. Maybe he'd stick to his promise to be no trouble to Fenella.

'OK! Guys!' Mike called everyone to order.

They were in the marquee and a cold May wind was making the sides billow slightly. The weather had gone back to being changeable.

'Today's task!' He had to raise his voice to make himself heard and to get everyone's attention. 'It's going to be done over two days and is about using really local produce.'

Cher turned round to look for the cameras and found there weren't any, or rather the cameras were all switched off at this point. The others focused on Mike. They were more united now they'd got the initial task out of the way.

'The first bit is sourcing your produce,' Mike explained, referring to a sheet of paper. 'You'll have a list of local suppliers, some money, and you'll be put in groups to be driven to them. This is to make sure you really do stay in the very local area. If you have a car, can you hand in your car keys? To make sure there's no cheating.'

'And then what?' asked Bill. 'What are we to do with our local ingredients?'

'Working on your own, you're to produce a really good three-course meal. The budget is generous so you don't need to watch the cost but you are a bit limited by it needing to be local.'

'What about things like olive oil?' asked Shadrach, the fanatical cook, sounding panicked. Daniel nodded in agreement. 'Salt and pepper?'

50

'I was coming to that,' said Mike. 'There is a list of exceptions to the local rule. Oil and salt and pepper are on it. I'm going to hand out a list of suppliers now and the rules about what counts as local that you can refer to. You've got an hour to think about what you want to cook, then the cars will come to drive you to where you want to go. It would be a good idea if you could get into carloads – about four people – so we can co-ordinate where we're going. You'll be filmed at the various suppliers. Oh, and you'll be given your packs before you get in the cars.'

Zoe felt excited. The challenge was right up her street really. 'I think that sounds fun,' she said to Cher, who happened to be nearby.

'What? Local food? Exciting? I don't think so. What round here is going to be half decent? A few carrots and a bit of old cow.'

Zoe looked around anxiously in case anyone remotely local had heard this insult and was offended. She walked slowly back to the room, reading the list of suppliers as she went. Her problem would be choosing what ingredients to go for, there was so much available. She was slightly surprised that Cher didn't follow her but not unhappy.

An hour later, armed with her requisite notebook and bag, Zoe walked back up to the front of the house. A fleet of taxis was drawn up and Fenella was on the steps with her phone in her hand looking flustered.

'What's up?' asked Zoe.

'I don't think they've sent enough taxis,' said Fenella. 'I do wish the production company had asked us which firms to use.'

'Well, it's not your problem, is it?' said Zoe. There seemed to be plenty of cars to her. People were climbing into them, their packs tucked into their clothing.

Mike came up to her. 'Ah, Zoe! I thought there was someone missing!'

'I got up here on time,' she said, aggrieved.

Mike looked at his watch. 'Yes, I suppose you did, but they didn't send quite enough cars—'

'Told you!' said Fenella, perversely pleased.

'—which meant everyone had to squash up – three in the back. I don't think the taxi firm took in about the camera people going too.'

Fenella shook her head, more in sorrow than in anger.

'The problem is there's not enough room for you, Zoe,' said Mike, looking cross.

'What?' Zoe suddenly felt like the last girl picked for the team. 'I bet Cher didn't have to squash in the back. I bet she was fine.'

Mike looked sheepish. 'She did dash off with just a cameraman in the car with her.'

'You shouldn't have let her!' Fenella said indignantly. 'It's not fair!'

'I know,' Mike agreed, 'but frankly I thought there'd be plenty of room for everyone and I'm not fit enough to run down the drive and throw myself in front of a moving car. Look, it'll be fine. Zoe can go, all on her own, when the first cab comes back. I'm sure you won't have to wait long.'

'It's outrageous!' said Fenella, taking Zoe's arm and leading her down to the kitchen. 'And it needn't have happened if only they'd let me tell them which local people are reliable.'

Gideon was in the kitchen, chatting to Rupert, and seeing him, Zoe tried to reverse back out of it. She couldn't seem to avoid him. There was an overnight bag in the corner of the kitchen and she presumed he'd been given the seal of approval and allowed to stay at Somerby. She found she liked the idea.

'No need to run away just because I'm here,' he said. 'I don't bite. Or at least, only about once a month when the moon is full.'

Rupert laughed.

'Poor Zoe got bumped off the taxis because they didn't send enough,' explained Fenella.

'You thought that might happen, didn't you, love?' said Rupert. 'Zoe, have a cup of coffee to compensate. I've just made some. And we owe you at least that, with all the help you've given us.'

Fenella sent Zoe a shocked glance, intercepted by Rupert. 'Oh, don't worry, girls,' Rupert said cheerfully. 'I'm sure it isn't against the rules for Zoe to help with the washing up.'

'Oh no, of course not,' said Fenella. 'Sit down. I'll find some biscuits.'

'Doesn't that put you at a disadvantage?' said Rupert, handing her a mug of coffee that smelt like heaven.

'I suppose.'

'It'll mean they'll get to the suppliers first,' said Gideon. 'And will have longer to think up their menu.'

'Well, yes, I had worked that out but there's nothing I can do about it.' She sipped her coffee gratefully and decided to let the calming atmosphere of the kitchen at Somerby soothe her annoyance.

'Let's have a look at your list of local suppliers,' said Rupert, holding out his hand. Zoe produced it from the back pocket of her jeans. 'Hm,' Rupert went on, looking at the list. 'They've missed off a couple of good places. Why didn't they ask us who our suppliers are? They've been very dense about this. They should have consulted us far more.'

'Who have they missed off?' said Fenella, sipping peppermint tea.

'Well, the Roses, for a start, and although cider is their main thing, they do produce some wonderful pork,' said Rupert. 'And Susan and Rob aren't on here. They're a dairy, tiny but perfectly formed —'

'As they say every time we go,' said Fenella. 'How did they miss them?'

'Some researcher in London didn't find them in any directory,' said Gideon. 'But there's no reason why we shouldn't go there.' He looked at Zoe, who found herself blushing.

'We? I'm not allowed to go except in the official cars – we had to hand in our car keys to make sure we didn't break the "only local" rules.'

'These places are practically within walking distance,' said Rupert. 'Much more local than some of these suppliers.' He was still looking at the list disparagingly.

'I'll take you,' said Gideon. 'I'd like to check them out myself.'

'But isn't it against the rules?' said Zoe, finding herself very much wanting to explore these places with Gideon. 'It would be fraternisation or something.'

'I'm a judge, not the enemy,' said Gideon, looking intently at her.

'Same thing,' said Zoe quietly. 'Isn't it?'

'Well, we won't tell anyone,' said Fenella, 'and it's their fault for not sending enough cars. You'd be disadvantaged if you didn't go with Gideon.'

Gideon looked at her. 'Anyone would think you're keen to get me out of your hair.'

'How did you guess!' said Fenella, laughing. 'I've got a team of decorators about to hit your bedroom any minute. We have to have that bridal suite ready double quick!'

He frowned. 'Oh. I hope my staying doesn't hold you up.'

'Not at all,' said Fenella. 'They can work round you. If you don't mind of course.'

'Fine by me.' Gideon smiled. Fenella and Rupert were doing him a favour after all.

Fenella turned to Zoe. 'Now finish your coffee and then go. And bring me back a leg of pork. I'll phone and tell them what we want. Oh, and some bacon . . .'

Chapter Six

❦

Zoe got into Gideon's car feeling a mixture of excitement and nervousness. She felt she'd got to know him a bit while they were drinking cocoa but being suddenly so close to him was somehow a shock. She knew she was attracted to him – fancied him even – but she hadn't realised quite how much till his arm was only inches away from hers. She really hoped she'd be able to concentrate. She didn't often find people attractive like this and it was making her feel a bit light-headed.

'Have you got the directions?' Gideon asked.

She gave herself a mental shake and engaged her brain. 'Yes. It looks quite straightforward.' Rupert had scrawled a map that Zoe now examined. 'Which one shall we go to first? Pigs or dairy?' She was determined to sound completely professional and efficient. Which she was. Usually.

'Which do we come to first?'

'The dairy, but we don't want stuff going off in the car while we look at pigs. Maybe pigs?'

He nodded, having thought this over. 'OK, I'm in your hands but don't get us lost.'

As she began to relax a little and enjoy his company she felt she could tease him. 'Excuse me! You were the one who went down the wrong lane and got the car stuck turning round!'

She saw him raise his eyes to heaven in the driving mirror. 'I knew you'd never let me forget that.'

Zoe smiled. Something in the way he said that connected them, as if they were a team – or a couple out on an adventure together. She found she liked the idea quite a lot, but then chided herself. They weren't a team, he was a judge of a competition that was going – with luck – to be watched by millions and she was a contestant.

And anyway, she was mad to fancy Gideon. He would never look at her except possibly as a minor diversion when there was no one else around. He had the sort of looks – not exactly handsome but undeniably sexy – that implied he could get any woman he decided he wanted. Even if she wanted him – and if she were honest, she did – she'd be mad to give in to her feelings. She had to keep a grip on herself. She couldn't jeopardise her chances in the competition. She was a modern young woman, with aspirations she didn't want to sacrifice by getting distracted by a man, tempting though he was.

'I think it's here,' she said as they approached a turning, half hidden by overgrown hedges. The countryside was ablaze with that fresh greenness one only got in May. Zoe was really enjoying herself. 'Rupert said the sign is pretty hidden but it's by the blasted oak.'

'I didn't think they really existed but I see what you mean.' He changed down and turned where she indicated. With a throaty roar they headed down a less-than-smooth half-dirt track. 'But if you've taken us down a long cul-de-sac I expect you to get us out.'

'Don't I always?' She sent him a challenging look.

His answering glance suggested to her that he was not used to being challenged. She decided to do it as often as possible – for his own good, of course. She also realised how much she loved flirting.

The lane was bordered by orchards with black pigs snuffling underneath the trees – an idyllic picture that made Zoe sigh for a more rural life. The town where she had lived up until the competition and where her parents still lived wasn't exactly a metropolis but there was something wonderfully appealing about the real countryside and not the chocolate-box version of it.

'Presumably those are cider-apple trees,' she said out loud, to disguise the sigh. 'I expect the apples would flavour the meat wonderfully.'

Gideon laughed. 'As long as they didn't eat too many and get drunk.'

'Can pigs get drunk?' asked Zoe.

'Oh yes, they really can. Not sure if they get hangovers though.'

The idea tickled her imagination. 'Imagine having to serve hangover cure in buckets, Alka-Seltzer billowing over the top.'

'Which would be followed by little piggy belches,' said Gideon. 'Rather sweet.'

Zoe stole a quick glance at him as he parked; a man who thought that pigs could be sweet could not be all bad. Not that she thought he was bad . . . She sort of wished he'd stop saying things that made her like him more.

Gideon got out of the car. There was no one about. 'Have they got a shop?' he asked Zoe. 'Or a bell?'

'We'll ring the front-door bell and hope someone comes.' She sighed. 'I haven't much experience of farms but I can imagine there's hardly ever anyone around. They're always off somewhere, doing something.'

Fortunately they didn't have to wait long, enjoying the sunshine and inspecting the flowerbeds on either side of the front door, before they heard a voice. 'Can I help you?'

A woman in her thirties appeared wearing a shirt and

a pair of jeans stuffed into wellington boots. Her hair was held back by a band and she had no make-up on. Her broad smile made further adornment unnecessary. 'Sorry, I was feeding the babies – piglets.'

'Oh, can we see?' said Zoe.

'Don't coo over anything you might eat,' said Gideon, following the two women to the babies.

'I'm not going to eat any of these, am I?' said Zoe.

'I was just saying . . .'

The woman she was following sighed. 'You sound just like my husband. I'm Jess Rose, by the way. Fen and Rupert sent you? They rang and said you were on your way. Here we are.'

There in a pen was a sow as big as an average family car and twelve little piglets like silken sacks with legs.

'Oh my God, they are so adorable!' said Zoe. Gideon raised an eyebrow but she could tell he thought they were adorable too.

'Yes they are,' agreed Jess. 'And yet we do eat them. We give them the very best, most natural life possible and then they die.'

'You don't give them names?' Zoe almost whispered.

Jess shook her head. 'Not the piglets, only the breeding sows.'

Zoe dragged her eyes away from the wriggling snuffling creatures that reminded her of Labrador puppies. 'This is no good! We're on a mission. Apart from picking up some things for Fen, I want some really wonderful pork product for a cookery competition.'

Jess smiled broadly. 'Come with me. I might have just the thing!'

They followed her to a shed. Hanging from the roof were half a dozen pieces of meat. 'It's from the belly,' said Jess. 'This is my homemade pancetta!'

Gideon and Zoe exchanged glances. 'Did Fen know about this?' Zoe asked.

'Nope! I wanted to see if it worked before I told anyone, but it does.'

'I must have some!' said Zoe.

'How would you use it?' asked Gideon.

'I don't know! And if I did I wouldn't tell you!' said Zoe only half aware how silly that sounded. 'Is it terribly expensive?'

They drove away from the farm with several packages on the back seat. 'I'm so excited about the pancetta,' said Zoe. 'No one else will have it!'

'You will have to do something special with it,' said Gideon. 'Having good ingredients is only the start.'

'Oh, stop being so sensible. Let's find the cheese place now.' But a memory of something in one of her mother's cookery books written in the seventies came back to her.

After twisting and turning through a few more country lanes they arrived at their next destination. Zoe was really enjoying herself. Gideon was very easy to be with and it was a lovely early summer's day. All was well with the world – for Zoe at least.

They parked round the back of another picturesque farmhouse, walked through the farmyard and past some cows with interesting white stripes down their backs, and rang what they hoped was the right bell. After a few minutes, while they wondered if they were at the wrong door, the door was opened by an attractive woman who smiled at them warmly.

'Fen rang and said you were coming,' she said. 'Welcome! I'm Susan. Fen said I was to show you everything, not just cheese and cream but that first. Come this way.'

As Zoe followed Susan and Gideon she felt inspired. This woman would have wonderful produce, things the others wouldn't have access to, and it would give her a bit of an advantage. Although she knew she was a good cook, she suspected that there were others in the competition who were better. They hadn't really had a chance to shine yet. She'd have to have some other edge for her to win.

'Do you want to see where we make it? Or just the shop?'

Gideon looked at his watch. 'Well, we've been out for a while.'

'We've been looking at baby pigs and buying bacon and pork,' said Zoe. 'And cider.'

Susan laughed. 'I know where you've been then. If you haven't time for the grand tour – and I haven't time really either – come and look at the shop.' She led the way to a small building and opened the door. 'This was once a cowshed.'

'Oh, I'm sleeping in a cowshed at the moment,' said Zoe.

'Rupert and Fen have been so imaginative, haven't they? Now, have a look. Almost everything here has been produced either on our farm or on the one next door.'

With her main course decided and an idea for a starter, it was the pudding that Zoe needed to think about. She wanted to do something original, which meant no summer fruits.

Gideon wandered off to look at the business end of the cheese-making process, leaving Zoe to examine the stock without his inhibiting presence. Was this whole expedition together against the rules? Although to be fair to herself, there was nothing in the sheet about not finding other suppliers, accompanied by a judge. It was just that she wouldn't be filmed.

'Is there anything particular you need?' asked Susan

after Zoe had walked all the way round the shop without choosing anything.

'The trouble is, I don't know what I need, except ingredients for a pudding that is original, and local of course.'

'The strawberries are lovely.'

'I know but I think everyone will be using strawberries or raspberries.' She picked up a jar of honey.

'Uncle Jim's honey is very special.'

'I'll have some anyway. I love honey.'

'So do I! And it goes awfully well with cheese.'

This caught Zoe's attention. 'Does it?'

'Yes! Here, let me show you.'

Susan opened a fridge and produced some cheese and then a jar of honey. She spread a little honey on the cheese. 'Here, taste this. This is not really a single Gloucester because we're outside the area where it can be produced, but it's the same method.'

Zoe put the cheese and honey into her mouth. While she was chewing, Susan went on. 'A friend I met on a cheese-making course makes it and it's one of my favourites. We call it Single Littlechurch. We keep the Gloucester cattle because they're a rare breed.'

Susan dived back into her fridge. 'And here's the one we make that's like a Brie.'

'What's that like with honey?' asked Zoe, her brain whirring.

Susan smiled. 'Try it!'

Zoe couldn't speak for a few seconds. 'That is so wonderful! I need that too!'

'Have you got an unlimited budget?'

'Not unlimited but fairly generous.' She chewed and thought some more. 'Although for a pudding, I probably need something a bit acidic, fruit of some kind, but not red ones.'

'Would it have to be fresh fruit?'

'I don't suppose so.'

Susan made a gesture towards her shelves. 'Have a look at the bottled fruit then.'

'Bullaces? What on earth are bullaces? I've never heard of them,' Zoe said a few moments later.

'A sort of wild plum. They grow in the hedgerows and we had masses last year. My mother does the bottling.'

Zoe picked up the jar and inspected the small yellow fruit that looked like golden opals. 'I'll definitely have some of these. Now, do you do cream?'

'Of course I do! And I defy you to find any better in the county.'

After a little more shopping, mainly in farm shops, they arrived back at Somerby. Zoe was relieved they hadn't bumped into anyone on the way. Not that she was doing anything illegal but she still felt she probably shouldn't have been spending so much time with one of the judges. She was delighted with her purchases and, what's more, although Gideon had been there, he didn't know exactly what she planned to cook. She found she liked the idea of surprising him in particular. Fenella and Rupert had organised tea for them all and Zoe was looking forward to cream tea – one that she had nothing to do with making.

Gideon parked in front of the house and Zoe got out. As she did so Cher appeared from beside the house. That girl had a sixth sense, thought Zoe guiltily.

'Oh, hello. We wondered where you were. You found a lift then?'

Now Gideon got out causing Cher to stare and then bridle.

'Oh! I see!' She giggled fetchingly. 'Isn't it against the rules to get pally with the judges?'

'It's against the rules to make it impossible for contestants to source their ingredients,' said Gideon calmly.

'Did I do that?' Cher was all innocence.

'You got in a cab all by yourself which meant there wasn't room for Zoe,' he explained.

'Duh! Sorree! There seemed to be loads of cabs.' Her fake remorse involved looking at Gideon upwards under her false eyelashes and smiling.

'Well, never mind, I've got what I need now,' said Zoe.

Just for a second she felt she'd rather do without anything to cook with than watch Cher flirt with Gideon, but then she gave herself a mental shake. That was ridiculous. Gideon seemed impervious to Cher's wiles and anyway she, Zoe, had no claim on him.

Their carefully marked packets of food handed in for safe-keeping, ready for the challenge the next day, and a wonderful spread consumed, everyone wandered back to their accommodation. They had some free time before dinner.

As Cher had got into the shower while Zoe was giving Fenella her shopping, Zoe switched on her laptop while she was waiting, aware Cher might take a while. Zoe was looking for a recipe. She'd just about tracked down the one she wanted when Cher emerged wrapped in a towel and peered over her shoulder, her nearness causing a drip to land on the keyboard. Zoe closed down the site and switched off her laptop.

'Being a bit precious about what you're planning to cook, aren't you?' Cher said.

'Am I? What are you planning then?' Zoe asked.

'Oh, not telling! Unless you tell me, of course. We wouldn't want to be doing the same thing, after all.'

Zoe was not a natural games player but she was

beginning to learn. 'Oh, OK,' she said brightly. 'It does make sense. You go first.'

Cher's expression hardened almost imperceptibly as she dressed. She didn't seem to mind doing so in front of Zoe but then with a body like hers she had nothing to hide. 'No, you.' She was now preening herself in front of the mirror.

'Right. Well, I thought I'd do this thing that was in a book of my mother's. Basically it's choux pastry that you deep fry.'

Cher made a face. 'Dreadfully fattening!'

'That won't matter. We don't have to eat them. What about you?'

'Oh, I haven't decided yet. I need a bit more time to think about it.'

Zoe considered protesting but the truth was she hadn't decided on her entire menu herself. Fortunately deep-fried choux pastry was only one of her ideas.

The minibus took everyone down to the pub in the village but only some people wanted to stay late. Cher was an early leaver, catching a lift with a local she'd found in the bar and trusted enough to take her home. But although Zoe arrived back less than twenty minutes later, when she got back to their room, she found the door firmly locked.

'This is bloody ridiculous,' said Zoe, after banging on the door for several fruitless minutes and searching through her list of contacts on her phone in the faint hope that she had Cher's number and could ring her to ask her to unlock the door. 'Cher?' she shouted. 'It's me, Zoe. You can't be asleep already! Let me in!'

There was no answer. It was all so quiet Zoe wondered if she was actually in there. For a few moments she worried whether Cher, having accepted a lift from someone she didn't know, had actually been kidnapped. But he'd seemed well known in the pub and had spent a lot of time talking about his wife and children.

Still, a few scenarios went through Zoe's mind involving Cher being hideously murdered before she spotted a hairclip on the step. She was fairly sure it hadn't been there when they left, which made her confident Cher was inside.

She shouted through the door again but got no answer and then she walked round the building, trying to find a window or something she could climb through. There was nothing, although a good peer through one of them revealed Cher's bag. She hadn't been murdered – yet!

She didn't want to wake up the other contestants who were on the premises and anyway, what could they do? There was only one thing for it: they would have a spare key at the house. She walked up there, but she was very annoyed. It was well after ten and she knew Fenella was getting to bed as early as she could. Rupert might be up though.

This optimistic thought faded as she approached the back door. There was no light on anywhere downstairs. She could see one high up on the second floor, but the basement, where the kitchen was, appeared to be deserted. Although she knew it was pointless, she tried to open the back door. Of course it was locked.

'This is so stupid!' said Zoe and marched back to the cowshed, determined to make Cher wake up this time.

She banged on the door until her fist felt bruised. No response. She decided she would have to throw stones at the light in the Somerby window and get Rupert up. There was an incline to the front of the house and she walked up it briskly, fired by irritation that was bordering on anxiety. What would she do if she couldn't get into her accommodation? She had to sleep somewhere!

As she arrived, puffing slightly, at the front door, a car drew up. Relief flooded over her. Here was someone who could help. She was even more relieved to see it was Gideon. Although he would think her mad or incompetent for not being able to get into her little house, she did at least know him.

'What are you doing here?' he asked. 'Have you just prepared your food for tomorrow or do you have an assignation?'

'Neither! My bloody room-mate has locked me out and I need to get into the house to find another key.' She paused. 'There must be one.'

'I haven't got a key to anywhere but I know where the one to the back door is. Let's go round.'

Zoe began to feel calmer. Soon she would be able to go to bed. She'd kill Cher in the morning.

The key was on the top of a thick old door that led to a cellar and Gideon soon had the back door open. As they walked up the passage to the kitchen Zoe rubbed her head and found she was sweating.

'God, I need a cup of tea!' she said, sounding desperate, as they entered the kitchen. She moved the kettle on to the hot plate. It was an emergency and tea was always a good thing at such times. Despite the sweat she was also rather cold. 'Do you want one? Then we can look for a key to my cowshed.'

'Tea would be great.' Gideon pulled out a chair and sat down at the long table.

They drank tea in companionable silence. Zoe felt calmer now, convinced that when they got up they would go into the passage and find a key cupboard, with all the keys neatly labelled. Everything seemed much better now she had someone else there to help her.

They found a key-cupboard, but sadly, under 'Cowshed' there was no key.

'I can't believe they don't have spares,' muttered Zoe on a sigh of desperation. 'What am I to do?'

'Well, first we'll go back to the cowshed and make sure the door really is locked, not jammed or anything. Then we'll have another go at waking Cher.'

'I really tried!' She rubbed her wrist, remembering how sore she'd made it hammering on the door.

'And if that plan fails, we'll revert to plan B.'

'Which is?' she said, trotting after him.

'I'll tell you when I've thought of it.'

Oddly, Zoe was relieved when Gideon couldn't get into the cowshed either. She'd have felt incredibly stupid if the door had just sprung open, having been unlocked all this time. 'OK, time for plan B,' she said.

He laughed softly. 'I do have one but you won't like it.'

'If it involves me getting a night's sleep, I'll love it,' said Zoe, yawning.

'It involves sharing my room, which is massive,' he said.

'Fine. I feel I could sleep on a rail just now, let alone in a massive room.'

'There is only one bed though. It's massive too.'

Zoe paused. They were nearly at the back door. 'You're joking, aren't you?'

'No.'

'I can't believe there isn't another room I could sleep in,' said Zoe. 'This house is enormous.'

'It's also under restoration and lots of rooms are being decorated. But most importantly, they don't have beds.'

'Ah,' said Zoe. 'I do need a bed.'

'So, back to plan B. But I've got the bridal suite, which is being done up. The painters were in there today. The bed is as big as a tennis court – obviously in case the wedding night doesn't go that well.'

'Right.'

'I'm not offering to sleep on the chair,' he said firmly. 'For one thing we both have to work tomorrow and need a good night's sleep, and for a second thing, there isn't one.'

'What? Nothing to leave your clothes on?'

'There's a stool for the dressing table.' He opened the door. 'Come on. There's no other reasonable solution.'

Reluctantly Zoe followed him into the house and up two flights of stairs to the bridal suite. Half of her was terrified by the idea of sharing a bed with him but the other was excited. She'd already admitted to herself she fancied him. This was obviously God's way of testing her. At the door she stopped. 'I haven't got a toothbrush or anything to sleep in.'

'I've got those bottle brush things you can fiddle about with and I'll lend you a shirt. Now please stop being prim about this. As I said, we've both got a heavy day tomorrow.'

Having given up all resistance (which she had to admit wasn't that strong by now) Zoe found you could do quite a good job without a toothbrush with a tiny bottle brush, toothpaste and a towel. And the shirt was fairly decent provided she kept her knickers on. She would have liked some sort of moisturiser but didn't mention it. He didn't seem quite metrosexual enough to have any.

Gideon was sitting up in the enormous bed. He was wearing a towelling dressing gown. She didn't ask him why. She assumed it was because he usually slept naked and was sparing her. She appreciated it though. For a moment the thought of what was underneath his robe flashed through her mind and she blushed. She got in the other side, keeping as near to the edge as she could without actually falling out. There was about two feet of unused bed between them. It would be fine. All she had to do was imagine Gideon was a fellow student or something. Then there'd be nothing odd about them sharing a bed platonically. The trouble was, the words 'platonic' and 'Gideon' didn't compute in her brain. She fancied him far too much. And he was kind. He'd put himself out a lot for her. That didn't make her like him any less.

'There's only one bedside light, I'm afraid.'

'It's all right, I haven't got my book with me anyway. I don't want to read.'

'I'll put the light out then.' He sounded strangely formal considering they were sharing a bed, although he gave the impression it was perfectly natural for them to be doing so and wasn't at all embarrassed.

'Thank you. Good night.' She lay down on her side, assuming the position she always adopted to sleep in. She felt him turn over too.

But his action had caused a tent, so she shuffled back a bit. Then she closed her eyes.

Tired as she was, sleep wouldn't come. She wanted to turn over but as there was no sound from Gideon she assumed he'd gone to sleep and she didn't want to disturb him.

She tried to focus on what she had to do the following day. She had her menu pretty much worked out and knew where to find the recipes but the ingredients she had brought from the cheese place were tormenting her. They were so good and unusual.

She had hundreds of recipes stored in her laptop and they'd been told they could bring recipes into the challenge. In theory, all she had to do in the morning was print out the ones she needed courtesy of her mini printer. But there wasn't a recipe using soft cheese, honey and bullaces on there.

Knowing that her ingredients were excellent and she might have a couple of things the others wouldn't have was reassuring. It was well within her abilities to produce a first-class meal but her original thoughts for a pudding seemed very predictable.

These thoughts did nothing to help her relax. In fact, they were making her more tense and further from sleep.

She searched her mind for something soothing – counting backwards (boring), seeing how many of her recipes she knew by heart (too closely connected with the competition), all her school mates' birthdays (pointless as they were all on Facebook).

There was a rustle from the other side of the bed. 'You're not managing to get to sleep, are you?' said Gideon into the darkness.

'Sorry! I'm trying to keep still.'

'You are still but you're very tense. I can feel it.'

'I don't know what to do about that. I can't stop thinking about the competition tomorrow. If I don't sleep I won't function well.' She exhaled sharply.

He thought for a minute. 'What would you do if you couldn't get to sleep at home?'

'It hardly every happens! I have no techniques. All the ones I've just tried make it worse.'

She felt him move again and the bedside light went on. 'Tempted as I am to suggest some mad passionate sex is what you need to relax you, I don't think it would.'

'No,' she squeaked. Was he joking? Just him saying that added a new layer of tension. If the circumstances had been right, and she couldn't just this minute imagine what they might be, she'd have leapt into his arms with enthusiasm. But not now.

'Right. I'm going to do what my mother used to do with me when I was ill as a child.'

'Oh?' This sounded suitably safe, assuming his mother wasn't a witch or anything.

'She read to me. And I've got something you might like.'

He got up and she could hear him rummaging in a bag. He brought the book back and got into bed.

'Now you'll have to snuggle up a bit – part of the relaxing process. Put your head on my shoulder.'

It took a bit of wriggling for Zoe to get herself comfortable but she did find the human contact took away some of her stress. There was nothing sexual about his offer now, of course. He was being kind and very practical. They both needed to sleep and by helping her he'd help himself. She felt a slight flicker of disappointment and then concentrated on enjoying the feeling of closeness.

'Right, now close your eyes.'

He started to read. After a few moments she said, 'I know what this is! Elizabeth David! Old school but lovely writing. Which book is it?'

'Don't worry about that, just listen.'

He had a beautiful voice, more beautiful now he was reading and not being masterful. The combination of that and Elizabeth David's wonderful prose made Zoe stop wanting to go to sleep. She just wanted to listen.

Zoe woke once in the night and immediately worried about the following morning. Turning up at the Somerby table in yesterday's clothes smelling of Gideon's shower gel might take a little explaining.

She turned over and went back to sleep, fully intending to get up early and be out of the way before Gideon woke in order to avoid any awkward 'you first, no you first' conversations about the bathroom.

Instead, she was woken by Gideon, fully dressed, putting a mug of tea on the table next to her and handing her a piece of toast on a plate.

'Morning. Get your laughing gear round that.'

She stared up at him. Last night he had soothed her to sleep with his beautiful voice and tales of Mediterranean food. This morning it was the worst sort of slang. She took the plate, grateful. His vulgarity took away any potential embarrassment.

'Thank you. Is it late? I meant to get up early.'

'It's half past seven and Cher still isn't opening the door. But Fen's looking for the spare key. I thought you might as well have some breakfast while she finds it.'

Zoe sipped the tea. 'That was kind of you. Did Fen say anything about me sleeping here?'

'Nothing to make you feel awkward. I don't think Cher is her favourite person. She did say we should have woken her though.'

'What, Fen? No we shouldn't!'

'Rupert agreed with us. Anyway, I'll leave you to it. You should be able to get to your toothbrush fairly soon.'

Alone again, Zoe lay back on the pillows and closed her eyes. It had been lovely sharing a bed with Gideon. In spite of finding him almost unbearably sexy they'd shared a closeness that was separate, special. At least that was how she felt. Yet this morning he was all brusque efficiency. He was infuriatingly hard to read.

Now she had to face reality: embarrassment; and the knowledge that sleeping with a judge, however innocently, was definitely against the rules. She was so anxious about the task ahead that her contentment slowly leaked away, like cold water seeping from a burst hot water bottle. It's hardly noticeable at first but soon the cold is too uncomfortable to bear and you have to get out and strip the bed.

As if the bed really was damp and cold Zoe got out and ran to the bathroom. A hot shower would sort her out.

Thankfully Fenella and Rupert hadn't been around when she let herself out of the back door and scurried over to the cowshed. Cher was in the shower when Zoe let herself in in. All the fury she had felt last night came back to her. She shouted through the bathroom door.

'Cher? What the hell happened? Why couldn't I get in? Why did you lock the door?'

The shower stopped and Cher, possibly aware she couldn't avoid an angry Zoe for ever, came out, wearing a towel. 'Oh God! I'm sooo sorry! Nightmare! I had a headache and took some tablets and then I just sort of passed out.'

'But why did you lock the door? You knew I wouldn't be long behind you?'

'I just did it automatically, I suppose. I am so sorry!'

Zoe brushed past Cher and went into the bathroom. Perhaps brushing her teeth with a proper toothbrush and putting on some make-up would make her feel more charitable.

A change of clothes helped too, and, believing she could now at least share a space with Cher without wanting to kill her, she went to her laptop to download her recipes. Except her battery was dead – which was odd because she'd left it plugged into the mains. But now everything was unplugged and her computer completely unresponsive.

'Cher? Have you done anything to my laptop?'

'Why would I? I have my own laptop.'

Frustrated and confused Zoe went to plug her computer into the mains. They didn't have long. They had to be ready to cook soon. But her mains lead was missing. She hunted for it. There wasn't even time to fall on Rupert and Fenella's mercy and ask to use their computer. She asked Cher if she'd seen it but she just shrugged.

'Does this mean you have to cook without your recipes?' she asked.

Zoe just growled.

Chapter Seven

After a somewhat chilly five minutes' silence, there was a banging on the door. 'Come on, girls,' said Mike. 'Time to get on the bus.'

Certain that Cher had deliberately run down her laptop battery and hidden her mains lead, Zoe kept silent. She had no time or energy to waste on Cher. She had to get her head together. She snatched up a notebook and pencil and stuffed it in her bag. She not only had to think up a pudding using her wonderful cheese and honey, but a starter as well.

Cher locked the door behind them, an action that reminded Zoe she had to give Fenella the spare key back. She ran up the incline to the back door, threw the key on the table in the empty kitchen and joined the minibus, the last one to do so.

'I saved a place for you,' said Cher, all solicitude. 'Poor old Zoe got locked out last night,' she went on. 'I passed out by mistake and she couldn't wake me.'

Zoe was forced to take the seat next to Cher as there was nowhere else.

'And so where did you sleep?' she asked in Bambi-eyed innocence with just the hint of a calculating glint.

Zoe hadn't had time to think of a credible story so she trimmed the truth. 'I found somewhere in the main house.'

'Oh!' Cher sounded surprised. 'I thought they couldn't have contestants because of the renovations?'

'I slept in a room that was still being decorated,' she said. 'Fen sorted me out.'

'Oh! I heard Gideon telling someone he was sleeping in the new wedding suite that was being painted. Is there another room?'

'Cher, if you don't mind, I've really got to focus. As you know I haven't been able to print off my recipes so I've got to do some thinking now.'

'You haven't got your recipes?' said Becca, sounding completely horrified.

Zoe was more and more convinced that Becca would win. She was obsessive and the way she talked about cooking and food told Zoe that although she hadn't seen the evidence of it herself yet, she must be a brilliant cook. If she was going to beat her she'd need help from the angels.

'Yes, my laptop battery was completely run down and I couldn't find my mains lead. Funny that.'

There was a shocked silence. 'I hope you don't mind me saying this, but I do think you should have been a bit better organised,' Becca said.

Zoe bit her lip. She'd just have to brazen it out. It wasn't her fault her computer wasn't working. And she was fairly sure it wasn't an accident either. 'You're right, I should have had the recipes on paper as well as on the computer, but I hadn't decided – I wanted to keep my options open.'

Becca nodded. 'I brought half a ton of recipes with me. It probably seems like overkill.'

'Nothing wrong with being prepared,' said Alan. 'I've learnt a lot of recipes by heart. It's sort of a habit with me, learning lines.' He smiled at Becca. 'I was an actor in a previous incarnation.'

Becca nodded, smiling shyly.

'Learn your recipes by heart?' said Bill. 'I couldn't remember my own name if it wasn't written on my vest.'

Everyone laughed but this banter just made Zoe even more worried about having to work with only her memory and her cooking skills to rely on.

At this point the minibus arrived at the field that, with the aid of very superior tents, had been turned into the competition kitchen. Zoe went to her allocated space with its own cooker, worktop and various kitchen gadgets, including knives. She, like many of the others, would have preferred to bring her own knives but the organisers had decided random people carrying knives wasn't safe. She remembered Dwaine at the restaurant who'd somehow smuggled his in: they had a point.

'OK, people!' said Mike. 'You know what you have to do. Three perfect courses using only the local ingredients you sourced yesterday. Other basic permitted ingredients are at your stations. You have three hours. The judges will wander between you and talk to you about your menus. Go!' Zoe fell on her pad and wrote out her menu as planned. *Pignatelli*: choux pastry with cheese and bacon deep fried, as a starter. At least she knew how to make it. Pork fillet with a cream and local calvados sauce, salad leaves and sauté potatoes. Then her pen stopped. Pudding. What was she going to do for a pudding? If all else failed she could make a fool from the bottled bullaces and the cream, but that was hardly competition-standard food.

Aware she was wasting valuable time, she decided to focus on what she could do. She stared at the list. Her pork didn't really require a recipe but although she'd made *pignatelli* hundreds of times she suddenly panicked that she wouldn't remember how to make choux pastry. It would be easy to mess it up.

The judges came up to her while she was still writing, still undecided.

'So, what are you up to?' said Fred, the friendly television chef beloved by the nation.

'I'm just trying to work out my recipes.' Suddenly noticing the camera behind the judges, she added a smile at the last minute.

'Don't you have your recipes with you?' Anna Fortune was easily the most scary of the three judges, although Zoe had to admit she rather admired her.

What was she to say? She was going to look like an idiot! On the other hand, if she told the truth at least she wouldn't have to be duplicitous as well incompetent. 'I had them on my laptop but when I went to print them off this morning I found that the battery was dead and my mains lead was missing.' The smile this time was probably more of a grimace.

Gideon raised an eyebrow. 'How did that happen?'

'I don't know.' She didn't, for certain. She only suspected Cher. 'Of course I would have done all this last night, after I'd bought my ingredients and planned my menu, but I was locked out of my accommodation and so couldn't.' She didn't bother to smile this time. She didn't trust herself to look at Gideon.

'Well, what are you going to do?' asked Anna Fortune.

'I'll be fine,' she said hurriedly, realising whatever she said she'd either look unprofessional or a snitch. She sought an unhappy compromise. 'I have a very good memory.' This was telly, she'd have to wing it.

'So, what is your menu?' asked Fred. 'Or what would it have been?'

She smiled at him. He was very reassuring, like a teddy bear, cuddly and uncritical. 'I was going to do something called *pignatelli*, which means pine cones. It's a retro seventies sort of starter I haven't seen except in my mother's house.' She smiled.

'It sounds ideal!'

'I should be able to remember how to make it.' She tried to keep the doubt out of her voice.

'Ah,' said Fred. He went on quickly, as if to get over a sticky bit. 'What about your pudding?'

'I haven't decided.' She tried to look as if this wasn't a problem at all.

Anna Fortune frowned. 'Well, you're going to have to make some decisions quickly. You haven't unlimited time. Chefs who are always behind time are a pain as well as being totally unprofessional.'

She had a clear and carrying voice and Zoe could see Cher listening to Zoe's telling off with a satisfied smirk.

'I'll be on time,' said Zoe with a confidence she didn't feel.

'I hope so.'

Anna Fortune and Fred moved on but Gideon stayed behind.

'Did you leave your laptop on all night, not plugged into the mains?' he asked, frowning.

'No. Of course not. It was like that when I finally got into my room.'

'Ah.' He paused. 'So what are you going to do? You have some wonderful ingredients, pancetta, cheese, eggs . . .'

Just hearing him say those words sent her back to the previous night when he had read to her to make her sleep. She shivered. 'Soufflé! I'll make a soufflé!' she said as inspiration suddenly struck.

'But you'll never do that without a recipe.' He spoke definitively.

She smiled sincerely for the first time in ages. 'Yes I will. It's not as unusual as my original idea but I've made them far more often. If it comes off . . .'

'A very high-risk strategy, if I may say,' said Gideon who, Zoe felt, would have said something quite different if the cameras hadn't been around. 'And what about your pudding?'

'Haven't thought of what to do yet. I have such wonderful things to cook with, something is bound to come to me!' Aware of the cameras she smiled brightly. 'If you'll excuse me, I must get on.'

Feeling slightly less pressured when the judges and the cameras moved away, Zoe went through the ingredients that were waiting for them. Puff pastry! There was puff pastry, ready rolled and easy to use. Her pudding problem was solved! And she could get it done straight away.

Although she'd sounded confident when she was talking to Gideon the thought of making a soufflé without a recipe was terrifying. All her other dishes had gone well. The cream sauce had to be finished and her pudding, using the blessed puff pastry, looked amazing. She had whipped and flavoured some cream to go with it. It needed glazing with a blow torch just before serving but otherwise it was done. There was only the soufflé to do now.

She prepared the dishes carefully, brushing the butter in vertical lines up the sides. Then she lined them with very fine toasted breadcrumbs, grateful that bread was one of the permitted basic ingredients. Finally she grated her cheese and fried her pancetta before chopping it finely. She'd never made a cheese and bacon soufflé before and she was not at all sure that Elizabeth David, credited with teaching the British how to cook, would approve, but she'd sourced the pancetta, she was determined to use it.

At last, she set the timer and cleared her work station, silently praying that the right things were going on in the oven. She was aware of the others bustling about at their stations, although she resolutely avoided looking over at Cher. She was sure to have created perfection and be smiling sweetly at a passing camera by now.

Zoe inspected her pudding. It was she felt, extremely appealing. She had made three circles of puff pastry with a hollow in the middle. Into these she'd put slices of the Brie-type cheese. Then she'd added a spoonful of what she thought of as 'Uncle Jim's honey'. On top of everything there were three bullaces. They looked delightful, three golden globes like paler, miniature apricots. She had dusted the tarts with icing sugar and glazed them so they looked extremely appetising. She was pleased with herself. She just wished she hadn't had to think on her feet. (Thankfully, she was quite good at it.)

'Please come to me first,' she prayed, and then looked through the glass door of the oven. 'Or better, second.' The soufflés had risen but not quite enough for Zoe. They looked as if they could go a bit higher.

Gideon came up and peered into her oven through the door. Obviously feeling the same he said, 'OK. I'll just have a word.'

Cher, whose beautifully garnished chicken liver pâté had already been filmed, was looking across to Zoe, her mouth compressed with anger and her eyes flashing. 'He's giving you special treatment! It's outrageous!'

Gideon, who was passing her bench with the other

judges said, 'We hope to be fair to all contestants, Cher. Zoe had an unfortunate accident and she had to work without recipes.' He glared at her in a way that made Zoe hope she would never be at the other end of such a look. 'To be truly fair, we'd have made you all work without them.'

Cher blushed and pouted and didn't say any more.

Under the steely eyes of the judges, Zoe retrieved her soufflés, certain she'd drop them on the floor even if they didn't drop by themselves.

'Well, they look delicious,' said Anna Fortune, sounding a little surprised. 'What are they?'

'Cheese and pancetta,' said Zoe.

Anna picked up a fork and made her way into the puffy goldenness before her. 'Mm! And so far no one else has had pancetta. Where did you source that?'

Zoe produced the leaflet from the farm showing its address. Anna Fortune looked at it. 'It doesn't mention pancetta.'

'It does cider apples and pork. Also Calvados, bacon and sausages. The pancetta was an experiment. I was lucky to get some.'

'OK, let's move on to your main course . . .'

Fred forked up most of a soufflé. 'There's no point in leaving it hanging around,' he said. 'It'll have sunk completely before the camera crew have a chance.' The camera crew, who were moving in for a close-up, muttered.

Gideon tasted the remaining soufflé and grunted.

'Very nice pork,' said Anna. 'You can taste the pigs were reared on apples. Sauce is fine, hasn't split. Now your pudding . . .'

Zoe produced her tarts.

'They certainly look very pretty,' said Anna, going in with her fork. 'What are they?'

Zoe didn't answer immediately. She wanted the flavour of the Brie, which would be unexpected, to reach Anna's palette before she told her what was in it. Anna was nodding and Fred's fork attacked another tart. Gideon went last.

'I'm getting some sort of cheese, and then honey,' he said. 'What are the fruits? Plums?'

'Bullaces. They're a sort of wild plum. I've used bottled ones from the place that provided the honey and the cheese.'

'An excellent combination,' said Fred. 'I like that very much.'

'I think this recipe could be worked on a bit,' said Anna, 'but altogether not bad at all. You were the one working without recipes?'

Zoe nodded. Anna didn't speak but Zoe thought her expression indicated approval.

'Well done!' said Gideon quietly, and then the judges moved on. It looked as if she wouldn't be going out just yet!

At last Zoe was able to relax and she started cleaning her station. When she looked up she saw that Cher was being judged. She couldn't hear exactly what was being said but the judges' expressions told her they were pretty pleased with what she had offered them. Her good mood dipped somewhat; the thought of living with Cher for at least two more days was not a cheery prospect.

Zoe was able to text her mother 'Still in!'

One of the lads went out: Daniel. He claimed, as they had a consoling drink in the pub afterwards, that he couldn't be hemmed in by petty regulations and had he been able to cook what he wanted to cook (molluscs, mostly) he'd have been blinding. 'I can't be bothered with all that local and seasonal stuff. If I want asparagus in January, I'll have it.' He glared at the group, suspecting not all of them were on his side. 'And if anyone mentions global warming or food miles I'll f—' He paused, possibly aware of Muriel, who wouldn't hesitate to tell him off if he swore too badly. '—bloody punch them!'

'So you did rather well, considering,' said Cher to Zoe, sending her a smouldering look across the table. 'I reckon Gideon likes you.' She made a dismissive little sound. 'Not sure why, unless there's something you care to tell us.'

'I don't think any of the judges showed any signs of favouritism,' said Becca, whose confidence had been boosted by some very nice compliments from the judges. 'I think Zoe just did a really good job with her ingredients. I thought her pudding was lovely.'

'Not that lovely,' Cher persisted 'I happen to know something about her and Gideon the rest of you don't!'

'Please don't talk about me as if I'm not here,' said Zoe, feeling suddenly desperately tired.

'Well, if you don't want me to tell everyone where you slept last night, you'd better do it yourself!' said Cher. She'd had a couple of glasses of wine and it seemed to have made her more aggressive than usual.

'No one is remotely interested in where I slept last night!' said Zoe. 'Can you just leave the subject alone?' Damn Cher, she obviously wasn't going to give up lightly.

'I think people will be interested if it affects your chances in the competition!' Cher looked around, making sure everyone at the table was listening now. 'So tell us!'

Zoe sighed, aware she had to say something.'Because Miss Zonked-out here couldn't be woken to let me in, I had to find somewhere in the main house to sleep.

Which I did. Now why is that anybody's business but mine?'

'Why are you making such a fuss about this, Cher?' asked Muriel. Zoe could have kissed her. 'It sounds to me as if it's a story that doesn't put you in a good light.'

'Never mind about me!' said Cher, determined to finish what she'd started. 'Make Zoe tell you!'

'I really don't see—' Zoe began, frantically trying to think of something she could say that wasn't too incriminating.

'Did you, or did you not, sleep with Gideon Irving?' Cher banged on the table for emphasis.

'Oh, for heaven's sake, don't be ridiculous, Cher. You could get a job standing in for Jeremy Kyle, you could,' said Muriel. 'Now can we move on? Anyone got a clue about the next challenge?'

Zoe, who did have a clue in that she knew a wedding was coming up, didn't answer.

Muriel went on, 'Well, let's think what we've done so far. Teamwork in the restaurant . . .'

'An individual challenge,' said Becca, 'which I preferred. I find relying on other people too nerve-racking.' She glanced at Cher.

'I like teamwork,' said Alan. 'In the theatre you have to rely on each other. I'm used to it.'

'I still think Zoe should tell us where she slept last night,' said Cher doggedly.

'Oh, let go of the bone, Cher!' said Alan. 'She's told us. The main house. Lucky her. It really doesn't make a difference to any of us if it was the second-best bedroom or the bridal suite.'

Zoe felt herself blush because it had been the bridal suite. 'It is a huge house. There are loads of bedrooms, although most seem to have the floorboards up or

86

something. What I want to know is what the rest of you would do if you won the competition? I want to open a deli. What about you, Alan?' She knew, of course, but she was desperate to change the subject.

'Oh, definitely the gastro pub, somewhere lovely, where all my muckers from the old days would come,' said Alan, suddenly dreamy. 'I can see it now. I might even buy a few vines in France, produce my own wine and sell it in the restaurant.'

'That sounds fun,' said Muriel. 'I just want a small restaurant in my own area where people can go out for a jolly good meal and not spend a fortune.'

Becca shuddered. 'I love cooking but I do not want to run a restaurant – or even work in one.'

'Why not?' demanded Daniel, emerging from his pit of failure. 'I love the buzz, the excitement—'

'I hate being shouted at and from what I've seen, there's a lot of shouting in restaurants,' Becca explained.

Zoe nodded. 'You're dead right. I don't think people work well under that sort of pressure.'

'You're both wusses!' declared Shadrach. 'I really get off on that stuff.'

Zoe and Becca exchanged glances.

'What about you, Cher?' asked Zoe, wanting to get back at her for her earlier harassment.

'Oh, I don't know,' said Cher. 'I don't need the money – it's not all that much anyway. I'd just use it to help my career in some way.'

'So how do you think you're going to cope if you don't like stress?' demanded Daniel, looking at Becca.

Becca looked around for an answer.

'Leave her alone, Daniel,' said Zoe. 'It's nothing to do with you any more!'

'That's so unfair!' said Cher. 'You can't pick on Daniel

just because he's not in the competition. He shouldn't have gone out! You should!' Cher's eyes glittered with resentment.

'Why should she have gone out, Cher?' asked Muriel calmly.

'Because . . .' She glanced at Zoe, possibly assessing her chances of getting away with what she wanted to say. Zoe's expression hardened. She went on: 'Because she didn't even cook from recipes!'

'Oh come on,' said Muriel. 'I hardly ever cook from recipes. Zoe's a good cook. She kept her place through being good, not through sleeping with one of the judges or whatever you were trying to imply earlier.' She raised an eyebrow at Zoe. Zoe warmed to her even more.

'You can believe what you want, Muriel. I know what I know!' Cher flounced off to the loo and Zoe breathed a sigh of relief.

'I'll get another round in,' said Alan.

'Good idea. I could do with something to take my mind off that unpleasant little scene,' said Muriel.

Zoe looked at her gratefully, glad of her support.

'You did brilliantly, Zoe,' said Becca. 'No one thinks you shouldn't still be here.'

But suddenly, Zoe wondered that herself. Should she? She pushed away the thought but accepted the top-up of wine that Alan was now offering. She glanced around the table and wondered if the kind words from Muriel and Becca and the silent backing of Shona actually reflected the expression in their faces. She was fairly sure they'd meant what they'd said about her cooking, but did they think she'd slept with Gideon?

She glanced at her watch. She wanted to go back to the cowshed, suddenly uncomfortable with the company. She liked the other contestants – well, most of them anyway.

Usually she rather enjoyed their free-time chats (they'd all decided Anna Fortune was the one they had to watch) but tonight she just wanted to be alone to sort out her feelings.

Cher had returned from the Ladies when Mike came over and sat with them for a bit, nursing the last inch of a bottle of beer as he had to drive the bus back later.

'So, are you all geared up for tomorrow's challenge?' he asked.

'No! We don't know what it is yet,' said Cher. 'They're not telling us until tomorrow.'

'Obviously I don't want to spoil the surprise,' said Mike. 'But I'll warn you, it's a team effort and a tough one.'

'Mikey, darling,' said Cher, linking herself to him and stroking his forearm. 'Do give us a little tiny hintette.'

'Wellies,' he said, enjoying the attention. 'You'll probably need wellies.'

They'd all been told to bring wellington boots without being told why.

'Oh God!' groaned Cher. 'We're going to have to cook in a f—' She too glanced at Muriel and moderated her language. '—flipping field!'

'That's it!' said Mike, finishing his drink. 'Now time to go home unless you want to walk back.'

Zoe was first on the bus. On the short journey she found herself thinking not of the cooking over bonfires she'd done as a child but of Gideon. And she wished she'd had the courage to sleep with him properly. If she was going to get blamed for it, she might as well have had the pleasure. She fancied him so much and it would have been something to remember forever.

Zoe woke once during the night to shut her window, which was dripping on her. It had started to rain and she

89

just had time to realise this would mean the field they were to cook in would be muddy before she drifted off to sleep and dreams of sexy food critics and Elizabeth David.

Chapter Eight

Zoe's phone awoke them at seven the following morning and they got ready without speaking beyond 'do you want tea or coffee?' Zoe decided to try and stop worrying about Cher trying to sabotage her – it was just too difficult to share a house otherwise.

Cher peered out of the window. 'It's bloody pouring with rain. Why is it today we have to cook in a field?'

'Just the way it is. Anyway, we cooked in a field yesterday.' She went on, 'Have you done anything like that before?'

'Are you joking? As if!'

Zoe wasn't surprised. She didn't see Cher as the Girl Guide type. Glamping would be the nearest she ever got.

They ate their breakfast cereal in silence and headed for the bus.

'OK, guys!' said Mike once they'd arrived at a beauty spot about half an hour away and were safely under canvas. 'Two teams of four. The judges will decide who goes where and will tell you what's going on.'

While they waited for the cameramen to do their thing, Zoe crossed her fingers that she wouldn't be in Cher's team. It wasn't that she was afraid of Cher over-salting her potatoes or anything – if they were on the same team she wouldn't risk jeopardising their chances – but rather that she'd probably be hopeless in conditions without electricity and running water.

'Good morning, contestants!' said Anna Fortune. 'I hope you all had a good night's sleep because you've a tough challenge before you today.'

Zoe felt herself blush but decided she had to get over it. Cher might have worked out where she slept the other night but there was no reason to think the judges – apart from Gideon, obviously – had any inkling. 'You're going to be cooking a hearty lunch for two groups of ramblers. They will have walked up to seven miles and will be hungry – and wet! They'll want soup, main course and pudding, but at twelve o'clock on the dot. That gives you three hours. The winning team will be decided by the walkers, but we'll decide which of you, from the losing team, will go out. Fred, will you tell them who they're working with?'

Fred smiled benignly and produced a piece of paper from his pocket.

'OK, we have two team leaders, Muriel and Bill. Bill's team is Shona, Alan and Becca. Muriel has . . .'

Zoe didn't listen to the names. Once she'd realised she'd be working with Cher her spirits slumped. Still, they had Shadrach, who seemed to be brilliant, although how he'd cope without anything except knives and chopping boards had yet to be seen and he was rather messy. Zoe knew that Muriel would be all right, and she would be too. Her own experience as a Saturday girl in a small, ill-equipped café meant she was used to depending on sub-standard equipment.

'There are ingredients over there.' Fred made a gesture towards a section of the tented area where piles of boxes could be seen. 'Decide what you want to cook and get down to it. It's up to the team leaders to decide who's doing what. Their decision is final so no arguing. You have three hours.'

'Right, team,' said Muriel. 'Follow me to help carry back the food. I'll choose what to do.'

'I don't peel potatoes,' said Cher.

'What do you mean you don't peel potatoes?' said Zoe. 'Are you genetically different from the rest of us?'

Cher scowled at her. 'I don't do peeling. Just saying.'

Zoe heard Muriel muttering as she strode towards the food, Shadrach at her heels.

'Come on, we must go and help,' said Zoe, tugging Cher's sleeve.

'I so don't want to do this!' Cher said.

'Look, we're all in this together,' said Zoe. 'If we lose, one of us will go out. If you don't pull your weight, it'll be you!'

Finally convinced, Cher followed Zoe to where the others were grabbing provisions and piling them into a basket. She was muttering as she went, but as soon as a camera panned in she was all smiles. The moment it moved to the other group her scowl returned. Zoe couldn't help marvel at Cher's chameleon ability to switch the charm on and off and also to sense when the camera was on her.

'Right,' said Muriel, 'we missed the chicken so we've got stewing steak. That'll be a casserole then.'

'We could put a pastry top on it,' suggested Shadrach. 'Pie is better than just stew.'

'Good point!' said Muriel. 'Let's hope we have time. There was lots of flour and butter to make it and we have butternut squash, so that's our soup option.'

Zoe had a private groan fearing she would be left cutting up the squashes and that they were very tough. With luck there'd be a potato peeler.

93

'So what are we doing for sweet?' asked Cher.

'I don't know. We have some lovely dried apricots so we could do a crumble,' said Muriel.

'I heard the others say they were doing crumble,' said Cher. Perhaps her knack for overhearing things had some good uses, Zoe thought.

Muriel sighed. 'What else can you do with apricots that isn't a pie or a crumble or a mousse or a soufflé?' she added, looking at Shadrach the designated expert, who shrugged.

'Bread and butter pudding,' said Zoe. 'With apricots. I think I saw bread and we've loads of butter and eggs.'

'I don't like bread and butter pudding,' said Cher. 'It's so carby.'

Muriel speared her with an eye that revealed her past career as a teacher. 'I think I'll put you on veg prep, Cher. Now, you have to be quick because if we don't get the stew on, the meat'll be chewy.'

'Shouldn't we do the soup first, seeing as it's the first course?' said Cher, who, in response to Muriel, had turned into a stroppy teenager. 'The hint is in the name?'

'No, butternut squash is quick to cook. We need to get the meat on. Shadrach, you chop that, the rest of us will do the veg.'

'This is quite fun, actually,' said Cher to Zoe a bit later. She was dicing an onion into perfect cubes. Zoe was in agony watching her, she was being so slow.

'Just as much fun if you go a bit faster,' said Zoe, who was taking a cleaver to a butternut squash the size of a loaf of bread.

'No, it's only fun if you do it really precisely,' said Cher and Zoe decided it wasn't her job to try and make her speed up. The squash fell into two and she raised her cleaver again.

'Hey, watch what you're doing with that, you'll have your fingers off,' complained Muriel. 'I can't afford to have you out of action.'

The judges chose this moment to swing by. Gideon, seeing Zoe with her cleaver, sucked in his breath and took it out of her hand. He picked up her board and tutted. Then he found a cloth, wetted it, spread it out, and put the board back on top. 'If you were in a professional kitchen and didn't do that, the chef would slaughter you,' he growled. 'I told you before!'

'Yes, chef,' muttered Zoe.

'And the same goes for you too!' He sent his scorching glance towards Cher, who flapped her hands and her eyelashes.

Zoe experienced an unexpected moment of sisterhood with Cher and cursed Gideon for taking away her cleaver

It was very stressful watching the ramblers file by since they were going to decide which team won. Every dish was to be tasted by everyone and marked. Then they could fill up on their favourite. They were mostly in late middle age, hale and hearty, but there was the occasional more elderly one, who hadn't been on the walk but was probably a parent of someone who had.

'That old woman won't have eaten butternut squash before,' muttered Cher, 'and her teeth won't manage the stew.' They hadn't had time to do a pie in the end.

'Yes they will, it's very tender, and tasty,' said Zoe, who had tried it earlier. 'I'm more worried about the pudding. They'll think it's not proper because it hasn't got sultanas in it.'

'It was your idea. We did have sultanas,' said Cher. Their brief moment of sisterhood hadn't lasted beyond the time it took for Zoe to get her cleaver back.

'At least there was no fat on the meat,' Cher went on. 'I hate meat in stews with fat on it.'

'Actually, so do I.' Zoe hesitated and then added, 'Cher, I really do think we should try to be friends. I know we're competing with each other but everyone is; we can still be mates.'

'Oh Zoe!' Cher flung up her hands and rolled her eyes. 'Of course we're mates!' She hugged Zoe and kissed the air near her cheek. 'We're in this together and if we play our cards right, one of us will win!'

Zoe wasn't so sure. She was confident in her abilities but there was tough competition. A couple of the others might one day become Michelin starred chefs. She was much more of an all rounder. But still, she was going to do her utmost to win!

The tasting took for ever, and the continual sound of the rain drip, dripping on to the tent didn't help. The food was going cold and the people seemed to eat agonisingly slowly.

'If only they could get on with it!' said Muriel. 'This is driving me mad.'

'What do the other team's dishes look like?' said Cher.

'They did Queen of Puddings,' said Muriel. 'We have to hope the meringue goes soggy.'

'Oh, we could have done crumble after all,' said Zoe, doubting the apricot bread and butter pudding now.

At last the tasting was over and the testers, who must have been starving by now, having walked for miles and then only been allowed tiny amounts of the food on offer, really tucked in.

'I feel like I'm working in a school canteen!' said Cher.

'I like feeding people,' said Zoe. 'I just don't like getting marks out of ten.'

'Tell you what,' said Muriel, 'I'm going to walk up and

down among them, and see if I can find out if they liked ours.'

She came back a few minutes later. 'Mixed opinions. Some thought the soup and the stew were both too spicy. I suppose we shouldn't have had two spicy things.'

'Old people can't cope with spicy food,' said Cher.

'These people are not old!' said Muriel. 'Some of them are my age!'

'Sorry,' muttered Cher.

'What about the pudding?' asked Zoe, feeling responsible.

Muriel made a face, '"What's wrong with sultanas?"'

'We did have sultanas,' said Cher, glaring at Zoe.

'I know! You said!' Zoe sighed and wiped her perfectly clean station again. She couldn't remember now why she'd insisted on leaving them out. She just hoped it hadn't cost her a place.

At last the diners were ferried away, many of them taking the trouble to tell the contestants how much they'd enjoyed their lunch.

'At least we had some happy campers,' said Muriel.

'Ergh! Don't say the "C" word! Can't imagine anything worse,' said Cher.

'So what do you do when you go to a festival?' asked Zoe, curious.

Cher shuddered. 'I don't. Pyramids of poo first thing in the morning . . . puhleese! This is the nearest to camping I intend to get.'

Zoe chuckled. 'At least you've cooked under canvas now.'

Cher made a face at her.

Mike came up. 'OK, guys, if you'd like to make your way to the dining area, we'll give you the results and I'm afraid one of you will be going home.'

The mud had got a lot worse now the ground had been churned up by the walkers. They slid a bit as they made their way to the judging.

'God, I hate this!' said Cher, clutching on to Zoe and nearly pulling her over.

'The mud is the easy part,' said Zoe.

'Right,' said Mike when everyone was assembled. 'We had some very satisfied customers there, so well done everyone. It's a shame there has to be a losing team really, when both teams have done well. Isn't that so, judges?'

'Up to a point,' said Anna Fortune. 'Some of you have appalling knife skills – or rather no knife skills – to the extent that the judges would be considering giving lessons if time weren't so short.' She paused ominously. 'Gideon and I were just saying we'll be lucky if we get through this competition without anyone losing a finger.'

The director came and joined them. 'Not sure that's exactly what we'd want televised to the world. Could we be a bit more upbeat?'

'No,' said Gideon. 'Anna is right and it's important that the viewing public knows how important knife skills are.'

The director sighed. 'OK, have it your own way, but I warn you, that bit may be cut.'

'Can we get on?' said Mike. 'The minibus people have another appointment and we don't want anyone having to walk home.'

Anna Fortune shrugged in a way that reminded Zoe that she was half Italian.

'Shall we do this now?' said Gideon. 'We don't need all the fake waiting when we've made our decision, do we?'

'This is television,' Fred reminded him.

Gideon made a growling sound and turned away.

'And the winner is . . . the Blue Team!' cried Mike.

Cher squeaked, Zoe sighed with relief and Muriel smiled 'Oh, that's us!' she said. 'Well done, team!'

'So someone from the Red Team—'

'We know!' said Cher, embarrassingly loudly. 'One of those losers goes.'

It was nervy Shona who had to leave. She cried, but as apparently she'd been crying during most of the challenge this wasn't much of a surprise.

'Right now, dinner in the pub again tonight but the buses are leaving at nine thirty sharp so if you miss them, you walk, OK!' Mike's initial jolliness seemed to have worn thin.

'If we miss it we can get a lift,' said Cher with the confidence of a pretty girl who didn't mind using her looks to get her through life.

Zoe considered not going to the pub. She wasn't really in the mood for group jollity. But on the other hand there was nothing to eat in their accommodation and she didn't want to scrounge from Fenella and Rupert.

'Oh come on, Zoe!' said Cher, sounding genuinely friendly. 'It won't be half as much fun without you!'

Hunger and this encouragement, with nods from the others, convinced Zoe and she went with them all. She'd wondered if they might mix with the camera and production crew but the powers that be obviously wanted to keep them all separate.

Cher continued to be so pleasant throughout the evening that Zoe was beginning to wonder if her early hostility had been nerves. The winning team were all in a good mood and did their best to encourage the losers so it was a cheerful evening. Zoe did wonder if she should have drunk so much cider. That, and the water she felt obliged to drink with it, meant constant trips to the loo which was across an alleyway and each journey made her a little wetter from the rain, which refused to let up.

'At least you won't get a hangover,' said Muriel, 'which is the main thing. There's something awful about the self-inflicted wound.' She sighed. 'I'm far too sensible to get them now, of course!'

'That sounds like a challenge, Muriel!' said Shadrach, who'd really shone for his team and had become bumptious.

'Oh no, not tonight,' said Muriel. She looked at her watch. 'It's time to get in the minibus. They won't wait.'

'We'll stay for another one,' said Cher, including Zoe in her statement. 'We'll get a lift.'

'Cher? I'd rather get back! I don't want to get a lift with a stranger.'

'Don't be a piker, Zoe! I just want a shot. Maybe two.'

'What, in the head?' said Shadrach.

Cher gave him a look. 'Come on, Zoe, let's go into the other bar and see who's there.'

Although her every instinct was telling her she was mad, Zoe followed Cher in the hope that maybe some girlish foolishness together would make living with her easier. Of course, she might not have to do that for too much longer, she thought gloomily, following Cher's bright hair through the passages to the Snug, where, she gathered from Cher, the friendly locals did their drinking. Tiredness, the weather and witnessing just how good Becca and Shadrach in particular were had dampened her usual optimistic spirits. The competition was definitely hotting up.

They staggered out a bit later in the wake of a cheerful member of the Young Farmers' Association. As there were two of them and only one of him, Zoe felt reasonably safe, and as he was in training for some sort of event that involved hurling oneself over hedges and ditches, he hadn't been drinking. He dropped them by the gate and they linked arms as they made their way to their cowshed. Zoe had enjoyed the evening in the end, amused by Cher's blatant flirting and the high spirits of the other punters. Just before they reached their front door, Cher slipped in the mud, pulling Zoe over on top of her.

'Sorree!' she said. 'You can have the shower first!'

Zoe was not entirely sober, and she did feel she and Cher were friends now, yet something didn't seem quite right about this generous offer. But as they giggled their way along she decided she was being unnecessarily suspicious.

Taking off their wellingtons seemed to take a long time. They sat on the step, pulling at them ineffectually as they slipped out of their hands. Eventually they were free of them and made their way into their little home.

'I'll make tea. You have a nice long shower,' said Cher.

Again Zoe felt a prickle of suspicion, but as the thought of a long hot shower was too tempting to resist she took herself in the bathroom.

'Your turn!' she said as she came out. 'I hope I haven't left too much of a mess.'

'Don't worry, you're all right.'

Zoe went to her bed to hunt out her pyjamas from under her pillow. At the same time as she put her hand on the bed and found that it was wet she saw that the window, which she clearly remembered shutting, was open.

'No!' she shouted. 'My bed is soaking. Cher!'

As she was wearing only a towel, she hunted in her rucksack for another pair of pyjamas and put them on, then she thought what to do.

Convinced it was Cher's fault her bed was wet, she felt she should take over the double bed and let Cher cope with sleeping on the tiny sofa without any bedding. But what was the point? It would just mean hours of shouting and fighting and upset. And there was no way she was sharing a bed with Cher even if Cher would countenance it (which she wouldn't). No, she would go over to the house – she knew where the key was now – and snuggle up on the sofa in the kitchen. It would be warm and safe and she could think what to do about Cher in the morning. The woman was clearly deranged – all that business about them becoming 'bessie mates' when really she was trying to blow her chances in the competition. But why tonight? They didn't have to do anything until nearly at least midday. They had a morning of rest and recuperation. As she got her things together she wondered if she was using Cher's weird behaviour as an excuse to go to the house, in the hope that she'd see Gideon.

She had to ask herself the question, but she knew she'd be mad to try and see Gideon deliberately. She'd got away with spending the night with him once, by the proverbial skin of her teeth: she couldn't chance it again.

But her bed was wet, and given that the room where he'd been sleeping was still being decorated he probably wasn't there. This thought was a relief and she finished packing her day sack. Her one act of revenge was to take Cher's wellington boots. They were bigger than hers and easier to slip on. Cher would never fit her size seven feet into Zoe's size fives.

Zoe opened the back door as quietly as she could and replaced the key. For a moment she hesitated. If Gideon was there, it could be desperately awkward, not to mention get her thrown out of the competition. Then she shivered and realised she couldn't go back. She stepped out of the wellingtons and tiptoed into the kitchen, hoping there weren't dogs in there who were likely to bark.

She needn't have bothered to be so quiet. The kitchen was occupied.

'Hello, Zoe!' said Rupert, looking up from a loaf of bread he was slicing. 'What can I do for you?'

'Oh!' Zoe was so convinced that the kitchen would be empty she hadn't prepared anything to say. 'Um, is Fen still up?'

'Yes. We're upstairs in our little sitting room eating sandwiches and drinking. Why don't you join us? You could carry the wine, and we'll need an extra glass. I've lit the fire. There's something wonderfully decadent about a fire in summer, don't you think?'

'Oh no, I don't want to intrude . . .'

'You wouldn't be intruding and you said you wanted Fen. She'd love to see you. Come on, pick up that bottle and follow me.'

Zoe took the bottle Rupert indicated. She followed him up the stairs and along the landing. Rupert opened a door. 'This would have been a bedroom, but we've turned it into a little room for us when the house is full, or in this case being decorated. Go in.'

The first thought that occurred to her was that by no one else's standards would it be described as a little room. Although to be fair it was smaller than the reception rooms she'd caught sight of and been in briefly at the beginning of the competition. The fireplace at one end seemed large for a bedroom and a log fire burned brightly in it. Two substantial scuffed leather sofas were pulled up at each side and a large low coffee table covered in clutter was in between.

On one of the sofas, looking completely at home, was Gideon.

Her heart did a jolt that told her she was pleased to see him but her brain told her to turn around and go straight back downstairs to the kitchen, revert to Plan A and sleep on the sofa.

No one seemed to notice the battle between her brain and her heart. Fen had her feet up on a large pouffe and was laughing at Gideon as if they'd known each other all their lives.

'Here's Zoe,' announced Rupert. 'I found her in the kitchen.'

'Zoe!' Fenella waved enthusiastically. 'Come in. I can't move, I'm afraid, but this is so nice! I was wondering how you were getting on and didn't think I could ask Gideon.'

Gideon got up. After a moment's pause he smiled, seemingly glad to see her. 'Come and sit by the fire. You look a bit chilly. And you're wearing your pyjamas,' he added, surprised.

Zoe felt herself enveloped in warmth, from the fire and from the welcome she received.

'Hello! I didn't mean to crash a party!' she said. 'Unless it's a pyjama party.'

'Oh it is!' said Fenella. 'It's all I wear these days. Rupes, get her a drink. Gideon, shove up so she can sit down.'

Gideon moved and patted the seat beside him. 'Oh, you've got bare feet,' he said when she was seated. 'Why?'

'I was wearing wellies when I came over but I took them off at the back door. They were terribly muddy.'

'We're not overly fussed about mud in this house unless we have proper guests,' said Fenella. 'Not like Gideon, who's not proper at all.'

Gideon gave Fenella a look that meant he took this as the compliment it was. Then he took a rug from the back of the sofa, tucked it under Zoe's feet and then lifted them on to the sofa. Zoe was touched by this gesture, although she tried to compose herself. Her emotions were all over the place. 'So what are you doing here?'

'I came to see if Fen was still up.'

'Problem?' Fen asked.

'Yes.' Zoe accepted the glass of wine Rupert held out to her.

'What?' asked Fen.

Zoe had hoped to tell Fenella privately what had happened. Now there was nothing for it; she'd have to tell them all. 'My bed got wet while I was out today,' Zoe said.

'You didn't leave the window open, did you?' Fenella asked, clearly horrified.

'No, I didn't!' said Zoe.

'Was it that little cow Cher?' asked Gideon. 'She is pure poison.'

'It must have been her because I clearly remember shutting it,' Zoe went on. 'I didn't want to share a bed with her and was planning to sleep on the sofa in the kitchen, if you weren't up.'

'Oh, you don't need to do that!' said Fen. 'We'll find you a corner. Look, have another glass of wine for me.' She paused. 'It's not really the alcohol I miss – at least I hope it isn't – it's the mateyness, the fun of sitting round with friends getting slightly pissed.'

Rupert topped up Zoe's glass. 'I'm afraid that ship has sailed,' she said. 'We went to the pub earlier and then Cher wanted to do shots.'

Gideon took the glass away from her. 'You don't want a hangover tomorrow.'

She took it back. 'I know. I drank loads of water.'

'Have a sandwich,' said Rupert. 'We've all eaten supper too but got hungry again. Or rather, Fen did, and so we didn't want to be left out.'

Zoe sipped the wine and nibbled the sandwich, her legs curled under the rug on the sofa. Gideon put his arm round her in a casual way making her feel part of the group, but also rather special. Yet again she pushed away her anxieties about fraternisation with judges.

But she really was tired. The various stresses and strains of the day had finally caught up with her. She put down her glass and refused more wine. Really, she should break up the party and find somewhere to sleep. But that would involve Fenella moving too, and she was obviously having a very nice time.

Her eyes closed and somehow, Gideon pulled her closer to him so she was more comfortable, snuggled under his arm. She gave in to the lovely feeling of warmth, the delicious smell of his cologne, the friendly chatter between him and Fenella and Rupert and was soon lost in a deep and dreamless sleep.

Chapter Nine

❧

She realised she must have dozed off when she heard the others talking about her.

'She's dead to the world,' said Fenella, 'and I didn't find her anywhere to spend the night.'

'Not sure where you'd planned,' said Rupert. 'There isn't anywhere. All the rooms are either uninhabitable or full of stuff for the day after tomorrow.'

'We could just cover her in blankets and leave her here,' suggested Fenella, but didn't sound keen. Zoe felt this was a very acceptable option. She was all ready for bed after all. It would be nice not to have to move. She kept her eyes closed.

'Don't worry, I'll look after her,' said Gideon.

There was a pause – a pause in which Zoe knew she should stir and gently wake up and not continue to eavesdrop.

'Well, I hope you do,' said Fenella, sounding stern. 'I like Zoe.'

'It's all right,' said Gideon, 'so do I. She can share my bed. As it sleeps six comfortably, she can be perfectly chaste.' He didn't point out they'd done it before and she was thankful Fenella and Rupert obviously hadn't known.

'It's not just that,' Fen went on. 'She's a contestant, you're a judge. If anyone found out, she'd have to leave in disgrace and you might too.'

'Trust me. I'll protect her. No one will find out.'

There was a silence. Zoe tried to imagine the concerned glances. Then there was a sigh. 'I don't want to make things awkward for you,' said Gideon eventually.

'It's not that . . .' said Fenella. 'Oh – give me the last sandwich and I'll forgive you.' There was silence, presumably while Fenella chewed.

Her anxieties seemingly soothed, she went on. 'Sarah's coming over tomorrow to make final wedding plans. I do hope your contestants are going to do a good job with the catering,' she said to Gideon.

'They're perfectly capable, and as the TV company is paying for all the food and wine, I don't think the couple will have cause for complaint.'

'I know that really,' Fenella went on and then groaned. It sounded like she was trying to get up. 'But I still don't want people having a bad time under my roof.'

'They won't.' Gideon sounded confident. 'With people like Zoe and Muriel, who are really efficient and jolly good cooks too, there'll be no problem.'

'I want to employ Zoe,' said Fenella. 'She'd be perfect to take over from me while I'm out of action with Buster here. I'll ask her in the morning. Heave me up, Scotty, and transport me to bed!'

'And I'd better take Sleeping Beauty,' said Gideon.

Another cue for Zoe to wake, but she didn't want to. She wanted to stay being cared for by Gideon even if it would be embarrassing if he couldn't lift her. She'd obviously wake up then. But it would really spoil the mood.

Maybe she'd lost weight recently because he got her into his arms without difficulty. But it was very hard for Zoe to stay completely relaxed, lolling her head and relaxing her arms. As they progressed out of the room she suddenly worried in case the position of her head caused her to dribble. She decided if anything like that looked like happening she'd stir, moan a little and say, 'Where am I?' She hoped it wouldn't be necessary. Although it would have been nice to use this famous cliché perfectly genuinely, it would be nicer to be tucked up into Gideon's bed.

She'd had plenty of time to think about sleeping with Gideon and come to the wicked, foolish conclusion that she was not going to waste this second opportunity. If she could persuade him, with it looking completely natural and as if it was his idea, she would. She had a major crush on him and felt she would regret it for the rest of her life if she didn't make the most of the situation. And she was in a reckless mood tonight. Nothing seemed to matter but this moment.

Fenella was escorting Gideon and opening the doors. When they reached his bedroom he said, 'Can you put the bedside light on? And now pull back the cover? Thanks.'

Gideon laid Zoe gently down and pulled up the duvet. It was all she could do not to put her arm over it as she always did, but she thought sudden movement might show that she was awake.

'I'm not entirely happy about this,' Fenella whispered.

'I could put a line of pillows down the middle of the bed if it would make you any happier.' Zoe could hear that Gideon was smiling.

'No, you can't because I'd have to find some pillows and it's too late for that. Just don't break her heart!'

'Aren't you worried that she'll break mine?'

'No. I imagine you've got a heart as hard as rock.'

'I'd like to think that was true, of course.'

Zoe lay so still that if anyone had looked at her they might have thought she was dead. She was willing him to go on, say something more revealing.

'You mean it isn't true?' Fenella was obviously intrigued.

'As a general rule but in this particular instance . . .'

Zoe thought she would either stop breathing entirely or burst into some huge noise – a sneeze, a howl, hysterical laughter.

'I do have a bit of a soft spot,' Gideon went on. 'Which means I have to be harder on her than any of the others in the competition. Fortunately she's good. I couldn't save her if she was due to go out.'

Zoe wanted to hug herself but kept perfectly still.

'Well, I'm glad to hear you've got morals,' said Fenella. 'I'll say goodnight now. See you for brekkie in the morning. I'll invent somewhere Zoe could have slept to save her reputation.'

Too late for that, thought Zoe. Cher already thinks I'm sleeping my way to the top. I might as well get some fun out of it even if it does make him harder on me.

To Zoe, waiting anxiously for his return, Gideon seemed to take a long time in the bathroom. When he did emerge he stood over her for a few seconds. Then he adjusted a curl lying on her face – a tender gesture that nearly caused Zoe to scream – got into bed and turned out the light.

This was her moment, she decided. She wriggled a little in her pretend sleep and moved a bit nearer to him.

He seemed to freeze. She inched a little nearer. As he didn't edge away she did a bit more wriggling.

'Zoe.' His voice was quite loud enough to wake her even if she had been asleep.

'Oh, hello,' she said, as innocently as she could. 'Am I having an attack of déjà vu or am I in your bed again?'

'You are in my bed again and if you don't go over to your side you may live to regret it.'

She snuggled in closer. 'I don't think I will.'

110

'You know what will happen? I'm only human. Those pyjamas are very erotic.'

'Are you sure?' She put her head on his shoulder. 'They're Cath Kidson. I always thought they were very respectable.'

'Well, you were wrong. And I'm not sure I can cope.'

'You don't have to cope. Or at least, you don't have to cope with . . .' Unusually for her, she didn't know what to say.

'What are you telling me, Zoe? I need to be very clear.'

'I'm trying not to have to put it into words.' Golly, this seducing thing was much harder in real life than it was in the movies!

'I don't want you do to anything you'll regret.'

Gentlemen were harder to deal with than cads. If anyone tried it on with Zoe and she wasn't keen she had no difficulty in making them understand exactly how she felt. But how was she going to get Gideon to do anything without actually leaping on him?

'You're wearing a dressing gown,' she complained. 'Do you always go to bed in one?'

'Only when I'm in bed with you,' he said.

'Is this a habit you could break?' She fingered his lapel.

'It's not a habit, it's a dressing gown.'

It took her a second to get the joke. 'Very funny.'

'Zoe, if I take off my dressing gown you know what will happen, don't you?'

'Of course! But I'm beginning to think nothing will!'

'And you want something to?'

'Should I employ a sky writer to tell you? What else do I have to do?' She sighed in frustration. 'I'm obviously not cut out to be a temptress.'

'Oh, you're tempting all right, I just—'

'Listen to me! I want you! I'm in your bed. If you don't

111

want me just say! If you do – well, it would help if you weren't wearing half a ton of towelling.'

He chuckled under his breath. 'OK, I can take a hint . . .'

Shortly after this the half-ton of towelling and the Cath Kidson pyjamas were on the floor.

The sun was pouring in through the curtains the next morning as Zoe slid out of bed. It was a wrench but she had to think of a way to cover her tracks before the world awoke. The quickest shower on record plus the skimpiest tooth brush and she was on her way downstairs. Gideon was still lying in bed. Zoe had hardly dared even look at him. A tiny glimpse of his body, half under the duvet, his hair rumpled and his beautiful mouth very slightly open made it hard enough to leave. If he stirred and spoke to her she'd have been lost.

She'd like to stay there all morning. She'd never felt like this before and was pretty sure that the bubble in her stomach and her inability to breathe properly was what everyone went on about. She had it bad, she realised. It was wonderful but also slightly scary. She felt so completely thrown, as if she was sickening for something. It was her own fault – entirely. If she hadn't slept with him she could have kept her emotions in check. But she'd made her decision and now she had to live with it. She also had to make sure her rashness didn't mean she got thrown out of the competition because her mind wasn't on her cooking. Or because someone found out what she and Gideon had done. She'd have to make sure beady-eyed Cher couldn't pin anything on her.

She got back into her pyjamas and crept down the stairs. She stopped as she heard voices in the kitchen. There was nothing for it, she'd just have to brazen it out.

She heard Cher's voice through the open kitchen door.

'I came because I was so worried about Zoe. She went off last night because her bed was a bit damp – I think she must have left the window open – and didn't come back. I wondered what had happened to her.'

Zoe was forced to admire Cher's acting ability. She sounded quite genuine, although as Zoe had spent the night in the house before and Cher hadn't worried it obviously wasn't real concern.

Zoe opened the door before Fenella or Rupert had to say anything that wasn't quite the truth.

'Hello, Cher! What are you doing here?'

'Zoe! I was so worried! What happened to you? Where did you sleep last night?'

So Cher obviously just wanted to catch her out. Zoe said, 'I don't know how it happened but I fell asleep on the sofa in the little sitting room. I must have been so tired!'

'We were having a drink and a snack,' said Fenella, possibly trying to give the impression that it had been hot milk and digestive biscuits not wine and enormous sandwiches.

'Yes,' Zoe went on. 'One minute I was with Fen and Rupert and the next thing I knew I was covered in blankets. It took me a minute to work out where I was when I woke up.'

'But you slept OK?' asked Fenella.

'Oh yes. That sofa is really comfortable.'

Although none of what she had said was untrue, Zoe felt herself blush. She *had* fallen asleep on the sofa in the little sitting room, she *had* wondered where she was when she woke up, but quite a lot had gone on between.

Cher's eyes narrowed. 'You're not stiff or anything?'

'Why should I be?' She was a bit stiff actually, but it wasn't from sleeping on the sofa.

'Oh, you know how it is when you fall asleep somewhere funny.'

Zoe felt as if Cher could see marks on her body that would betray her but she hadn't seen any in the shower. 'Anyway, can't stay here chatting, I'd better get dressed.'

'Come back and have breakfast,' said Rupert. 'I'm doing a bit of a fry-up. You too, Cher,' he added.

'Are you going to grill the bacon?' Cher asked daintly.

'No, fry it. The hint is in the name,' said Rupert, smiling.

'Agas do great breakfasts,' said Fenella. 'Sometimes I do the bacon in the oven but Rupert likes to make fried bread . . .'

Zoe left the room just as Cher gave a little scream of horror at the thought of carbs and bacon fat in the same toxic mouthful.

When she returned, Gideon was sitting at the table attacking a huge plate of breakfast. He looked up when Zoe came in and winked so quickly no one but she noticed. At least that's what she hoped. She pulled out a chair. Cher was sitting next to him and she saw her slide a rasher of bacon on to his plate and look up at him coyly.

'Are you trying to bribe a judge with bacon?' he asked, looking down at Cher in a way that stabbed Zoe, although she knew perfectly well she had no reason to be jealous. Had she?

'Of course not. I could never compete with Zoe in that department but I couldn't eat another scrap.'

To Zoe's eternal gratitude Rupert came in immediately. 'But you've hardly eaten one scrap! One streaky rasher and a tomato. You won't be able to get through until lunchtime on that.'

'Oh, I never eat much. I get full really quickly.' She looked pointedly at the loaded plate Fenella had put in front of Zoe as she sat down.

'But you're a cook,' said Rupert. 'Surely you have to taste things?'

'Only a bit. And I hardly ever eat a full meal.' She looked across at Zoe. 'I can't think why Rupert thinks you need to eat all that.'

Zoe, who had no body issues and never thought much about her weight suddenly felt like a hippopotamus – a loved-up guilty hippopotamus. She stole another look at Gideon. She felt a foot gently touch hers. She couldn't be sure if it was accidental or not or even Gideon's but the smile he gave her hinted that it was. Part of her felt a thrill at the danger of it all; part of her wanted to admonish him. There was more than her place in the competition at stake here. 'I think Rupert is just generous,' she said.

'Yes!' agreed Fenella. 'He's a feeder. That's why I'm so enormous. Cher, what was the weather like when you came over?'

'It's clearing up nicely,' said Cher.

Zoe suddenly felt hugely grateful for the British obsession with the weather.

'That's good. With the wedding tomorrow it would be nice if everything could dry off a bit first. Darling?' Fenella turned to Rupert. 'Sarah and Hugo will be here in a minute. Is there anything left to feed them on?'

'About half a pig. Now everyone, what about toast?'

'Golly, not for me!' declared Cher as if anyone who wanted toast had to be second cousin to Gargantua. 'But I'm sure Zoe could fit in a couple of rounds.'

'I'm still eating sausages, Cher,' said Zoe, irritated.

'Well, you are what you eat!' Cher trilled and Zoe could have kicked herself for giving her the opportunity.

'Girls,' said Rupert sternly. 'No need to bicker.'

As she hadn't been bickering, Zoe felt aggrieved but accepted he couldn't just pick on Cher.

'That was the most amazing breakfast, thank you very much,' said Zoe. She got up from the table, gathering nearby dirty plates. 'I'll just put these in the dishwasher.'

'You don't have to,' said Fenella weakly. 'There'll be another lot when Sarah and Hugo get here.'

'Is that the Sarah Stratford who arranged Carrie Condy's wedding?' Cher said. 'I saw all the pictures. Her dress was amazing.' She continued to sit while Zoe cleared.

'Yes,' said Fenella. 'It really got us started, didn't it, Rupes?'

'Sure did. Zoe, that's very kind of you.'

'It's just habit,' said Zoe. 'Now I'd better go and sort out my bed.'

'Oh, stay and meet Sarah and Hugo,' said Fenella.

'We're meeting them at half past eleven anyway, aren't we?' said Zoe, who felt she'd intruded quite enough on Fenella and Rupert.

'But you'll get ahead of the game if you stay,' said Rupert.

'I'm staying!' declared Cher. 'Hugo Marsters is a celebrity photographer.'

Fenella frowned slightly. 'He is celebrated certainly but I don't think he takes photos for *Hello!* magazine.'

'Oh, whatever,' said Cher.

Zoe decided she couldn't cope with watching Cher flirt with this photographer as well as Gideon. Besides, she needed some time on her own to process what had happened and to enjoy the feelings. It had been so, so special. Nothing like that had ever happened to her before. She suddenly got the point; she knew what sex and love were about for the first time.

'I need to do something about my bed,' said Zoe, getting up with determination.

'Well, don't worry about the mattress, we have spares,'

116

said Fenella. 'My lovely cleaning ladies are coming today. They'll find you a new one and put the wet one in the boiler room to dry.'

'Great. I'll drape the bedding about the place.'

'Really, don't worry about it.' It was Fenella being firm now.

But Zoe did tidy up a bit and have a calming walk round the garden before she grabbed her pad and headed towards the reception room where they were all to be briefed on the wedding the next day.

'Right! Everybody!' Mike's rallying call was familiar now but it still made Zoe nervous. 'Sarah Stratford, who's in charge of the wedding, is going to tell you what she wants you to do. Sarah?'

The contestants, production and camera crew and the judges were all assembled in the reception room where they'd been first briefed on the competition.

Sarah, who managed to look remarkably efficient at the same time as being slightly nervous about being on television, cleared her throat.

'Hi there. As Mike says, I'm Sarah and I'm the wedding planner, and I have to confess I'm very anxious about you lot doing the food for a wedding I'm in charge of.' Her warm smile made everyone laugh, as they were meant to do.

'It's a champagne and canapés event, but they have to be substantial. We don't want everyone falling down drunk after five minutes. That's scheduled in for later.'

Her audience laughed again.

'I want you each to make ten sorts of canapé and ten of each kind so we end up with seven hundred. That'll be ten each for every guest, which should be enough to keep them upright. The wedding is at twelve tomorrow.

117

The couple are getting married here, in the chapel, and so the guests will want feeding at one o'clock. Now I'm going to hand you over to the judges to give you more details.'

There was a ripple of excitement in the room. Weddings tended to have that effect although the men in the group were a little less enthusiastic. Sarah went to join an attractive man standing at the side. He put his arm round her and kissed the top of her head. Zoe assumed it was Hugo. Gideon stepped forward.

'Right. We want five hot and five cold canapés. You need to think what you want to make, look up recipes etc. and then get your ten canapés passed by any of the three judges or by Sarah. Then you can start cooking, but remember lots of them will need to be very hot out of the oven, or assembled on the day so they don't go soggy. There are a lot of ingredients here' – he indicated a long table piled high with food – 'but if you want anything that isn't here and you have time to go shopping, feel free. We'll give you money.'

Cher put her hand up. 'But what's to stop us buying a lot of sausage rolls from the shop and just heating them up?'

'The fact that we'd know you'd done that and you'd be disqualified. Any more questions? No? Fine. Oh, one thing you'll be pleased to learn: there's a certain amount of ready-made puff pastry on the table but not enough for everyone. We don't want too many vol-au-vents.' Gideon paused. 'And if we've passed something pastry-based for too many people, you'll have to think of something else. We want variety and originality. Thank you.'

It was terribly hard to think when you were in love, Zoe discovered, but she had to put Gideon out of her mind and just focus. She didn't bother to join the race to

118

the table to bag the pastry. She got out her notebook and started to write.

Pignatelli, rice balls, beef in Yorkshire puddings, miniature pizzas – not very exciting but vegetarian – *frittatas*, she wrote. That was five hot canapés. What could she do cold? She had to be quick or other people would get the ideas and then she'd have to think of something else.

After a few minutes frantic thinking and writing, she ran over to the judges.

Anna Fortune took her list. 'No to beef in Yorkshire puddings, frittatas and if anyone else offers me asparagus with parma ham I shall scream.'

'Sorry,' said Zoe, although it wasn't really her fault.

'And what are these rice balls?' Anna regarded her through narrowed eyes.

'Italian. Ham and cheese with some veg maybe, in rice, deep fried in egg and breadcrumbs.' She used to do this without the ham quite often for friends. They were tasty and very cheap if you didn't mind the calories.

'*Arancini*,' said Anna.

'Or *supplì*,' put in Gideon. 'Elizabeth David called them *supplì*.'

Just hearing him say 'Elizabeth David' made her stomach turn over with lust. Really, it was coming to something if one of the most famous and important names in the culinary world was a trigger for her desire. Just for a nanosecond their eyes met. There was hardly a flicker in his but she knew he was thinking what she was thinking. Oh, he was lovely! she thought, but then realised that lovely as he was, he was a judge and she hardly knew him. In the little time she'd had to herself since their night of passion she had come to the conclusion he probably wasn't a keeper. Or rather *she* wasn't. She'd keep him, no question. But he wouldn't keep her. She doubted she was more than a diversion for him. Someone who was fun to be with for a while but only while she was there, in front of his nose. But that was OK. She knew that's how it was. She'd be sad when the competition was over, or rather was over for her, but she wouldn't regret her affair with him. She would enjoy it to the maximum while it lasted and then move on knowing she'd had a wonderful time with a wonderful lover.

She gave him a very tiny wink, not closing her eye but twitching the corner of it. He responded with one of the same. She felt her mouth move in a betraying smile. She clamped it shut and focused on what Anna was saying to her. It all felt deliciously illicit.

Eventually she was dismissed by Anna. 'Go and see what ingredients are left and if you can make what you've chosen with them, fine. If not, think again!'

There were too many ingredients missing for Zoe to be able to do many of her chosen canapés, which immediately made her wonder if there had been enough food provided – and if there had been, whether Cher had concealed it somewhere. Mind you, given the skimpiness of her outfit it clearly wasn't up her jumper. Zoe had to change her plans and so one of her cold canapés, using smoked salmon, had to become soup in a shot glass.

There were no shot glasses provided but Zoe had an idea that Fenella might well have some. She had a ridiculous amount of equipment, she had told Zoe. As there was nothing else Zoe could be getting on with, she went over to the house to ask.

She reached the kitchen and found a powwow going on. Sarah, looking tight-lipped and strained, was talking to Fenella and Rupert.

'I just can't believe it. This woman is supposed to be reliable – she's one of the top suppliers in the country according to all the glossy magazines. And to just forget to do it? Does that make sense?'

'Well . . .' Fenella seemed to think it was a possibility. Not Sarah.

'The woman is running a business! This cake represents a lot of money! And she's forgotten to do it!'

'Don't get in a fret, old girl,' said Rupert, 'I'm sure we can get another one made. Or pop down to Waitrose—'

Fenella and Sarah turned on him. 'There isn't time to make a cake that size, let it cool, ice it, decorate it and have it ready by noon tomorrow!' said Sarah.

As Zoe had listened to this exchange a plan had formed in her mind. She liked challenges and before she could help herself she jumped in. 'Excuse me,' she said.

'What?' Fenella, usually so placid and helpful, seemed a bit impatient.

Sarah, who Zoe remembered too late was one of the judges for this task, looked as if she was only a second away from snapping Zoe's head off.

'Cupcakes,' said Zoe. 'We could all make them. I'm brilliant at icing them. Set up a production line and we could get seventy cupcakes done really quickly. We just need the cases, of course.'

Sarah breathed deeply, possibly for the first time for several days. 'That is a bloody brilliant idea,' she said eventually, after Zoe had become convinced her head was going to be cut off and used in place of a wedding cake. 'It's not what the bride wanted but it'll save her several hundred pounds and as the dress went way over budget she'll be grateful.' She suddenly giggled. 'Talk about a meringue! She's got the whole bloody Pavlova!'

'But what about the competition?' objected Rupert. 'If Zoe's making cupcakes, she won't be able to focus on her canapés. Just sayin',' he finished.

'I'm a judge! Surely if she makes cupcakes for a wedding cake, for my wedding, she'll have to go through to the next round.' Sarah looked at Rupert, her expression more diffident than her determined words. 'Won't she?'

Chapter Ten

While Sarah was overseeing arrangements in other parts of the house, Zoe asked Fenella about shot glasses.

'Oh yes. Loads of them. Certainly enough for the wedding.'

'Good. I'd better get back and do some cooking then.' Zoe frowned. 'I don't think they provided enough food, you know.'

'They'll get more. I hope! I'm not having a wedding at Somerby that's under catered. And Sarah won't have it either.' Fenella had to sit down to recover from this thought and the anxiety of the missing wedding cake.

'Maybe they did provide enough and people snaffled more than they needed,' muttered Zoe.

'Cher! I'm sure it's her! You should have seen her with Hugo – and Gideon.' Fenella paused in the way women do when they're longing to ask another what happened the previous night but don't quite like to. Zoe could tell she was burning with curiosity.

Zoe, who was trying very hard to function while deeply distracted by a barrage of emotions she couldn't exactly identify, was tempted to confide. She trusted Fenella and without her best friend Jenny on hand she was the next best thing. 'Gideon is *lovely*,' she said, blushing.

Fenella was indignant. 'And so he lied to me? He didn't leave you to sleep, "perfectly chaste" as he said in such a wonderfully old-fashioned way?'

'Er – no. But to be fair, it was my fault.' She gave a shuddering sigh as she remembered the night before. 'I did sort of jump on him.'

'But he didn't mind?' Fenella said, less indignant now.

Zoe giggled. 'Don't think so.' She stopped giggling suddenly. 'I do know I'm mad. And you don't need to give me the whole "will he still respect me in the morning" speech. While I do think he'll respect me and everything, I'm not letting myself get carried away.' Not in her head, anyway. She couldn't speak for her heart on this occasion.

'That's good,' said Fenella, blatantly not believing her. 'But are you sure? He seems very nice but . . .'

Zoe gave a bright smile. 'Oh, I'm sure to break my heart a little, but that's part of the fun, isn't it? You get those moody moments, a few songs that make you well up a bit, and a concert ticket or something that you keep in a box. But that's all right!'

'Have you ever actually had your heart broken?' asked Fenella. 'I promise you, it's not to be taken lightly.'

Zoe considered, thinking that she might well be about to experience it, although a spark of hope that it might be more than just a fling burned steadily inside. 'Well, no. But I did break someone else's heart – or at least he said I did. I don't think it lasted terribly long.'

'Well, real heartbreak is truly horrible,' said Fenella. 'Before Rupert and I got together we had a bit of a blip and I've never been through so much torment. Even thinking about it now, when we're married and so happy, I get remembered pain.'

'I will try to carry my heart about very carefully.'

'"Lock it up in a box of golden," as the folk song says.' Fenella chewed her lip, obviously considering how to go on. 'I like Gideon, I really do. I think he's a nice man . . .'

124

'But?'

'I'm not sure he's the settling-down kind. I mean – he's so dashing and attractive, and you're a lovely girl. You're not like him in that way.'

Zoe sighed deeply.

'I may be quite wrong. I don't know him all that well.'

'It's all right. I know exactly what you mean. You mean you see him with someone more sophisticated, who's like him.'

Fenella put her hand on Zoe's. 'I think I'm trying to say he's not good enough for you.'

'Unfortunately, it's too late for the warning. We have had sex and I fully intend to have it again, as much as I can before it's all over.' She heard the defiance in her voice and hoped Fenella didn't think she was being too brazen.

'But don't risk the competition, Zoe. No man is worth that. If anyone, particularly Cher, finds out they'll tell the world. You'll have to leave and that would be dreadful. You're so good at this. And if Gideon is a good man he'll wait until it's over.'

Zoe nodded, thinking that when the competition was over she would probably never see Gideon again. She felt a flutter of anxiety. Although she'd breezily told Fenella she was fine with a moment of passion, her heart persisted in saying otherwise.

Fen squeezed Zoe's hand again. 'Although it's not as if we say to ourselves "I will fall in love" or "I won't fall in love", it just happens. We have no choice. But please be careful – about everything!'

'I'm glad you understand. I've never fallen in love before,' Zoe admitted. 'It's terrible timing, I know, but . . . Anyway, you won't say anything, will you? Not even to Rupert? Well, maybe you can to him but not to anyone else?'

'Of coure I won't. But I really don't want to see you get

hurt. Maybe Gideon is Mr Right and will stay with you for ever.'

'You don't believe that and nor do I,' said Zoe.

'It could be true! Everyone wants to settle down sometime. Look at me and Rupert.'

Zoe sighed. Fenella and Rupert were so perfect together, would she ever be part of a couple like that?

Sarah appeared in the kitchen, panting slightly. 'I've spoken to the other judges and told them about your solution, and they want you to come up so they can film the whole "can the team make the cupcake wedding cake" thing. Apparently it will be brilliant telly. I don't care about the telly, but I do want a brilliant cake.'

'It will be, I promise you.'

Sarah wrinkled her brow. 'I'm sorry to ask, but I'll have to on camera, and I do want to know, have you made a cupcake wedding cake before?'

'No, but I have made loads of cupcakes. I used to do them for the café I worked in. Once you've got that swirl and know how to make good butter icing, it's just a matter of displaying them nicely. Isn't it?' she added, seeing Sarah was still concerned.

'Fen, do you have a cupcake stand anywhere about your person?' Sarah asked.

Fenella smiled. 'I might have. But not for seventy cupcakes, I don't think.'

'Couldn't we have a huge square box to put lots of them on and then have the cupcake stand on top?' suggested Zoe. She suddenly felt passionate about her idea. She'd make it work even if it killed her!

Sarah nodded. 'Fen, I'm sure you've got some lovely tulle or something somewhere to drape around the table. Don't worry, we can do this. But honestly, that bloody cake-maker! I'll never use her again!'

'There may have been a good reason . . .' Fenella began but then said, 'Oh, OK, she's hopeless. Never use her again.'

'If they want us to go and film, hadn't we better get on?' Zoe interrupted

'Oh, OK,' Sarah agreed. 'Let's do it then.'

Zoe had got used to the couple of cameramen and their cameras who hovered over her when she cooked by now, but she wasn't quite used to being the centre of attention without a prop in her hand. She felt a bit hot and realised she hadn't put any make-up on that morning. She muttered about this to Mike

'Don't worry! You look great, Zoe!' he said. 'Really glowing. A touch of mascara and you're good to go.'

Fred was the judge designated to do the interview. At least it wasn't Gideon. 'So, Zoe, you were the contestant who found a solution to the drama of the missing wedding cake.'

She laughed in self-deprecation. 'I just happened to be there when Sarah discovered she didn't have a cake. Any of us would have made the suggestion, I'm sure.'

The camera panned round the faces of the other contestants. 'Baking's not my thing,' said Bill, the proficient but burly ex-builder.

'So, Zoe, are you going to make the cupcakes on your own? You do still have to complete the canapé challenge too, you know.' Fred looked rueful.

'Well, I'm hoping we'll all pitch in with the cupcakes. Set up a production line. I'm sure we can do it in time.'

'I'm not making bloody cupcakes,' said Cher.

'On television!' muttered Muriel out of the corner of her mouth. 'Remember to be nice!'

Zoe could hear her irritated sigh and hoped that the

camera couldn't. 'Of course I'll help!' said Cher, loudly and brightly. 'But this is a competition. We have to remember that.' She was clearly upset Zoe was getting all the attention. It must be torture for her, especially when she'd paid particular attention to her hair and make-up that morning, thought Zoe bitchily.

'So, Zoe, how do you picture the cupcakes? I mean, this is for a very special occasion. It needs to be more than a few buns, doesn't it?' Fred was his usual benign self but he obviously didn't think cupcakes were going to cut it as a wedding cake.

'I'm only the cook here,' said Zoe, after a moment of panic she hoped wasn't too apparent, 'so dressing it up isn't really my job —'

'But it is. A chef is responsible for how his food looks. It's a vital part.' Fred wasn't going to help her, obviously. 'Think of the amazing ice sculptures some chefs produce.'

This was way above her pay grade, Zoe thought. In the nick of time she remembered the tulle. She paused and launched in. She had nothing to lose. 'OK, what I see in my mind's eye – although it might not be possible to do – is the cakes looking like a bridal veil?' She was thinking on her feet.

'Sounds very girly,' said Fred, 'do go on.'

As the words came out of her mouth the picture formed in her mind. 'Well, I picture a cluster of cakes at the very top, as if they were the tiara. Then, with tulle or net or something cascading down the back, there'd be half moons of something holding the cakes, getting bigger and bigger towards the bottom.' Relief at having made some sort of response even if it was totally impractical made her feel exhilarated. 'And if would be great if the decorations on the cakes could be sort of mirrored on the veil. So we'd have a co-ordinated effect.'

Out of the corner of her eye she saw Sarah listening intently, a slight frown of concentration on her face. An encouraging smile from Gideon nearly threw her off but she managed to keep her cool.

'That sounds very pretty. Sarah?' Fred turned to her. 'You're in charge of this wedding and your regular cake-maker let you down—'

'Not my regular cake-maker,' Sarah corrected him. 'She wouldn't have let me down. This was one chosen by the bride. Anyway —'

'Yes. Now do you think Zoe's idea would work? It sounds very complicated to me.'

Fred was so sceptical that Zoe was plunged into anxiety.

'Oh, I think it will work well,' Sarah was saying. 'I've seen something like that before and it looked stunning. We can copy some of the flowers in the bouquet and make them in icing – another way of linking it all together.'

When the cameras finally moved away, after Zoe had had to repeat herself several times, she found she was sweating.

'Will it really work, do you think?' she asked Sarah.

'Oh yes! It's a brilliant idea! Now you get on with your canapés and I'll track down a stand and fabric for the cakes. I'll also get hold of the cases. The minute I've got those, maybe you could get cracking?'

'I won't have to do it on my own, will I?'

'I'm sure we'll get someone to help you,' Sarah said, sounding reassuring. And Zoe was reassured until she went to her station and realised how much she had to do even without the cakes. No one would risk losing because of inferior canapés to help with a cake that wasn't part of the competition.

Feeling overwhelmed, she went to the table where the ingredients for the canapés sat, looking sad, not picked to be in the team by anyone. The others had wandered off for a coffee break in the barn. Zoe didn't have time.

She was gloomily inspecting some camembert, wondering if she would be allowed to bake it whole so people could dip in, or if every canapé had to be a bite-sized piece, when someone came up behind her and kissed her neck. She jumped six feet in the air.

'I knew you were responsive, but it was only a kiss.' Gideon's voice in her ear caused her to shiver all over and make her knees go weak.

Just for a second she allowed herself to enjoy the feeling of him pressed against her body, then she forced herself to be sensible. 'Someone might see us!' she breathed.

'I checked. We're blissfully alone. Shall we take advantage?'

She knew he was teasing but she longed to take him up on his suggestion. She was becoming obsessed with him, she realised, and she couldn't afford to be. She just wanted to hold a part of him and never let go. She dragged some sense up from somewhere. She wanted to win the competition, or at least get through this round with her dignity intact. She was not going to blow it all just for a few moments of bliss. 'No! Someone could appear at any moment. I have so much to do! I haven't time for anything . . . extra-curricular. I'm not sure who will help me make the cupcakes and I'm sure my canapés will be dried up and horrible by the time anyone eats them. I have to make them first,' she explained, in case he hadn't got that she had twice as much to do as anyone else. 'I mustn't mess this up! The competition is the chance—'

'Of a lifetime. OK, I get you. I'd better leave you alone then. I'm planning on doing some painting anyway.'

'Painting? That's a bit surprising. I don't see you with an easel and a floppy hat.'

'Not that kind of painting! Decorating. Rupert told me he's frantically trying to get a coat of paint on their bedroom before the baby comes and I thought I'd do some for him. I'm not busy at the moment and they're both up to their eyes with the wedding.'

Zoe gave a little sigh. He was not only sexy, charismatic and flatteringly into her, but he was also kind. Kindness was not a characteristic she usually associated with powerful, attractive men – no wonder she was infatuated. She allowed herself to stroke his arm in appreciation. Then she gave another, shuddering sigh. 'I really must get on.' What she must not do was make a fool of herself on television because of a man. She could cope with not winning but not with looking unprepared and stupid. Not even Gideon was worth that.

Gideon headed for the entrance to the marquee, turned back and blew her a kiss and then left her to it.

Collecting herself, she took what ingredients were left and put a tray of hazelnuts in the oven to roast. She didn't know what she was going to do with them but having another look at the camembert, which actually smelt rather delicious now she was closer to it, she thought of the honey she had used for her 'local and seasonal' challenge. She had some left.

Rather than waste time finding Anna Fortune to ask if she could use other ingredients she decided just to carry on. She'd have to stop work on the challenge the minute Sarah came back with the cases for the cupcakes. Zoe hoped she wouldn't have to make the stand for them on her own. She picked up a ciabatta to see if it was going stale already.

The others had returned to their stations and were now busy preparing their own canapés. The marquee was full of noise and bustle. She had to think quickly. Cher was watching her carefully; the cameramen were milling around. Zoe briefly noted that everyone else's canapés all looked wonderfully professional and near completion. Hers were put to shame and what's more she had barely started. Could she get it all together in time?

'OK! Stop what you're doing! I've got the stuff for the cupcakes!' Sarah and Fenella sounded excited as they came up to Zoe at her station a little while later. 'There is an amazing shop—' Sarah went on.

'That I told her about,' put in Fenella.

'Whatever. We've got what we need. But I think we should make them—'

'We? Isn't it just me then?' asked Zoe hopefully.

'It's just you for now,' said Sarah after a pause.

'We did ask the others but no one is prepared to sacrifice their chances in the competition to do extra,' said Fenella. 'You're the only one who seems to care about the actual wedding.'

'Muriel said she'd help when she'd finished,' said Sarah. 'And Becca said she'd decorate if she had everything done.'

'So why am I the mug? Why am I sacrificing my chances in the competition?' Zoe looked at the two women who seemed to expect so much from her.

'Because you're nice and we're desperate?' said Fenella tentatively.

'And I will do my best to make sure it doesn't damage your chances,' said Sarah, although she didn't sound completely convinced she could do this. She paused. 'I think we should do it in the Somerby kitchen, not here. It'll be easier.'

Zoe sighed and as they walked back to the house she asked herself the question she had just asked the others.

Her answers were complex and not very flattering. Yes, she did care about the wedding and genuinely want to help, but she also knew while she was competent she had good cooks to compete against. Maybe gaining some brownie points might actually work better for her. Also she wanted Gideon to be impressed. She wanted him to think well of her.

'You've cleared the table!' said Sarah, as they went in.

'I shoved everything on it on to a chair,' said Fenella, 'if that's what you mean. I thought Zoe needed space.'

'I do!' said Zoe. 'Space and time and – well, anything else you're offering.'

'Tea?' suggested Fenella, holding up the kettle.

Zoe nodded.

To her enormous relief, Fenella had a recipe book that gave quantities for that many cupcakes so she didn't have to do complicated multiplication that might not have worked anyway. She rapidly weighed out the ingredients and Fenella handed her a pile of bowls. 'And here's my KitchenAid! Isn't it heaven? I don't actually use it often but I love looking at it.'

Zoe inspected the powder-blue machine that was giving Fenella such aesthetic pleasure. 'Actually, have you got a hand mixer?' Zoe asked. 'I think it would work better than that. I'll use the KitchenAid for the icing,' she added, by way of compensation.

Fenella and Sarah laid out seventy-five cupcake cases. 'Thank goodness you've got this huge table,' said Sarah. 'I'd never be able to do this at home.'

Fenella shook her head. 'But you wouldn't be doing it at home, would you? You'd get a caterer.'

'Or Bron,' said Sarah, referring to a mutual friend. 'I'd have got her to do the wedding cake in the first place only the bride wanted her favoured cake-maker.' Sarah was obviously still furious about it. 'So,' she went on. 'Is there any chance we can get the colours that were going in the original cake?'

'Which are?' Zoe felt a film of sweat form as this cupcake idea just got harder.

'Deep crimson, the colour of dark red roses, and a sort of very pale yellow. I do have samples of fabric.' Sarah's expression was encouraging, as if this would definitely be helpful.

'I have dried rose petals exactly the right shade,' added Fenella. 'And, if it helps, it just so happens that we have a rose out with petals exactly the right yellow. I don't know why yellow roses always seem to be the first to come out, but they are.'

'If you're doing the wedding-veil thing we could use them to help decorate the cakes,' said Sarah.

'Will the cakes be white?' asked Zoe. 'Or cream-coloured?'

Sarah cleared her throat. 'The kitchen shop was pretty good. It had colouring. Is there any chance you could do coloured icing?' She produced the colours as if giving a present she wasn't certain of.

Zoe inspected the pots, read the tops and nodded. 'I could do red cakes, like roses, pale yellow, ditto and' – she paused – 'two-tone cakes. Well, the icing is two-tone.'

'Wow!' said Fenella. 'How do you do that?'

'Easier than it sounds. I'll show you if you're around when I'm doing them.'

Sarah came round the table and hugged her. 'You're a star! I don't know what we'd do without you!'

Zoe accepted the hug. 'All part of the service.'

About twenty minutes later she said, 'Now, I think I'm about ready to fill the cases.'

'OK, as you fill them we'll put them on trays and put them in the oven,' said Fenella. 'Are you sure you don't want to use the Aga? It's the perfect temperature to do cakes at the moment.'

Zoe was torn. The woman she'd learnt about cupcakes from said that range cookers were a nightmare for cupcakes. But it would be much quicker if they could use all the oven space available.

Zoe looked at Sarah hoping for a decision. 'You could try a trayful,' Sarah said, possibly reading panic and indecision in Zoe's eyes. 'It would speed up the process and it will be OK if you keep an eye on them.'

'Yes, but don't open the oven door within the first ten minutes or they'll sink for sure.'

'We'll set the timer,' said Fenella. 'I make cakes in the Aga all the time. I'll keep a close eye.'

'All right,' said Zoe. 'But it'll be your fault if it all goes wrong! If the cakes are cooked too hot they turn into volcanoes. Then we'd have to cut the tops off and it would take ages.' She peered at the thermometer and relaxed a little. It wasn't too hot.

'That's OK,' said Sarah, using tones well practised on the anxieties of brides' mothers and sometimes bridegrooms. 'We'll keep an eye. It'll all be fine.'

At last all the cakes were in the oven and Zoe dashed back to her canapés at her station in the cooking tent. As she passed the other competitors and saw what further beautiful creations they had produced while she'd been baking she felt she'd never survive the round. She just hadn't had the time.

Adrenalin made her work fast but she kept looking at her watch. Although Sarah and Fenella were both in the kitchen with timers and her number on their phones so they could ring the minute the cakes were cooked, she was still worried about a batch getting burnt and her having to make them all over again.

She got the call just as she was trying to think up a last canapé, aware she'd wandered off the list she'd originally given but trusting that not having the ingredients would be sufficient excuse. Abandoning some toasted ciabatta and slices of camembert, she galloped over to the house and checked that all the cakes were golden brown.

'They look amazing!' said Sarah firmly. 'Just check in case you don't believe me and then go back to your day job. You can't ice these until they're cool.'

'OK,' said Zoe, slightly out of breath. 'I'll make the icing after the judging.'

The contestants had had to prepare as far as they could, given that many of the canapés would have to be cooked just before serving. They'd been told that a sample of everything had to be ready so the judges could taste it all but they wouldn't make their final decision until the following day, just before everything was ready to serve.

They walked along the line, tasting, exclaiming, making noises of appreciation. Zoe was horribly aware how rushed and rustic her offerings looked.

There was a silence as they arrived at her station.

'She's just made seventy-five cupcakes for the wedding cake,' said Sarah after a panicked moment. 'She's rescued the whole wedding.'

'We can't judge her differently from the others because she's used her time to do different things,' said Anna Fortune.

'Try a cupcake,' said Sarah. 'Obviously it's not iced. We'll be doing that tomorrow.'

'And is Zoe doing that?' Anna asked, addressing Sarah, not Zoe.

'Yes. We're hoping some of the others will help.' Sarah spoke with a confidence she might not have entirely felt.

'But why should they jeopardise their chances in the competition to help ice cakes?'

Gideon, who had been standing back, stepped forward. 'The challenge is about a wedding. Surely the cake is a major part of it. I think the cupcakes should be taken into consideration.'

Zoe looked away. She was finding it hard being around him in public and was terrified she might reveal her feelings for him. And him sticking up for her now made her feel that even he thought her canapés were hopeless.

'I say,' put in Fred, with his mouthful. 'These are delicious!'

'What are?' Anna and Gideon regarded the plates with sudden interest.

Fred finished his canapé and pointed. It was to the ciabatta with melted camembert. Zoe had drizzled honey over them and added ground-up hazelnuts. They had been a last-minute, desperate attempt to come up with something to make up her required number of items. If the sample had worked, she'd make them just before the service tomorrow.

Gideon and Anna both took one. They nodded and Gideon widened his eyes, indicating his approval.

'Well,' said Anna eventually, 'the final judging isn't until just before the wedding tomorrow and those are very delicious and unusual. Maybe we don't need to throw Zoe out just yet.' She gave a smile that convinced no one but did at least mean that Zoe was off the hook for now. She let out a very long breath.

Chapter Eleven

❧

Zoe had her phone on vibrate and had set her alarm for half past five. She wanted to be in the Somerby kitchen by six to make the butter cream and start icing. She had given up hope of getting any of the others to help her. Far better to do it herself and know it was done than to trust her fellow competitors.

She also wanted to avoid Cher as much as possible. She had been worrying at Zoe like a dog after a flea the night before, trying to get details of what had been going on when Zoe had been out of sight of everyone else. For the most part she'd been dashing to and from her cooking station in the marquee and the Somerby kitchen being all things to all men, but she had snatched a quiet moment in the secluded walled garden where Gideon had happened to chance upon her and snatch another kiss. It had felt wonderfully decadent but foolhardy. Luckily none of the windows faced on to it. When Fenella told Zoe how important it was that she should be careful, she had been preaching to the converted. She must not jeopardise her chances in the competition for a man – any man – but particularly not one like Gideon. He might be sexy, he might even be kind – in fact he definitely was both those things – but was he ever going to settle down with a girl like her? She didn't even want to settle down! She had a competition and a career to think about *it*. So she must not let her wayward hormones (which was probably all it was really) get in the way of this amazing chance.

So however much she yearned to sneak over to Somerby for another night of passion she stayed in her own narrow single bed. The thought of what had gone on the night before had distracted her from Cher's gentle but persistent snoring from the other side of the room and then the anxieties of the day had waned and she'd fallen into a deep sleep. The fact that she might catch a glimpse of him at breakfast had absolutely nothing to do with the spring in her step as she ran over to the house in the morning. If only Gideon hadn't made her feel as if she'd had a whiff of some wonderful gas that made her heart fizz and sing and her feet feel they couldn't just walk they had to dance.

Somerby was bathed in a lovely early-morning light as she crossed the courtyard. It looked wonderfully romantic, but then everything had a romantic glow at that moment. She greeted the dogs and let them out and then went to the scullery where all the cakes were laid out, covered in muslin cloths. She lifted a cloth, dreading to see them too brown, or risen in the middle. But no, they had all risen evenly and wouldn't have to be trimmed off or baked again. Fenella and Sarah must have watched over them with stopwatches in their hands.

The butter had been left in the kitchen overnight so it wasn't too hard and Fenella's KitchenAid was soon whirring away, creaming the sugar and butter together. Zoe added several drops of vanilla essence.

Sarah had not been able to provide disposable piping bags, which was a shame but, undaunted, Zoe carried on.

Firstly she prepared the cream-coloured icing, which needed only a tiny touch of yellow, just to deepen the natural creaminess of the icing. Then she made up the dark red icing, which was more or less the same colour as the dark red rose petals. Finally, she made a large sausage of cream-coloured icing and a much slimmer one of dark red and laid them next to each other on clingfilm. This would make the cream coloured with a crimson blush that she felt would produce the very prettiest cupcakes of them all.

She was just inserting a clingfilm sausage into a piping bag when Rupert, rubbing his eyes and looking bleary, appeared in the kitchen, his feet bare, wearing pull-on pyjama bottoms and a Bart Simpson T-shirt.

He looked across at what Zoe was doing, faintly horrified. 'Isn't it a bit early for that sort of thing?'

'Morning!' sang Zoe cheerily, partly to be annoying. She was slightly disappointed that it wasn't Gideon but then thankful. She couldn't afford to be distracted.

'Did you sleep here again? Is your middle name Cinderella? Have you had tea? Coffee?'

'No, no, and yes,' said Zoe, laughing. 'I wanted to get started early. If I can get the cakes iced they can be decorated later. Maybe some of the others will help.' Cher was more likely to help sprinkle on spangles than she was to do anything harder. 'Do you know when Sarah is likely to turn up?

'Soon, I'm sure. She's staying a little way away with a friend of Hugo's. She would have stayed here only we're in such chaos.' He put the kettle on and rubbed the back of his head. 'Fen isn't feeling too brilliant.'

'Oh?'

'Bit of backache. I'm trying to convince her that she doesn't need to hurl herself out of bed. I'm hoping a cup of tea and some ginger biscuits will help.'

Zoe sipped her tea and then went back to her icing as Rupert headed back upstairs. For a moment she wondered if she had time to slip upstairs herself with a cup of tea for Gideon before doggedly returning to the task in hand.

Her next interruption came just as she finished. It was Sarah. She came in through the back door, laden with carriers. 'Oh wow!' she said when she saw the cupcakes all iced in rows on the table. Zoe had even added touches of edible glitter and spangles. 'Oh wow!' she said again. 'Now all we have to do is get them to the marquee. I've got the tulle. When do you have to carry on with your canapés?'

'Now really, but I'll do this first.'

Sarah took on an anguished expression. 'I do feel guilty. Supposing you go out! It'll be all my fault!'

'Don't be silly! I probably won't win anyway, I don't think I cook as well as some of the others.'

'I bet you cook better than some too!'

'It's hard to tell. You don't get to taste each other's food all that often.' Zoe sighed. 'But I would like to get through to the next stage.'

'I'll try and make sure you do,' said Sarah, sounding grim. 'It won't be fair otherwise.'

'Well, don't stick up for me too much or the others will suspect something.'

'What is there to suspect?'

Aware she'd said too much – she didn't want Sarah knowing about her and Gideon unless she absolutely had to – Zoe shrugged. 'Oh, you know, that I've helped out.'

Sarah was still looking confused when Fenella appeared.

'Hi! Everyone got everything they need? Will you look at those cakes! They're amazing! Can I eat one?'

Zoe laughed. 'There are spares. I had to do extra for the judging so you can eat one if you can face butter cream so early in the morning. But let me get you a cup of tea or something. Rupert said you had a really bad night.'

'I've had better but don't you look after me. I'm not completely incapable. Yet.'

'I'll make you tea,' said Sarah. 'You sit down. If you're going to have a cake eat it at the table.'

'Actually, I'm not sure I can face one just at the moment.' Fenella sat. 'They look lush though, don't they? We haven't had a cupcake wedding cake here before although I know they are popular.'

'They're easy to serve and some cupcake companies provide boxes so people can take them home,' said Zoe.

'What's worrying me is getting them over to the marquee,' said Sarah, 'we'll need helpers.'

'I'm not trusting my cupcakes to the competition,' said Zoe. 'I wouldn't put it past Cher to drop them on purpose.'

'I agree,' said Fenella. 'She's a madam.'

'A pretty madam,' said Sarah, 'and one who knows how to use her charms.'

An hour and a half later Zoe stepped back and admired the cakes. She and Sarah had carried them all over to the marquee in trays. It had worked out just as she had imagined it in her head. The very top layer of cakes was like the tiara on top of the veil, clustered like roses. The tulle billowed out beneath, pinned in places by clutches of cakes, in stages. At the bottom cakes were grouped in twos and threes to look like cut roses. In between the cakes were rose petals, either dried, in deep red, or real pale yellow ones. Sarah was taking pictures with her phone.

'Any bride who had that as their cake would be over the moon,' said Fenella.

'I think she'll be delighted,' said Sarah. 'Her original cake was quite dull really. Just pale yellow with deep red piping. And this'll be free.'

'You've played a blinder,' said Rupert, who'd been part of the team ferrying the cupcakes.

'I'm glad you're pleased. Now I've got to sort out my canapés,' Zoe said, throwing off her apron and hurrying off to the marquee.

The judges circled the competitors like wolves round a sickly deer calf, Zoe felt. At last, having tasted and commented they gathered everyone together. Gideon stood up to make the announcement.

Having him as the spokesman was unusual and it made Zoe even more nervous.

'I'm afraid to say that we haven't been able to come to a decision,' said Gideon, looking uncharacteristically stressed. 'An announcement will be made after the wedding.'

'But it's obvious,' said Cher. 'Zoe should go out. Her canapés are dreadful!'

'They're not bad at all,' said Fred. 'Those ones with camembert and honey are delicious.'

'I thought my *supplì* were quite good too,' said Zoe, seeing as everyone was having their say.

'They tasted good,' Anna Fortune agreed, 'but your presentation is not up to standard. People would not be willing to pay one pound fifty each for them.'

'But they're free!' said Zoe.

'It's a competition,' Anna Fortune reminded her firmly.

'It's also a wedding,' said Sarah equally firmly, 'and without Zoe we wouldn't have a cake.' She looked at her watch. 'Now, I must go. If everyone could bring their canapés over to the marquee that would be helpful. And then start cooking the hot ones in about an hour and a half. The guests will start arriving for food at about one.'

'Do you want us to help serve?' asked Muriel. 'I have a friend in catering I help out quite often. It's fun.'

'Personally, I'm going for a lie-down,' said Cher, 'and I should think Zoe needs one too. Heaven knows what she's been up to all night.'

'Making cupcakes mostly, I should think,' said Muriel. 'Zoe, I had a peek earlier, and they are amazing. I love that it looks like a wedding veil with the cupcakes pretending to be roses. Did you design it yourself?'

Zoe smiled. 'I did – with a little help from my friends!'

'Well, it's beautiful,' said Muriel.

Becca, who didn't often comment on others' food, spending all her concentration on her own efforts, came up. 'It's lovely. I hope it doesn't mean you go out of the competition.'

Zoe sighed. 'If it does, it does. I don't think I'm going to win anyway. I think you're going to do that, Becca.'

Becca blushed. 'Cooking's the only thing I've ever been remotely good at.'

'And you're very good at it,' said Muriel.

Zoe's feelings were a whirr of confusion. Excitement and anxiety seemed to add to the constant feeling of longing for Gideon which seemed to underwrite all her other emotions. But mostly, she wanted the bride to like the cake.

It wouldn't be very long before the wedding party and the guests would arrive for the reception.

The large marquee that the contestants had been using had been sectioned off so that a row of cookers, where the cooks could finish their hot canapés, were separated from the guests.

Standing in the marquee, one would never guess that behind one of the walls six people were anxiously pulling things out of ovens and putting them back in again. Zoe, who trusted the alarm on her phone would tell her when she had to rush back to her oven, stood looking at the flower-decorated space whose focal point was the cake.

Someone had lit it so it looked like a work of art. Zoe didn't know who had done this or if this was usual for wedding cakes but it made her gasp. She took a photograph on her phone to send to her mother later. She felt a surge of pride. Whatever happened she'd created something beautiful and she wanted a record of it.

'Looks good, doesn't it?' said Fenella. 'I think Hugo – Sarah's husband? – did the lighting. The roses and the cupcakes exactly the same colour look magical. I do hope you're pleased.'

Zoe nodded. She felt a bit overcome and couldn't speak. She cleared her throat. 'Even if I get knocked out for my untidy canapés I don't regret doing it.'

Fenella kissed her cheek.

Once the wedding party began to arrive there was no time for contemplation or feeling pleased. All the contestants turned into waiters, carrying trays of hot food out into the crowd. They didn't have to help but wanted to: for one thing handing round their canapés was the best way to see how they were received. Sarah did tell Becca off at one point for standing over a couple for rather too long while they ate her miniature Yorkshire puddings and rare roast beef, but mostly they mucked in.

Zoe was way behind the others but decided it didn't matter if not all the food was ready at the same time. But when the last tray of *supplì* was out of the oven where they'd been keeping hot, and the last lot of ciabatta with honey and camembert was done, she found a clean apron and took her food out into the crowd. People were being called to order for the speeches so she slipped between them, glad people were still hungry enough to take them.

She was stuck at the back, alone in the crowd, when someone put a glass of champagne into her hand. It was Gideon. 'Have this, you deserve it.'

Zoe sipped, relishing the sharpness of the bubbles on her tongue. She'd been drinking from a bottle of water while she'd cooked; but it had got warm. This was delicious and palate-cleansing. He stood behind her.

'Someone might see!' she whispered, anguished.

'No one will notice. They'll just think I happen to be here.' He rested his hand gently on her waist and pressed in to her.

'Don't!' she said, fear and desire making her dizzy.

'Then come outside with me and let me kiss you.'

'I think that's blackmail,' she breathed.

'So?'

She finished the champagne and put the glass on a nearby table. The best man was just clearing his throat. The way he looked at the bride made Zoe hope the woman didn't get embarrassed easily. It appeared as if all her girlhood follies were about to be exposed, with embellishments.

Gideon led Zoe to an exit between two walls of the marquee and out into the fresh air. There were other people standing about; perhaps they were finding the marquee a little hot as the May sunshine beat down on it. He held out a hand but she didn't take it, not daring to risk any contact between them being seen. But she followed him between two buildings to where a rose rambled wildly over what had once been a pigsty and was now elegant accommodation.

She felt suddenly shy and, seeing it, he murmured something and pulled her close, kissing the corner of her mouth. 'You've done so well, Zoe. That cake is sensational.'

'Thank you,' she said quietly as she leant into him. And then he kissed her more thoroughly.

She allowed herself a few seconds of bliss before pulling away. 'Really, Gideon, this is too risky.'

He looked as if he was about to argue but then he said, 'You're right. There's such a lot to lose if we were found out.'

She looked up into his eyes and felt glad he understood. He could have talked her into kissing him more, or even going somewhere for more than kissing, but he didn't. It made her like him more. He wasn't using his power over her for his own ends. Unless he didn't realise how she felt. She sighed and smiled, glad to think her feelings weren't too blindingly obvious.

'I'd better go back. People will wonder where I am.'

'Go on then. I'll see you later.'

'Thank you for the champagne.'

'Next time, there'll be a bottle.'

Zoe made her way back to her oven, her heart singing. She didn't even mind that there was a blackened tray of something she'd forgotten about. Gideon obviously liked her, for herself and not just for sex, or he wouldn't have let her go. She found herself smiling and couldn't seem to stop.

The last guests were still wandering round the grounds waiting for buses to take them to the evening do, which was taking place somewhere else.

The contestants were herded together with the film crew to be addressed by the judges. The marquee, so beautiful only hours before, was now being cleared of tables and chairs and flowers and returning to its origins as a tent.

At the far end furniture was still being shifted and Sarah, as the main judge, had to raise her voice slightly.

'The bride and groom are delighted with how it all went,' she announced. 'I'm so relieved, I can't tell you. The cake was beyond their wildest dreams,' she said, looking for Zoe, who was trying to hide behind a flower-decked pillar.

'But we must remember the challenge wasn't about a few cupcakes,' said Anna Fortune, 'it was about the canapés.'

There was a pause which sent Zoe's nerves into orbit in spite of the nice things Sarah had said about the cake, while camera angles were altered.

Gideon was muttering into Anna's ear and Zoe hoped he wasn't standing up for her. It would draw attention to them if he was and Cher would say – quite rightly – that Zoe was getting preferential treatment.

Zoe felt a stab of guilt. She hadn't received any advantage (or hardly any) because of what was going on between her and Gideon but it was still wrong. Her conscience was on a hair trigger.

Fred waved at the camera in a cheerful way. 'I think this used to be described as a judgely huddle,' and he joined Anna and Gideon in their discussion. Sarah stood slightly outside the circle with her arms folded. She did not look pleased. A part of Zoe felt this would make really good television – a bit of dissension among the judges. The other part felt a stirring of panic: things were obviously not going her way.

Sarah broke in to the group and the discussion went on.

'They'll have to cut some of this,' said Shadrach. 'It's getting boring.'

Zoe wasn't bored but she was in an agony of suspense.

At last the judges broke away from each other, the

cameras were set up again and Sarah was centre stage. She repeated all she'd said before and added, 'Although some of the canapés didn't look quite up to standard, they did taste delicious. Zoe, the judges loved your ciabatta, cheese and honey with hazelnuts but your rice balls looked a little rustic.'

'So is she going out?' Cher asked loudly and inappropriately.

There was a long pause as the judges looked at each other. Zoe's heart thumped loudly. Now that it seemed inevitable she would go out she realised how much she wanted to stay.

'It's been decided that no one will go out,' announced Fred at last. 'You've all done a very good job and Zoe, whose canapés were the weakest – visually – produced a wonderful wedding cake.'

'Zoe would have gone out otherwise,' said Anna Fortune, looking at her with gimlet 'I won't let you get away with anything' eyes.

'Excuse me!' said Cher. 'No offence, Zoe – but if her canapés weren't up to standard, it's not fair to keep her in when we all worked really hard to make ours good.'

Zoe couldn't stop herself looking at Gideon, whose eyes glittered in a menacing way.

'The judges have made their decision, Cher,' said Anna Fortune. She may have shared Cher's opinion but she wasn't having a mere contestant questioning the judges, Zoe could tell.

'Which brings us to our next challenge,' said Gideon. 'Cooking in a top London restaurant kitchen. It'll be very, very challenging. Good luck!'

There was a gasp from the contestants as the judges swept out of the marquee, the camera crew following closely behind.

Chapter Twelve

༄༅༅

The next day had been a day of rest. Zoe had chatted to the others for a while and then found a quiet spot in the garden and tried to distract herself with the novel she'd bought with her. She hadn't had time to read even a page since the competition had begun. She had half hoped she'd be able to spend some time with Gideon but he'd gone off with the other judges to look over the footage taken so far with the producers. And anyway Cher had been keeping her beady eye on her, hanging on to her arm as if she actually liked her. Eventually Zoe had had to say she needed some time alone. Cher had ended up sunbathing in a deckchair on the other side of the garden, still within sight.

They were now on their way to London for the fine-dining challenge.

'I'm going up to the quiet carriage,' said Zoe at the station while they waited for the train. 'I want to read.'

What she actually wanted was space for thought and to flick through some diagrams of knife skills; this session in a professional London kitchen was going to test her to the limit. She knew if she sat in the same carriage as the others she would be talked at.

As she gazed at the passing scenery, thinking how pretty it was, she realised that the twinge of conscience she had felt yesterday was intensifying, clouding the bubble of happiness which had been lurking under her apron almost from the start of the competition. It didn't make her feelings for Gideon any less intense – in fact it might have increased them – but she had to examine her actions and see if guilt was justified.

She opened her folder with the diagrams in and noted the 'claw' position for holding narrow things, like shallots, so they could be chopped with the sharpest knife without the fingers being threatened. Although her eyes and a small part of her brain was on the picture, most of her was asking herself just how wrong it was to be sleeping with one of the judges during a competition.

She thought about the big ones – *The X Factor*, *Strictly Come Dancing*, *Britain's Got Talent* – and pictured one of the lovely young things sleeping with one of their judges. If she heard about that she'd be appalled. And would John Torode sleep with a *Masterchef* hopeful? No, of course he wouldn't, even if he wasn't a happily married man. It was wrong. Whichever way you cut it (her eye was caught by a dangerous-looking practice in which you drew the knife towards the fingers holding an onion – one slip and you'd be wearing blue plasters for days) what she and Gideon were doing was wrong. She should give him up, simple as that. She should just go to him and say, 'It has to stop!'

But *did* it have to stop? Had he used his influence and charm to keep her in the competition? Her mind went back over the various rounds until it came to the canapés. Her canapés, although generally declared delicious, certainly lacked finesse. Anna Fortune would have had her out.

Yet it wasn't Gideon who'd saved her, although he had probably added a few words of encouragement, it was Sarah. Sarah would have protected her against any judge because Zoe had saved her wedding. And quite right too!

Zoe thought defiantly. Without a cake the wedding would have been a disaster. As it had turned out it was almost the star of the show! Sarah had told her later that she'd been emailing pictures of it to her friend who made cakes so she could offer it to future brides. Zoe smiled as she remembered the conversation. Sarah had tentatively asked her if she planned to make wedding cakes like that again herself; Zoe had replied that if she never saw another cupcake it would be too soon. It wasn't quite true but she certainly didn't fancy making them to earn her living.

Round and round went her brain, dipping out occasionally to check her folder. Gideon was such good company. He made her laugh, he laughed at her jokes in return and she felt they would have got on even if they hadn't shared such powerful sexual chemistry. But although she really, really liked Gideon – more than liked – she still wasn't completely sure about him. And was it worth risking her chances if he was only going to say 'thank you and goodbye' at the end of it and she was left loveless and sent off in shame? She tried concentrating on the booklet again.

She opened the section on fish, which was where her skills and lack of experience would really let her down. The diagram showing how you turned a squid inside out and back again – several times – in order to make it edible made her eyes swim and her brain ache. She hoped fervently that it would be easier to understand if she actually had a squid in front of her. Filleting a flat fish didn't look easy either. She could imagine the shouting that would go on if she wasted half of an expensive Dover sole.

But this was just a distraction, she knew. What she really should be doing was thinking how to tell Gideon that they had to stop the lovely, flirtatious and delightful thing they'd both enjoyed so much. She could no longer steal moments alone with him and she certainly wouldn't sleep with him – not until she was out of the competition, at least. A shuddering sigh went through her as the pain of her decision hit her brain. Would she – could she – be strong enough to carry through this resolve? If she told them not to, would her knees not go weak when she saw him and her body start to respond to him even while they were several feet apart? She doubted it. She had no faith in her body where Gideon was concerned.

And maybe the decision was out of her hands. This service at a top-flight, 'fine-dining' restaurant could be beyond her.

But when she thought back over the days and considered what she had achieved she realised she'd learnt a lot and developed in confidence. She wasn't ready to throw in the towel just yet. She found she did mind the thought of not winning. Or at least of not making it through to the final. And she felt an ache at the thought of never seeing Gideon again. Why was life so complicated? Couldn't she have her cake and eat it? Plenty of people did. But in such cases things usually turned out badly in the end. There really was no doubt about it. She must finish it.

Cher, Muriel, Becca and Zoe got into a taxi, only Cher worrying about the cameras filming her short skirt. Muriel and Zoe were wearing jeans. The men had chivalrously let them take the first taxi and were now climbing into the one that arrived shortly behind. Their overnight bags had been taken separately to their hotel. 'So it's to Pierre Beauvère we go!' said Muriel, trying not to sound nervous.

'At least we have this afternoon to learn the ropes before we have to cook for actual people,' said Zoe. 'I must admit I'm terrified. It's like being asked to sing at Covent Garden if you've only ever been in the school choir.'

'Not quite as bad as that, surely?' said Becca nervously.

Zoe shrugged. 'Almost.' Although, she realised, the slight sickness she felt might be partly due to her decision about Gideon. 'I'm far happier cooking in a field.'

'Well, I've worked in a fine-dining restaurant before,' said Cher, exuding confidence and checking her make-up in her compact mirror. 'I'm just hoping I don't have to wear one of those chef's caps. They look cute at the time but your hair looks awful afterwards.'

Muriel took a deep breath. 'Cher, I can't believe you're worrying about what you might look like after service when you have to cook for a Michelin-starred chef who is not the pleasantest, by all accounts!'

'Television! Duh! I care about my appearance.'

'And we don't?' said Zoe.

'I don't think so. I don't think I've ever seen any of you in a dress.'

Zoe subsided into the seat. 'I have worn a dress,' she said after a moment's thought.

'Obviously not a memorable one,' said Cher.

Zoe sighed but inside she was smiling. Cher might spend all her waking moments thinking about how she looked but she, scruffy old Zoe, was the one who had caught the attention of Gideon. She tried not to feel smug at the thought of how wasted Cher's efforts had been on that score. Then she reminded herself that she had to stop thinking about him.

As they were filmed, several times, getting out of the taxi and going up the steps to the restaurant, Zoe tried to focus on the task ahead of her. But she was extremely nervous.

She'd heard what horrible things they did to people in professional kitchens. She gave herself a talking to: just because you're a girl, and are going to be filmed, and are likely to get all sorts of extra help, it doesn't mean they're going to put your head in a bin full of fish guts.

Unconvinced, she smiled weakly at the others as she pushed open the door – for real this time – and entered the place of torture that was masquerading as a shrine to good food and perfect service.

Since the start of the competition the film crew had always been there but somehow were always forgotten about. Now, away from the familiar surroundings of Somerby and its environs, they felt like friends. When they left Zoe felt she was being abandoned at school by fond parents. The boys had now arrived and all seven contestants were huddled by the door, waiting for instructions.

They were greeted by seven people, six men and a woman. Zoe was pleased to get the woman: she looked the friendliest.

Although they had arrived after lunchtime service and the kitchen was relatively quiet, there were still things going on: people in chef's whites prepping piles of parsley or chopping onions. A couple had their elbows on the benches, peering at things. Another was scraping the seeds from a vanilla pod.

If she hadn't been there to work, Zoe would have loved it, but for the first time in the competition she felt genuinely daunted. She knew her skills weren't as a chef in a professional kitchen and just at this moment she couldn't think what she was good at. Being handy with half a ton of butter cream and a piping bag wouldn't count for much here.

'Hello.' A man, tall, hostile, with a foreign accent came up to her. 'You're the girl for the TV?' He grunted in response to her nod. 'Sylvie will look after you.'

Sylvie nodded. 'Yes, chef!'

'Find her some whites. I can't have her here in those clothes.'

Zoe saw him go to give the others the same warm welcome in turn and moved a little closer to Sylvie.

'Follow me,' said Sylvie. 'Now what sort of shoes have you to work in?'

As the judges had checked everyone's shoes before they left, Zoe swung down her rucksack and showed the clogs within.

'Fine,' said Sylvie. 'Pierre will have your guts as a garnish for monkfish if you don't have proper shoes.'

Zoe laughed, relaxing a little. 'We had the shoe talk early on. Gideon was particularly fixated about it.' Inwardly she cursed herself for mentioning his name. It was 'mentionitis' and she mustn't let herself do it!

'Gideon? Gideon Irving? The food critic?'

'That's him. Have you heard of him?'

'God yes! He's a fairly famous critic, you know. But I used to work with him years ago.' Sylvie went a little dreamy. 'Broke my heart, the bastard.'

As she said this without rancour Zoe felt obliged to press for more information. 'Oh?'

'Yes. He's a handsome devil and we were working together.' She sighed. 'Not his fault really, I don't think. Emotionally, he just wasn't engaged. He hid it well, but I knew.'

'That sounds very sad,' said Zoe, thinking of herself.

'Yes. There'd obviously been someone he'd never got over. I heard she went off to America to pursue a career in TV.'

'And?'

She wanted Sylvie to say what a nice man Gideon was in spite of it all, but Sylvie misunderstood.

'She made a go of it, I think. But my theory about him is – was – he never really got over her.'

'Oh.' Since she hadn't got the reassurance she craved, Zoe tried to think of something to say before Sylvie realised that she had feelings for Gideon. 'Were you . . .' she paused. 'Were you broken-hearted long?'

Sylvie shrugged and laughed. 'Well, he is kind of hard to get out of your mind and your head once he's in there, but he's not the settling-down kind and I always knew that, in my heart.'

Zoe's heart, which suspected that too, felt a little bruised. 'Oh,' she said for the third time. She couldn't think of anything else to say and didn't quite know what to think. Did he make a habit of wooing women he worked with and then leaving them? Was she just another notch on the chopping board for him? The thought made her feel sick. But Sylvie had said it was years ago so perhaps he'd changed. She clung on to the notion.

'So just don't you go falling in love with him!' Sylvie chuckled. 'Not that you would, him being a judge, but he is attractive and you're young and lovely.'

Sylvie didn't seem to suspect Zoe had feelings for Gideon. She was determined to keep the conversation light. She summoned her best Oscar performance and laughed.

'He certainly is a judge!' she said, as if the idea of even thinking about having any kind of relationship was completely beyond her. 'And I may not be the youngest and I'm certainly not the loveliest.'

'That's OK then. Now let's get you kitted up.'

Thankfully Sylvie was fooled and Zoe was relieved she'd soon be too busy to dwell on all the maelstrom of emotions Sylvie's comments had thrown up.

Chapter Thirteen

Once she'd kitted Zoe out in a chef's jacket, apron, check trousers and hat (which made Zoe realise that Cher was the only one they looked cute on), Sylvie took Zoe back to Pierre. As they left the changing room Zoe saw Cher protesting prettily against the hat. Sod's law would mean she didn't have to wear one.

'I want her on the fish section,' said Pierre, scowling.

Zoe felt he must have read her mind. Not only did he sense she was totally distracted but he knew she also couldn't do fish.

And being looked after by an old flame of Gideon's who'd made it quite clear that having anything to do with him would end in heartbreak didn't help.

'She can prepare the monkfish,' he continued and then went away, sneering Gallicly, hygiene regulations possibly being the only thing that stopped him spitting.

Sylvie took hold of Zoe's arm. 'You may have picked up that he's not over keen on this TV thing,' she said, leading Zoe to the fish-preparation area. 'He's been forced into it by the executive chef – who's a friend of Gideon's, naturally.'

'Why naturally?'

'He's a feared food critic but people like him. Women too. As we've discussed.'

While she was obviously trying to imply she was fine about it now, Zoe got the impression that Sylvie's heart was still a bit battered, if not actually broken.

'So, the monkfish? I'd like to be able to do something before the crew come back.' Zoe didn't want to talk about Gideon any more. Thinking about him every second was bad enough and she had to try and concentrate. It was more important than ever that she didn't go out through being too distracted to give it her best.

'OK. Well, at least you don't have to worry about the head,' said Sylvie, 'as they're cut off at sea. They take up far too much room. And the skin is OK too, what you need to really worry about is the membrane. It's practically invisible and sticks like glue.'

Fifteen minutes later Zoe was still struggling. 'I can't get the bloody stuff off!' she said, forgetting the crew had returned and her bad language and frustration was going to be shown to thousands of people. 'I can still pick up the fillet with the membrane!'

'Just tug it with your fingers. There's a bit of a knack to it. But don't leave any on or Pierre—'

'I know, you said: use my guts as a garnish.' She got hold of another bit and managed to get it off. 'I thought the skin was tough, but at least you can see it.'

'You're doing well,' said Sylvie, but Zoe didn't believe her.

'How many do I have to do?' Zoe asked in horror.

'Not many. Only half a dozen.'

Six! She had to struggle like this five more times. She got off a piece of membrane, which encouraged her to ask. 'So how will I cook this? Do you know?'

Sylvie laughed. 'Oh, you won't be cooking this. Pierre says monkfish is far too expensive for amateurs. You'll be cooking mackerel.'

Zoe managed to stay silent this time and just made a face. 'I suppose you're going to tell me he's lovely really.'

Sylvie nodded. 'He is, actually. He just has very high standards and really cares about food.'

'So do we all,' said Zoe sharply. 'It's why we all work so hard.' Then, feeling guilty for snapping, she added, 'What will I be cooking?'

'Fishcakes,' said Sylvie.

'I think I can manage them,' said Zoe, somewhat mollified.

'We serve two fishcakes per portion. You'll need to do about fifty.'

Zoe made a little sound like a kitten needing milk. Sylvie laughed. 'I'll be there to help you. Pierre wouldn't risk you messing up. And you can start really early in the morning and give yourself plenty of time.'

Only Cher was still perky after her afternoon at the restaurant, having been doing pâtisserie at which, with her delicate touch, she was maddeningly good. Everyone else was exhausted. Becca had spent her time boning tiny birds and looked ashen. Shadrach had been shaving vegetables so finely you could see through them. Everyone had some horror story to relate but Zoe was sure she was the only one who had nearly been reduced to tears – or if she was, she was the only one admitting it. Zoe went with the others for a quick drink in the bar but was the first to leave. She needed to be in the kitchen at dawn the next morning or she'd go out of the competition – and then she might never see Gideon again.

The next day in the restaurant didn't go much better. Although gutting the mackerel was a lot easier once she'd got the knack of pulling out all the innards by the head, she burned several of them by having her grill too hot, and later burned her fingers trying to flake them when the flesh was too hot. Before she could think about cooking the fishcakes she had to clean off her fingers, which, in spite of trying very hard, had become banana-sized, covered with flour and breadcrumbs. Yet in the end she was privately pleased with the neatness and uniformity of her fishcakes, and when Pierre had seen them he had just grunted, which was equal to high praise in Zoe's eyes.

By the time they came to cook the first portion, Zoe was feeling her lack of sleep. Fear and nerves had kept her going in the beginning but now the fact that she had spent most of the night turning her pillow over and over in an attempt to get comfortable interspersed with bouts of thinking about Gideon meant she felt slightly dizzy.

The atmosphere in the kitchen was getting to her too. It was exciting but also terrifying.

'You either get off on the adrenalin or you don't,' said Sylvie. 'Me, I love it. I love the tension, the sense of theatre, all that. But if you like to be calm with nobody shouting, a restaurant kitchen is probably not for you.'

'Maybe I'll get into it,' said Zoe, forcing enthusiasm into her voice and bouncing around on her toes hoping to get into the mood. 'You know, I'll be stressed at first and then I'll really get into it and come away flying!'

'Maybe,' said Sylvie, looking doubtful.

Cher as ever had been infuriatingly perky. The others were quieter but no one seemed as nervous as Zoe was.

Pierre loomed like an evil apparition just as she was cooking her test batch of fishcakes. She'd already had to do a piece to camera about it all and Zoe had noticed Pierre scowling at her out of the corner of her eye. He was willing her to fail.

She lowered the first fishcake into the sizzling oil.

'You've got that too hot,' said Pierre. 'It's burning the fishcakes. Throw it away.'

Zoe didn't dare argue although she felt a slightly browner fishcake would still be acceptable. It was his restaurant and she did understand that the filming thing was taking up a lot of time and space. She took out the fishcake and moved the pan to the side so it could cool down a little.

'Now try another one,' said Pierre.

This time the sizzling was a little quieter.

'Perfect,' said Pierre when she removed the fishcake. 'Now I'll try it.'

Zoe swallowed, hoping against hope that she'd seasoned it correctly – which, in chef's terms, she had discovered, meant lots of salt.

'Mm, not bad,' said Pierre having taken a bite, opening his jaw like a boa constrictor to do so. 'Carry on.'

'There! I told you he was a sweetie really!' said Sylvie.

'I do not think saying "not bad" and "carry on" exactly defines being a sweetie, but hey, I'll take what I can get.'

'It means he's impressed. If he wasn't happy there's no way he'd let you serve those fishcakes.'

There was just time to do a quick 'how are you all feeling about the challenge' piece together. Afterwards Zoe found herself huddling in a corner with Muriel and Cher while the others went off to the loo or for a sneaky cigarette.

Muriel looked suddenly ten years older but Cher was glowing. She'd been doing well at pâtisserie and her nimble fingers combined with a very kind and susceptible pastry chef meant she'd been producing genuinely beautiful pastries.

'Pierre's a sweetie, isn't he?' she said, sipping water from a bottle. 'He was so kind about my little confections.'

'Is that what they're calling them these days?' said Zoe, before she could stop herself.

'Ooh, saucer of milk for table eight!' said Cher, laughing in a way that made Zoe feel patronised and catty at the same time.

'Personally I find Pierre a complete bastard!' said Muriel, after a hasty look over her shoulder to check he couldn't hear. 'I swear there wasn't one scrap of fat on that lamb bone but he had to go and find a huge slice of it.'

'Well, he's not going to put up with incompetence, is he?' said Cher. 'I mean, this is his restaurant! He's got a reputation!' Another sip of water went down. 'I saw him reporting to the judges.'

'We won't be judged until after the lunchtime service,' said Zoe.

'No, but for some of us, I think you'll find the decision has already been made.'

Then she swept off, cool and immaculate in her whites, not a hair out of place and no chef's hat.

'I feel like an actor about to go on stage to play *Hamlet* without knowing the lines,' said Zoe to Sylvie as she returned to her work station.

'Don't panic. You've practised. You'll be good at them now!'

She stood at her station feeling like a horse about to run the Grand National, only with other horses setting off first. Other starters were ordered. At first it seemed no one wanted fishcakes. Then the first order came. She managed to remember to shout back, 'Yes, chef!' and then she got started. She tested the oil was the perfect temperature and carefully lowered in her fishcakes.

'Great!' said Sylvie as Zoe took them out and laid them on paper to drain. 'Now just plate them up and add the mayo and the garnish and you're done!'

She still dreaded hearing 'fishcakes' being called from the pass but as they were called more often she speeded up until she was waiting, almost eager.

She also learnt to calculate exactly how long they would

take so if she was asked she could say, 'Two minutes, chef,' with total confidence. She didn't notice the camera team getting a close-up of the sizzling pan, or the judges, she was just focused on getting out the fishcakes, perfect and on time. It was exhilarating and terrifying at the same time, the only things keeping her going being high-octane adrenalin and a determination to succeed.

She was aware of others struggling. As she went to the chill room she passed the meat section and saw Muriel floundering, surrounded by half-cooked racks of lamb, and Cher screaming as she dropped a plate of pastry cases on the floor. She was fairly sure that no one but her saw Cher put the unbroken ones back on the plate, but she didn't say anything. Time and the restaurant was the greater enemy just now. Her battles with Cher were not to be fought during a challenge. Besides, she had to get back to her own station.

'OK, guys, service is over!' a voice boomed above the din.

It seemed to Zoe as if a great machine had been turned off. The show was over but, very much to her surprise, Zoe was still exhilarated. Somehow during that long, hot morning she'd got in the groove and enjoyed herself. She looked around. Chefs of all degrees were still cleaning up their stations, sluicing down their working areas with hot soapy water and wiping up repeatedly. Kitchen porters carried teetering piles of baking trays, bowls and pans to be washed up. People started to talk; the air had gone out of the balloon.

Pierre came up to Zoe and she tensed; although she knew she'd been fine really, her body expected her to be castigated if not actually beheaded. 'You did well. You need to speed up considerably, of course, if you're ever to work in a professional kitchen, but otherwise – not bad.'

He moved on, having smiled like a snake spotting a baby rabbit. Zoe lost some of her exhilaration. He obviously thought the chances of her working in a professional kitchen were slim.

Mike, their producer, came up to them. 'Right, everyone, we're going to do the judging now. They're waiting for you in the restaurant.'

'Can we tidy up a bit?' asked Muriel. 'Ourselves, I mean, instead of this goddamn kitchen.' That was the first time anyone had heard Muriel use an expletive. The challenge had obviously really got to her.

Mike shook his head. ''Fraid not. We want it completely natural, just as you are. Come along please.'

They filed out of the kitchen and into the restaurant to meet their fate.

'Where's Gideon?' asked Muriel in a whisper.

Zoe had noticed he was missing almost before she could see he wasn't there. 'I don't know!' she said, and then realised she'd sounded a bit panicked. She forced a smile. 'Oh well, one less person to try and impress.'

'OK, guys,' said Anna Fortune. 'Firstly, you'll notice that Gideon isn't with us. He's gone to New York to see about making this programme over there.'

Zoe moved her dry lips together, trying to moisten them. New York! Wasn't that where Sylvie said his one true love had gone? Then she mentally kicked herself. New York was huge, and if he was going to follow her he'd have done it years ago.

She forced herself to focus on Anna, who went on: 'But you'll be glad to know he sampled your cooking and he'll be back to judge the rest of the competition.'

Zoe was indeed glad to hear that although what she would do if she went out now, she didn't know. She had no way of contacting him and he had no way of contacting

166

her, except through the production company and she couldn't risk that in case they wondered why. She hoped he wouldn't ask, either. Zoe was discovering it was possible to have a lot of deep important thoughts in a very short space of time. She rather wished her brain would just stop though as the thoughts were making her feel sick.

'You've done really well, on the whole, with a couple of exceptions . . .' Anna went on, her low, modulated voice managing to cause panic in several breasts.

She seemed to be going on for ever. And then Fred had his say, and then they read out the notes Gideon had made before he left for the airport. And then Pierre came on and in spite of apparently hating the whole television thing, seemed intent on dragging out his five minutes of fame as long as possible.

Everyone was extra nervous. Zoe could feel Muriel beside her almost trembling. This was harder on her, Zoe told herself firmly, to stop self-pity creeping up from her aching feet and swamping her. Muriel was older than the rest of them, she probably didn't have the same stamina. But Muriel's heart wasn't involved. Or if it was, she had kept it well hidden. She crossed her fingers and prayed, very hard.

At last Fred said, 'This is the end of the line for one of you. But when you leave, leave with your head high knowing you cook better than most people in this country and you've learnt more in this past fortnight about cooking than many people learn in a lifetime.'

It was a bit clichéd, thought Zoe, but he was trying to boost the morale of whoever did have to make the walk of shame, taking off their apron, unbuttoning their chef's jacket.

'And the person not going through to the next round is . . . Muriel!'

At first Zoe just felt shocked. Muriel couldn't go! She

was her friend! Her ally! If Muriel went it would just be just Cher, Becca and the boys, Shadrach, Bill and Alan, left.

Then she realised if it was Muriel, it wasn't her. Relief followed by guilt threatened to swamp her. She turned to Muriel and hugged her. They both started to cry.

'I'm all right, really,' Muriel said, recovering first. 'I'm just tired! I'm so happy to have lasted this long but I didn't cope well in there . . .'

There was a lot of hugging and weeping and general congratulation before they were lined up again to do the final shot, when the remaining contestants looked relieved as Muriel walked away.

'Well, I thought that was fun!' said Cher as they gathered in the foyer of the hotel, waiting for the taxi to the station. 'I don't know why you all thought it was so hard!'

Zoe was very glad Muriel had already left. A car had driven her to her home where her family would be there to greet her.

'We weren't all fiddling about with bits of whipped cream and pastry,' said Becca, empowered by her recent achievements.

'There's a lot more to pastry work than just that,' said Cher seriously.

'Whatever, we're lucky to be left in. Muriel was a great cook,' said Alan.

'Not as great as all that,' said Cher. Zoe didn't have the heart to reply.

Shadrach yawned and stretched so widely Zoe heard his joints crack. 'Well, I'm glad we've got a few days off. I want some of my mum's home cooking.'

'What do you want most?' asked Zoe, curious.

'Macaroni cheese with crispy onions and bacon on top,

with breadcrumbs,' said Shadrach instantly. 'I've been dreaming of it for days.'

Zoe considered. 'I think it has to be apple pie for me. With pastry top and bottom. My mother makes great pastry.'

'Baked beans with hot chilli sauce stirred into them,' said Bill. 'Hey! I'm hungry!'

The others laughed. At least the competition hadn't put them off food – apart from Cher, that is, but she didn't eat much anyway. Zoe realised she'd grown rather fond of everyone. She'd miss Muriel. She couldn't help wishing it had been Cher who'd been knocked out. She just seemed to get more and more smug. Perhaps after a few days away from her Zoe would feel more charitable and less irritated.

They'd arrived back at Somerby, collected a few belongings and gone their separate ways. Cher had been picked up in an expensive-looking car, giving them all a cheery little wave as she went. Bill had given Becca a lift to the station. Alan and Shadrach were leaving in the morning. Zoe said a quick hello and goodbye to Fenella and Rupert, who were delighted she was still in the competition, and then got into her little car and headed home.

Chapter Fourteen

꧁ꞈ꧂

As Zoe pointed her car into the drive behind her mother's Golf she felt she'd aged ten years since she'd left home.

Her mother, hearing her car, came out of the house to greet her. 'Darling! You look shattered.'

'Thanks a lot, Mum!' said Zoe, returning her mother's hug with equal force. 'Oh, it's good to be home!' She meant it. She felt as if she'd been living in a very intense bubble for the last week or so. It was good to break free for a few days.

Her mother took her bag and they went into the house. Zeb the dog had to be greeted and even the cat came up and rubbed itself round Zoe's legs.

'Jenny is very keen to meet up. She wants to hear everything.'

Zoe yawned. 'Maybe tomorrow. I'll definitely want an early night tonight.'

'Well, Dad'll be back soon so we can eat early.'

'What are we having?' All the talk of home cooking the evening before had made her extra interested.

'Shepherd's pie, little peas, then apple pie,' said her mother promptly.

Zoe gave her mother another hug. 'You know me so well!'

'So I should hope.' She looked at her watch. 'Dad won't be home for a bit yet. Do you want a bath or anything?'

'Well, given that before I went back to Somerby to pick

up my car I was at a very swanky hotel I'm not actually dirty, but a bath—'

'With bubbles?'

'And a book, would be lovely.'

Zoe's mother laughed. 'It's just like when you used to come home after uni.'

After a wonderfully cosy and restorative evening with her parents, Zoe felt up to meeting her best friend Jenny the next day. The trouble with Jenny was Zoe couldn't hide anything from her and she would weasel all the details about Gideon and how she felt out of her before they were halfway down the first glass of wine. But Zoe didn't mind. She wanted to talk about him. It was a symptom of being in love – or whatever she was: you wanted to talk about your love-object all the time. And while she was close to her mother, there was no obvious happy ending with Gideon and she didn't want her to worry, or take on that concerned look that always made Zoe feel bad. And she'd always shared everything with Jenny – they'd known each other since primary school.

Jenny claimed there were no troubles that couldn't be solved by being close to a horse, so when Zoe had called her the night before, she had suggested that Zoe go over to the livery yard where she kept hers; and Zoe had felt it was worth the early start. Jenny's horse, Prince Albert – Bert for short – was tied up to a rail in the yard while she mucked out his stall. Zoe went straight over to him for an initial chat. There was something definitely comforting about his solid presence, and he'd known Zoe quite a long time so they were old friends.

'Hey Zoe!' called Jenny, wheeling a barrow to the muck heap. 'How are you?'

'Good thanks. You? And lovely Bert?' She stroked the massive head which leaned into her shoulder and whispered into her ear with lips like velvet.

'We're fine, but we haven't been in a cookery competition. I want to hear all about it.'

Zoe was aware of Jenny's knowing eyes on her as she and Bert communicated with strokes and caresses, hot breaths, snorts and murmurings. Jenny had an uncanny ability to sense when Zoe had something to hide.

'I do love Bert. He's just there for you. He doesn't ask questions,' said Zoe.

'I'm sure it's mutual. I also love you. But I do ask questions. Get a broom and help me muck out.'

Zoe set to with enthusiasm. It was somehow easier to get her thoughts in order while she was being active. She had done nothing but think about Gideon on the way home but everything was a jumble in her head. Mucking out helped clear the fog.

'So, what are the others like?' Jenny asked, tossing a pile of muck into the barrow with one deft action.

'Most of them are really nice. My favourite went out last time though. It's a girl I don't like who bothers me.'

'But you always like everyone!'

'I know, but not her. It's probably because she doesn't like me.'

'So? Tell me about her.'

Zoe concentrated on getting her broom into an awkward corner. 'She's very pretty, very focused and has at least twice tried to sabotage my chances.'

'Drama! Did you tell anyone? The judges?'

'Er – no. I'm not in a good position to do that.'

'Why not? Are they unapproachable? Swear a lot? Or what?'

Zoe bit her lip. 'Or what.'

'Which means?' Jenny stopped work and looked at her friend intently.

'One of them is rather gorg.'

'Oh! You mean you fancy one of the judges? Bet you didn't see that coming!'

'And it's gone a bit further than just fancying him.'

'Ah.' Jenny thought for a moment. 'Tell you what, let's tack up. You take Bert and I'll borrow Buzz next door. Annabel won't mind. I'll just text her.' Jenny pulled out her phone.

'But I haven't ridden for ages!' Zoe protested, half excited and half nervous at the thought of being on a horse again.

'There's nothing to it!' said Jenny, heading for the tack room. 'It's just like—'

'No, it's not like riding a bicycle!' said Zoe. Didn't they say that about sex too? God, her mind seemed to be on little else these days.

'It is a bit,' said Jenny, 'and you'll be fine. Bert will look after you. We'll just go up in the woods where we can ride abreast and have a good old chat. I want all the gory details.'

They made their way through the woods to where they used to ride together when they were thirteen years old. Zoe found it was familiar being on Bert's back.

'I'd forgotten how lovely it is up here,' she said to Jenny as they reached a clearing at the far end of the copse.

'You should get up here more often. Annabel is always glad for Buzz to be ridden and you and Bert are a team.'

'It's the old enemy, time,' said Zoe, her eyes raking the plants and bushes, remembering the happy times she and Jenny had spent. 'Oh look, wild garlic,' she said. 'It's late for that, isn't it?'

Jenny shrugged. 'I suppose it depends where it's growing. I made some great pesto with it the other day.'

'Oh? So you're into cooking a bit more now?'

'Only a bit. Now come up beside me and tell me what you've been up to. And don't leave anything out!'

'Well, I think it sounds lovely. Really romantic,' said Jenny when Zoe had finished her story. It was a relief to talk about Gideon to someone, especially someone she trusted implicitly and knew her so well.

'But it's so wrong! He's a judge! And he probably only wants me for a little fling because according to Sylvie he's in love with some childhood sweetheart.'

'He'll be over that by now!' Ever practical, Jenny was impatient with the thought of childhood sweethearts. 'But he sounds nice. You know, not only after one thing.'

'Does he? I'm glad you think so. When I'm with him I find it quite hard to work out if he is really nice or if I just fancy him so much I can't think straight.' She sighed. 'But what I absolutely must not do is let him stop me focusing on the competition. I didn't expect to last this long, Jenny, but now I have, I feel perhaps I can make it. There are some great cooks still in the competition. There's a girl called Becca who's brilliant, but sometimes her nerves let her down.'

'But you manage to control yours?'

'Mostly. It's not always easy, but I can.'

'Well, I'm impressed!' She pulled Buzz round and said, 'Fancy a gentle canter up this incline? I know Bert would love it.'

'OK, but you heard the gentle part, didn't you, Bertie, darling?'

'He did. You'll be fine!'

*

When Zoe finally got back to her parents' house after her ride she felt much more at ease with herself and the situation. She'd known it would help talking to Jenny. Her friend hadn't thought she'd done a terrible thing, just reassured her that you couldn't help whom you fell in love with but that it was important to concentrate on the competition. Like Fenella she'd said that if Gideon really liked Zoe, he'd wait.

Zoe was now more determined than ever that she would focus on her cooking. She also resolved not to allow herself to have any private contact with Gideon until the competition was over – or at least over for her. She knew she could do it. She had strong will power when she wanted it. In fact, she told herself, she wouldn't give him a moment's further thought.

She went to sleep dreaming of him.

Chapter Fifteen

❧

As the remaining contestants gathered in the marquee waiting for the judges Zoe noted that everyone looked better than they had done the last time they'd seen each other. Then they'd been hollow-eyed, greasy-haired, verging on the hysterical. Now they'd all had a rest and had probably been cooking in their own homes, reassuring themselves that they really could do it, and they did have enough left in them to continue the competition. They had arrived back at Somerby during the day and now, before they were bussed off to the pub for supper, they were going to be told their fate: the challenge for the next day.

But there were only five of them. A quick look round told Zoe Alan wasn't there. She hoped he hadn't left because he was ill or had a family emergency. She liked Alan. In fact she liked everyone – apart from Cher.

It was ironic, thought Zoe, that the closer they became as a group of people (excluding Cher, of course) the more direct the competition felt between them.

'It's like being gladiators,' she muttered to Becca, who happened to be next to her. 'We're all a team but we have to fight against each other.'

'What?' said Becca, who obviously hadn't seen the relevant films.

'Never mind. I'm nervous, I'm rambling. Here are the judges.'

Except that Gideon was missing. In spite of all her resolutions, the plans she had declared to herself as well as to Jenny and Bert for keeping him out of her mind at all times vanished. All she could think of was why he wasn't there.

'Gideon is still in New York,' said Anna Fortune, looking straight at Zoe and making her feel extremely anxious. Did she know anything or – worse – was she a mind-reader? Were they about to be exposed, and on cameras? Thank heavens this wasn't live.

'And Alan has been offered a part in a soap, starting immediately, which is why he's not here. It's very good news for him.' Somehow she managed to imply he wasn't going to be getting good news about his cooking skills, so he might as well join a fictional community in the North-East. Everyone murmured and smiled.

'Now Fred is going to tell you about the next task.'

'Well, chefs,' said Fred, smiling and friendly as usual, 'this is going to be a real challenge to some of you. It's to make just one course . . .'

'Easy!' said Cher from behind Zoe.

'. . . from what you find on a foraging trip that you'll take under the watchful and informative eye of Thorn here.'

He indicated a dark, bearded man, who could have been an extra in a Narnia film. Thorn was wearing a selection of clothing that seemed grown on or half sloughed off: leather, tweed and various unidentifiable fabrics that could have been rescued from a recycling bin.

'Good evening. I'm an experienced forager, I live mainly on what I find for free and have done for years.'

Zoe thought, unkindly, that he possibly hadn't come across much soap in his foragings, or even the plants that were purported to serve the same function.

'Tomorrow morning, bright and early, we'll meet up here and I'll take you for a walk in the woods that I'm confident will change your cooking lives for ever.'

There was no denying the fanatical glint in his eye as he said this. The mutterings behind Zoe became louder and more obscene.

'I'm sorry, I don't do weeds or fungi: they kill people,' said Cher.

'Then you'll be out,' said Bill. 'Don't be such an idiot.'

'Don't worry. I'll be checking everything you find. You won't be allowed to eat anything harmful,' said Thorn.

As Thorn and Cher contemplated each other Zoe thought they hardly seemed from the same planet. Thorn was like a faun, wild, almost animal. Cher, glossy and pale, looked even more mannequin-like than usual beside him.

'And you'll be glad to hear that there'll be a good selection of ingredients you can add to your wild food,' said Fred. 'Thorn here wouldn't have permitted adding things you hadn't gathered, but we persuaded him. And we do have to eat what you cook.' He smiled to indicate he'd made a joke and everyone laughed politely.

When everything had been explained, several times, with the cameras and without, they were dismissed and wandered over to the minibus. 'Shame for you Gideon's not here,' said Cher to Zoe. 'How will you manage without your pet judge?'

Zoe said nothing. Muriel, who always managed to put Cher in her place, was no longer there to stand up for her. But Cher's casual jibe made her think. Had he in fact fought for her specially? Was she good enough to get through the next round without him there?

'You'll be able to have the cowshed to yourself though,' Cher went on. 'I got Mike to put me in a room at the pub. A bit more what I'm used to.'

Cher's slightly sneering tone managed to imply the cowshed still sheltered cows and hadn't been turned into luxury accommodation.

'That's fine. I like to be on hand myself,' said Zoe.

'So you can go sneaking up to the house whenever you want to.'

'That's right!' said Zoe, hoping Cher wouldn't see her blush. Why on earth had she thought absence might have made her heart fonder towards Cher? If anything she disliked her even more.

'Well, you do seem very keen to help out.'

'I like Fen and Rupert,' said Zoe, trying not to sound defensive. 'And what's wrong with being useful?'

'The fact that you need to ask that means you're just not a winner. Haven't got the right personality. But hey!' She flicked her hand in a way that showed off her French manicure to best effect. 'There's only room for one at the top and that place has a great big reserved label on it – with my name underneath.'

Zoe shook her head and smiled, hoping she looked pitying of Cher's uber-confidence. Part of her admired Cher for her self-centred ambition. And another part feared she was right – maybe she, Zoe, wasn't a winner. The thought stiffened her resolve. She'd bloody well make herself one!

After a warm welcome back from Fenella and Rupert, Zoe had enjoyed a blissful Cher-free night in the cowshed. It was just a shame she'd had to get up so early. She shifted from one foot to the other and scrunched her toes inside her wellies. She was cold and although the scenery was beautiful, five o'clock was just too early to enjoy anything. Everyone felt the same, she could tell by the way they were hugging their arms and muttering. At least Zoe hadn't been to the pub with the others the night before.

The rain didn't help. It wasn't torrential and they'd been warned to wear boots and waterproofs, but it made the unearthly hour seem as if it was still night-time. It *was* still night to most sensible people.

They'd been driven in four-wheel-drive vehicles to a wood and then made to get out. Cher moaned the loudest but for once Zoe had to agree with her. She had more sense than to agree out loud, though.

But Thorn, who seemed to be even more made of moss and bark than he had done yesterday, was convinced it was the zenith of the day and mere wetness couldn't dampen his enthusiasm. 'Don't worry about the rain, people. The sun will come out in a moment.' His soft voice and ancient-hippy demeanour seemed to give him magic powers because at that moment the sun did come out. There was just time for a rainbow to form before the rain stopped.

'Oh wow! That was so amazing!' said Cher, doing a movement with her hands more suited to a fifties musical than a foraging expedition.

The others agreed and Zoe's spirits lifted a little. When the alarm on her phone had beeped her awake she'd been ready to resign from the competition, having concluded that never seeing Gideon again was by far the best option. With the sun turning raindrops into tiny diamonds and the prospect of learning new skills she decided to give it her best.

'Now, we're going to have a walk through the woods together,' said Thorn, 'and then you're going to go off and gather things for your meals. I'll check everything first to make sure no one's going to poison themselves.'

It was a revelation. Zoe knew that there were lots of edible things apart from blackberries but Thorn seemed to pick anything and everything. He wasn't a cook but he knew what things tasted like and soon everyone was chewing on bits of leaf – except Cher who seemed to find the idea of eating random bits of greenery weird and faintly disgusting.

'OK, folks. Go forth and forage,' said Thorn at last.

Zoe walked as fast as she could in the opposite direction to the others. She didn't want to get stuck with Cher saying 'eewu' and 'yuck' all the time. Once out of earshot of the others she paused for a few seconds, to worry that she might not find them again before starting to look for food. She began to enjoy herself. It was strangely absorbing and she was reminded of sloe-picking with her father.

She'd found some sow thistle, which would apparently make a nice salad but, more importantly, was easily recognisable. She also spotted some reachable ash keys but decided she didn't want to make pickle. They didn't yet know how long they'd have to cook their foraged dish. Beginning to worry that it was all a con and there was nothing edible in the wood, she went down into what might have once been a quarry and up the other side again. To her relief she spotted some coltsfoot, its huge semi-circular leaves reminding her how it got its name. At least she'd have one vegetable, she thought, and began to pile it into her basket. Then she heard a noise. She turned round. Gideon was on the top of the quarry, the place she had just come down from.

'Zoe!' he said.

Her heart gave a jolt and her brain could hardly take in what she was seeing. She had managed to put him out of her mind for at least half an hour, and she'd thought he was in the States so had stopped hoping to see him. Now that he had appeared her brain could hardly take in his presence.

Her instinct was to fling her basket into the bushes and

clamber up the quarry and into his arms but her last remaining gram of sense stopped her. They could so easily be seen. A moment of impulsiveness could throw her chances of winning as easily as she could have chucked her basket. Her mouth had gone completely dry and her legs shook a little.

But then he smiled and started down towards her. Suddenly nothing seemed to matter, not Sylvie's warnings, not the competition, not the potential shame, nothing. She moved to join him, barely aware of how she got there.

He was holding her in his arms before she remembered her resolution to give him up. Just before his lips met hers she realised all her virtuous plans had no chance. She was in love with him and if she got her heart broken so be it. Her passion swept all logic away.

They stayed welded together for long minutes, then at last broke away an inch or two.

'God, I've missed you,' he breathed into her hair.

Zoe gave a shuddering sigh. Now he was with her all her doubts disappeared. So what if he'd once been in love with someone else? So what if their being together meant that she might be thrown out of the competition? His arms were round her; nothing else was important. 'How did you find me?' she asked.

'Rupert knew where you'd been brought. I found the others, saw you weren't with them and went exploring.' He paused. 'Maybe it was my soul calling to your soul that helped me locate you.'

She giggled. 'Silly!' she said, but in her heart she wished he'd meant it. Wanting to get nearer to him again she pushed her arms under his coat so she could press her face against his shirt front. He smelt lovely. His arms encircled her more tightly and he lowered his head so he could rest it on her hair. Eventually she said, 'I dropped my coltsfoot.'

'I'll help you get more.' He paused, suddenly serious. 'Actually, if I help you, would you mind going back early? I've got the car.'

For a moment Zoe thought he was about to suggest something romantic, but he seemed concerned, as if he'd remembered something that was bothering him. 'Why? What's the problem?'

'It's Fen. I think the baby might be coming.'

'Goodness, but that isn't a problem, is it?'

'I don't know. They wouldn't really tell me.'

'Now you're not really telling me!' Zoe was starting to worry. 'What's going on?'

'I'm not sure, but Rupert said he'd find out if you'd mind coming back early, and then Fen said, "No, Rupes! We've already made her mess up one challenge, I'm not doing it again." So Rupert said, "Oh, OK." But he looked worried.'

'But you don't really know why?'

He shrugged. 'It might be because Fen was frantically cleaning the kitchen and muttering about beds and things.'

'Women about to give birth do clean,' said Zoe, glad that she knew this and so needn't worry about it.

'I don't think this is to do with nesting,' said Gideon, 'but more because Rupert's parents are coming. I gather they're not easy guests. Rupert would have asked Sarah but she's up to her eyes in weddings. It's her busiest time of the year.'

Zoe began to understand. Rupert thought Fenella ought to go to hospital but Fenella didn't want his parents arriving and finding the place in a state. But nor did she want to ask Zoe to help, because she was in a competition. 'I tell you what, let's pick as much as we can for me to make something and then go back.'

'Good idea. You mustn't risk your chance in the

183

competition. That would be a real waste when you've done so well so far.'

His words brought her up short. When she first saw Gideon again she had thought 'all for love and the world well lost', only for her it meant the competition rather than the world. But now she realised it was madness. Gideon was right. The competition was important, but so was Fenella. She'd find a way to do both. She had to.

'I don't want to let Fen down. She's become a real friend.'

'You won't let her down if you pick a few more weeds,' said Gideon.

She was diverted by his sceptical expression. 'Not a fan of foraging, then?'

He shrugged. 'I think it may be a fad, but you didn't hear me say that. It's possible someone may create a dish one day that doesn't taste of compost.'

Zoe received an instant shot of extra enthusiasm for the task. She had to impress Gideon and convince him that she could make anything taste good.

They found plenty of coltsfoot and more sow thistle and filled up the basket with dandelion leaves. 'You know the French call this *pis-en-lit*, don't you?' asked Gideon, putting a handful in the basket.

'Doesn't everyone?' said Zoe. 'And they sell it in France. We get it for nothing.' She inspected her booty. 'I think we've got enough. We can't fit anything else in.'

'Good, then kiss me instead.'

They had just started back when Cher appeared from behind a tree. She was holding her mobile phone and as there was no reception in the wood Zoe suddenly panicked that she might have seen her and Gideon.

'Hiya!' Cher trilled. 'Just taking some piccies of the

plants, in case I need to pop out and get more later.' She paused. 'That and other interesting things.'

'Good idea,' said Zoe, ignoring her last comment.

'So, Gideon,' said Cher. 'You're back from the States.'

'Obviously,' said Gideon pleasantly.

'And how did you manage to find Zoe?'

'I just came across her by chance. I was lucky.'

He spoke so calmly and with such a complete lack of guilt that Zoe felt that Cher would be forced to accept this as the truth. At least she hoped she would.

Although Zoe wanted to go straight to the house to check on Fenella, Gideon insisted she went to the marquee. 'Babies take ages. Find out what you need to do with your potential compost heap and then see Fen.' He paused, seeing she was still concerned. 'I'll go to the house and if I think she needs you urgently, I'll come and get you.'

She sighed. 'OK.' The fresh green plants that had looked so appetising when she gathered them had begun to wilt a little. She hoped she could prove Gideon wrong and turn them into something delicious.

Rupert was in the marquee providing tea for the judges and contestants.

'How's Fen?' asked Zoe the moment she was near enough.

Rupert sighed. 'Cleaning the guest bathroom.' His opinion on his wife's choice of activity was evident by the way he slammed a tin of biscuits on the table.

'But Gideon said the baby was coming? said Cher.

'I think it is, but she won't go to hospital yet. I did ring the midwife, because she's started having contractions, but she said if Fen's still speaking it's OK to hang on for a bit – but not to leave it too late.'

'Helpful,' said Anna Fortune.

185

'I'll take my tea up and see her, if that's all right,' said Zoe, looking at Anna.

Anna shrugged. 'It's up to you. You're missing out on thinking time but it's your choice.'

'I have got a bit of an idea . . .' Zoe lied.

Anna relented a little. 'Well, everything you've picked has to be checked by Thorn to make sure it's not poisonous, so go and see Fenella if it'll make you feel better.'

Rupert walked back to the house with her. 'I'd be grateful if you could talk her into going into hospital. I don't want her having it here with only me in charge.'

'God no!' said Zoe, suddenly worried.

'She keeps telling me first babies take ages,' he said on a sigh. 'I do hope she's right!'

'I'm sure she is. Everyone says that.'

'So, what are you going to do for your foraging challenge?' He paused. 'Sorry! You don't have to tell me. I just wanted a bit of distraction.'

'I don't mind you asking and I'm not really sure. How do you make any of it taste nice! I do wish it wasn't a bit too late for wild garlic. There was some growing when I was at home just now, I saw it when I went riding, but it's over in most places.'

'Ah ha!' said Rupert proudly. 'We still have it! It's in a gloomy bit that never gets any sun. I'll show you.'

'Oh, that would be fantastic! I could do pesto and pasta with a weed salad. At least I know that would taste nice.'

'Then come this way.'

After she had gathered a generous amount she suddenly said, 'You don't think it's cheating, do you?'

Rupert shrugged. 'I have no idea. Maybe you'd better trot back and ask?'

Zoe didn't trot, she galloped. She raced up to Fred and Anna. 'I've just come across this amazing wild garlic.' It was only half a lie. 'Can I use it?' They exchanged glances. Zoe could see that Fred would have said yes instantly but Anna was thinking about it. Gideon was busy with the others. They applied to him and after a shrug from him Anna at last said, 'OK, it's wild. Thorn will have to check you haven't made a mistake and picked lily of the valley or anything toxic, but otherwise, I don't see why you shouldn't make use of what's growing here and not in the wood.'

Having expressed her gratitude and added her garlic to her basket, she went back to the house more quickly than she'd gone to find the judges.

Fenella was on her hands and knees in the bathroom making noises that Zoe had never heard a human make before. When she became aware of Zoe she apologised. 'Did I swear? Sorry! It's just when the contractions come it helps.'

'Shouldn't you go to hospital? Rupert is really worried he's going to have to deliver the baby himself – with the house full of people!'

'I can't go until I've finished this. Rupert's parents are coming and they think I'm a first-class slut.'

'Well, if you're going to be a slut, be a classy one!' said Zoe, joking to cover her anxiety. But Fenella was not in the mood for jokes. 'Seriously, Fen,' Zoe went on. 'I can do this.'

'What about the competition? I can't let you jeopardise your chances for me again. The cupcake thing was bad enough.' Then she clenched her eyes shut and panted, in obvious pain.

At this, Zoe decided she couldn't bear to go on arguing about it. 'I can do both. Right now, you and the baby are more important and if you need to go to hospital, you should go. If you can't go without sterilising the bathroom first, I'll do that for you.'

187

'I can't let you do that!'

'I'm only doing pasta with pesto made from the wild garlic Rupert showed me and a salad. It won't take long. Give me the Marigolds and the bleach.'

'Are you really sure?' asked Fenella, handing them over.

'Yes! We can't start anything yet because Thorn has to go through every bit of weed and stick in case it's hemlock. That'll take ages.' Although Zoe now had what she needed to finish the bathroom, Fenella showed no signs of moving. 'Shouldn't you go now?'

Fenella shook her head. 'I really don't want to go too early. It would just mean hanging around for ages. I'm better off here.'

Zoe raised her eyes to heaven. 'How far away is the hospital?'

'Not far! Only about half an hour. The midwife said don't come in too soon.'

'Fen, that's miles – ages away.' Zoe pulled on the rubber gloves. 'I think this is just the right time!.'

'I don't want to go before Rupert's parents get here. They're so difficult.' Then Fenella settled into another contraction that seemed longer and more painful than the last Zoe had witnessed.

'Why did you ask them to come?' said Zoe when Fenella could speak again.

'Ask them? Ask them? I didn't bloody ask them! They said they were coming and nothing Rupert could say would stop them. They say they want to help.'

'And will they?'

'Good God no! They need to be waited on hand, foot and finger. Rupert's mother's idea of helping is to knit a shawl that needs to be washed by hand in early morning dew gathered by virgins.'

'Goodness!'

'And vests. Hand-knitted vests.'

'But it's nearly summer!'

'Oh, don't worry, they will have shrunk to postage stamps before it gets really warm.'

Zoe shook her head. 'I'd leave the house and barricade the door if I were you. They'd go home eventually.'

'Zoe, they need you,' Rupert called up the stars. 'It's time to start cooking, I think.'

'OK, everyone, settle down!' Mike clapped his hands, making him seem more like a teacher than ever. 'Anna is going to talk to you. Cameras!'

'Well, chefs, all your baskets have been checked. In a minute you can help yourselves to the other ingredients and then Fred will start you off on your next challenge. But before we do that, I just want to tell you about the challenge after that. I know it's usually a big surprise but we've had to schedule another break.'

'Excuse me, why is that?' Cher broke in through the murmurs of confusion from the others. 'If you don't mind me saying so, we've just had a break. Is this another scheduling problem?'

Anna glared at Cher. 'No. The next challenge is fine dining at its most demanding. It's the grand finale and you will be cooking a four-course meal for Michelin-starred chefs, judges and celebrity judges. The reason for the extra break is two-fold. One, you will need time to devise and practise your menus: practise and practise until you can do them in your sleep.' She sniffed in a way that implied sleep was for wimps. 'The other reason is that the judging is slightly different for the final challenge. It won't be just the three of us. And the judges we want can't make it sooner.'

Fred then stepped forward. 'And after the finale we're

throwing a big party. Everyone's invited, and the best thing of all is that it won't be televised.' He paused and then went on, 'So, for the final challenge we need a first course, a fish course, main and a pudding. You'll order your ingredients beforehand, or bring anything of your own you want. You'll have all day to do it. And I'm sorry, but we won't divulge who the final judges are.'

'Oh go on, we won't tell anyone!' said Cher.

Fred shook his head. 'I think we should crack on. We still have to eliminate someone. Only four of you will be competing in the last round.'

Zoe stifled a yawn. They'd all been up since dawn and even the thought of the final challenge couldn't distract her from her concerns for Fenella.

'So, those of you who don't have cars will be taken to the station immediately after the judging, or sent back to your accommodation if there isn't a suitable train,' said Fred. 'Mike's got it all worked out. Anything else we need to tell them?' He looked at Mike, who consulted his clipboard.

'I think that's everything.'

'OK,' said Fred. 'Choose your ingredients!'

Zoe worked as if the devil was waiting for his dinner and it was her job to provide it. She knew what ingredients she wanted and because they were simple, she just grabbed them. Then she cooked like a demon, glad that her knife skills had vastly improved since the restaurant challenge.

At last, the cooking and the judging was over. Zoe stayed in because hers tasted the nicest although it was judged as the least adventurous. Bill made the mistake of cooking cleavers – perfectly edible, even health giving – but in this case, improperly prepared; they had made the judges gag.

'In our house we call this wild Sellotape,' said Fred, 'or goosegrass.'

Thorn was disappointed in Bill for not preparing this delicacy so it tasted good. His opinion of chefs went down a bit.

They all commiserated with Bill and then as soon as she decently could Zoe went back to the house. A quick dash upstairs revealed Rupert frantically searching for Fenella's pre-packed bag and Fenella insisting in between contractions that she didn't want to go to hospital. When she saw Zoe she said, 'Did you stay in?'

'Yes. Mine tasted nice, so thank you for telling me about the wild garlic.' She looked at Fenella, who seemed to have something else on her mind.

'What are you going to do now?' Fenella asked.

'Actually, we've got an unscheduled break,' said Zoe. 'We're supposed to go home and practise our recipes. They told us about the final challenge.' She gulped. 'It's doing four courses in front of top chefs as well as the judges.'

'Oh!' Rupert looked at Fenella, a shocked expression on his face.

'Why? What's the matter?'

But neither Fenella nor Rupert took any notice. 'No,' said Fenella firmly. 'We can't—' What she couldn't do disappeared into a contraction.

'Actually, Zoe, while Fen's distracted, I'll ask you. Would you stay here for a bit? Keep an eye on things? I know Fen isn't going to hospital because she's worried about leaving—'

'I am still here, you know,' said Fenella, panting.

'And I'm here for you,' said Zoe firmly. 'Now, what is it you need me to do?'

'No!' said Fenella. 'You need to practise your dishes!'

'I can do that here perfectly well,' said Zoe.

Fenella and Rupert exchanged glances and then Fenella sighed. 'Well, I'd feel so much happier about Rupert's parents being here if they couldn't let themselves in and rampage over the house complaining what a state everything is in.

'And think!' Fenella went on, 'Gideon might stay too and you could – you know – be together!'

'Darling, Zoe might not want to . . .' broke in Rupert.

But Zoe had been doing some thinking. She could practise her dishes here; in fact in some ways it would be better because she wouldn't be taking over her mother's rather small kitchen. And if Gideon was able to stay too, it would be heaven. Provided no one found out about it, of course.

'Don't worry. I understand, and I'll stay here as long as you need me to. Now you just get in the car. The hospital's expecting you.' Zoe accepted Rupert's grateful look, which was followed by a hug.

'You've been a total star,' he said. 'I don't know what we've have done without you.'

Chapter Sixteen

The others had long since left. Cher had waved imperiously from her father's Jag, after ceremoniously giving Zoe an air kiss and hissing, 'May the best woman win.' No one had questioned Zoe on what she'd be doing for the two weeks they had free.

Zoe's first action was to let the dogs out from the room where they lived when the house was full of strangers or people who weren't keen on them. While they obviously liked their space well enough, they were pleased to see her and ambled into the kitchen.

Then Zoe decided to go upstairs and have a good look round. With Rupert's parents on their way she'd need to know where everything was and as Fenella had got into the car she had insisted she felt free to go everywhere and find things she needed.

She couldn't resist going to the bridal suite first, hoping for some sign of Gideon. But there was none. The room looked as if it had never been used it was so tidy. She couldn't tell if he was planning to come back or not. She knew he didn't travel with much, but a toothbrush or something would have given her a little hope she might see him again.

The guest bedroom was next to the bathroom she had helped Fenella clean. The airing cupboard was next to that. She went on opening doors and discovered a door at the end of the passage. There were a couple of rooms beyond it. One was small but useable if you overlooked the bare floorboards and cracked wash basin but it had a single bed in it. Next to it was a larger room full of tools and ladders and a disconnected bathroom suite. Zoe guessed that the small room would be the bathroom for this room when it was finished.

Zoe made sure she knew where things where before she went back downstairs. She began to feel sympathy for Fenella – no one would want picky in-laws staying when the house was part way through such a major refurb.

After she got downstairs she cleared up the kitchen, which was looking a bit like the *Mary Celeste*: abandoned in the middle of a meal. As she worked she wondered about Gideon. Would he just drive home after the judges had done whatever they did after a challenge? She wasn't even sure where home was for him. Or would he come and see her? He'd know where she was.

She very much wanted him to come and find her and not go home. Not only did she desperately want to see him again she wasn't sure if she wanted to sleep in such a huge house on her own with only the dogs for company, with the threat of Rupert's parents hanging over her like a Sword of Damocles.

She poured herself a glass of wine and toasted herself. She never thought she'd make it this far – to the final. She texted her mother with the good news. Her mother phoned her and they chatted for a bit while Zoe explained what she was up to. Then she went back upstairs to make sure the guest accommodation was ready for Rupert's parents. Glad it wasn't the bedroom that she and Gideon had shared and having found a lot of matching bed linen dumped on the bed, waiting to be put on, she enjoyed herself making sure everything looked immaculate, if a little hotel-like.

She wondered about picking some flowers but she didn't really want to leave the house even for a short time. Gideon or Rupert might ring. She compromised by taking a few sprigs from the flowers in the big arrangement in the hallway, which was beginning to drop a bit anyway. She pulled out the deadest blooms leaving only the best bits. It did make rather a mess on the floor but she would hunt for the hoover and deal with that later.

She went back down to the kitchen once more and, her wine finished, made a cup of tea and looked at the pictures on the wall. There were some of Fenella and Rupert and others of Somerby. Then she examined the array of cookery books perched on the bookshelf that adorned one of the corners of the room. The house was very quiet without the usual bustle going on and she found she didn't like it. She was beginning to think that Gideon had decided to go straight home and was torturing herself with thoughts that he'd come to his senses and taken the cowardly route by not even saying goodbye to her. She had just reached a very low point when chopping an onion seemed the only way to regain some sense of perspective when the back door opened and Gideon himself walked in.

'You *are* here. Rupert texted me to say you were. I'm so sorry I was so long! I had to take Becca and the train had gone from the nearest station so I had to drive to Hereford and I got lost in the lanes coming back.'

She walked into his arms and felt she was in the right place. It was familiar and exciting, comforting and thrilling. He had meant to come back to her. She laughed at her wild imaginings.

She raised her face to his. After a deliciously long, luxurious kiss, he led her out of the kitchen and up to the room where they'd shared their night of passion. Neither of them spoke. He lowered her on to the bed, kissing and undressing her by turns. Zoe began to melt as lust coursed through her. They seemed welded together, unable to part even long enough to finish getting undressed. Just as Gideon was at last taking off his belt, all the bells of heaven and hell and a lot of banging was unleashed on the front door.

'Oh damn!' he breathed, not letting her go although she tried to pull away.

'Rupert's parents?' Zoe asked.

'Yup,' said Gideon with a sigh.

The banging started again. 'We'd better let them in before they take all the paint off the door,' said Zoe, her voice muffled by Gideon's chest.

'Or go through a panel,' said Gideon, still holding Zoe as if she were a lifebelt and he was a drowning sailor.

She gave a shuddering sigh and broke free. She ran into the bathroom, did up her bra and took a moment to make sure her hair wasn't all over her face. Leaving Gideon to compose himself she rushed downstairs and pulled open the door.

'Thank Christ someone's in this damn money pit!' announced a tall man in a hat. 'Why they have to live in this godforsaken *hole* I have no idea! And why can't they get a nanny like normal people do?'

'Oh, Algy! We've been through this and they obviously have got help which is something.' The woman following the man was strangely similar to her husband. 'Good evening, we are Lord and Lady Gainsborough. And you are?'

'Zoe Harper.' Just for a second Zoe contemplated telling them that she was not paid staff but just then the dogs pushed through to greet the visitors and the moment passed.

196

'Get off, you brutes!' shouted the man. 'Haven't they got a damn kennel? Dogs should never be kept in the house.'

Zoe wrangled the dogs back inside, feeling everything would be better if only he'd stop yelling. 'Do come in. Do you need help with your bags?'

Just at this moment Gideon appeared. He looked much more presentable than he had five minutes ago although he was still tucking his shirt in. 'Can you take the luggage?' demanded Lord Gainsborough of him. 'Are we permitted through the door? Or would that make life too inconvenient for you?'

Sarcastic as well as loud, thought Zoe, amused as well as annoyed. 'Of course. If you follow me I'll show you your room, unless you know the way?' They might be frequent visitors, although judging by Fenella's panic at the thought of their arrival they probably weren't.

'We never know where we're going to be able to lay our heads,' said Lady Gainsborough. 'Only half this pile is actually habitable.'

'Your room is delightful,' said Zoe. She picked up several of the many small cases that now littered the hall and set off up the stairs.

'So Fenella finally did the sensible thing and got some staff,' declared Lady Gainsborough. 'I never thought she'd do anything so intelligent. She's got all these mad ideas but I expect you know all about *them*!'

Zoe didn't feel in a position to comment.

'Hmm,' Lady Gainsborough went on as Zoe showed her the room. 'Not too foul, I suppose.' Zoe was thrilled by the effect of the flowers, the side lights which she'd thought to turn on, and the general effect of calm luxury the room gave.

Lady Gainsborough went on, 'But of course we can't share a bed. He snores.'

Zoe indulged in a moment of panic. 'OK, I'll just make up another room for you. Fen – Mrs . . .' Fenella's surname deserted her. 'She didn't say you needed two rooms.'

Lady Gainsborough snorted. 'It didn't used to be so bad. I probably should have mentioned it,' she added grudgingly.

'I'll just go and see which bedroom is most suitable,' said Zoe. She'd need another quick snoop round this floor to find another room. She really hoped Gideon's wouldn't be the only usable option.

'And if you can bring up a bottle of whisky and some glasses that would help,' her ladyship went on.

'I'll ask Gideon,' said Zoe.

Lord Gainsborough arrived in the bedroom before she could get out of it.

'Can't sleep with her ladyship, she snores like a train,' he announced. Gideon, who was carrying the rest of the many cases, gave Zoe a look that could easily have sent her into fits of giggles.

'I'm just arranging another room,' said Zoe. 'I didn't know you needed separate ones. And Gideon, could you bring up a bottle of whisky and some glasses.'

'And if the fireplace actually functions, which would be a small miracle, maybe you could light the fire up here?' Lady Gainsborough added.

'No. The fireplace is out of action. The chimney needs attention,' said Zoe swiftly as a vision of her and Gideon trailing up and down the stairs with buckets of coal added to the horror. 'Excuse me, I'll just sort another bedroom for you.'

It turned out that the only other remotely suitable room on this side of the house *was* Gideon's. He could have the little single room at the back she decided. She had her room in the cowshed still. She didn't feel Lord and Lady Gainsborough would appreciate Gideon and her sharing a bedroom. Every floor creaked; they'd be sure to hear if they tried a midnight tryst. Her heart lurched. It would be too cruel if they were kept apart by Fenella's vile in-laws.

Zoe thanked her stars that she'd found where the airing cupboard was earlier and she was extremely relieved to find lots and lots of good quality bed linen in it. She supposed it was to do with having bridal suites with beds in them, and it didn't take her long to assemble some bedding for the room where she and Gideon had shared so much. Lord Gainsborough could do without flowers.

She went back to the first bedroom where Rupert's parents were now knocking back whiskies large enough to float a battleship.

'I've got the other room ready,' she said, envying Gideon for having escaped and Rupert's parents for the strong drink.

'Thank you,' said Lady Gainsborough, who was obviously planning to keep the room with the sofa and chairs. 'Now when could we eat? We don't need much but we are hungry so if you could call us down when it's ready? Half an hour do you? Fenella said she'd make a stew before we came so you could just heat some of that up. Oh, and a baked potato and some sort of green veg. No peas or beans though.' She paused. 'They make him fart.'

Zoe went down into the kitchen where Gideon was topping up her wine, having made himself a cup of coffee.

'They want stew, baked potatoes and a green vegetable, not peas or beans, in about half an hour.'

Gideon nodded. 'And you haven't seen a stew?'

Zoe shook her head.

'We could search the freezer.'

She nodded.

'And defrost it in the microwave?'

She nodded again. 'And if there's nothing suitable in the freezer, pray to God there's something green in the garden.'

'But before you go looking . . . come here, you little gypsy.'

She had just gone into his arms for the second time when they were disturbed by a distant jangling. Zoe sighed. 'They have a sixth sense, they know the minute we go near each other.' She frowned. 'That's not the front door, is it?'

Gideon shook his head. The jangling continued. Then he laughed. 'Look!'

Zoe looked at where he was pointing. An old-fashioned bell indicator showed one of the little windows waggling.

'I don't believe this!' said Gideon. 'I really don't!'

'I'd better go,' said Zoe.

'I'll go if you like,' said Gideon, apparently giving up on his plans for Zoe. 'But there's something I must—'

Zoe interrupted him. 'No, I'll go, but could you look in the freezer for the stew?'

'Where is the freezer?'

'Oh! Well, I think there's a chest one in one of the sheds but otherwise the fridge freezer is in there.' She pointed towards the scullery where the washing machine and fridge lived along side tins of olive oil and jars of jam.

'I'm not going into any shed,' Gideon warned her. 'If I draw a blank, they'll have to have an omelette.'

'Or spaghetti. You know, that's just what I fancy. A really plain spaghetti with just some olive oil and garlic.'

'And a bit of chilli?'

Zoe nodded. 'Oh yes. But we'll have to wait. Now I must go and see what her ladyship wants.'

'So the bell works, does it?' said Lady Gainsborough. 'We weren't sure. So little does work in this barracks.'

'What can I do for you?' Zoe felt she was in a play. She knew she'd be tempted to curtsey when she left the room, even if that wasn't what a real maid would do.

'Can you bring some bottled water? I assume there is some? I have pills to take.'

Zoe glanced towards the bathroom wondering why she couldn't float her pills down on whisky. 'There are glasses. I checked.'

Lady Gainsborough shook her head. 'Don't trust the water here. I think the plumbing is probably all lead pipes.'

'I'll see what I can do,' said Zoe. 'Sparkling or still?'

'Still please.' Lady Gainsborough turned away, which meant she wouldn't see if Zoe curtseyed or not.

As she ran downstairs Zoe was grateful there were bottles of water left from the filming. And if none of them still had water in them, well, the taps worked just fine. Personally, she didn't care if Fenella's mother-in-law died from lead poisoning or not. She hadn't even had time to wonder how Fenella was doing at the hospital!

'Nothing remotely stew-like in the freezer,' said Gideon, 'but I did find this in the fridge.'

It was a Pyrex bowl full of greying meat with some whole shallots and mushrooms sticking out of it. On the top was a bay leaf and a small bundle of sticks.

'I bet Fen or Rupert made this, put it in here to cool right down and then forgot to put it in the freezer,' said Zoe.

'But when was it made?' asked Gideon.

'Smell it,' suggested Zoe.

'You smell it,' said Gideon.

Wrinkling her nose in advance, Zoe sniffed. 'It smells a bit winey. You try.'

Emboldened by Zoe's reaction, Gideon took a proper smell. 'I think it's probably all right,' he said eventually. 'They probably won't notice if it's a bit off.'

'OK, let's put it in a pan and heat it up. But don't ask me to eat it.' Zoe, suddenly overcome with tiredness, yawned hugely. 'Sorry. My early morning has got to me.'

'It has been a long day.' Gideon put his arm round Zoe's shoulder and rubbed her arm. 'Poor darling. We could tell "them upstairs" to take a running jump and fend for themselves. Quite apart from wanting to make love to you hard enough to loosen your teeth, I need to tell you something, but it'll keep.'

Zoe hoped it was something nice and was quite happy to wait – for the mad passionate love-making too if she had to. 'I promised Fen I'd look after them. And besides, it's sort of fun. A challenge: can we make them happy?'

'Nothing daunts you, does it?' he said, his head on one side, with an expression in his eyes she didn't have time to respond to. 'No matter what happens, you come out fighting and win.'

'I don't know about that.'

'But you always find a solution, you never just give up.'

Zoe considered. 'Well, I always feel if you've started something – a job, a competition, even just cooking a meal – you might as well give it your all or why bother doing it at all?'

'That's always been my attitude,' said Gideon as he selected a pan from the stand in the corner and put it on the heat. 'I always wanted to be a food writer but I knew it wasn't really a way to make a living so I did other things first. But I never lost sight of my ambition.'

'And now you've achieved your dream.'

'Not quite. I picked up other dreams along the way. As you know I want to really educate the public about food. I want to get the supermarkets on side so that a busy person doesn't have to read the backs of every packet to check what's in it, or where it comes from. They'll know they can trust it to be ethically sourced.' He tipped in the stew, which looked even more unappetising now.

'That's what I'd like for my deli. Ethical, delicious, and no one being ripped off along the way.' She looked up at him, excited to find they shared something that was important to her. Then she looked at the stew. 'Are you sure it's OK? We don't want to deal with them if they got food poisoning.' The thought made her turn pale with horror.

Gideon, who'd been hunting round for a wooden spoon, looked at her. 'That really would test your friendship with Fen and Rupert.'

She was loving this time together. They were like a team pitted against an enemy. She felt she could cope with anything if she had Gideon by her side.

Zoe sniffed the stew. 'I'll add a slug of wine. That should disguise any off tastes.' She gave him a look. 'I know you shouldn't put wine into a dish and not cook off the alcohol but this is an emergency.'

He held up his hands in surrender. 'I wasn't going to say anything!'

Zoe nodded. 'Good, then I'll start the baked potatoes off in the microwave. I'll crisp the skins in the oven. I can imagine the uproar if they thought the potatoes had been cooked in a microwave.'

'But they can't expect baked potatoes in under an hour.'

'I don't think they have any idea how long a baked potato takes to cook,' said Zoe. 'I don't imagine they've ever set foot in a kitchen except perhaps to deliver something they've just shot.'

She was in the garden on the hunt for green veg, since the freezer contained exclusively peas, beans and sweetcorn, when Gideon called from the door. 'Come in! It's Rupert. He wants to talk to you!'

203

Clutching the colander full of green stuff to her, Zoe hurried to the house. She very much wanted to talk to Rupert too. How such a nice man could have such difficult parents was a mystery.

'Rupert? How's Fen? Has she had the baby?'

Rupert laughed. 'Not yet, I'm afraid. She's having an epidural in a minute though, so at least she won't be in so much pain.'

'But everything's OK otherwise?'

'Yes. Everyone's being brilliant. But how are things at your end? Are my parents being a nightmare?' Correctly interpreting Zoe's silence as a reluctance to tell a man his parents were the guests from hell, he went on, 'You can see now why poor Fen got in such a state about them. They insisted on coming to help with the baby though we'd have been fine on our own. Are they treating you like staff? Tell them you're not! Don't put up with being ordered about.'

'It's fine. It's easier to be staff than try and be friends.'

'Yes, well, I can understand that bit.' Rupert chuckled. 'Did you find the boeuf bourgignon?'

'Oh, was that what it was? Yes.'

'In the freezer? I made it a while ago now.'

'No, in the fridge. But I think it's all right. Smells OK now we've added some extra wine. Do you want to talk to your parents?'

'No. I'll ring Mater direct on her mobile.'

Zoe paused and then said, 'Tell me, Rupert, please, that you do not really call your mother Mater.'

He laughed but didn't answer immediately. 'Only some-times. Fen sends love, by the way.'

'And mine to her! We're thinking of you!' Zoe suddenly found herself getting quite emotional at the thought of Fenella having her first child.

*

'I really don't want them eating dinner down here,' said Zoe firmly when she'd let Gideon know there was no further news. 'We'll have to find somewhere else.'

'The dining room is as big as a football pitch,' said Gideon. 'We could just clear one end of the table.'

'No! We'd have to make conversation, or hover behind their chairs. I'm not up to either of those options just now. I'll have a scout round for somewhere else.'

She went into the room that Fenella used as an office. Apart from the desk, which was a tottering heap of paperwork, it was perfect. There was a round table without much on it, two suitable chairs and – miraculously – an obviously working fireplace. It wasn't really cold, it being May, but a fire would brighten everything up. A cloth over the desk would sort the mess in seconds.

The fire-lighting fairy, or possibly Rupert, had left kindling in the basket on top of some logs. It was all very dry. Zoe, who liked making fires, didn't take long to get a blaze going. She made sure it had really taken and then put the guard in front of it and went off in search of tablecloths and cutlery.

She thought she'd sit down in the kitchen on the sofa, if only for a minute, before Rupert's parents needed clearing up after. She'd made Fen's office look really cosy, and the stew actually smelt quite nice by the time Gideon took it through. He'd obviously been delayed. Maybe they were complaining that their knives and forks weren't quite as shiny as they might have been. It was true, they weren't, but Zoe had been pleased to find the real silver and thought, in the candlelight, a little tarnish might not show. The candlesticks themselves she had given a quick rub over.

She settled a cushion into the curve of her back and pulled a mohair throw over her, just for comfort. Then she closed her eyes.

'You're beginning to make a habit of this,' Gideon said softly a little while later.

Reluctantly, Zoe opened her eyes. 'I only sat down for moment.' She smiled sleepily up at him.

'I know. The same thing nearly happened to me. We were up early.'

'Did they like their dinner?'

'Loved it. Particularly the greens. I didn't recognise them. What were they?'

Zoe had to think what he was talking about for a minute. 'Oh! Oh you know! Coltsfoot! I suppose they look different cooked. There was nothing else that I could find. Thorn said they're really good with sesame seeds. You'd better not tell them though.' She paused. 'I'd better get up.'

'Stay there for a minute.' Gideon put his hand on her shoulder. 'I've got kind of used to watching you sleep.'

Zoe swallowed. She no longer wanted to sleep quite so much now Gideon was with her.

'You know, I will have to go home at the crack of dawn tomorrow. I've got work to do.'

The thought of them being parted was horrible. 'What sort of work?' Zoe asked, although the moment she'd spoken she realised it was a silly question. He was a writer – that was his work.

'I need to do a piece for a cookery magazine. I've left it really late.'

'Do you have to go home to do that? Don't you just need a laptop? You could use mine.'

'I always feel sharing a computer is more intimate than sharing a toothbrush,' he said.

Zoe didn't know how to respond. She felt like that herself, a bit, but didn't want to make her suggestion seem like too big a deal. She managed a shrug. She'd have offered to share a life-support machine with him if it meant

206

he stayed with her. 'Whatever. The offer's there,' she managed eventually.

Gideon regarded her seriously. 'That's very kind of you, but I have my own laptop. It's my notes I'll need.'

Zoe felt abashed. Of course he'd have his laptop with him. No writer – or in her case chef – would travel without one if they were in a car. And if they went by train they'd have a netbook.

'I can make a start without notes,' said Gideon. 'You have another snooze. They won't be needing us for a bit.'

As Zoe closed her eyes she thought how cosy it was – Gideon working and her dozing. To her it meant that they were friends and not just lovers.

She was still in a reverie when she heard the door open. It was Lady Gainsborough with some dishes.

'We did call but no one came. Is there any chance of some pudding? We do like to end the meal with something sweet. Not raw fruit. That makes him fart too.'

Zoe sat up abruptly.

'But if you're in separate rooms . . .' Zoe said, her drowsiness making her forget her role as unquestioning family retainer for a moment.

'I'll be able to hear it,' said Lady Gainsborough, frowning slightly to indicate she wasn't used to being questioned. 'Now what about the pudding?'

'I don't think there is any,' said Zoe, deciding to be firm.

'Well, can't you make something? Are you a cook or aren't you?'

Zoe sighed, forced to acknowledge that given the challenges she had risen to lately, making a pudding was hardly difficult. 'I'll bring something through as soon as I can. How do you feel about ice cream?'

Lady Gainsborough shook her head. 'Only if there's nothing else, but Algy will complain.'

'OK, I'll find something.'

Lady Gainsborough left, naturally without saying thank you, and Zoe peered into the fridge. Gideon abandoned his laptop and peered over her shoulder.

'I bet you can't make anything half decent out of what's in here,' he said, looking at a muddle of butter, cheese, leftovers and jars of jam and condiments.

'How much do you bet?' said Zoe, who'd spotted a half-eaten bar of white chocolate. It was stuck right at the back and had the air of having been there for some time.

'Fiver,' said Gideon.

'Done!' They sealed the deal with a kiss. Then Zoe sniffed at a carton of cream. It smelt OK although it was a little crusty round the edges.

Encouraged, she took these things and went to the fruit bowl for apples.

'What are you going to do with that lot?' said Gideon.

'Wait and see. And take a last loving look at your fiver. It won't be in your wallet for much longer. But don't stand over me. Go and write your article.'

It didn't take her long to make a pancake batter and a few crêpes. Then she fried a couple of apples in butter, added a slug of calvados and then turned her attention to the white chocolate and cream.

Gideon's bet was a fillip to her enthusiasm. She didn't greatly care if Rupert's parents had something delicious to eat, but she did want to impress Gideon.

She put the broken-up chocolate into a bowl and whisked it over a pan of water until it was melted. She added some of the cream and tasted it. Perfect! Just custardy enough, she decided.

Gideon was engrossed in his writing but occasionally looked up and smiled, sniffing the air appreciatively as the delicious smells wafted down to his end of the kitchen.

Roughly twenty minutes later, she summoned him from his corner.

'Come and look at this! And pay your debts!'

On each of two plates lay a perfect crêpe filled with fried apple with a little pot of white chocolate custard on the side. She had sieved a little icing sugar over the pancakes and they looked almost restaurant standard.

'Hmm, not everyone likes white chocolate. In fact some people don't think it should even be called chocolate at all.'

Zoe swatted him playfully on the arm 'Come on! Cough up!' she demanded, knowing he was just teasing her. 'And I'd better take this in now.'

Biting back a 'ta da!' she put a plate in front of each of Rupert's parents.

'What's this?' demanded Lord Gainsborough. 'Custard? I only like Bird's custard.'

'But you love pancakes,' said his wife. 'Stop being so fussy.'

Zoe left the room before she giggled.

'Did they pass the test?' asked Gideon. 'If they don't like it I don't have to pay up.'

'Well, the custard wasn't Bird's, which was a bit of a downer, but apparently Lord Gainsborough loves pancakes. His wife told him he did.'

'In which case . . .' He reached into his back pocket, opened his wallet and took out a five-pound note and handed it to Zoe.

'I wish I'd got you to bet more now.' Zoe took the money and tucked it into the pocket of her jeans. 'It could have been a nice little earner.'

'I wouldn't have risked any more than that,' said

Gideon. 'I know you're both a good cook and very resourceful.'

'Thank you, kindly,' she said, in a way that meant he wouldn't guess how much his words meant to her.

'So are you going to let me sample the pudding? I feel as I've paid for it.'

'You'd pay far more than a fiver for that pudding in a restaurant,' said Zoe, 'but there's plenty of batter so we might as well use it up.'

They had cleared the plates and made hot drinks for his parents (filter coffee and peppermint tea) when they heard a car. The dogs began to bark and Gideon and Zoe looked at each other.

'Who . . . ?'

'Do you think . . . ?'

Chapter Seventeen

❧

The kitchen door banged and Rupert appeared. He had the broadest grin Zoe had ever seen on his face.

'It's a girl!' he said, his voice high with emotion and relief. 'Mother and baby doing fine!' He embraced Zoe as if she was his oldest friend.

'Oh, Rupert, that's wonderful!' cried Zoe. 'I'm so happy for you both!'

Rupert was on a high. He hugged Gideon too, saying, 'I never want to go through that again, but it was amazing. Just amazing. Poor old Fen! Seeing her in so much pain was ghastly.'

The words spilled out of him. They listened smiling and nodding as he went on to describe the labour, contraction by contraction, and then the epidural and the birth. He even showed them a couple of pictures he'd managed to take of mother and baby which they dutifully oohed and ahhed over. At last he stopped. 'I need a drink of water,' he said hoarsely.

'I'd need something stronger if I'd just gone through all that,' said Gideon, looking a little pale.

Zoe handed Rupert the water. 'You'd better tell your parents you're home.'

Rupert downed the glass of water in one. 'God! I'm all over the place – I haven't even told them Fen's had the baby yet! Look, would you mind asking them to come through while I find some champers? We must celebrate! Where are they, by the way?'

'I turned Fen's study into a dining room. We couldn't quite cope with having them in here.' Zoe paused, aware she was going to say something that might be hurtful. 'I mean, I don't think they're used to kitchens.'

'No, they're not. But they can put up with it this time.' He disappeared briefly into the back regions and reappeared holding a couple of bottles. 'I put these to chill before I left.' He unscrewed the wire on one of them. 'So would you be a love and fetch them?' he asked Zoe. 'They should be here when the cork is out.'

Zoe knocked on the door of the makeshift dining room and went in. 'Rupert's here. He wants to talk to you.'

'Ah! The baby!' Rupert's father got up. 'Though what he knows about it, I don't know.'

'He'll have been there, darling,' said Rupert's mother. 'You knew he was going to be.'

Rupert's father made a sound like an irritated lion. 'I do not understand this modern fashion for fathers in the labour ward. Quite unnecessary and very unpleasant for all concerned.'

'Absolutely. Never happened in my day,' said Lady Gainsborough, shaking her head in disapproval of modern habits. 'The men kept out of the way and only saw the mother when she was all cleaned up and tidy.' She put down the petit point she was doing, possibly to make a change from knitting little handwash-only garments. They followed Zoe to the kitchen.

'It's a girl!' announced Rupert, pouring champagne into glasses.

'Ah,' said his father, brought up short. 'Well, never mind, old chap. She's young enough to have another go. You might get a boy next time.'

Now Zoe understood Rupert's delay in telling them. He must have anticipated that they'd want him to have a son and heir.

'It's a shame,' said his mother, shaking her head, somehow implying that with a little more organisation and foresight, and less concession to modern mores, this blow could have been avoided.

'Actually,' said Rupert, sounding annoyed, 'we're thrilled to have a little girl! She's absolutely beautiful!'

'Oh come on, darling,' said his mother. 'All babies look the same. I'm glad you're putting a brave face on it, but there's no need. We're your parents. You can be honest.'

'I am being honest! We're delighted to have a girl and she is beautiful!'

'There, there,' said his mother, 'no need to get upset. I'm sure she'll be very pretty in a year or so.'

'She's beautiful now! And if you want champagne, pick up a glass.'

Gideon picked up two and gave them to the reluctant grandparents.

'Have you thought of names?' asked Zoe, partly for social reasons and partly because she wanted to know.

'Honoria, Eugenia, Arethusa,' said Rupert, clutching his glass grimly.

His mother frowned. 'But none of those are family names. What are you thinking of? Or was it Fenella's choice?'

'We talked about it together,' said Rupert, having downed half the contents of his glass in one and topped it up.

'Women are prone to mad ideas when they've just pupped,' said Lord Gainsborough. 'She'll see sense eventually.'

His wife nodded. 'We offered to pay for a monthly nurse, one who'd get the baby into a good routine. But oh no, the silly girl is going to breastfeed.' She shook her head, revolted by the very idea.

Gideon raised an eyebrow and started on the wire of the second bottle. Zoe caught his eye – she longed for them to have a quiet moment together. She'd reluctantly come to the heart-wrenching conclusion that with all the drama there was no way they could spend the night together discreetly.

Rupert went on determinedly. 'We have to get the birth registered before six weeks are up and we've chosen our names.' He looked at Zoe, his eyes glittering dangerously. 'Is there anything to eat? I know I shouldn't ask you but—'

'Why shouldn't you ask her?' said his father. 'For God's sake! These bloody communist ideas!' He drained his champagne glass. 'Now I'm going to bed, if no one objects!' He said this as if people were likely to protest against losing his company. When he got to the door, he ground to a halt and turned back. 'By the way, that's a jolly decent claret your girl served us. You must tell me where you got it.'

'Another time, if you don't mind,' said Rupert.

'Wait for me!' Rupert's mother called to her husband. 'I'm coming too! You can help me up those death-trap stairs!'

Only a moment passed before Zoe began to giggle. Tiredness, champagne and the ridiculousness of Rupert's parents got to her.

'Are you drunk?' demanded Gideon, trying not to laugh himself.

'Maybe! I don't know!' Zoe continued to laugh although she knew it wasn't really that funny.

'I do apologise for them,' said Rupert, sinking down into a chair at the table. 'We don't see a lot of them, as you've probably gathered, and I forget how appalling they are.'

'I'm sure they have some endearing qualities,' said Zoe, serious at last and determined that Rupert shouldn't feel obliged to apologise further. 'And they've been a good challenge, I must say. Feeding them was fun. Talking of which – stew?'

Rupert frowned. 'Stew? Oh my giddy aunt!' (Zoe felt he probably had a real giddy aunt.) 'I made that ages ago. I can't believe I was so organised.'

'You weren't quite organised enough to freeze it, but your parents thought it was nice,' said Gideon.

Rupert put his head into his hands. 'Oh my God, I do hope I haven't poisoned them.'

'It wouldn't have been you that poisoned them,' said Zoe, sounding calmer than she felt, 'it would have been us.' A thought occurred to her. 'Will they sue?'

Rupert chuckled and shook his head. 'Oh no, they're old school. A gippy tummy is a gippy tummy. No real cause for alarm.' He paused. 'I'll give the stew a miss though. I'll just make myself a snack.'

Gideon pressed him back down into his seat. 'We're staff; you've just had a baby. We can rustle something up.'

'Of course!' said Zoe. 'I could make you a sandwich or an omelette or something.' He looked hungry but nothing she'd offered him apparently hit the spot. 'Or you could have a crêpe filled with apple and calvados with a white chocolate custard.'

Rupert beamed. 'Now you're talking!'

When, a few moments later, she put the plate in front of him he gave a satisfied sigh. 'God, you're good!' he said.

'She is, isn't she?' said Gideon and Zoe glowed.

'You don't fancy a job, do you?' said Rupert, looking hopeful.

Zoe laughed. 'Not just at the moment, thank you, but I'll bear it in mind.'

215

'She's got a competition to get through before she can start thinking about jobs. It's important she doesn't get distracted,' said Gideon firmly.

'I know, I was only chancing my arm,' said Rupert. 'What do you plan to do if you win?'

'I want to open the perfect deli,' said Zoe. 'You know, the usual, with olive oil and balsamic but also made dishes, so locals and visitors can buy ready meals and cakes and things, but properly home-made.'

'You wouldn't fancy making food – ready meals – to sell to supermarkets?' Rupert asked. He'd gone on to the plate of cheese and biscuits that Zoe had found.

She shook her head. 'No. I like the people aspect of it all. I'd enjoy getting in the special tea for the picky customer and making the dishes for the person with food allergies.'

'Fair enough,' said Rupert. 'I do get that. I like the people aspect of this business too, most of the time. Getting it right for them is sometimes a problem but when you do, it's very satisfying.'

Zoe nodded. 'I like solving problems too. It's one of the reasons I entered the competition, really.'

Gideon refilled their glasses. Rupert toyed with his for a few moments. 'I'm not quite sure how to put this, but Fen would be really grateful if you were here when she comes home with the baby. She can't cope with my parents at the best of times and when you've just had a baby you're very vulnerable. The midwife told me,' he added before Zoe could ask how he knew this.

Gideon shook his head. 'Zoe's got to practise for her fine-dining challenge. She's good but she will need to think about what she's doing and make sure she can do it.'

Zoe was torn. She wasn't good at saying no and she

was very fond of Rupert and Fenella. 'I could practise here,' she said. 'This kitchen is far bigger than my parents' kitchen is.' She looked at Gideon, to make sure he understood. 'I was in a rented house before the competition and I gave it up – or at least didn't renew my lease.'

'If you could we'd be so grateful. You've seen what my parents are like. They just don't understand how much work they make and they've always had servants. They live in a different era to the rest of us.'

Gideon shook his head. 'It's amazing you're so normal, really.'

'Mm.' Zoe nodded. She wanted to add, 'So calm, so good-natured, so undemanding,' but felt that while it was OK for him to go on about his parents, she and Gideon should keep their complaints to the minimum.

'That's what Fen said when she first met them. She wouldn't come home and face them at all until we were engaged. She only did then because she absolutely had to. I'd talked to her about them rather too much.'

'Really?' asked Gideon, his interest piqued. 'So what happened when you did bring her to meet them?'

Rupert shook his head with remembered embarrassment. 'It was pretty awful until they found out that Fen's ancestors are actually quite a bit posher than mine, in spite of the title. So they stopped thinking I was marrying beneath me.' He paused. 'They still don't get her, though.' He shook his head sadly.

Zoe and Gideon exchanged glances and Zoe realised that Gideon shared her slight fear that Rupert was going to get maudlin and sentimental – understandable but not helpful.

Zoe spoke bracingly. 'I'm sure they'll love her when they see her being a brilliant mum, and she's bound to be one of those. You can sort of tell.' Not being a mother herself Zoe was making this up as she went along but she thought it was quite probably true.

Rupert smiled and got to his feet. 'It doesn't really matter though. Can I tempt either of you to a brandy? I think I need one.'

'Um,' said Zoe, not sure how much longer she could keep awake.

'Not for me, I'm afraid,' said Gideon, 'I've got to get some sleep. I have to be on my way early in the morning.' He looked at Zoe as he said this.

Zoe felt instantly bereft. Awareness that this short idyll of being together without having to be furtive was already over made tears prick her eyes. She knew it was tiredness that was making her react so strongly but she couldn't help it. 'Actually I might join you in the brandy, Rupert.' She looked at Gideon, unable to keep her expression bland, although she tried. She had no rights over him – she couldn't question when or where he went. He was a free agent, as was she. She sipped the brandy Rupert had passed across the table, hoping it would make her brave.

'But, Gideon,' said Rupert, 'you can't leave the party now. It's just getting fun!'

'I must, I'm afraid. As I said, I've got a fearsomely early start. I have to get home, finish an article, put some things in a bag and get myself to the airport to catch an afternoon flight.'

Flight? What flight? Where was he going? Why hadn't he mentioned it before? Was that what he'd been trying to tell her before? Zoe panicked slightly and then took a deep breath. He had been so loving in their brief time together this evening in between their running around after Rupert's parents. She felt tears prickle.

'I'll miss all the traffic and . . .' He looked down at Zoe and Zoe longed for them to be alone, but she couldn't think how to engineer it.

'Zoe?' said Gideon softly. 'Could I have a word before I turn in?'

She followed him out of the door, fighting tears. But by the time she'd got up the stairs and joined him in his room she looked calm even if she didn't feel it.

'I don't want to go, I really don't,' said Gideon the moment they were through the door. 'But I've had this meeting set up for ages. They're a group of olive-oil producers – a tiny consortium. I'd really like to buy from them if I can.' His voice tailed away.

Zoe nodded, glad she'd had the brandy, which had given her the strength she needed. 'Of course you must go. There's no earthly reason why you shouldn't.'

'Isn't there? Well no, not really. You'll be all right.' He stated a fact. 'But, Zoe, you're to promise me you will practise your cooking? You mustn't just turn into a slave for Rupert's parents, or even for Rupert and Fenella and the baby. The competition is important.'

'I know it is. I will practise. I want my pâtisserie to be as good as – the other competitors,' she added, stopping herself from saying Cher's name in case it made her look vindictive.

He kissed the top of her head. 'Good girl. I'm so proud of you. Now you go and keep Rupert company. I wish . . . but we can't . . .'.

From the depths of her sadness came a dimple of mischief. 'Oh? Why's that?'

He ruffled her hair. 'You know perfectly well why. Not with this houseful.' He drew her to him. 'This is a deposit for next time we meet.' He kissed her hard and long until Zoe was breathless and had almost forgotten that

219

he was leaving. 'I'll claim the rest when we're together again in private,' he said. He was breathless too.

Fighting a confusing mix of sadness and unfulfilled desire, Zoe rejoined Rupert in the kitchen. He seemed to still be full of adrenalin caused by seeing his daughter born, but at least had moved from brandy on to tea. Zoe made herself a mug, blessing the kettle that was almost permanently boiling that made this the work of moments.

'So tell me,' she said, pinning on a smile. 'What are you really going to call the baby?'

He gave a shout of laughter. 'So you weren't fooled? I'm glad!'

'So?'

'Glory. We're going to call her Glory. Short for Glorianna.'

'Oh. That's a lovely name!' Once she'd had a second or two to get used to it, Zoe discovered that she did think it was a lovely name. 'And when will your parents find out the truth?'

'Oh, I don't know. At the christening probably.'

Zoe smiled. 'And when does Fen think she'll be allowed home?'

'A day or so. She needs to get over the birth and all that, but she's longing to get back.' He paused. 'There was a time, during labour – transition I think they call it – when she said that unless I got my bloody parents out of the house first, she'd never come home.'

'She'll feel different about that now she's had the baby, I'm sure,' said Zoe, although she wasn't confident about it.

'She'd better. When my parents decide something – like they're here to help with the baby – they stick by it.'

'I hope this doesn't sound horrible but your mother doesn't come over as a hands-on granny.'

Rupert laughed. 'She wasn't a hands-on mother, why would she change? Good point! But she has a sense of what's right.' He stood up and yawned hugely. 'Shame Gideon has to go. He's a good bloke. Thinks very highly of you.'

Zoe blushed. 'Well . . .'

'Really! Says you're the best all-round cook in the competition.' He frowned. 'Said he couldn't go on about it too much though. People might talk. Anyway! Better go to bed now. Damn tired. You must be too,' he added. Zoe loved him in that moment for being so British and not prying.

'I am pretty much hanging.'

'Well, don't worry about the parents' breakfast. I'll give them one of my fry-ups. That'll keep them quiet for hours. Get up when you feel like it.'

'OK, but really, I quite enjoyed being a maid. Or maybe it was a cook general?'

'You're neither! You're a friend!'

'It's all right. I do know that. I was just saying . . .' What she was saying escaped her and she yawned hugely. 'I'm going to bed. Night night. And congratulations!'

Chapter Eighteen

Zoe slept late the following morning. She had woken once in the early hours, and realised it was Gideon's car that had disturbed her. Sadness washed over her again, but her long day meant she didn't stay awake for long and awoke again after nine. She showered and then went up to the house.

The kitchen was full of bustle and noise. The news of the baby had leaked into the ether and half the neighbourhood seemed to have arrived to wish Rupert joy. His parents, seated at the table with mountains of bacon and eggs in front of them, seemed far less bossy and imposing than they had the night before.

'Morning!' she said when she could make herself heard among the half-dozen people seated at the table. Only three of them were eating breakfast, but they all had mugs of something in front of them.

'Zoe! Sweetheart!' said Rupert, getting up and engulfing Zoe in his cashmere sweater. 'Everyone! This is Zoe! She's staying to help with the baby for a bit.'

In among the 'hello, Zoe's Zoe heard Rupert's father say, 'I thought she was staff, not Rupert's bit on the side.'

'Don't be ridiculous!' said his mother. 'He wouldn't let her in the house if he was sleeping with her.'

Glad no one else seemed to have heard this, Zoe pulled up a chair and accepted a large mug of something put into her hand by a smiling Rupert. It turned out to be coffee. The lovely warm atmosphere of the kitchen softened the blow of Gideon's departure at little. If nothing else Zoe felt she'd made real friends here.

'So you're in that cookery competition they've had here?' asked a friendly woman sitting next to Zoe. 'I don't know how you cook in front of the cameras. I'd turn into a heap of nerves and drop everything.'

'It's like that to begin with but you forget the cameras frighteningly quickly,' said Zoe.

'Well, rather you than me,' said the woman, shaking her head and pushing back her chair. 'Rupert, I must go. Give my love to Fen and the baby. I'll be over again the moment she gets here. But don't let her have too many visitors, she'll get exhausted.' She sent a look up the table that was missed by Rupert's parents but observed by everyone else.

'I should go too,' said almost everyone, and the big table was soon nearly empty, leaving only Rupert's parents and Zoe. Rupert was showing people out.

Zoe got up and started gathering dishes as Rupert's parents left the room.

She was about to check everything had been cleared from Fenella's study when she realised it was occupied. Rupert's mother was having a few words with her son.

'Darling, I know you have all these bolshie ideas about how to treat servants but really and truly they need to know their place! They feel comfortable with that! God knows what Winterbotham would have done if we'd used his Christian name! Had forty fits, that's what.'

Zoe had to listen although she knew perfectly well she shouldn't.

Rupert was amused, she could tell, and wondered if his mother could too. 'Mater! Zoe is not Winterbotham! She's a dear friend who is helping out! She's not a servant.'

223

'Well, she was putting on quite a creditable impression of one yesterday!'

Zoe nodded smugly.

'Although that spinach she served with dinner was a little odd. I didn't know you grew spinach and strange to have it at this time of year.'

Zoe could hear the frown of confusion in her voice.

'You know, Ma, I have no idea what you're talking about,' said Rupert.

'Typical man, never remotely interested in the garden. But what I'm saying is, if you keep your distance with her, she'll be really quite useful. But this "all friends together" nonsense is just that! – nonsense!'

'But if I treated her as a servant I'd have to pay her,' said Rupert.

Zoe stiffened. She couldn't take money from Rupert and Fenella, not unless she had a proper job with them.

'Oh, she's free, is she? In which case, my darling, forget I ever spoke!'

Zoe went back to the kitchen. So Rupert's mother was mean as well as demanding. Poor, poor Fen!

Rupert was adamant that Zoe did her own thing after breakfast, at least until he had got the kitchen tidy. So, after a brisk walk to clear her head, she sat down at her laptop in the cowshed and started researching recipes. But eventually she accepted that she couldn't concentrate; all she seemed able to do was think about Gideon. She couldn't decide if Gideon really liked her – in a long-term, meaningful way – or if she was just a convenient armful. How she wished they had had another night together. If they'd been together for longer she might have learnt more about him. When they were together she felt so sure of him, but when he wasn't there doubts rushed in. Doubts that said she was mad to be with him when she'd been warned against him and knew for herself she was risking her heart.

She got up from her computer and went back to the house. There'd be loads to do there. She was doing no good sitting on her own, dreaming.

Rupert insisted on roasting a joint of beef for supper, getting it ready before he went to visit Fenella and the baby.

'So how's Fen liking it in hospital?' asked Zoe, wrapping up the paper of potato peelings and putting them in the compost.

'She says everyone is brilliant but she's homesick,' he explained, dusting half a cow with mustard and flour. 'She wants me to buy chocolates or something as a thank-you for the staff.'

'I could make cupcakes, if that would be any good. The nurses probably get quite a lot of chocolates. Cupcakes would be a change.' It would also keep her busy.

'Oh Zoe, I couldn't ask you to do that!' said Rupert.

Interpreting this as a 'yes please' Zoe said, 'You didn't ask, I offered. And I'm very happy to make some. There are cases and things left over from the wedding.' She paused. 'It'll give me something to do in between bell-answering duties.'

Rupert gave her a look of embarrassment mixed with despair. 'I know! I'm so sorry! I have explained but they don't understand that you're a friend and not a servant.'

'It's fine, really it is! It's quite funny actually, and I like trying to second guess their requirements and make them happy.'

'You're a star.' Rupert closed the oven door behind the joint.

'And as such, would you like me to pick some more

coltsfoot? It went down OK yesterday. Or will they object to having the same vegetable twice in succession?'

'Frankly, I'd give 'em peas and beans and to hell with the farting!'

Then Rupert gave her a hard squeeze and a kiss on the cheek before going off to see his wife and daughter.

Chapter Nineteen

❦

The reception committee for the baby was rather like the line-up of servants in *Downton Abbey*, about to receive an important guest. Zoe felt as if she was starring in a television period drama. Except this time of course there were no cameras rolling.

It happened because Fenella's parents had sped down from Scotland the moment they discovered that Rupert's parents were there.

'Fenny swore she didn't want anyone,' Fenella's mother said. She was far friendlier than Rupert's mother in spite of being more grand. She even insisted Zoe call her Hermione. 'She said she and Rupert would manage fine and we could come down when it was a bit more convenient to us!' This she had told Zoe while Zoe chopped onion and carrot to make cottage pie with leftover beef. 'But frankly, my dear, I think Rupert's parents are ghastly and don't want my daughter unprotected from them!'

Zoe, who was already fairly fond of Hermione, nodded. She and Hermione weren't quite at the stage where they could share bitchy remarks about Rupert's parents but it wouldn't be long.

'And have you heard the latest?'

As Rupert's parents thought of Zoe as below-stairs they hadn't made her privy to whatever the latest was.

'They want the christening immediately!'

Hermione was obviously appalled and so was Zoe. Poor

little Glory wasn't even home from hospital! 'Why so soon?' Fairly sure Rupert's parents wouldn't like it, she added a bit of garlic to her vegetables browning in the pan.

'Because they want to go on a world cruise and they've brought The Christening Gown with them!' Hermione's eyes flashed. 'We have a lovely christening dress which I bet is far prettier than theirs, but apparently it has to be the Gainsborough robe that's used.'

'But couldn't the christening be after they get back from their cruise?' A couple of good shakes of Worcester sauce went on top of the veg.

'Apparently not! They are so old-fashioned I'm surprised they even drive. They were even muttering about Fen being churched!'

Zoe, who was piling meat and vegetables into a dish, put down the frying pan. 'I'm sorry, you've lost me.'

'Exactly! That is my point! Who on earth gets churched these days?'

'Maybe if I knew what it meant . . . ?'

'Oh, it's an ancient custom whereby a mother who's had a baby is purified in church because childbirth is obviously disgusting.'

Zoe turned to her mashed potato. She had a pile the size of a small pillow and she started blobbing it on the meat and vegetables. 'Why?' She wouldn't put it past Lady Gainsborough to insist.

'There is no real why! But Rupert's parents come from the ark and probably do think giving birth makes a woman unclean.' Hermione paused. 'Although to be absolutely honest I don't think they meant it too seriously.'

'Good.' Zoe opened the door of the Aga and slid in the dish. Would large dishes of food made out of leftovers feature in her fine-dining menu? Somehow she doubted it, although it was well within her skill set.

'Now you've done that, bless you, let's go upstairs and wait for Fen and Glory,' said Hermione. 'They shouldn't be long now.'

Rupert's parents had obviously had the same thought, or perhaps they were worried that they needed to be the first to see the baby, but it transpired that they all ended up on the steps of Somerby.

'Well, at least we've got a good day for it!' said Fenella's father, making the best of things. 'What do you think about the name?'

'I've never heard anything so ridiculous in my life,' said Lord Gainsborough. 'Arethusa! For God's sake!'

'Apparently that was some sort of joke on Rupert's part,' said his mother. 'But Glorianna is even worse! I only *hope* we can make her see sense before the christening. Why she couldn't choose a proper family name, I don't know.'

Hermione was bristling. 'Well, I think it's a good choice. It took me a little while to get used to the idea but now I have, I think it's a lovely name. She'll be called Glory, anyway.' Hermione scowled at her co-grandmother and Zoe hoped they would never have to spend Christmas together.

'Isn't this sun bliss?' said Zoe, who had perched on one of the steps leading to the front door. She spoke with her eyes shut so anyone or no one could reply. No one did. She could feel the tension bristling between the two grandmothers.

'Oh, that's them,' said Fenella's father and everyone stood in silence as they watched the Range Rover come up the sweeping drive to the house.

'Where's the baby?' demanded Rupert's mother the moment they could see inside the car. 'Why isn't Fenella carrying it?'

229

'It would need to be strapped in,' snapped Hermione. 'She, I mean.'

'Health and safety gone mad!' said Rupert's father, and Zoe realised she'd have been disappointed if he hadn't said it.

'I don't think Fenella's got any idea of how to look after a baby,' muttered Rupert's mother as Rupert pulled up. 'I offered her the best nurse there is, but she wouldn't have it.'

For Fenella and Rupert's sake, Zoe was very glad that the sound of gravel and the handbrake meant that Hermione didn't hear.

'Oh wow!' said Fenella, sliding out of the car. 'What a reception committee! I feel like the Queen! Mummy! Daddy! I didn't expect you too! How lovely!'

Rupert's parents were much more interested in the baby so Fenella was able to hug and be hugged. Rupert went round to the back seat of the Range Rover where the baby was lying in her car seat, fast asleep.

'Never seen anything so ridiculous in my life,' said Rupert's mother. 'It's at least twice the size of the baby!'

Fenella, released from her parents' embraces, joined Rupert by the back seat. 'We bought this with some of the cheque you sent us,' she said, unclicking the straps and scooping her baby, swathed in lacy shawls, into her arms.

'Now let's get you inside,' said Rupert. 'Would you like a glass of fizz?'

Zoe, the bystander, saw the look of fierce, protective love on Rupert's face and felt Fenella was the luckiest woman on the planet. Her heart did a little flip.

'Not sure I should have fizz,' said Fenella, frowning a little. 'It might upset Glory.'

Rupert's mother made a noise that was a combination

of disgust and despair. 'Please don't tell me you're going to try and feed the child yourself! It'll be an utter disaster! Trust me!' But she was talking to herself as no one else was listening. 'What you need is a strict timetable, no cuddling, and routine, routine, routine. I've got a book. Tells you all about it. Potty trained by three months. If you won't have the nanny . . .'

Once they were all safely inside, Hermione took charge. 'Now go straight to bed, darling,' she said to her daughter. 'You'll be exhausted.'

Zoe felt a little sorry for Fenella. Bringing your baby home for the first time should have been a celebration not a social minefield. If her in-laws hadn't been there she probably would have pottered out into the garden with the baby and had a glass of champagne until she felt tired and wanted to go to bed. But instead of being able to do this simple thing, she was hedged in with relations, some of them hostile.

'Shall I put the kettle on? Make some tea?' Zoe suggested brightly.

'Thank you!' said Fenella in a way that made Zoe wonder if she was about to cry.

When Zoe brought up the tea, with a plate of cupcakes, Fenella was established in bed. There was a crib on a stand next to her and in it Glory still slept, unaware and uncaring of the war her small person had caused.

'Don't stay marooned up here if you'd rather be down-stairs,' Hermione was saying.

'What happened to good old-fashioned lying-in!' said Rupert's mother. 'When I had Rupert I hardly stirred from my bed for three weeks.'

'It's a bit different nowadays,' said Hermione. 'Mothers get back to doing things far more quickly.'

'I'm sure they do,' agreed Rupert's mother. 'But is it a good idea?'

Zoe cleared her throat. 'The men are downstairs opening bottles of champagne and whisky. I think they want advice as to which one they should start with.'

By some miracle, both women left the room almost immediately.

'Blimey, Zoe! How did you do that? Actually I would quite like to see Mum but I can't cope with her and Rupert's mother hissing over me like two mother cats with a single kitten. Rupert's mother doesn't like me! Why is she even here?'

Zoe put the mug and a plate of cake where Fenella could reach them. 'Shall I pop down for a bottle of champers? Rupert seems to have bought a crate of it.'

Fenella shook her head. 'Tea is just what I want now. And cake.' She took a huge bite and chewed blissfully. 'Everyone who looked after me loved the ones you sent in. I don't think they get a moment to eat a lot of the time.'

A murmur from the crib made both women start.

'Ooh, she's waking up,' said Zoe, having looked at the stirring bundle for a few moments. 'Does she need feeding?'

'I expect so.' Fenella paused. 'Can you hand her to me?'

'OK, in a minute!' Zoe ran to the en suite and washed her hands manically for a few minutes during which time the murmur had become almost a cry. Then, bravely, she burrowed among the blankets and found Glory. After briefly noting how tiny and vulnerable she was, she handed her to Fenella. 'That was scary!'

'I know! They are pretty tough but it's still nerve-racking.'

'Do you want me to go? A bit of privacy?'

'Good Lord no! Little babies are always eating. I'd never speak to a soul if I felt I had to be alone to feed.' She unbuttoned her shirt and then unhooked the front section of her bra. 'Here you are, little one.'

Zoe couldn't help thinking that it was an awful lot of breast to stuff in a very small baby-mouth but Glory seemed to chomp down on it happily and soon was sucking away making little noises of contentment. They presented a lovely picture, mother and daughter sharing a blissful moment of peace together.

'I'm going to get your mum,' said Zoe after a few minutes. 'I think she'd like to be here. And don't worry, I'll keep Rupert's mother away.'

'Isn't she a nightmare?'

'Tell me about it! Although I have to confess, because she's not my mother-in-law, I find her funny.'

'I wonder what Gideon's mother is like?'

Zoe stopped, halfway to the door.

'Have I said something wrong?' asked Fenella. Zoe shrugged. She'd had plenty of time to think about Gideon and their relationship – if it was one and not just a fling. Was it the end of the affair or just the beginning? She felt she could be honest with Fenella though. 'No, not really. I mean, I don't know. He had to go and now . . .' She paused. 'I feel a bit funny about it, as if I'm not sure of him any more. I haven't heard from him at all since he left.'

'I'm sure it's fine,' said Fenella firmly. 'He's a nice guy. He wouldn't just forget about you because he's gone away.'

'No. No, I'm sure he wouldn't do that.' Although she wasn't entirely sure she felt Fenella could be right. She said more brightly, 'Right, I'll go and get your mother.'

But as she went down the stairs to the kitchen the little cold feeling of doubt lodged in her. Gideon was out of her league: he was a successful, sophisticated man. She was a little cook in a competition. What did she really have to offer him? Sylvie's words kept coming back to her with irritating regularity. Although absence was making her heart fonder, it might be out of sight, out of mind for him.

Suppressing her doubts, for there was nothing she could do about it right now, Zoe went into the kitchen. There were bottles open and Rupert was filling glasses. Hermione was squashed between her husband and Lord Gainsborough with Lady Gainsborough next to him. Considering it was such a big room and they obviously didn't like each other that much, they were strangely close. It would take skill to extract her.

Zoe positioned herself just behind them. Tempted to tug on Hermione's sleeve like a child, Zoe cleared her throat. 'I think Fen wants company.'

A second later she wished she'd said, 'wants her mother', but it had sounded so needy in her head she hadn't. But as Lady Gainsborough instantly pulled away from the group, Zoe realised her mistake.

'I'll go up,' said Lady Gainsborough. 'I've got a book for her. It would be a good opportunity for me to give it to her along with some sound – old-fashioned, I'll grant you – advice. Otherwise she'll have that baby ruined in no time.'

'No, I'll go,' said Hermione tightly. 'She's my daughter, after all.'

'Well, no one's stopping you coming too,' Lady Gainsborough said, obviously wishing she could.

'I'll come as well,' muttered Zoe, thinking that Fenella would need a referee.

'Why would my daughter-in-law need you?' Lady Gainsborough looked at Zoe in surprise.

'I just thought—'

'You're not a nanny, are you? Never had any experience of children? I thought not. You stay down here and clear up before dinner. That would be really useful.'

There was no arguing. Lady Gainsborough was right. While she probably knew less about looking after a baby than most primary-school children, she had at least had a couple.

'I'll be up to clear the tea things in a minute,' said Zoe firmly, thinking there had to be some advantages in being the help.

The men wandered into the garden to smoke the cigars that Rupert had produced. As they left Zoe heard Lord Gainsborough saying, 'An Englishman's home is no longer his castle if he can't smoke in it! You're ruled by the petticoats, Rupes old boy.'

'No more than you are, Dad,' Zoe heard Rupert reply. She smiled.

Zoe cleared up the kitchen in record time and set the table, then she rushed upstairs to Fenella's room, hoping there wouldn't be blood on the carpet, or worse. As she opened the door Lady Gainsborough practically knocked her over. 'You going to have to brace up, dear. Crying isn't going to help!' she declared as she swept past Zoe and on down the stairs.

Once in the room, Zoe was confronted with two women, one's eyes bright with tears, the other's glittering with anger.

'You have to get Rupert to ask them to leave!' said Hermione. 'She and I cannot stay in this house together!'

'I can't, Mummy! It would make life so difficult for Rupert. We have to all try to get along. Oh, Glory! Your nappy needs changing.'

Hermione took the baby from Fenella and probed her nappy. 'It is a bit wet.'

'I'll pass the things,' said Zoe, just in case anyone thought she knew how to change a baby.

By the time the bed was covered with a changing mat, several yards of cotton wool, a bowl of warm water and a towel, Fenella was looking less tearful. They all watched as Hermione unwrapped Glory, her little scarlet legs kicking and her arms stretched and moving.

'She's so adorable,' said Zoe when Fenella had done the necessary. 'Absolutely adorable.'

'Isn't she just?' said Hermione, fastening the snaps over Glory's nappy and picking her up. 'To think that woman says we shouldn't cuddle you.' She gave her grand-daughter a kiss.

'What do you mean? Did she really say that?' Zoe realised that Hermione hated Lady Gainsborough far more than she did.

'She didn't say it, she gave Fenny a book.' With the hand that wasn't holding the baby, Hermione picked up the book and handed it to Zoe.

Zoe took it and went to the window seat to glance through it. First of all, it was old. Zoe had been expecting something new and fresh-looking, but this one had been on some shelf for years and years. A quick glance at the front told her it was published before the Second World War. Surely even Lady Gainsborough wouldn't expect anyone to use such an ancient manual?

'You're not considering reading this, are you?' she asked Fenella.

'That's what I said!' announced Hermione.

'I'm not going to follow what it says,' insisted Fen, 'but I thought I ought to flick through it.'

'Listen, darling, even if this book wasn't totally against everything I know about babies, it's archaic! I can't under-stand why she's given it to you.'

'She's cross with me for refusing the monthly nurse she offered to pay for,' explained Fenella, almost snatching her baby from her mother and proceeding to offer her the other breast.

'At least a human would have been better than that frightful book,' said Hermione.

'I don't think so. Rupert's sister, who's on the strict side of Ghengis Khan when it comes to bringing up children – all slapping and going to bed without supper – said the nurse my mother-in-law paid for was too hard core.'

'Blimey,' muttered Zoe from her seat by the window, fascinated by the number of tiny garments that were considered necessary, including things called binders.

'I can ignore the book!' said Fenella. 'A woman would have been much harder.'

'At least Glory's a summer baby,' said Zoe, still hypnotised by the book, 'putting out in her pram for "airing" wouldn't be quite so chilly.'

'And now she's insisting on having her christened because if she died now she'd go to hell!' wailed Fenella.

'She's not going to die and she's not going to hell,' said Hermione crossly, though not with her daughter. 'And if you don't want to have her christened now just say so.'

'I can't say boo to a goose at the moment,' said Fenella, sniffing. 'I keep crying. It does nothing for my sense of resolve.'

'I'll say no for you then,' said Hermione. 'I'm well up for a row with that woman!'

'No, Mum!' This obviously wasn't helpful. 'I can't have people rowing. If they want to have Glory done now, I don't mind. Just as long as Sarah and Hugo can come and I don't have to arrange it.'

'You won't have to do a thing, darling, I'll see to that.'

'Me too!' chimed in Zoe. This was ground she felt

comfortable on. 'Although I think Rupert will have to make arrangements with the vicar. Is he nice?'

'He's lovely!' said Fenella, suddenly beaming. 'And he's a woman! I mean, she's a woman, but that's brilliant because it will really piss off Rupes' parents. They're dead against women priests. Very high-church Anglican.'

'I thought you didn't want conflict?' said Hermione, confused.

'Well, I do and I don't. I don't want to have to keep the peace between you and them, but I wouldn't mind if something made them go off in a huff as long as Rupert didn't have to spend weeks and weeks building bridges.'

Hermione sighed. 'OK then. Glory can wear the hideous Gainsborough robe and not our lovely one.'

'Is it hideous? I haven't seen it. And it's a baby dress, how can it be hideous?' asked Fenella.

'It's bound to be. That family has no taste,' said Hermione.

'Rupert is lovely though,' said Zoe.

'Well, to be fair' – it was obviously an effort – 'old christening dresses usually are pretty tiny so if you want Glory to wear the Gainsborough robe – or even ours – it had better be now.'

Fenella got up for supper. Rupert carried his baby daughter down to the basement as tenderly as Zoe had ever seen anyone carry anything. Zoe carried the stand for the Moses basket in one hand, and the basket in the other. Fenella was allowed to carry an extra cushion to sit on.

'Is this wise?' demanded her mother-in-law the moment Fenella appeared. 'I'm sure – thing – here' – she flapped a hand at Zoe – 'could have brought you up a tray.'

'I wanted to join the rest of the world,' said Fenella.

'And *Zoe* has spent quite long enough looking after me.'

Lady Gainsborough said, 'If you say so, dear,' with a silent 'don't blame me if it all goes hideously wrong' expression.

'Fenella, m'dear,' said her father-in-law. 'Have a glass of claret. Good for the blood.'

'Yes, have a drink!' Fenella's father encouraged.

'I'm not sure I should really,' said Fenella.

'Why not?' demanded her father-in-law, who obviously thought abstinence was a surer sign of insanity than anything else.

'Breastfeeding,' said his wife as if it were a euphemism for drinking vomit.

'Oh, darling, I'm sure one glass wouldn't hurt,' said Rupert.

When everyone had full glasses and Rupert was back in charge of the Aga (the cottage pie having been removed sometime previously), Lady Gainsborough banged a fork against a glass, calling the meeting to order.

'Honestly, we're only family,' Hermione muttered to Zoe behind her hand.

'Er, excuse me?' Lady Gainsborough had heard the mutter. 'We need to make a few decisions.'

Zoe got up to help Rupert. She didn't want to be caught taking sides.

'Actually only Fen and Rupert need to decide anything,' said Hermione, playing with a salt-cellar in a way that implied she could throw it with speed and accuracy if necessary.

'I beg to differ,' said a woman who had never begged for anything, ever. 'This is a family decision.'

'What is?' asked Rupert amiably, cheerfully unaware of a whole lot of undercurrents.

'Which christening robe is to be used,' snapped Lady Gainsborough. 'As the baby is a Gainsborough it's important that she's in the family robe.'

'I don't see that,' said Hermione, although she'd privately agreed it would be the best choice. 'Our robe is far prettier.'

'It's probably too small,' said Lady Gainsborough. 'Fenella's baby' – she obviously couldn't bring herself to use the name – 'is on the large side.'

'Are you saying my baby is fat?' said Fenella, stung.

'Seven and a half pounds is never fat, sweetie,' said Rupert. 'It's a lovely healthy weight.'

'Can I make a suggestion?' said Lord Gainsborough loudly, making sure everyone heard him. 'That we postpone the matter of which gown the baby wears until tomorrow? It is only a girl, after all.'

Fortunately Rupert and Zoe contrived to put large plates of food in front of the main protagonists before war could break out.

Chapter Twenty

To everyone's satisfaction, the vicar was delighted for the christening to be held during morning service the following Sunday. Fenella and Rupert were delighted and extremely grateful. Sarah and Hugo, who were to be godparents, had the weekend free.

Zoe suggested to Fenella that she should go home, that she wasn't needed any more and that as she wasn't a family member, she was just in the way. She didn't mention that she had to practise for her fine-dining challenge.

'Oh God, I've been so selfish! I didn't think about you wanting to go home. Of course! You've got to practise! Do go if you want to. We'll manage somehow.' She frowned slightly. 'You couldn't practise here, could you? No, of course not. Forget I asked.'

Fenella's anguish made Zoe laugh. 'Oh, Fen! I don't particularly want to go home. I'm sure I could practise if no one minded eating the food. I'm having so much fun here.' She'd looked up some recipes on her laptop when she wasn't busy being helpful and she really needed to actually test-run some of them, but she hadn't felt comfortable about using the Somerby families as guinea pigs – not that she'd had time. But she really ought to get on with it; she felt the responsibility even more keenly because she'd promised Gideon.

As, somehow, she and Gideon hadn't exchanged numbers in the rush of him leaving, Somerby was the only place where he could get in touch with her. She felt horribly disappointed that he hadn't – and nor had he called Rupert to see how the baby was. She ached for him. She felt rather lonely in the cowshed on her own, not that she wished Cher was there with her. But at least she'd have been a distraction.

'Do you really need me?' she said.

'Need you? Yes! God! After you'd cleared out that chest of drawers for the baby clothes even Rupert's mother said that you weren't a complete waste of space. That's code for "absolutely invaluable". And if she thinks you're useful, the rest of us are utterly dependent! But you mustn't, whatever you do, jeopardise your chances of winning the competition because you haven't had time to practise.'

'I'll make time,' said Zoe, relieved and pleased. She felt closer to Gideon being here where they had last been together. She'd stay for as long as she was wanted.

'And of course we do need a christening cake, not to mention lunch.'

'Lunch?'

'We're having Glory done during morning service, so everyone will come back here for lunch. With luck we can set out a couple of long tables under the trees and pretend we're in France.'

'Oh, that does sound lovely!'

'Yes. Rupes will poach a couple of salmon and do his trademark side of beef. We'll have salad, bread, cheese, various bits of cured pig. Soft fruit for pudding and a cake.' She smiled hopefully at Zoe. 'I know it's a bit cheeky to ask but what sort of cake would you like to make? Is there anything you'd especially like to practise? We know you're ace at cupcakes, so I don't expect you want to do them?'

'Not really. I probably need to practise some sort of pâtisserie . . .'

Fenella thought for a moment. 'Not sure if it counts but I've always yearned for one of those tower things made of profiteroles . . .'

'A croquembouche?' Zoe's eyes widened. 'Choux pastry? I've never made one.'

'Oh, just make whatever you like! I'm sure anything would be lovely.'

'No! If you want a croquembouche, that's what you shall have. I think it would be really good for me. Although time-consuming, if you need me to do other stuff.'

'I'll make sure I won't. You've done far too much already.' She took Zoe's hand. 'I can't tell you how grateful I am. You've been an absolute star. And Mum will pitch in and it's going to be very simple, but I would just love that cake. I can just picture it. All French and lovely.'

'Let's do it then!'

Zoe worked out that she'd have to make at least a hundred choux buns and after discussion with Fenella decided to fill them with flavoured cream and stick them together with caramel. She'd find some pink flowers or rose petals to finish the decoration. That sort of dramatic pudding might be just what she needed for the final challenge. She thought of Gideon. He'd be pleased she was getting down to it at last.

She did her choux buns in batches, when the kitchen wasn't needed for anything else. She and Fenella wanted to keep it a secret as long as possible, although Hermione fairly soon realised there were going to be a lot of cream puffs at this christening.

'If you're not peeling potatoes or doing something else for those gannets . . .' She paused to make sure Zoe knew who she was talking about. '. . . you're making choux buns. What's up?'

Zoe chuckled. 'It's not really a secret although Fen and I are trying to keep it dark so we get maximum effect, but we're making one of those tower things as the cake.'

'You mean you are? You're an absolute treasure. Poor dear Fen only seems able to make milk for that baby! Talk about hungry. She never stops eating!'

'I'm sure it's all right. Fen seems to like it. Whenever I take her a snack she's cuddled up with Glory, reading,' said Zoe.

'Yes, and of course You Know Who says it's mad and she should only feed Glory four-hourly. I never had a baby that went for four hours between feeds.'

'As long as it works for Glory, what else matters?' said Zoe, who was beginning to feel she knew quite a lot about babies now. Feed them and change them and bath them sometimes seemed to cover it.

In spite of everyone's insistence that it was all going to be very 'simple' Zoe knew enough to realise that 'simple' usually meant 'incredibly well thought out and planned'. Thus, everyone was busy, sourcing food, ordering it and, later, collecting it. Zoe went off to fetch at least a gallon of double cream from Susan and Rob's dairy and then on to pick up some home-made salami. It was going to be a feast. Although she knew she was not being tested and as long as it looked more or less all right no one would mind if her croquembouche didn't look as if it belonged in the window of a French pâtis-serie, she had her pride. She also needed to feel she was working towards her goal of winning the competition and not just having a lovely time with friends, however tempting that idea was.

*

Zoe was gathering her profiteroles, having taken the latest batch out of the oven, Hermione was making fairy cakes and Fenella was ensconced on the sofa, with Glory in the Moses basket, when Rupert's mother came into the kitchen.

'What is going on?' she demanded, making Zoe feel like a schoolgirl whose midnight feast had been discovered. 'We won't need all those cream puffs! Why on earth did you make so many?'

'I'm just making the christening cake,' said Zoe, sounding more confident than she felt.

'But why? Haven't you got the top layer of your wedding cake?' Rupert's mother directed her wrath at Fenella.

Fenella looked bemused. 'I don't know.'

'Oh!' said Hermione, 'I think I have got it somewhere. It's in the freezer.'

'But it should be used as the christening cake. It's traditional.' Now Lady Gainsborough looked bewildered. 'Surely you know that?' She turned to everyone in turn except Zoe, who was staff and so not expected to know anything.

Zoe put down the gold circle on which she was basing her creation, wondering if she should leave it until she was alone. It was tricky enough to do, but with World War Three going on around her, it would be almost impossible. On the other hand, it would be good practice to be thoroughly stressed out when she assembled it.

'I can't believe you didn't know that about the christening cake,' Lady Gainsborough repeated.

'Well, I might have known it, but when we came down we didn't know we were going to be bounced into a christening, so we didn't bring it with us!' said Hermione, with right on her side. 'If you hadn't been in such a hurry—'

'You should have been prepared! As I was with the dress!'

'Well, I couldn't have had a cake posted down here,' said Hermione.

'We can use the wedding cake next time,' said Fenella diplomatically, although through gritted teeth.

'I suppose so. And you might have a boy then, too,' said Lady Gainsborough. She left the room. The 'as you were' was tacit but obvious.

Zoe had filled the profiteroles. She had arranged them in size order and she had made the caramel that was going to stick them together. It was the next part that worried her. YouTube had been quite useful and she had spent a lot of time watching it. But the advice wasn't unanimous. Some sites used hugely expensive steel moulds, others depended on toothpicks and polystyrene. And one, which had less lordly ambitions, just built it up without anything to support it. But the most pressing problem was having to do it surrounded by people, some of whom wanted to cook other things. Although the pressure might be massive when she cooked for the competition, she would at least have space to do it. She went to find Rupert and explained her problem.

'Oh, no worries,' he said easily. 'There's a room outside the chapel. We had it built in case people needed to wait there for any reason. It can be your dedicated croquembouche room. We'll add it to the list of the facilities we offer.'

It was late Saturday afternoon. Zoe was beginning to assemble her masterpiece. Sarah and Hugo were due to arrive at nine the following morning, in time for church at eleven. Everyone had sorted out outfits, and

Fenella had lent Zoe a very pretty dress which was a bit longer on Zoe than it was on Fen, but was just right for the occasion.

She had made caramel and it was the perfect consistency. She had filled over a hundred profiteroles with cream flavoured with vanilla and brandy and she had her gold circle as a guide and base. It was now or never. She had to get going.

Three times she had dipped a profiterole in caramel and placed it on the circle and nothing bad had happened. She was gaining confidence and had picked up a fourth when Fenella came in. She was crying.

'I can't believe what my mother has done!'

Zoe, by now a huge fan of Hermione, was surprised. 'What? What has she done?'

'She's washed the Gainsborough robe!'

'Oh!'

'Flavia said she wasn't to. She said it was too delicate to be washed, and my mother washed it!'

'Has it fallen apart?' This was bad. No wonder Fenella was crying.

'No! At least I don't think so! But it's quite a different colour!'

'Don't tell me your mother put it in with a red sock and it's gone pink!'

In spite of her distress, Fenella giggled. 'It's not that bad! She washed it by hand, very gently, in baby shampoo.'

'But? What's the problem?'

Hermione came in looking self-righteous and unapologetic. 'There is no problem! The dress is perfectly all right.'

'But, Mummy! Flavia said it wasn't to be washed and you washed it!'

'I wasn't going to have my granddaughter christened in a filthy dress!'

247

Fenella wailed and clutched her hair. 'That's all very well but she's going to find out and then she'll kill me!'

'She won't. Well, she might, but at least the dress will be clean. Really, it smelt disgusting. You wouldn't have wanted Glory to wear it. Now it's clean it is actually quite pretty.'

'Maybe she won't find out you washed it,' suggested Zoe, who really wanted her designated space to herself so she could build her creation.

'She can't not notice it's not that dingy yellow any more,' said Fenella. 'It's bleedin' obvious!'

'Language, darling,' said Hermione.

'It's all right for you, Mummy. You don't have to face her!' Fenella looked down at the table and gasped in horror. 'I've put my hand on a profiterole. Is it all right if I eat it?'

'It had better be,' said Zoe. 'Now if you two don't mind, I'd sort of rather do this on my own.'

Eating her cream puff, Fenella led her mother away, still arguing about the dress.

Zoe went back to her croquembouche.

Zoe got up very early on the Sunday and as she made her way from the cowshed to the main house she was thrilled to see there was the sort of mistiness that promised fine weather. Part of her felt she could have lived here for ever – but only if Gideon had been there. Fenella's dream of a large party sitting at long tables under the trees would be fulfilled. The rainy-day alternative, which was to have everything in a marquee, had never been a runner, as no one had done anything about putting it up.

Zoe took some scissors from the kitchen drawer and set off round the garden, looking for pale pink roses. Once she'd sourced her decorations she'd help Rupert set up the tables and chairs.

She found the perfect rose. Her mother would have known what variety it was but it was enough for Zoe that it was fragrant, with pale pink petals, and it was out.

Nearer the time, she planned to spin sugar round and round the cake so it sparkled and shone in the sunshine. It was going to be beautiful!

Lured to the kitchen by the need for tea, Zoe found Fenella with Glory over her shoulder. 'Oh, can I have a hold?' Zoe asked.

Fenella handed her over. 'Yes, do. I'll make you a cuppa. I bet that's why you're here.'

'I thought I'd get one in before everyone else arrived wanting breakfast.' Zoe patted Glory's back loving the feel of her velvet head against her neck. She was wearing only a vest and a nappy and looked just perfect. 'I don't think she needs a swanky dress to look gorgeous.'

'Nor do I, but it's kind of like a wedding. A big dress is expected.' Fenella handed Zoe a mug. 'Sit down and have it before everything goes mad.'

Glory gave a huge yawn and Zoe found herself doing the same. 'I was up early,' she explained.

Fenella nodded. 'Us too, but I feel OK. I'll be dead by teatime.' She patted first one breast and then the other. 'If you'd like to hand her to me, I'll feed her. If I feed her now she'll be ready by about ten, then she should last through the ceremony.' She unbuttoned her shirt. 'I have this dread of having to feed her in church.'

'I'm sure it's happened before and no thunderbolts came down from on high,' said Zoe, deciding she needed toast. She pointed at the loaf with the bread knife to see if Fenella wanted some.

'Oh yes please, and I know the vicar would be absolutely fine, but think of the in-laws! They'd die.'

'Give it a go then! We could have a quick funeral while the church is booked.'

Fenella giggled. 'It's going to be a bit chaotic when we all come back from church. Rupert will give everyone drinks but we'll all have to rush around getting stuff out of the fridges.'

'That's OK, I'll do all that while you're in church.' Zoe spread a piece of toast with butter. 'What do you want on this?'

'Marmite please,' said Fenella. 'But you're coming to church.'

'I know you invited me and it's terribly kind of you to include me—'

'Considering you're "staff",' put in Fenella with a smile.

'But I'd rather get sorted here. I want to do the spun sugar for the croquembouche absolutely at the last minute.' She crunched into her own toast. 'It'll be much easier for you if it's all ready when people get here.'

'Actually, could I have another bit? I'm constantly starving,' said Fenella, 'and while I agree it would be much easier if it was all out ready, you have to be in church with us.'

'Why?' Zoe handed over the second slice of toast.

'Because . . . well, I probably should have mentioned this to you before, but Rupert and I want you to be Glory's godmother.'

'But Sarah—'

'Girls usually have two. You've played such a big part in her arrival and have been such a support since, it only seems right.'

Zoe suddenly felt tearful. 'But really, Fen, usually it would be someone you've known for years.'

'No, it's someone you wouldn't mind looking after your baby if the worst happened.'

Just for a moment, Zoe was completely overcome. Hot tears spilled out of her eyes no matter what she did to keep them in. Then she found a tissue and blew her nose. 'I don't know what to say!'

'Just say yes,' said Fenella. 'Oh, and maybe make me another mug of tea? Just to seal the deal?'

If this was a film, thought Zoe, following the christening party into church, Gideon would appear at the end, see Glory in her arms, and realise she was the one for him. And if the timings had been different and if he hadn't known about Glory, he would be confused but delighted and then a little disappointed that Glory wasn't his and hers. Sometimes things are better in films, she decided sadly, forcing Gideon from her thoughts. Almost always really.

But the trouble with trying to force someone from your thoughts was that it involved thinking about them quite a lot in the first place. Fortunately, once Sarah and Hugo had arrived and Fenella's father started planning who should travel with whom, Zoe did find herself distracted and privately convinced it would be easier if she just drove herself to church in her own car.

Zoe thought it was a delightful service. Rupert's parents almost turned to stone at the thought of having to shake hands with people they didn't know during the Peace, and in this church the Peace involved everyone moving around shaking hands and quite a lot of kissing. They looked as if every handshake was potentially fatal.

The baptism part of it was wonderful too. Everyone got involved and slowly but surely Rupert's parents were forced to unbend and take part.

Zoe did find it all very emotional. She wasn't sure if it was because being a godmother had been sprung on her (although the abject horror expressed by Lord and Lady

251

Gainsborough made it absolutely worth it) or because her feelings for Gideon did seem to colour everything. She couldn't help envying Fenella, with a husband who adored her and the sweetest baby imaginable. Even her in-laws didn't make her any less fortunate in Zoe's eyes.

But as everyone was tearful, Zoe could dab her eyes with the tissue helpfully provided by the vicar (who needed one herself) and pretend it was only the miracle of birth that was making her weep. Seeing Fenella and Rupert cradling Glory lovingly in their arms was enough to make the hardest heart weep and she noticed even Lady Gainsborough dab her eye discreetly with a mono-grammed, lace-edged hanky.

As predicted, it was a complete shambles when they got back to the house. People stood in the way trying to be helpful, those who knew where the food was forgot about the garnishes and to remove the clingfilm. Glory's grand-fathers stormed about looking for drink, and Rupert's mother stood in the path between the walk-in fridges and the table demanding staff.

Fenella and Glory sat at the head of the table, ignoring everything, just being together, Glory having a post-baptismal snack.

Then suddenly it all fell into place. Platters of food marched up the centre of the table, punctuated by bottles. Plates for food were in each place, there were enough chairs, everyone had a full glass. Toasts were drunk, proposed by almost everyone. Eventually Fenella said, 'Oh, do please eat, I'm starving!'

Zoe left the table before the puddings, abandoning the clearing-up and swapping from one course to another to other people. Instead she retreated to her designated croquembouche room to decorate her masterpiece. First she reheated her caramel on the little one ring electric cooker Rupert had provided. When it was the perfect temperature, she made some circles on baking parchment, then she spun it round and round the tower of profiteroles and added the circles. It looked like a golden cone or a comet. In fact, it looked so like a comet, Zoe hastily created a star out of caramel. She glued it on and sighed with satisfaction. Then she went back to the party.

She was just about to sit down for a breather when Fenella said, 'I think we're ready for the cake now, is it ready?'

'I'll go and get it. Can you make sure there's room on the table?'

It was the perfect setting. People in pretty clothes sitting at the long table under the trees, having eaten and drunk just a bit too much. Rupert had cleared a space for the cake and Sarah helped Zoe carry it.

'It's amazing!' said Sarah, 'I must suggest it for wedding cakes when people want something special that's not all chocolate.'

'You can put chocolate on it, but I think caramel is prettier really.'

'And it suits Glory somehow, it being golden,' said Sarah.

They reached the space and set it down.

'Oh wow,' said Fenella. 'This really is fantastic, better even than I expected it to be. You're a genius, Zoe!'

'Really, not too foul at all,' said Rupert, smiling in a way that made Zoe glow with pride.

'It is quite pretty,' said Lady Gainsborough, 'and we can have the wedding cake when they have a boy.'

'But until then, we'll keep on with the croquembouches,' said Fenella. 'Now how do I cut this thing?'

After everyone else had exclaimed at Zoe's beautiful

creation and said what a pity it was that they had to cut into it (although they were dying to try a piece), Hugo took some pictures. He'd been snapping away throughout the christening and had promised Zoe a few pictures for her portfolio – and a particularly sweet one of her and Glory. Zoe couldn't help wishing Gideon was here too. Perhaps she could send him the picture some time – or perhaps not; it might ensure she never saw him again.

Finally, Rupert dared to do the deed and they served it from the top, saving the caramel star for later. And it was delicious. The puffs broke and then melted, oozing flavoured cream. It really was a triumph.

'That girl is not a bad cook,' Zoe overheard Lady Gainsborough say to one of the other guests. 'Although making her godmother is taking gratitude a bit far.'

Sarah and Zoe were doing the last of the clearing-up. The guests had gone, Rupert had taken his parents for a drive and Fenella and Glory had retreated to bed for a glorious nap.

'That was a triumph,' said Sarah. 'It's lovely when those plans actually work. So often it rains, or the food isn't that good, or the salads flop or someone disturbs a wasps' nest, but that was perfect!'

'I'm so glad, for Fen's sake. It was all so rushed, from her point of view. It's brilliant that it worked so well.'

'They can always have a big party for all their friends a bit later, when Glory can wear what she likes.'

'Although she did look adorable!'

'Yes, but it was a bit worrying, everyone holding her with sticky fingers!' Then Sarah stopped reminiscing. 'So, Zoe, what are your plans?'

'For now? Or after the competition?'

'After. I imagine now you'll be planning menus and

practising like mad. I do think you should do a croquem-bouche for your pudding though. That worked so well.'

'I probably will. It demonstrates my skills: choux pastry, caramel – tricky things.'

'So?' Sarah seemed genuinely interested.

'Well, if I win – and it is a big if – I'd like to open a deli.' She went on to tell Sarah all that she'd told Gideon and, like him, Sarah seemed to approve.

'I do think that sounds excellent but I had wondered if you'd like to be a wedding caterer? You're obviously good at it.'

'I wouldn't mind doing that on the side, to supplement my income – golly, don't I sound grown up? – but basic-ally it would be part of the package, not the main event. It's a deli I really want.'

'Well, let's keep in touch.' Sarah paused. 'What will you do if you don't win? Although all the signs are that you will.'

'Oh, don't jinx it! If I don't win, I'll just get a job – cooking in a pub, doing a spot of catering, I don't know.' She sighed deeply. 'I do want to win. When I first entered I thought I just wanted the experience, the exposure, but now, I really, really want it!'

Chapter Twenty-One

'Are you sure you have to go?' Fenella had Glory clutched to her chest, standing on the steps of Somerby, while Rupert loaded Zoe's bags into her car.

'Yes! My family thinks I've emigrated and, anyway, you don't need me any more.' Zoe did have mixed feelings about leaving Somerby and Fenella and Rupert but now all the extra family had gone, there was no excuse for her to stay. And as Gideon hadn't called anyway – maybe he didn't have the Somerby number either? – there was no particular point.

'Well, I'll say it again, if ever you want a job – as almost anything – there's sure to be one here,' said Fenella. 'We'll need a catering manager or something quite soon.'

'I'm really grateful—'

'But, of course, when you win the competition you'll open your deli, so you won't need a job,' Fenella went on. 'If ever you need a reference . . .'

'I might not win! In fact I probably won't and I might be very grateful for a job.'

Rupert strode over to Zoe and put his arm round her shoulders. 'I expect you want to leave now. Fen would keep you here for ever if she could.'

'I'm glad you liked me staying so much. I'm very grateful too. I've had a brilliant time and I now have all sorts of useful experience. But I'm going now, or I won't be home in time for lunch, and my parents are expecting me.'

It was a wrench leaving Somerby. It was so tied up in her mind with Gideon. They had met there – or nearby – she had fallen in love and they had got to know each other there.

She refused to get neurotic about the fact he hadn't been in touch. There'd be some perfectly reasonable reason why he hadn't.

In spite of this sensible attitude, the worm of doubt continued to crawl about in her brain from time to time. Was she just the girl who was handy and quite amusing? Were her feelings not reciprocated? Was it all on her side? She thought back to some of their shared moments: playing butler and cook to Rupert's parents, the stolen moment in the woods, their last, passionate kiss. No, she couldn't have read the signs so wrong. It must be all right.

So, as she drove along the high-hedged lanes she tried to feel happy about it. It had been a joyous affair, full of fun and kindness and one glorious night of mind-blowing sex. She mustn't worry that it had ended. It hadn't. It was just taking a break!

As she got nearer home, she found herself dithering about what, if anything, to tell her mother. Her mother might well ask. And while she was happy to talk about Gideon all day and half the night, her mother would worry about the fact he was a judge. Zoe was worried too. But she probably wouldn't get away with not saying anything. It was the way of mothers that they could recognise if their daughters had undergone some sort of change.

Both parents were on the doorstep when she drove in. She was surprised to see her father.

'Not working, Dad?' she said as she hugged him.

'No, I wangled the afternoon off.'

'It's lovely to see you, darling,' said her mother, hugging just as hard.

'Hey, you two! I haven't been away that long!'

'I know, but you've been through a lot,' said her mother, ushering her into the house. 'I thought we'd just have a snack in the garden for lunch, as it's so sunny.'

Over the wine and the salad Zoe kept her parents entertained with tales of Somerby, Rupert's parents, the croquembouche and, in an expurgated version, Gideon. When her father went off to his study to catch up on a bit of work her mother made tea and set the mug firmly in front of her daughter; she wanted details.

She listened in silence while Zoe went through the description of how they'd met and how outrageously and utterly gorgeous and stunningly sexy he was. She went on to say how different from other people he was and how his hopes and ambitions coincided with hers, to a certain extent.

Her mother left a long, tactful silence before saying, 'So, doesn't the fact that he's a judge make him completely off limits?'

Zoe sighed and nodded. 'But you can't always choose who you – fancy.' She stopped but she knew her mother wasn't fooled. She sensed it had gone further than just fancying.

'I'll put the kettle on again,' her mother said.

After her mother had come through with the refilled mugs of tea and had produced a packet of chocolate digestives, she went on: 'Couldn't you put it all on hold until after the competition?'

'That's what we are doing, more or less. We haven't actually discussed it yet. I haven't heard from him since he went away anyway. I'm fine about it' – she smiled to hide her fib – 'and maybe he was thinking the same thing, maybe that's why he hasn't tried to get in touch. Maybe he thinks it's better if we don't see each other until it's all over.'

'It does seem a shame to risk—'

'I know, Mum! You don't need to remind me. I'm determined not to risk my chances in the competition.'

Zoe's mother seemed a bit sceptical but only said, 'Oh! How could I have forgotten! There was a something in the post for you a couple of days ago. It might have information about your final challenge.'

Glad that her mother was distracted from Gideon, Zoe followed her mother into the house. 'How exciting! We know it's fine dining but not all the details.'

'Here you go!' She handed Zoe a couple of envelopes, with the one she considered important on the top.

As Zoe took the envelopes and the letter opener her mother passed she noticed the second envelope was handwritten. She didn't recognise the writing but she knew instantly who it was from. Her heart sang and she gave an ecstatic little sigh, hoping her mother wouldn't notice.

'Actually, Mum? Would you like another cup of tea? I'll make it.' She was awash herself but her mother had no limits to her capacity.

When she came back she was fully in charge of her feelings and focused on the competition.

The official envelope was large and full of bits of paper. The first thing Zoe picked up was a printed invitation. 'Wow!' she said, passing it to her mother.

'An after-show party! How nice! Do you think it'll be full of celebs?'

'Maybe,' said Zoe, examining it. 'But I'm not asking Jamie Oliver for his autograph, even if you beg me.'

'Oh, OK,' said her mother. 'Alan Titchmarsh?'

'It's a cooking thing. He does gardens.'

Her mother sighed in resignation. 'All right, so what are you going to wear?'

'Mum! What I wear isn't important! It's how I cook! Look!' She pulled out a sheet of paper on which was written the next challenge and handed it to her mother. Really she was longing to get to what she was sure was Gideon's letter but she felt she must give her professional life precedence.

'"A celebration meal for six: two chefs, two critics, a food-loving celebrity and one of the original judges",' her mother read aloud.

'Oh my goodness,' said Zoe, reading over her mother's shoulder. Seeing it all in print made it scarily real. 'Four courses and top, fine-dining food.' She had a moment of panic. She'd lost valuable practise time at Somerby, even if it had been in a good cause. She had a lot to catch up on!

'But you can order what ingredients you like. They do say good food starts in the shop,' said her mother, reading.

'Or with the producer,' said Zoe. 'There are some great ones near Somerby.'

'But still, I hate to say this, but I'm so glad it's you and not me!'

Zoe pulled out a chair and sat at the garden table. 'It's all right. I've got this far, I can do it. And I already know what I'll make for pudding – a croquembouche.'

'Oh? Like you did for the christening. Good idea!'

Zoe's enthusiasm grew. 'I'd quite like to put gold leaf on some physalis fruit – you know, cape gooseberries – or something, so I can put little gold balls in between the profiteroles.'

'Will you have time? It sounds awfully fiddly. And would gold leaf stick? You know how the toffee always falls off the toffee apples unless you're really careful. And what would you do as a starter?'

Zoe gathered the papers together, including the hand-written envelope. 'Actually, Mum, I need to have a bit of a think. I'll take this lot upstairs and reread everything and then we'll hit the cookery books.'

Clutching the papers to her she ran up to her bedroom, dumped everything on the side table but took the envelope and sat on her bed.

She could open Gideon's letter at last. She was tempted to scrabble it open with her fingers, but as she'd picked up the letter opener with the papers she slit it open. She might want to keep the envelope intact.

Dear Zoe,

I am so sorry not to have been in touch. Still kicking myself for not exchanging numbers. I didn't even have the number at Somerby with me. I managed to get your home address by devious means!

I have a lot to tell you. Life has got even more hectic than usual. But we'll be together very soon and I can explain then.

I'm about to be whisked away to a meeting.

Yours, Gideon

As a love letter, it wasn't entirely satisfactory, but it was so much better than nothing. And it was really nice to see his handwriting. It was good writing and he had obviously used a fountain pen. Most people texted or emailed these days; it was very special to have something tangible she could keep for ever. It was just like Gideon to have written to her. There was no tender sign-off though. How long does it take to write 'lots of love'? Hardly any time at all. But was 'yours' better? Maybe it meant more than just 'lots of love'. Zoe hardly ever wrote an email that she didn't put 'lots of love' at the end of.

She examined the paper again. It was from a hotel. Gideon hadn't given her his email address, his mobile number or anything. Perhaps he didn't want her to get in touch? Perhaps this was a 'keep at arms' length' letter?

She descended into gloom for a few moments and then reread the letter once more for luck. He'd gone to some trouble to find out her address. He didn't need to write at all. No, she decided to be happy. Being happy or unhappy was quite often just a decision, she realised, glad that she'd made it.

She got up and went downstairs. It was time to scour the culinary world for recipes.

Planning the menu was fun. Zoe's mother had a lot of cookery books, Zoe had even more, and then there was the internet. Her mother threw herself into the whole thing with enthusiasm and her father obligingly ate samples as they appeared.

'You're not a bad cook, Zoe,' he said, snarfing up a tiny tart full of finely chopped mushrooms and topped with a poached quail's egg.

Zoe was frowning. 'Thank you. We liked that too but I'm not sure. It's too small for a starter really.'

'Give them two, then!' Her father seemed to think this was the blindingly obvious solution.

Zoe shook her head. 'Two would look wrong, and three would be too much. I'll have to think of something else.'

'Oh, shame,' said her father.

'Don't worry, there's mixture over. We're having it for supper.'

Thinking up the different courses with someone who really wanted you to win was so much more fun than doing everything on your own. Her mother was a very good cook herself although she didn't fully understand about cooking in a competition.

'I know there is nothing more delicious than a perfect little cup of soup but it won't be enough at this stage of the competition,' Zoe explained.

Her mother sighed. 'I suppose I'm just thinking of lovely food that isn't too stressful to serve.'

Zoe thought back to some of the best restaurants she'd eaten at. They sometimes served a tiny portion of soup which was almost the best part of the meal. 'I suppose out of four courses I could have one simple thing.'

'As long as it was perfect?'

'And presented beautifully'

'You can have my wedding coffee cups if you like. I haven't used them for years,' said her mother.

Zoe didn't speak for a few seconds. Her mother's coffee cups were antique, Spode, decorated with pea pods and tendrils in the palest green with gold edges. Zoe had always loved them. 'But Mum!' She had to clear her throat, she was so touched by the offer. 'Supposing they got broken!'

'I don't expect they will. And at least they'd go in a good cause. I never use them, after all.'

'But they're so special!'

'I know. So it's right that you have them for this special occasion.'

Zoe could picture a pea soup, exactly the same colour as the cups, and how wonderful it would look. She hugged her mother. 'If you're really sure . . .'

'Of course! Now what are you going to do next? A starter? Or fish?'

'Fish, I think. They're looking for technique. They want fiddly and time-consuming. Anything remotely easy and I could get marked down. That said, I do think I'll risk it and do a simple fish – perhaps a John Dory, which would be two simple courses.'

'Well, you've got the choux pastry for the buns, that's quite technical.'

'Yes, and I've practised it loads.'

'I know!' said her mother. 'My book club adored those éclairs.'

'But I should maybe have another go at the caramel and spun sugar.'

Her mother chuckled. 'What other skills do you have to show off? Juggling?'

Zoe giggled. 'Boning, stuffing, something or other "three ways" – possibly something you wouldn't normally eat.'

'Like dormouse for instance?'

'That's it, only probably something that's not endangered. Rabbit, perhaps?'

'Do you like rabbit?' Zoe's mother seemed all set to enthuse about Miffy as food if she had to.

'Not really. I could do some sort of fowl – or game.' Zoe ran through every creature she could think of in her head but didn't come up with anything that inspired her.

'Or steak.'

Zoe regarded her mother as if she were mad for a few seconds and then her expression changed. 'Three ways with steak would be fairly unusual. I could do a miniature beef Wellington, a perfect pan-fried steak with Jenga chips – you know, when you stack them in a little tower like the game? – and may be steak tartare?'

Her mother nodded. 'But what about cold food on a hot plate?'

Zoe considered. Her mother had a thing about hot plates that no one else in the family understood at all. But she might have a point. 'Or a tiny, perfect burger? Deep fried crispy onions? Some perfect relish? I could probably make that beforehand. They say we can have six ingredients we haven't made ourselves, or made earlier.'

Planning the perfect menu took several days, sheets of paper, the internet, trips to the library and agonies of indecision. But it was fun, and when she wasn't thinking and wondering about Gideon, it occupied Zoe's mind completely.

At last she was happy with her menu and threw herself into developing the perfect relish and the best and lightest sauce for the fish. She spent quite a lot of money on edible gold leaf and physalises too.

When they weren't thinking about food, Zoe and her mother thought about what Zoe should wear for the party and the photo shoot. Zoe's mother didn't think she was paying the matter enough attention.

'But it's a food comp, Mum! Not *Britain's Next Top Model!*'

'Trust me, darling, if you don't make an effort you'll regret it for ever. And I bet that Cher will be going to town.'

Jenny, who had come over for lunch, mostly to weigh in on Zoe's mother's side, nodded. 'You need to look shit hot.'

Zoe's mother raised her eyebrows but nodded. 'What about that boy you're keen on? Isn't he going to be there?'

Zoe laughed at the thought of Gideon being described as a boy. 'I just thought I'd look more earnest and committed if I didn't try to compete with Cher for looks.'

Zoe's mother and Jenny exchanged despairing looks.

'OK! I want to look gorgeous. As far as I can, seeing as I'm quite short.'

'Petite, darling,'

'And thanks to Jimmy Choo, Louboutin etc., you don't have to be short any more,' said Jenny.

'For someone who mostly thinks about horses, you're very into shoe designers,' muttered Zoe.

'I don't live in a cave!' said Jenny.

'I rather like Emma Hope,' said Zoe's mother wistfully, possibly thinking of her youth.

'Maybe I should do something about my hair?' said Zoe, who was now quite keen on the idea of getting glammed up.

Jenny inspected Zoe's mop, which was as usual a bit on the wild side. 'I like it a bit longer but I do see you might want a good cut.'

Zoe took hold of a handful of curls. 'I wonder what I'd look like with it straightened?'

'Very high maintenance,' said Jenny.

'Why don't you go along and see Debbie,' her mother said. 'She's the best hairdresser in the county. All my friends go there.'

Zoe bit her lip, not sure the statement that 'all my friends go there' was quite the recommendation for her, seeing as she was a different generation.

'Oh yes,' said Jenny. 'She's really good. She did the hair for a friend's wedding. She'll sort you out.' She looked longingly at the last cream puff. 'Can I eat that? I know I've had two already but they are delish.'

Zoe pushed the plate towards her. 'Please! No one in the house can face any more choux pastry at the moment. I've been making it blindfold.'

'Really?' Jenny almost seemed to believe this.

Zoe tutted. 'No, not really! But I have made it a lot so it's one less thing to worry about for the competition.'

Debbie was brilliant. For a start, she was only a bit older than Zoe so knew exactly what was on trend and what would suit Zoe best. She came home with her head a mass of curls that she could pin back, or wear with a hair band, or just have tousled.

She couldn't help wondering how Gideon would react to it. He liked her unstructured look and he would probably like this. Or at least, she hoped so. She was so longing to see him again.

Her mother made and paid for an appointment to have her nails done. While she was there she had her eyebrows shaped. She briefly considered having her eyelashes extended but the girl said, 'Honestly, you don't need it. Your eyelashes are fine as they are.'

She shimmied home and twirled for her mother and later for her father who said, 'I think you look the same as you did before you spent all that money, but what do I know?'

He was pushed affectionately and dispatched to the sitting room with the paper.

'You look stunning, darling. You *do* look the same as you did this morning but sleeker, more groomed. Gamine, and sort of French. You'll give that Cher a run for her money.'

'Mum! It isn't a competition for looks, you know!'

'Oh yes it is,' said her mother. 'It always is.'

Two weeks later, with a case full of emergency changes of mind, esoteric ingredients that the TV company might not be able to source, and her mother's antique coffee cups to bring her luck, Zoe took the train to London.

'Just as well you don't have to change at Swindon,' said her father, as he helped her haul her luggage to the platform.

'No, and I only have to climb into a taxi at Paddington.'

'It's like when you went to uni only almost worse!' said her mother. 'Are you sure you don't want to take my Rescue Remedy? Just in case you get really nervous?'

'I'll be fine, Mum. Really. Or at least, as fine as I can be.'

'You just do your best. Dad and I are so proud of you!'

'Are you sure you and Dad can't come to the final judging and the wrap party afterwards?'

'Honey! In some ways I'd love to but your dad's got to be away for work and I'd hate being there on my own, even if I didn't have a whole lot of stuff it would be difficult to get out of.'

Zoe sighed. 'You wouldn't be on your own. I'd be there.'

'You'll be busy and I'd get terribly nervous for you. I'd just be miserable, and you'd worry about me.'

There was no denying the truth of this. Her mother was great with people she knew but she was shy deep down. She also suffered dreadfully with nerves on her daughter's behalf. Zoe didn't want to force her to come to something she wouldn't enjoy. 'OK, if you really don't want to.'

'Thank you, darling. It's honestly better this way.'

Zoe hugged her parents, hoping that either the train would come or her mother would go before she started to cry. 'If you want to do a bit of shopping you'd better not waste all your parking ticket on saying goodbye to me.'

'OK, OK, I can take a hint.' Her mother hugged her again hard. 'Keep in touch!'

Just as she settled into her seat her phone beeped. It was a text from Jenny. 'Good luck, can't wait to see it when it airs'. Zoe hadn't given much thought to the actual programme. Now she was forced to, she felt she might have to hide when that time came. She wasn't sure she'd be able to watch it. Although perhaps if she was watching it snuggled up next to Gideon it would be bearable. Then, chiding herself for daydreaming, she opened her folder and forced herself to think about three ways with steak.

Chapter Twenty-Two

Just as Zoe's taxi pulled up at the London hotel where they were staying she spotted Cher getting out of another one. She too had a lot of luggage, which took some time to get on to the pavement. When they'd both emptied their taxis Zoe looked up. Cher saw her and smiled.

'Hiya!' she said, unusually friendly. She was looking slightly odd. Zoe wondered if she'd done something to herself while they'd been at home but couldn't work out what.

'Hello! How are you?'

'Great, thanks.' She flicked her hair back over her shoulders; it was even longer, blonder and more streaked than ever. Then Zoe realised what was odd about her. Cher had had Botox. Her forehead, revealed by her new style, was smooth as paper.

Someone from the television company came up. 'Have you got your perishables there, girls?' he said. 'I'll take them out of the way for you.'

Handing them over took a little time but at last elegantly uniformed commissionaires took their cases and they went into the hotel.

Free of baggage apart from a handbag big enough to house a medium-sized poodle, Cher gushed all over again. 'Darling! Love the hair!' she said, kissing the air by Zoe's shoulder. 'You look like Amélie, sort of French.'

Zoe kissed Cher back and got a face full of extensions.

'Thank you! That was the idea. You look fab as usual. Fabber, maybe.' Cher was one of those irritating women who could really make a fake tan work. She was neither orange nor streaky.

'Thanks! I've been in the Maldives, working on my tan, and my celebration dinner of course.' Her laugh tinkled merrily, somehow turning this into a lie. 'But also getting a bit of R. and R. I've got loads to tell you,' she went on. 'Let's hope our suites are next door to each other!'

'Suites? Amazing!' said Zoe, suddenly yearning for a Travelodge, on her own.

'Yes, apparently there's a big deal going on between the hotel chain and the TV company. My uncle told me all about it. It's what he does.'

'If you two ladies would like to travel up in the lift together,' said a bell boy, 'the luggage will come up separately.'

'Fine!' said Cher. And as they travelled up in the mirrored, marble lift together, she mouthed to Zoe: 'Cute!' Zoe had to agree the bell boy was cute, but he could also see Cher mouthing so she didn't comment.

'Tell you what,' said Cher as she was taken to her door, 'let's get unpacked and then you come to mine and we'll assault the mini-bar. It's all paid for!'

'What time do they want us for the photo shoot? Didn't they say downstairs in the lobby for six?' Zoe knew perfectly well they did but wanted Cher to decide for herself that they'd need every second of the intervening time to get ready. She didn't want to get drunk with Cher first. It was not a hen night.

'We'll have time for a quick one. Nice to be relaxed for the photo shoot. We don't want to look like rabbits caught in the headlights, do we?' The implication was that only one of them was in danger of looking like that and it wasn't her.

'OK. I'll come to your room at quarter to. We'll be doing our own make-up, won't we?' Before Cher could answer, Zoe shot along the corridor as if desperate to get her eyelash curlers out.

Cher had ordered a bottle of champagne from room service, and handed Zoe a glass the moment she got through the door. 'Here, have this. You and me need to have a talk.'

Although Cher was being just as friendly as before, Zoe felt suddenly chilled. Maybe it was just the air-conditioning that was up a bit high.

Cher opened her laptop. 'I want you to look at some pictures.'

Zoe sipped her champagne, wondering if there was really time for 'me looking amazing on a beach' photographs.

Cher placed an elegant, French-manicured finger on the trackpad and a picture filled the screen. 'I took these on my mobile, so they're not great, but I think they're clear enough, don't you?'

Zoe peered at the screen. It seemed to be a weird close-up from a Ray Mears programme. Then she recognised her fleece. A second later she saw Gideon. They were kissing.

Several more photos of the same subject followed.

'There!' said Cher. 'What do you think?'

Zoe felt sick. Her knees failed her and she sank on to the sofa. A gulp of champagne didn't really help. What could she possibly say?

She fell back on trivialities. 'God! My hair! Did I really go round looking like that?' She was playing for time and was quite pleased with her effort.

'Never thought I'd say this, but it's not your hair you should be worrying about, sweetie.'

'You think I have a bit of a muffin top going on?'

Cher shook her head, pretending to be sad. 'It's who you're kissing. Gideon. A judge. What you're looking at is a major scandal. And not just your hair.'

Zoe clutched her glass as if it could somehow save her. She had a feeling Cher knew exactly what she was going to say next.

'So?' Cher looked at her with her head on one side.

Zoe shrugged. 'What do you want me to do about it?'

'Simple. Don't win the competition.'

'Cher! I'm not likely to! There are people better than me in it. You might win!'

'I might and I want to increase my chances. You're the one they're saying is tipped for the top. Not because of your cooking,' she sneered as if Zoe's cooking was beneath contempt, 'but because of your "general ability to cope in a crisis." I told you, I know all about it. So I want you out. These pictures are going to help.'

'Supposing I say I don't care? Supposing I say "publish and be damned"?'

Cher might not have got the Duke of Wellington quote but it didn't seem to matter. 'Listen, you can say to hell with it, and not care if you don't win. But if the show is tarnished with this sodding great scandal, it won't only affect you, it'll affect everyone and Gideon won't work in television again. His career?' She made a gesture with her hand nosediving towards the floor. 'Like that. You have to screw your chances of winning.'

'I could just pull out?' Somehow the thought of not giving it her best shot was far worse than not competing, although that was fairly dreadful. She'd worked so hard.

Cher shook her head. 'No. The reasons will get out and

the results will be the same. You just have to cook badly so you don't win. Shouldn't be too difficult.' Cher giggled. 'You might even do it without trying!'

This seemed like a lifeline. 'I may not win—'

Cher shook her head. 'No. You have to make absolutely certain you don't win. You've got to ruin a dish. I want your reputation as a cook shattered, on television, in public. It's only what you deserve.'

Zoe drew breath to protest but Cher held up a hand.

'No! You slept with a judge! That is wrong on so many levels. You have to make sure you don't gain from it.'

Zoe didn't feel she could protest that the pictures of them kissing didn't mean she had slept with him. It was irrelevant and, anyway, she *had* slept with him. 'Just tell me, you seem to know everything, did you ever get the impression that Gideon favoured me over the rest of you?'

Cher's little shrug told Zoe what she wanted to know. 'I'm not saying that, but he might have done. And sleeping with him is still wrong. You must see that.'

Zoe was silent. She'd always known that sleeping with Gideon was wrong, and yet the reality was that, even now, there was nothing she would have done differently.

'So you agree?' Cher might have been getting Zoe to agree which nightclub they should go to first.

Zoe nodded. She didn't know what else to do.

'Then cheers!' Cher refilled both glasses. 'It's going to be a great night!'

Chapter Twenty-Three

Cher was particularly WAG-like and charming in the limo that picked up the three female contestants and took them to the hotel where the photo shoot was to be held. The press conference and party were going to be there too. She patronised Becca in a way that made Zoe squirm but as she had her own internal maelstrom she couldn't do much to help, apart from the occasional sympathetic smile. Her feelings were so mixed up. She was going to be seeing Gideon, which was at once tremendously exciting and completely terrifying. Would she get a chance to speak to him? And, most importantly, how would he take the news that she was being blackmailed by Cher? She wished now that she'd taken the bottle of Rescue Remedy her mother had tried to press on her. What she really felt like was a tranquilliser. Maybe someone would offer her some brandy. Gideon would be furious. But he had a lot to lose too. Why oh why hadn't they been more careful?

'I'm going to get used to this lifestyle!' said Cher, stretching her long, perfect legs in front of her. 'After this competition, some of us are going to be stars!' She said the word with an ecstasy that made Zoe squirm. A glance across at Becca told her she felt the same.

'You might not win, Cher,' said Becca boldly. 'And we're chefs, not models.'

'I *might* not win,' she agreed, 'but it's unlikely. The thing is, your nerves will get the better of you and Zoe – well, she's not really up there, is she? And as for not being a model, I think I could quite easily step sideways into that role.'

'That's not fair!' said Becca. 'Zoe's done brilliantly!'

'But not as a cook. She's just a jolly coper, the helper in times of trouble, making cupcakes, being a little star, doing good deeds wherever she can. What this competition wants is a Michelin-standard chef, not a glorified Girl Guide.'

Zoe cringed in her seat. Cher's cruel statements were usually easy to dismiss but that hit home. She had been the helper – she *liked* to help! She also liked the challenge, the problem-solving. Maybe she'd been wrong to give in to this instinct. Maybe it marked her out as unprofessional. But, really, that wasn't the point. Her biggest, hugest, life-changing error had been to get into bed with one of the judges. She could be worthy of three Michelin stars right now but she still couldn't cook herself out of this particular hole.

'Becca is that standard,' Zoe said, forcing herself to say something to hide how ghastly she was feeling. She may be out of the competition but she could still root for Becca. She deserved to win it anyway.

Cher shook her head sadly. 'Nerves,' she repeated. 'They will get to you, won't they? Think of cooking for all those top chefs, under the lights, the eyes of the world on you. Your hands will sweat; they'll slip on the knife. You might actually cut yourself.'

'We've been cooking like that ever since the start of the competition,' said Becca, 'it's no different now. The best chef will win. And don't forget Shadrach. He's always cutting himself but it doesn't stop him cooking amazing food.'

'But messy. He won't win when his station is such a muddle.'

As Cher's station was always immaculate Zoe really hoped this wasn't true.

'You can't know that,' said Becca. 'It's the food that counts. He could easily win.'

To Cher's delight and the others' consternation they were made up before the photo shoot. But in spite of her inner turmoil, Zoe did find it rather fun and strangely relaxing.

All three girls were seated in front of a mirror and each one had a make-up artist hovering over them. Mentally awarding herself a saucer of cream, Zoe couldn't help thinking that Cher's Botox looked stiff and fake now she could see her reflected in the mirror.

'Tell me, Cher,' she said, deciding she liked cream. 'Why did you decide to have Botox? Were some little worry lines, possibly about the competition, creeping in?'

Cher wasn't remotely embarrassed. 'Oh no, nothing like that. I just wanted to look my absolute best. Because my appearance is important to me.'

'But you're only in your early twenties!'

'And your point is?'

Zoe gave up. Cher obviously thought there was nothing strange about injecting toxins into your skin even if the flaws it corrected weren't visible to anyone else. 'And do you feel it helped?'

Cher was indignant. 'Of course it helped! Duh! Look!' She pointed to her forehead. 'No lines!'

'No expression!' put in Becca, who'd gained a lot of confidence during the competition.

'Frowning's very over-rated,' said Cher, with a little moue of temper. 'Can we have false eyelashes if we want them?'

'Anything you like,' said her artist. 'You're the client.'

'I'm Susy,' said the girl assigned to Zoe. 'What sort of look would you like?'

'Hello. I usually go for quite a natural look.' Zoe was feeling that her make-up application skills were hopelessly amateur.

'You have really great hair! Are those curls natural? Amazing. So many girls iron their hair these days. Such a shame.'

Zoe might have imagined it but she thought Susy glanced at Cher in a disapproving way.

'Maybe, as it is all a bit special, I should have a more dramatic look than normal?' Zoe looked at Susy appealingly, hoping she'd tell her what was best.

'We can do that. A sort of enhanced natural, and you could have a few false lashes at the end of your own for added oomph, if you'd like that.'

It was with Becca that the change was most dramatic. She never wore any make-up but she'd given her artist free rein and while it wasn't overdone, she now looked like the pretty girl she was and not the anxious mouse who had first turned up as a competitor. The new look added to her confidence too. This young woman wouldn't succumb to gamesmanship.

In spite of her limited range of expression Cher managed to show displeasure at Becca's transformation; she wanted to be the prettiest, and not have a rival in the glamour stakes.

'And now, ladies, if you're ready, we'll do the photo shoot.' A glamorous girl in the skinniest jeans and the highest heels that Zoe had ever seen outside a celebrity magazine smiled approvingly at them.

Zoe longed for Mike and the friendly team they'd got to know at Somerby. These people were nice enough but they were strangers. The others had begun to feel like part of the family.

'I don't remember there being all this non-cooky publicity

for other cookery comps,' she muttered to Becca. 'You only ever saw them in their whites.'

'This show is much bigger than anything they've had before,' said Cher. 'My uncle told me all about it. We're going to be stars.'

'I'm sure we're not,' said Becca. 'Unless we win, and we can't all win. And even then, we'll only be famous for five minutes, and only because of our cooking.'

Cher gave her a knowing look which said, 'You know nothing, sweetheart.'

Zoe followed the others to the set-up for the photo shoot. It was a fake kitchen, with a big range cooker, lots of copper pans and jugs of herbs, right in the middle of the work surface. Pretty but really irritating if you actually had to cook there, she decided.

'Now we want you all together to begin with,' said the girl in charge. 'Come along, Shadrach, we'll have you in the middle, surrounded by the girls. That's right . . .'

It took for ever. At one point Zoe found herself lying on her tummy with her legs bent up and her chin in her hands looking – there was no other word for it – cute.

Cher excelled at it; she revelled in the attention and adored every extravagant request.

'I think if they asked her to sit on the hot stove with her legs apart, she'd do it,' said Shadrach.

'I need a drink,' said Becca, 'and I don't mean water!'

'We've just got a few shots for magazines to do now. All of you sit on the sofa together,' said the girl on the stilt heels, still upright, still in charge.

Zoe found she got used to smiling to order. After nearly an hour though her jaw was beginning to ache and her top lip kept sticking to her teeth. But at last they were released and glasses of champagne were put into their hands.

'Just a little time to wind down before you go home to get early nights before your big day,' said the girl in spiky heels. 'Or you won't sleep!'

Zoe had just come out of the loo before their taxi arrived to take them back to their hotel when she saw Gideon. He saw her at the same moment and they moved together like magnets hardly aware of the people milling around in between.

'Hello, you,' she said, breathless. All the love and lust she'd been telling herself wasn't real more or less since she'd last seen him came flooding back. Then she remembered Cher. 'Where can we be alone? We need to talk.'

'And the rest!' He laughed down at her, his eyes dancing.

'Oh Gideon, it's not that. I wish it was! I've got something I must tell you. But not here!'

He nodded. 'I know a place. Follow me. In here.' Gideon opened a door.

It was a small room full of stacked chairs and tables. 'How did you know about this?' asked Zoe, impressed.

'I opened the door by mistake when I was looking for the Gents.' His expression softened. 'Oh Zoe, I've missed you so.'

He pulled her into a hug and for a while they stayed with their arms around each other, not even kissing. It was bliss. Eventually she pulled away and looked up at him. 'I've got to pull out of the competition.'

'What? Why? What are you talking about?' He held her hands as if reluctant to let her go.

'I don't mean pull out really. I mean – deliberately fail.'

'That makes even less sense!' He was frowning now.

She moved away, aware that she was going to annoy him. She couldn't look at him; she felt so ashamed, besmirched, by what had happened. 'Cher has pictures.

279

Of us. Together. She took them in the wood, during the foraging.'

'So?'

She looked at him now. Why was he being so dense? 'So? So she said if I don't make sure I don't win she'll tell everyone that we've been having an affair. The show might have to be pulled for all I know. It'll be tainted by scandal!' Zoe fought not to sound hysterical but wasn't doing a good job. She wanted to pace the floor to get rid of some of her tension but there were piles of chairs and tables in every corner.

'But that's blackmail!'

'Yes! But we did have an affair and she has got proof. She's in a position to blackmail me.'

'Us. I was there too.'

'And your career will be affected, won't it?'

'Yes, I suppose it will.' He sighed. 'But you can't let this affect you now. You have a real chance of winning this competition.'

She shook her head. 'I really should have thought of that before.' Why, oh why hadn't she controlled her feelings? What had been so wonderful now just seemed unbelievably sordid. Then she felt a flicker of anger. He should have thought of it. He was there too. He encouraged her!

Gideon pushed his hand into his hair as if to help his thinking process. 'I know I've never shown you any advantage. That must count for something.'

'Nothing is going to count against the fact that you're a judge and I'm a contestant and we slept together.'

Gideon groaned. 'There'll be a way out of this, we just need to find it. Damn it. This is serious.'

'The way I see it, I have two options. Either I can resign, but then all the reasons for it would come out – Cher would make absolutely sure of it – or I make a mistake with one of my recipes, and just lose.' Zoe paused and looked up at Gideon. 'I probably wouldn't have won anyway.'

'I'm not having it! You're not throwing the competition because of Cher. She's not above trying to seduce the judges herself. I happen to know!'

This made Zoe feel even worse. 'Unfortunately I wasn't able to get photographs of you in bed together—'

'I didn't sleep with her, you idiot!'

'Don't call me an idiot! You're the one who can't see what is so bloody obvious.'

'Look, I'll sort it! You're not to pull out. '

'I won't pull out, but I will have to fail. I mean it. I'm not risking your career or the show.'

Gideon put his hands on her shoulders. 'And I won't let you. I can't believe you're prepared to give in to Cher like that.'

'It's my decision,' Zoe said, trying to stop her voice wobbling. 'You can't stop me. I have to do this.'

'Don't be a fool! Christ, I'm disappointed in you, Zoe. I thought you cared about this competition.' He looked thunderous, as if he wanted to shake some sense in to her.

'Stop shouting at me.'

At that moment the door opened and a young woman came in, obviously staff. Gideon was still glaring at her and obviously angry, so Zoe took the opportunity to escape. She couldn't deal with it any longer – any of it – least of all Gideon.

Chapter Twenty-Four

❧❦❧

By 8 a.m. the following morning, Zoe was wearing whites, with the logo of the cookery competition embroidered on her breast. She'd been given an area to work in and all her ingredients were in boxes around her, apart from those in the fridges and chillers. She felt numb. Gideon was furious with her. She'd just have to find time at the party to explain to him. He'd said he'd sort it, but she knew he couldn't. He'd be angry, and she might lose him, but the thought of what Cher might do with those photographs was far, far worse.

She had decided she was going to put every inch of heart and soul she had into creating this meal. At the last minute she'd do something – she didn't yet know what – to ruin it. But of course if something went wrong, she wouldn't have to do that, she could just make out to Cher that the mistake was deliberate. Gideon would just have to get over it. Once he'd had time to reflect he must realise it was the only thing she could do.

She was aware that 'three ways with fillet' wasn't usual, but she wanted to do it. She'd sourced some beef from her home area that had been hung a very long time and was sure it would be delicious. She decided to start making the brioche dough for the bun for the mini-burger. No one would expect a burger and with the mini beef Wellington it might be a bit filling, but her other courses were fairly light.

Once the dough was proving she started on her rough-puff pastry. She would have to roll it out and chill it several times. Next, the soup. Fresh peas, podded and without their skins, briefly cooked in chicken stock, thickened with cream. She would whizz it up at the last minute and serve it in her mother's coffee cups and call it cappucino. She made a pile of parmesan crisps, drying them over a rolling pin to give them the look of Pringles.

Next she made her choux buns for her croquembouche. The television company had hired her a mould at vast expense, which should be much easier than building it freehand had been.

She didn't want her meal described as heavy, or too much. She started on the big fat squared-off chips. She was going to fry them at least three times in duck fat for maximum crispiness. There was a deep fat fryer there for her.

She consulted her list. It was very important not to get into a panic and cook things out of order. Everything that had to be cooked in advance needed to be done but not so far in advance they'd be past their best. The chips would get their final fry while the judges were eating their John Dory. (The lemon thyme, from her mother's garden, was, like the coffee cups, another good-luck talisman.) She put the wild mushrooms that were going with the John Dory in a bowl of water to soak.

She was just beginning to feel she might get everything done by one o'clock, her slot, when along came the television crew and a celebrity chef to interview her about her menu. (Cher had been beside herself with glee at the line-up of celebrity judges they needed to impress.)

At least it wasn't Gideon. That would have been awful.

'So, Zoe, you've got quite an unusual menu here: cappuccino of fresh peas. That's just a fancy way of saying pea soup, isn't it?'

He was a chef known for his confrontational attitude but as Zoe felt she'd already lost everything she cared about she didn't flinch from straight talking.

'That's right. Part of fine dining is making the food seem as attractive as it can be. Calling it cappuccino and serving it in coffee cups is part of that.'

'So you're not giving us much soup?'

'No. When you have four courses you don't need much soup.'

'And is soup enough of a challenge to qualify as fine dining?'

'Any food can qualify as fine dining if it's done well enough.' She was pleased with this one.

He nodded. 'It's a bit eighties, but retro is in at the moment.'

'That's what I thought,' said Zoe promptly, who thought soup was soup and didn't know it could be retro.

'So then we have John Dory, simple enough, but three ways with fillet? Are you taking the – are you joking?'

Zoe laughed. 'Not at all. We have beef Wellington, a bit of steak, simply cooked in the pan, and a miniature burger.'

'That is a bit out of left field, if I may say so, Zoe.' The chef grinned. Perhaps he was coming round to Zoe's way of thinking. 'A burger? For a fine-dining meal?'

'Why not? What is more delicious than a perfect burger?'

'Will you mince the meat yourself?'

'I'm going to chop it finely. I'll have more control that way.'

'And serving it with . . . ?'

'A brioche roll and tomato and chilli relish. I'm using cherry tomatoes.'

'Small but perfectly formed, eh?'

'That's what I'm aiming for. I might make a mustard mayo to go with it. Oh, and micro herbs for a bit of colour.'

'OK, and then we have the croquembouche. That's a big pudding!'

'Yes. I could have made a smaller version but I thought, where's the fun in that? A croquembouche has to be big. That's the point of it.' As she talked Zoe felt her nerves subside. She was used to the cameras now. She could do this. She just hoped when it came to the crunch she didn't bottle it. Even if she had to bow out, she'd do it gracefully.

'You've made a croquembouche before, I assume?'

'Oh yes, for a friend's christening party. That time I didn't have a mould so I think it'll be easier this time . . .'

'And gold-leaf physalis?'

'Yes. I wanted little golden spheres, like jewels.'

'Well, good luck, Zoe. I look forward to tasting it all later.'

Zoe was on a roll. Putting Gideon out of her mind felt a bit like shifting Nelson's Column a little to the left, but she did it. Somehow her anxiety about him and their relationship (if they had one at all now), and the fact she was being blackmailed, focused her. It was all so awful she just blanked it out and used every corner of her mind for her cooking.

And everything went right. She felt as if she'd turned into a cooking robot that couldn't put a foot wrong. Her brioche dough for the bun was as light as air and crisp so no one could accuse the bun of adding lead to her dish.

She'd always had a knack for pastry but wondered, as she worked on her rough-puff, if her artificial calm made it even better. Cold hands were good for pastry; maybe a cold, shut-up heart also helped? She made tart cases with the leftovers, after she'd measured enough pastry for six little beef Wellingtons.

Then she started on her mince. Her knives were so sharp they might well have been able to cut a silk scarf had she felt this test necessary, and her mother's butcher hadn't let her down – the beef was perfect. It was so tender she had enough finely chopped in a very short time. She fried some off to taste it and decided to only season it lightly before making her burgers. She could have added onion or herbs but felt it was better just as it was.

And all the time the cameras focused on her, moving in for close-ups and pulling away. By now Zoe was so used to their presence she hardly noticed them, any more than you notice the noise of a fan or a fridge. They were just part of the background.

After some thought and experiment at home she had decided to wrap the beef for her Wellingtons in Parma ham, and to add onion and a little garlic to the duxelle of finely chopped mushrooms. She made this by hand too and not in a food processor so she could control exactly how fine the chopping was. She didn't want a purée.

Then, because she had the time, she did the initial searing for each piece of beef separately, so if she made a mistake she hadn't ruined all of them. As she tested the first one, she wondered why she was taking so much trouble when she had to lose the competition. But her pride meant she wanted to lose it on purpose and not because she was lacking in skill.

The croquembouche was almost easy, with a mould to help. She'd perfected getting all the little buns the same size and the end result was beautifully conical and didn't lean to one side or the other.

She glanced at her watch and checked she'd done as much as she could. She decided now was the time to get her cape gooseberries gold-leafed. Again it worked wonderfully well. She'd dipped the physalises in sugar

286

water to make sure they were tacky and then caught up some gold leaf to produce perfect little gold spheres. The turned back leaves of the physalises looked like wings. She wouldn't add them to the pudding until the judges were eating their fillet three ways. The spun sugar would also be very last minute.

She checked her list for the hundredth time and finally began to get nervous. While she'd been cooking she'd been totally absorbed but now she had to wait until everyone was seated before she could finish her dishes and get them out. And the thought of Gideon somewhere out there on the other side of the wall didn't help her nerves. She wondered if the others were nervous too. They were all working in separate rooms Zoe was glad she was going first.

She was also glad her parents weren't up in London, for the final judging and the party. Her mother had been right, she'd have worried about them. What with Gideon, having to 'fail' and everything else, she didn't need any more distractions.

At last Mike came into her kitchen. 'All right? All ready? You seem very calm and organised. You know you're the first up? When you're done, a car will take you over to the viewing theatre and you'll wait until all the contestants and everyone is there, and then you watch the show. Of course it's the uncut version but you get all the judges' comments.'

'I know.' They had had all this explained earlier, but she knew Mike was fairer than fair and wanted to make sure Zoe wasn't in doubt about anything.

'OK, get ready with your starter.'

Chapter Twenty-Five

Zoe had chopped some mint so fine it was like dust. This was to emulate the cocoa on top of the cappuccino. She added some peeled peas as the coffee beans. The parmesan crisps she served in a basket, as if they were tuile biscuits. Just for a second she was sorry she couldn't take a picture of the soup for her mother. But still, she'd see them on television if all went well. All going well, of course, meant her not winning.

'Service!' she called, getting her mind back under control, and the minute the trays were away, she focused on her fish.

It was like being two people, she decided. Half of her was really enjoying the challenge and how well everything was going. The other half was in agony because she knew she'd have to ruin something any moment now. Gideon would be furious but he would come round in the end, wouldn't he? She wondered how the others were feeling. She could almost sense Cher, demanding her to fail – or else!

It had to be the fillet. It was too late for the Wellingtons, wrapped up safely in pastry, Parma ham and finely chopped mushrooms, but as she lowered what she called Jenga chips into the deep-fat fryer for their third time, she decided she would heavily oversalt the steak and the burger. Then there could be no doubt about it. They might forgive one lot of seasoning being wrong, but not two.

She coated the burger in a fine layer of Welsh Rarebit mixture and flashed the blow torch over it. Then she picked up some salt from the salt-pig and, in a very cheffy way, holding it high, she put far too much on before adding the brioche top.

The soup cups came back. 'How are you doing?' said Mike. 'Are you nearly ready with your main?'

'Oh yes. Just one minute.' She oversalted the steak in the same way, took a chip away from the pile for Mike and then said, 'Service!'

'Didn't you put a bit too much salt on that steak?' Mike asked, crunching into the chip.

'Chefs always complain if you don't season things enough,' said Zoe. This was perfectly true, but she still knew she was lying. She couldn't let Mike know she'd thrown her chances of winning.

As the waiter carried the croquembouche through to the judges, she knew she couldn't have done anything to ruin that. Because she'd made it for Glory's christening, it had too many happy associations. Messing it up deliberately wasn't an option.

She did realise she'd taken a risk. With the spun sugar, the gold leaf and all the other things that could have gone wrong, she might not have had to oversalt her steak and her burger.

'They seemed to like that,' said Mike a little later, patting her shoulder in a friendly way. 'Now you go back to the hotel to change and then the car will take you to the viewing theatre. There'll be a restorative glass of champagne for you there. After the judging it's the party.'

Zoe did feel wrung out. Although everything had gone very well it had still been a lot of cooking. The thought of a shower and ten minutes on her bed was very tempting.

She woke with a start thirty minutes later and had to

rush. They'd been asked to wear chef's hats for the judging and Zoe snatched it up and put it in her bag as she whisked out of the room and down to the waiting taxi. She'd work out how to put it on without looking like a complete idiot later.

The first person she met in the foyer of the movie theatre was Fenella. She had Glory over her shoulder and was patting her back.

'Fen! How lovely to see you!' Zoe was tempted to snatch Glory from her for a comforting hug.

'Zoe! How did it go?'

'Oh. Fine, really!' Zoe put on a positive expression, suddenly desperate to confide in Fenella, but she couldn't. She just had to live with it on her own.

After quite a lot more cuddling between Glory and her godmother Zoe, they went into the cinema. The lights were up and people were chatting. The room was full of what Zoe presumed to be friends and relatives of the contestants, and film crew who weren't on duty. Glory, bored with the conversation, fell asleep.

Cher was the next contestant to arrive. She looked amazing, her make-up fresh and her chef's hat appealingly slanted.

'How did it go?' she demanded, plonking herself down next to Zoe.

'Oh! Fine!' It probably wasn't a good idea to tell Cher she'd oversalted her fillet with people all around, in case someone overheard.

'You're not going to win, are you?' Cher asked brightly.

'Who knows!' said Zoe. 'How did your meal go?'

'Oh great. What was your menu?'

Zoe told her.

'Soup? You did soup? Hardly difficult, is it?'

'Well . . .'

'Pudding?'

'Croquembouche.' Surely Cher would be impressed by that at least.

'That's so old-fashioned!' Cher smiled delightedly. 'You won't win with that menu.'

Zoe shrugged. She could neither agree or disagree.

Becca arrived looking flustered. 'Thank God that's over! I'm never going to cook in front of people again!'

'Ah, poor love!' said Cher, as sincere as a snake in the grass. 'What was your menu?'

Zoe thought it sounded horrendously technical but she had faith in Becca. She really wanted her to win because she was the best, not because she, Zoe, had deliberately blown it.

Shadrach turned up looking more than ever as if he'd had a run-in with a spiky hedge. 'You look a bit stressed,' cooed Cher.

He didn't reply, he just fell back into his seat and rubbed his hand over his face. Presumably he'd had a shower after cooking but he was still sweating.

'He's no competition, at least,' muttered Cher to Zoe and Becca.

Becca shared a look with Zoe. 'Her confidence runneth over,' she muttered.

At last, far too late for Zoe's nerves, it was time for the showing. Zoe was very glad she was first. Her agony would be over quicker.

It was weird, the contestants agreed, muttering together, to see what happened to one's food after you'd seen it on the pass. The waiters swooped into the dining room and placed the dishes in front of the judges. Only one judge from the show was there and, inevitably it felt, Zoe got Gideon. Cher pinched her arm the moment the cameras showed it was him.

He was with the cheery celebrity chef who had interviewed Zoe about her menu, another chef, two food critics, one of whom was famous for his tetchy reviews, and a woman Zoe didn't recognise.

Zoe focused on the food so hard it made her dizzy. She was glad she had something to stop her fainting or being sick or showing her emotions in some other embarrassingly physical way.

On the whole she was happy with the look of her pea cappuccino. It looked very pretty in her mother's cups and the mint did look like cocoa powder. But was the whole idea a horrible culinary cliché? She decided it was.

No one said anything for a few tantalizing seconds. 'It's good!' said one of the chefs. 'Surprisingly good.'

'Simple yet delicious,' one of the food critics agreed. 'But is soup too easy for this competition?'

'Let's see how she copes with the John Dory,' said the first chef.

'Yes,' said the blonde woman. 'It's a delicate fish. Easy to spoil.'

The coffee cups were removed and the John Dory brought in to replace it. 'This is good,' said Gideon, although speaking at all seemed to cause him stress. Was he waiting for something completely inedible or hoping Zoe had changed her mind?

'It's edible,' said the snippiest food critic, 'but I still think it's too simple for the standard of this competition. We're looking for Michelin standard.'

'Don't be so bloody ridiculous,' growled Gideon. 'It's a competition for amateurs, not chefs who've worked at their skills for years.'

Cher leant into Zoe. 'They'll cut that bit out.'

Zoe didn't reply.

'We do have a very high standard of cooking here,' said the chef. 'I'm very impressed.'

'The next course is going to be interesting,' said the snippy food critic. 'Three ways with fillet. I can't see that working. Pastry for the Wellington and a bun for the burger. It's bound to be very heavy.'

'Wait till you try it,' said one of the chefs. 'I think it's a fun idea. The pastry and the bun have been made from scratch. This girl has a good set of skills.'

Zoe was very pleased with how her main course looked on the plate. Of course she'd seen it on the pass, and had spent some moments arranging it and putting on the salad leaves, but somehow seeing it in front of a diner gave it a different dimension. But she dreaded seeing them eat it.

They all started with different bits. Gideon attacked his mini beef Wellington. 'I'm never quite sure about this "three ways with" thing,' he said. 'I feel it says more about the chef showing off than it does about producing a good meal.'

Zoe felt a bit deflated, forgetting for a minute that he mustn't like her food.

'This pastry is delicious,' said the first chef. 'Real melt-in-the-mouth stuff.'

'The steak is tender enough but very over-seasoned,' said the other chef, chewing with surprising enthusiasm.

'Never a fan of micro herbs,' said a food critic, 'but I admit they look pretty.' He took a chip. 'Excellent chips!'

'So why,' said the other food critic, 'by all that's holy, is the steak so damn salty?'

'And the burger,' said the woman. 'Otherwise it's perfect!'

Gideon was frowning. He looked up and it was if he was looking directly at her. He must know she'd over-salted the beef deliberately. She winced.

'Chips, excellent . . .' said the first food critic, making Zoe glad she'd supplied eight of them and not just six.

'Let's see what the pudding's like,' said the first chef.

'Oh wow!' said the judges when the croquembouche was brought in. There were some 'oh wow's from the audience too.

'Very clever,' muttered Cher to Zoe. 'But rather old school.'

Someone from behind shushed her, and Cher sat back in her chair with an angry wriggle.

'Well, this looks very beautiful,' said the blonde woman, 'but if those choux buns are soggy, the whole thing is just a big pile of nothing.'

'Croquembouche means "crack in the mouth",' said Gideon.

'I think we knew that,' said one of the food critics, frowning. Zoe wondered if they were rivals.

'I said it for the benefit of the audience,' said Gideon.

'Oh. Sorry, mate.'

'Well, this certainly cracks in the mouth,' said one of the chefs. 'This is some of the best choux pastry I've eaten.'

'And I love those little golden fruits,' said the woman. 'Flamboyant but completely appropriate.'

'This girl does have a flair for pastry,' said a chef.

'Hmm, pity about her totally unreliable palate,' said the other.

'Tell us, Gideon,' said the blonde, 'you've eaten all the food this girl has produced throughout the competition—'

'Her name is Zoe,' said Gideon and then paused. 'Audience!'

'Oh, sorry,' said the woman, who was really beginning

to irritate Zoe now. 'I forgot. So tell us, does she have an unreliable palate?'

Cher's nails bit into Zoe's arm. It was hard to tell which of the two were most on edge.

'I have to say that up until now her palate has been fine,' said Gideon with emphasis. He knew she'd done it on purpose.

There was a silence, during which one of the food critics had another portion of croquembouche.

'Well, we'd better write down our marks,' said the woman. 'Have you all got your score cards?'

There was a short lull between cooks, for technical reasons, and so there was time for the other contestants to congratulate Zoe. 'You did brilliantly!' said Becca. 'I do hope you win!'

'Don't you hope you win?' Shadrach asked her, surprised.

'Oh, I don't expect to win,' said Becca. 'I didn't do nearly as well.'

Cher was the next cook up. Gideon was exchanged for Fred, the cheery judge they had all loved. The other judges were the same.

'They're all going to discuss who wins at the end,' Mike explained to the room, 'but our original judges make the final decision.'

Cher's starter included foie gras, a sorbet and an almond emulsion. It all seemed desperately complicated to Zoe but Cher seemed confident and efficient.

The judges said nothing for an agonisingly long time.

'Very ambitious,' said one of the chefs.

The woman, who Zoe now knew to be Laura Matheson, the owner of a famous mini-chain of restaurants, speared some foie gras on her fork, inspected it and then put it in her mouth. She ate it but didn't speak for a long time.

The food critic threw down his fork. 'Well, I don't know about you lot but I think that sorbet tastes of slightly sweetened phlegm.'

'Gross!' said Laura. 'Did you have to say that?'

'How do you even know what phlegm tastes of?' said one of the chefs. 'There are real skills here!'

The argument went on but there was no consensus.

'Let's have the main course,' said Fred.

'Stripe me pink! A foam!' declared the food critic who'd said the sorbet tasted of phlegm. 'I thought the danger of foams was past. Apparently not.'

'You see foams on Michelin-starred menus!' hissed Cher.

It dawned on Zoe that perhaps Cher had copied her menu from a Michelin-starred restaurant. It was cheating in a way, but if she could pull it off, it would make her an awesome chef. And she couldn't help feeling sorry for her after the phlegm remark – it would be on national television.

'The calamari is well cooked,' said Laura, 'but the stuffing doesn't taste of much.'

'Hard to cook squid well,' said a chef. 'Got to congratulate her on that.'

'I've met him,' Cher whispered to Zoe, her mood improving. 'He's so sweet!'

Zoe didn't comment. She was the one being blackmailed and it seemed as if Cher was perfectly capable of sleeping her way to the top!

'Let's move on. We have time constraints,' said Fred after a nod from Laura.

'I know wood pigeon should be pink,' said the food critic, who obviously wasn't a fan of Cher's style of cooking, 'but a good surgeon should be able to bring this one back to life.'

'Oh come on! You're supposed to be a food expert! This is quality cooking!' said the chef Cher had met.

'The Brussels sprouts are very good,' said Laura.

'Yet more foie gras,' said one of the chefs. 'Has she got shares in a goose farm?'

'I want pudding,' said the food critic. 'And I hope it's a bloody good apple pie, or a crumble, something to counteract all this namby pampy half-raw food.'

It was a quartet of puddings. There was panna cotta, jelly, sorbet and a granita, all flavoured with either pear or lemon grass.

'Very delicate flavours,' said Laura.

'Too effing delicate, in my opinion,' said the food critic with nursery pudding tastes.

Cher was muttering loudly beside her as the judges moved on to the other two contestants. Becca and Shadrach watched in agony as their meals were judged. Zoe was in agony too. She had deliberately made a mistake but Becca and Shadrach – two very good cooks – both had little disasters. She might yet win!

Cher, obviously thinking the same thing, looked at her through narrowed eyes, her Botox preventing her from giving a nasty sneer.

There was a long, anguished hiatus after all the meals were eaten while the judges judged. Only the last part of this would be viewed tonight, when they gave their result. No one knew how long it would be before there was news. Cher yanked Zoe's arm and pulled her off to the Ladies.

'You did tell Gideon you couldn't win?' she demanded, having checked that none of the cubicles were occupied.

'Yes! And I oversalted my steak and my burger.'

'Oh, that was on purpose, was it?'

'Of course!'

'Not that you're likely to win anyway, your menu was so naïve and retro.' Cher checked her reflection in the mirror but made no changes.

'Then what are you worried about?' Zoe pulled at her curls and readjusted her chef's hat.

'It's you who should be worried. If they make the wrong decision . . .'

Zoe couldn't tell if Cher wanted to win more than she wanted to blackmail her. And as she still had the photographs, even if Zoe didn't win, it made her very anxious.

It seemed to take for ever. Everyone left their seats and wandered around, chatting, drinking and getting in a state.

'I don't know why I'm even thinking about winning,' said Becca as she started her second glass of champagne. 'I won't. You others were brilliant!'

'If you overlook the "slightly sweetened phlegm" thing,' said Shadrach.

'We'd all rather overlook that,' said Zoe. 'It makes me feel sick to think about it.'

'And you didn't have to eat it!' said Shadrach.

'Oh shut up! They didn't much like your collapsed soufflé. Why you even thought about putting a scoop of ice cream inside a hot soufflé, I don't know!' said Cher, her claws out.

'But it obviously tasted great!' said Zoe.

'It looked like sick,' said Cher, not to be outdone by a food critic on the cutting-remark front.

At last they were all called back to their seats to watch the final bit of judging. The celebrity chefs, restaurant owner and food critics were no longer there. It was just the judges they had come to know (and in some cases) love.

'I just think her whole menu was well balanced and nearly perfect,' Fred was saying, but no one knew whom he was talking about.

'There was some very good food there,' said Gideon. 'I thought the soufflé was fantastic.'

This gave Zoe a hiccup. Was she pleased he wasn't saying good things about her food? Or did she feel betrayed?

The discussion went back and forward until the end, when, wonderfully and horribly, it looked like Zoe was the front runner.

'I've always liked her food and she's always done brilliantly in very difficult circumstances,' said Fred.

There was a pause long enough to read *War and Peace* in. Then Gideon said, 'Can we forgive that horrendous over-seasoning on her steak?' He looked defiantly at the camera at this point and once more Zoe felt his gaze was really directed at her. She desperately wanted it all to be over so that she could explain to him she really didn't have a choice. She couldn't bear him to think badly of her.

Another pause, as long as the first, 'No,' said Fred. 'I don't suppose we can.'

'So our winner is Becca?' asked Gideon.

The other judges nodded.

There was uproar in the cinema. Cher gasped, 'No . . . no!' Becca disappeared under a crowd of friends and family, fighting to be the first to congratulate her. Zoe hardly managed, 'Well done! I knew you could do it!' before Becca was whisked away to be interviewed about how it all felt.

Cher regarded Zoe, her expression tight. She had herself under control now. 'You must be very relieved.'

Zoe nodded. 'And you must be very disappointed. You tried to blackmail the wrong contestant.'

299

Cher shook her head. 'Oh no. You've really upped your game, even with your totally old-fashioned menu. You'd have won if you hadn't oversalted the beef.' She smiled but it did not reach her eyes. 'I've still got the pictures, you know.' Her voice dripped with venom.

Zoe looked at her for a moment but didn't bother to protest and demand she deleted them from her phone in front of her eyes. She didn't want to give Cher any excuse to cause a commotion. So she turned and walked towards Mike, who was beckoning them.

'Back to the hotel to change and then on to the party!' he said.

'Do we get our make-up done?' asked Cher.

'No,' said Mike firmly. 'It's not being televised. Your make-up is down to you.'

Cher shook back her golden hair and shrugged.

Chapter Twenty-Six

As Zoe pulled her dress over her head she accepted that she had to go to the party although she was in tatters. She desperately needed to see Gideon and talk to him even if he was still ready to kill her. As she saw it, she'd had no choice but to do what she did and it was for him as much as herself. But would he see it like that? Or would he say – and he would have a point – that while Cher still had the pictures they still could be blackmailed and she had spoilt her chances of winning for nothing?

She wanted all her armour though. She wanted to be the perfect, elegant girlfriend. And it was nice to be looking glamorous for a change. He hadn't often seen her in a dress with proper make-up and good shoes. She couldn't compete with Cher, of course, who, tanned and Botoxed, plucked and shaped, was model-beautiful, but she didn't need to care about Cher any more. Did she?

By clever timing, she and Becca managed to get into the same cab. Cher was still titivating and Shadrach had gone straight from the movie theatre where they'd watched the programme to the venue. He was probably going to be at the party wearing his chef's whites, only in his case the word 'white' was no longer quite appropriate.

Mike came up to them. 'Becca! Zoe! You look amazing! Really lovely. Not that you didn't always, but now you look sort of – groomed.' He looked at Zoe particularly and she managed a smile.

'I am groomed. Really, there's not a hair out of place – anywhere!'

Mike laughed. 'Not too much information please! Becca, can I borrow you for a moment?'

Zoe would have liked Becca to chat to. She suddenly felt shy. The party seemed to be full of people shouting at each other and no one was familiar. Her mother really would have hated it.

Then she spotted Gideon. He was way over the other side of the room. She didn't want to be the one who went up to him but felt she should give him a chance to see her by moving nearer. She put on a purposeful expression as she 'excuse-me'd her way through the crowd.

As she approached her target she spotted Sylvie who'd supported her through the restaurant challenge and went to talk to her, grateful not to be 'Norma no mates' any longer.

'Hi, Sylvie! How are you?'

'Zoe! Hi! What a shame you didn't win! You would have done if you hadn't oversalted the steak. That's really not like you. I thought you had a good palate.' Sylvie seemed to take Zoe's failure to win personally.

Zoe shrugged apologetically. 'Oh, you know how it is. I got nervous.'

Sylvie shook her head still disbelieving. 'Your fish was perfect though, or looked it. I'm glad about that.'

'You were so helpful,' said Zoe. 'I'll always be grateful for what you taught me.'

'You were a good pupil!' Sylvie paused. 'What did Gideon say to you about oversalting the steak?'

'I haven't seen him to talk to since I did it,' said Zoe.

'He'll roast you alive,' said Sylvie calmly. 'He knows how good you can be. He's been telling everyone.'

This was a bit of a shock. It had never occurred to her that he would talk about her skills as a chef with other people. It seemed a bit indiscreet in the circumstances. In a moment of panic she wondered if he'd been indiscreet about anything else but realised a moment later that of course he wouldn't be. He wasn't like that. But it took her heart a moment to catch up with her head and stop fluttering like a wild bird in a cage.

Zoe braced herself. 'I'd better go and speak to him.' If Sylvie, only knowing half the story, thought Gideon would be furious then he was likely to eat her alive.

'I'll be here with a brandy and a wet towel if you need them,' said Sylvie. 'But making such a basic mistake . . .'

Zoe was just gearing herself up to have a conversation she knew wasn't going to be remotely pleasant when a very beautiful blonde woman approached Gideon from behind. Gideon, who was talking to someone, didn't notice her but Zoe and Sylvie were well placed to see how she planned to surprise him. She put her arms round him from behind and kissed his cheek. Zoe saw Gideon turn round in surprise, and then a big smile lit up his face as he took her in his arms in a bear hug.

'That's his wife,' muttered Sylvie beside her. 'I Googled him – you know, after we talked about him – in a stalkerish way, and saw it was her.'

Zoe felt herself sway and only just managed not to clutch on to Sylvie. She tried to force moisture into her mouth. She felt so sick and dizzy she wished she could faint to order. But she could hardly move. For some reason people were pressing nearer so she and Sylvie were crushed together. A discreet exit was out of the question. She looked at Gideon, willing him to glance in her direction and somehow make it all right. As she looked she saw the woman – his wife – pull him in closer. 'Darling!'

Zoe didn't know if she could hear the woman speak over the crowd or if she was just lip-reading but the woman's body language was clear as day. This woman was very, very fond of Gideon. And he seemed just as fond of her. His arm was still tightly around her waist as she leant in to talk to him. He laughed at something she whispered in his ear. Zoe couldn't bear to watch but nor could she move away. The press of people was just too much.

Then Gideon turned and saw Zoe. He smiled and beckoned her over. It was the jolt she needed to make her shift her paralysed limbs. He wanted to introduce her to his *wife*? How could he – how could anyone with any sort of heart do that?

'Not a good moment to have a chat,' she muttered to Sylvie. 'And I need the loo. Catch up later.' She started the process of escaping from the crowd but found herself looking at Gideon again.

He looked straight back at her, his expression bewildered.

He was unbelievable. Fighting tears she shook her head and began to push her way out through the crowd in earnest. She got out of the room and into the corridor. She was searching for the Ladies, wanting to be alone to get a hold of herself, when suddenly Gideon was in front of her.

He must have been far more forceful about getting through the throng than she had been. He looked confused – hurt even.

'Zoe, what are you doing? Where are you going?'

'Home!' she said instinctively.

'But we need to talk! I want to introduce you to—'

'To *your wife*? You must be raving mad!' She set off down the corridor as fast as her high heels would let her.

'For God's sake!' He chased after her and caught her arm just as she reached the corner. 'Zoe! You're being ridiculous!'

She shook her head. 'No I'm not. I'm being perfectly reasonable. You're married. Your wife is here. You obviously love each other. Let's not pretend it's anything different. We had . . .' She glanced up and down the corridor to make sure no one could overhear her. '. . . a fling. But I don't want to break up your marriage. I'm just going to go home and carry on with the rest of my life.'

'It's not like that!' Gideon looked down at her, frowning, his mouth compressed.

Zoe knew she was about to cry. She was tired, overwrought and very stressed. 'Oh, find a new scriptwriter! That line's very overused!' she threw at him.

'You're being so unreasonable!'

'Oh, am I? Well, I'm sorry I won't join in with your cosy little "ménage à trois" but I'm just too old-fashioned!'

'That's not what I meant at all!'

'It doesn't matter. I'm breaking off whatever it was we had.' Cruelly, her brain flicked back to their time at Somerby together when she thought they were a proper couple. She knew she wouldn't hold the tears back much longer.

'You can't just walk out on us!'

'Yes I can!' She paused long enough to unhook her shoes from her feet. By a miracle she spotted a sign to the Ladies and ran towards it. She could hear footsteps behind her and broke out into a sweat. She had to reach the door before he reached her.

Assistance came from an unexpected source. An American voice called down the passage, 'Gideon? Honey? There's someone you really must meet . . .'

It made him pause and Zoe got through the door.

She leant against it until she was sure Gideon wasn't following her in there and then took refuge in a cubicle.

She was splashing her face with water when Fenella and Glory came in.

'Oh, Zoe! I am glad to see you. It's such a crush in there I thought I'd never find you to say goodbye. I just want to change Glory's nappy and then we're off.'

'Oh? So soon?' Zoe suddenly felt as if her only friends in the world were emigrating, leaving her to live a long and lonely life on her own.

'Yes. We want to get back. Glory doesn't love being in the car. It's easier if we travel at night.' She put Glory down on the designated space and began unwrapping her. 'What are your plans?'

'Oh, I'll go home too, I suppose. If that is a plan.'

'Will your parents be disappointed that you didn't win?' Fen lifted up Glory's legs and slid a fresh nappy under her.

'Yes, but they won't make me feel awful about it or anything.'

'Do you feel awful about it?' Fen looked curious. 'You did so well!'

'No. No, not really.' Zoe felt so awful generally it was hard to tell how much she minded not winning when she knew if she hadn't been blackmailed she could have done – or at least had a fighting chance.

'So what will you do when you get home? Apart from having a rest?'

Zoe shrugged, really wondering if she'd ever have enough spirit to do anything again. 'Slump for a bit and then start looking for jobs, I suppose.'

'I don't suppose you'd consider coming back with us? We've a big do on at the weekend and I could really use your help. It's one of Sarah's weddings.'

Zoe considered. In some ways she wanted to go home, to be cherished by her mother, who had comforted her through every disappointment in her life. But on the other hand, at Somerby she'd be busy. She wouldn't have time to think about Gideon, or what might have been. 'I'd have to ask my mum, make sure she doesn't feel let down.'

'Give her a ring.'

Zoe got out her phone. Her call was answered instantly. 'Mum? Mum, I didn't win. I'm not at all surprised. Becca, the girl who did win, was wonderful and she finally got her nerves under control.'

'Ah, well, it was brilliant you got as far as you did,' said her mother. 'Were my coffee cups appreciated?'

'Oh yes, and they're coming back to you very soon. They're being sent by special delivery.'

'Aren't you going to bring them?'

Zoe paused. 'The thing is, I hope you don't mind, but Fen has asked me if I'll go back with them to Somerby. They've got a big do on and she needs help with the baby.' She took a breath and played her trump card. 'It would really take my mind off not winning.'

'Then of course you must go to Somerby, darling!' Her mother seemed relieved that Zoe had something nice lined up. 'And you never know, there might be a job in it for you!'

'Oh Mum, I won't stay too long, I want to hug you so much! But I do feel it's what I need to do just at the moment.'

*

307

'I'm sorry to drag you away,' Fenella apologised as they set off into the night. 'Other people's babies love their car seats and go to sleep instantly in them. Not our little Glory.'

'That's all right,' said Zoe. 'I'm glad to think I won't be running into Cher by mistake. I feel a bit like I'm escaping.' She hadn't gone back to the party. She hoped people wouldn't mind her not saying goodbye.

'Oh?' said Rupert, looking at Zoe in the driving mirror.

'Oh you know,' said Zoe, now hoping she hadn't betrayed herself. 'There's been so much publicity and things. And Cher and I have never really got on.'

'What about you and Gideon?' asked Fenella. 'Sorry to ask, but I couldn't help noticing he seemed to be with someone else at the party.'

'Yup,' said Zoe baldly. 'He's married.'

'Oh God, Zoe, I'm so sorry!' said Fenella. 'What a complete gobshite.'

Zoe nodded. 'Yup. All men are bastards, present company excepted.' She yawned loudly. 'I might close my eyes actually. I'm a bit shattered.'

'You do that,' said Fenella. 'I'm planning to do the same. We'll plot Gideon's ghastly death tomorrow.'

Zoe was tired but she wasn't sleepy. However, pretending to be asleep would mean she didn't have to talk.

The big Range Rover purred through the streets of London and on to the motorway, and in spite of her inner agonies, Zoe dozed off for real. When she woke up they were driving through the winding lanes of Herefordshire and nearly home.

Although it was summer, when they arrived back and Fenella had fed Glory, she insisted on giving Zoe a hot-water bottle and Rupert demanded she accept a stiff drink.

Taking both with her, she went up to her allocated bedroom which, unfortunately, was the one where she had slept with Gideon. Fenella put a sympathetic hand on her arm. 'I'm sorry, but the bed is made up and I don't want you going in the cowshed. I think you should be in the house, with us.'

Apart from the inevitable poignancy of sleeping in the bed where she'd been so happy with Gideon, Zoe was glad she was in the house too. The hot-water bottle and the whisky, as well as an exhaustion natural after all she'd been through, meant she drifted off almost immediately.

She awoke to birds singing and sunshine pouring in through the window. It took her a few seconds to work out where she was and why. Her feelings were so mixed she felt slightly sick, and she got up and went to the window, hoping the summer morning would soothe her.

Of course she was glad that she hadn't won so that Cher's threat of blackmail had nearly disappeared. (While she still had the pictures, Zoe couldn't completely relax.) And of course she was very happy to be at Somerby where no one could get to her. But the memory of the row with Gideon felt almost like a torn muscle or an unhealed sore. She could see his face, which had once looked at her so tenderly, full of confusion and despising her.

Not that it was all her fault. They were both responsible. But at least she had been a free agent. Gideon had a wife he hadn't mentioned. And Becca deserved to win. She was by far the best cook. But Zoe had had a good chance until she'd let her heart rule her head – and all for a man who forgot to tell her he was married.

Except she loved him. Until the parallel lines of her

head and her heart finally crossed, she would go on loving him. The trouble was, her heart didn't believe what her head knew perfectly well. She wasn't stupid, intellectually, but she couldn't convince her heart – or her body – that he was a bad man and she was far better off without him.

She had a quick shower, pulled on a sundress and went downstairs with her hair still wet and no make-up.

'I love summer,' she announced to Fenella and Rupert who were in the kitchen, 'you only have to put on about two items of clothing.' She was determined to put a brave face on it. She'd been a fool. And Fenella had warned her to be careful.

Fenella and Rupert laughed, as they were supposed to. 'Are you saying that you are only wearing two items of clothing?' asked Fen.

'Yes. You'll be relieved to hear I am wearing knickers.' She pulled out a chair and sat down. 'Where's my goddaughter this morning?'

'Still asleep.' Rupert picked up the baby alarm as if to check it was still working. 'She had a feed when we got in – which was quite late – but has, amazingly, slept soundly since. Now,' he said, rubbing his hands. 'Breakfast?'

Zoe agreed to eggs, bacon and sausages, a little surprised to find herself so hungry. Her relentlessly cheerful air was having the right effect. No one was looking at her pityingly or asking searching questions and she could just sip the mug of tea Fenella handed her and watch Rupert cook. She wasn't sure she was going to feel like cooking herself any time soon but just being in the Somerby kitchen was soothing.

'OK,' said Rupert, setting down two plates laden with food. 'Real toast or Aga toast?'

'Aga toast, definitely.'

'So, Zoe,' said Fenella, once they had all they needed in front of them, 'what are you going to do now? And why the hell did you oversalt the steak?'

'Fen!' said her husband indignantly. 'You said I had to be tactful and you go right on in with your green wellies!'

'What?' said Zoe looking between them, wondering if she could get out of this conversation.

'Fen said, "Now, Rupes, don't say anything. Be tactful! Poor girl,"' he quoted. 'And she just plunges in, no tact at all!'

'Ah.' Zoe sighed deeply. She'd been sure her sundress and jaunty attitude and enormous appetite would convince them that all was well in her world. Apparently not.

'What went wrong?' asked Fen. 'You were doing so well! There's no way you'd put on too much salt by mistake.'

'Do you think anyone else thought that?' This could be serious.

'What? That you deliberately oversalted the beef?' said Fenella, considering. 'To be honest, I suppose people who didn't know your cooking would have thought you just made a mistake.'

'But you didn't?' asked Rupert, fish slice in hand, having just added a slice of bread to the accumulated bacon fat in the pan.

'Of course she didn't!' snapped Fenella. 'She's a brilliant cook!'

'Maybe she doesn't want to talk about it,' said Rupert, pressing down the bread.

'I hope you're going to share that fried bread,' said Zoe, to put off the moment of truth.

'Of course! I'll wop it into the oven for a bit to crisp it up and get rid of surplus fat,' he agreed.

311

'I'll make more tea,' said Fenella, 'then Zoe can tell us everything.'

'Only if she wants to!' said Rupert, wopping in the bread as promised.

Fenella shook her head, set in her role as bad cop. 'Sorry, actually you don't get the choice. You have to tell all.'

'OK,' Zoe sighed. 'Tea and fried bread might be enough to make me spill the beans.'

'You can have marmalade on it if you like,' said Rupert, the good cop.

'That's all right. I'll tell.'

'The thing is – was . . .' said Zoe with her mouth full. '. . . Cher had taken photos of me and Gideon together.'

'How did she get those?' Fenella's indignation caused her to slam her mug down on the table and slop tea over the side. 'We've gone to so much trouble to make this place secure and discreet so people can come here and feel relaxed.'

'She took them while we were foraging in the woods,' Zoe explained. 'She didn't get into the bedrooms or anything.'

Fenella sighed and sat down. 'Ah.'

'You were caught frolicking in the woods, were you?' said Rupert, an eyebrow raised in mock disapproval.

'We were foraging,' said Zoe with dignity. 'But maybe we did have a little kiss.'

'That's the absolute pain of mobile phones with cameras on them!' said Fenella. 'Look at the trouble they cause!'

'That said, I'd never take photos at all if I couldn't do it on my phone,' said Zoe.

'True,' Fenella agreed. She sighed. 'So, she took photographs. When did you find out?'

'Not until we were in London before we cooked for the final challenge. She said if I won she'd take the photos to the press – I think she probably knows a paparazzo or something. Anyway, she or her uncle seem to know everyone. And she said it would bring the whole programme into disrepute, which it would, and ruin Gideon's career too.'

'What about your career?' asked Fenella.

Zoe smiled and bit her lip. 'I don't think she thought I had one. And, currently, she's right.'

'So did you tell Gideon? What did he have to say about it?' asked Rupert.

'He was furious. He said I shouldn't give in to blackmail. But as everything Cher was going to say was true, I didn't think I had any choice.'

Fenella put a sympathetic finger on Zoe's arm. 'And . . . did you fall out about it?'

Zoe almost laughed. 'He was incandescent! I couldn't make him understand that I had no choice. I had to mess up the competition.'

'I have to say, you could have done it a bit more thoroughly,' said Rupert. 'You actually cooked a blinder. That's what made me so suspicious about the salt thing.'

'Oh God, I see that now. At the time I just went into the zone – I knew I couldn't win so I didn't worry about winning, I just followed my plan. Then I decided what I was going to do to ruin it.'

'But the others made mistakes too,' said Rupert. 'You were consistently the best.'

'Rupert's a big fan of cookery competitions,' Fenella explained. 'Not sure why.'

'You're a big fan of property programmes,' he countered. 'I really don't know how you explain that. It's not as if we don't have enough property to cope with here.'

'But Rupert, do you think people will guess I threw it deliberately? This is worrying!'

'Everything else did go rather well,' said Fenella.

313

'It's mad! I know if I'd been trying to win all sorts of things would have gone wrong. I was just so worried that Gideon's career would be destroyed . . .' Her voice slowed as she realised she'd said a lot more than she'd intended. 'And then I found out about Gideon and realised I'd lost far more than a bloody competition . . .'

'I think we need more tea,' said Fenella, flapping a hand at Rupert but without looking at him. 'So you really love him?'

Zoe took a deep breath. 'It was bad enough that he was cross with me but then before I could talk to him about it, I saw them . . .' She tailed off, her throat closing up with tears.

'So you really love him?' repeated Fen gently.

Zoe nodded. 'But it's hopeless. Not only will he never want to speak to me again but he's married. I may be extremely dumb but I'm not going to waste my life being in love with a married man. Even one who did care about me,' she added.

Fenella didn't speak for a few moments. 'You're probably wise. But you did seem good together.'

'For a short while we were, although I could have done without all the guilt and stuff. And that was before I knew about his wife!'

'And don't worry about the competition thing,' said Rupert. 'Viewers wouldn't know what a good palate you have.'

Somehow this reassurance made Zoe feel worse. When the baby alarm showed signs of life she leapt to her feet. 'I'll go!'

'She's not really awake yet! You could leave her a few—'

But Fenella's words faded as Zoe flew up the stairs, grateful for an excuse to escape.

*

Sarah and Hugo arrived in time for dinner that night. Zoe acted as Rupert's sous-chef and made several sorts of potatoes and different vegetables. She wanted to keep busy and Glory could only be cuddled for a certain number of hours in the day, given that she had a mother.

They didn't talk about Zoe's situation much. They knew it would all be thrashed out later, round the table, with Sarah and Hugo. Zoe felt like a hot-air balloon with no hot air. All the cooking, the worrying, the practising and eventually doing so well had been all for nothing. Now all she had left was the sense that she'd been an utter fool, a silly girl dazzled by an attractive powerful man. Her self-esteem was about as low as it could go. Keeping busy was the only thing that could stop her flinging herself on her bed and sobbing for days.

Rupert's lavish hospitality meant bottles of champagne and Pimm's were offered when Sarah and Hugo got there.

'Have a King Pimm,' said Rupert. 'Cava and Pimm's – less sweet and four times as intoxicating.'

'I'd rather just have a glass of fizz,' said Sarah. 'Pimm's goes to my head so.'

'Have proper fizz then. We'll keep the Cava for the Pimm's.'

Zoe sipped her glass of champagne slowly. She was too worried to feel remotely celebratory. The jollifications lasted too long for her. She wanted to talk to Sarah and Hugo about her problem: Fenella had been so confident that they would have just the answer and Zoe remembered how interested Sarah had been in her plans before.

Hugo seemed to sense her anxiety and sat down beside her. He asked her gentle questions about the competition, her food and how she chose her menu while the others laughed, got knives and forks on to the table and opened bottles.

'Don't worry,' said Hugo. 'Sarah has a plan, and if Sarah has a plan, all will be well.'

Sarah's plan involved a friend with a deli. 'She's just taken it over from someone who wasn't much good at it. She wants to do a complete relaunch.'

This sounded interesting. 'Oh?'

'It's a nice little shop, in a lovely situation in a perfect deli-type town – you know, lots of foodie types who want weird—'

'Esoteric is the word we prefer,' said Rupert.

'Weird ingredients,' Sarah went on. 'But she's got a hell of a lot on. I gave her a ring this afternoon to see if she might fancy a lovely assistant . . .'

'And?' Zoe couldn't bear the suspense.

'She fell on my neck, so to speak. She'd love to have you.'

'But she doesn't know anything about me!'

Sarah shook her head. 'I told her you were a good cook, resourceful, and kept your head in a crisis. The only downside is she can only afford to pay you the minimum wage. You're worth far more but if the business goes the way it should, she'll be able to offer you more . . .'

It only took Zoe a second to make up her mind. It sounded perfect. She'd be busy and doing things she loved. It would also be good experience for when she eventually opened her own deli – which she was more determined than ever to save up for. 'It's exactly what I want. I don't mind too much about the money, I just want to be doing something. Hard work is the cure for almost everything!'

'Good for you!' said Rupert, putting a large hand on her shoulder.

'Yes, well done,' said Hugo.

Zoe put on a smile. 'So, where is this deli then? Not too far away, I hope.'

'Oh no, it's in the Cotswolds.'

'Whereabouts?' asked Zoe, pleased to think she'd be in striking distance of home and of Somerby.

'It's in Fearnley,' said Sarah. 'Just outside—'

But Rupert and Fenella had burst out laughing. 'We know where Fearnley is!'

'You do?' said Zoe. 'Where is it, then?'

'It's where Rupert's parents live!' said Fenella, getting hysterical. 'They'll probably go into the shop and you'll be serving them all over again!'

Zoe caught their amusement. 'Well, at least I know not to serve them peas or beans.'

Chapter Twenty-Seven

❧

'OK, Mum, you won't forward any letters from Gideon?'
'No, darling.'
'Or pass on my mobile number if he rings the house?'
'No.'
'Or tell him where I am?'
Zoe's mother took her daughter into her arms. 'Of course not! I know how hard this is for you. I'm not going to do anything to make it harder!'

Satisfied at last, Zoe got into her car. She'd forced the same promises out of Fenella and all at Somerby. Fenella had taken a bit longer to persuade, but it was harder for her, she'd met Gideon. She knew exactly how charming he could be. 'I won't get over him if I keep hoping for a letter or an email,' Zoe insisted. 'I must go completely cold turkey.' And for all she knew Gideon might not want to get in contact with her anyway. He was probably well and truly back in the arms of his wife and shuddering at his narrow escape.

These promises in place, just in case, two weeks after the competition Zoe drove into the little town of Fearnley. She'd been sad to leave Somerby and little Glory behind. She'd grown so fond of the whole family but she couldn't stay there. She could be found too easily and there were too many painful memories. A few days at home with her family, with Jenny on hand, had helped revive her spirits a little and now she felt a renewed sense of purpose. She might die an heartbroken old maid but she would have her own deli one day and helping Sarah's friend was a good start. She felt like two people: one carrying on as normal, a fully functioning adult, the other nursing a broken heart and wondering if she'd ever get over it.

As she looked for the shop she saw Fearnley was indeed the perfect town for a specialist food shop. A range of antique and gift shops punctuated the hotels and tea rooms and shops selling china, frocks and homewares. The town had been a tourist honey pot for hundreds of years; it was probably time it had something to cater for the second-home owners and the more enlightened retired army officers. She thought about Rupert's parents and wondered if they would buy loose tea, Bath Oliver biscuits and Gentleman's Relish if somewhere local provided it.

She spotted the shop, its windows whited out, and next to it, a little lane that led to the back of the shop and a parking space for Zoe. She parked next to a battered Transit van and got out, inspecting the back of the shop, feeling a little shy but also excited about this new phase in her life.

Astrid, her new boss, greeted her with a paintbrush in one hand and a cup of coffee in the other. She was wearing a boiler suit and a faint spattering of white emulsion.

'Hi! You're Zoe? Great! Grab a cup of coffee and then we can get started. Do you mind a bit of painting and decorating? We can talk and work.'

'I don't mind what I do, but I only do basic painting, no fancy bits.'

'Hooray! Sarah said you'd be happy to muck in and we don't want fancy bits. I just want everything fresh and white, before the chippies arrive to put up the shelving. I've got this mad idea that I want a huge long shelf right across the shop that I could put plates and decorative tins on – like you'd have in a kitchen.'

'It sounds great. I love that idea!'

Zoe wasn't quite as enthusiastic as she sounded, not because she didn't like the idea of a big display shelf running right across the shop, but because her heart ached. Just now, any enthusiasm had to be faked. But here she would be occupied morning till night. Maybe if she went to bed every night exhausted from physical activity she would sleep and not be forced to watch memories of Gideon go round in her mind on a loop.

Astrid, who knew how to delegate, soon found Zoe a boiler suit to match her own and found some pumping music on the radio. She gave Zoe the roller. 'There, do your worst with that big boy!'

Zoe smiled. She liked Astrid. Working with her would be fun.

When Astrid declared if she didn't eat something she'd drop dead from hunger, Zoe went out for sandwiches. She bought them from a small supermarket and they didn't look inspiring. A freshly made sandwich was something a good deli could provide; she decided to suggest it to Astrid if she didn't already have it as part of her plan.

'Oh God yes!' said Astrid, when Zoe put forward her idea. 'I have thought of sangers – as my grandfather used to call them – but any other ideas, however far out from left field they seem, I want to hear them.'

'Recipe cards? I could help you with them.'

'Great idea! We could gather together the ingredients and put them with a recipe. Real cooking but made easy for people! I'm so glad Sarah suggested you. You're perfect.'

'I don't know about that . . .'

'Hey, come and see what I did while you were out.' Zoe followed Astrid up the stairs. 'I made a start on the flat upstairs. It's where you'll be staying. I've just used it as an office up to now, but it has got furniture.'

While Zoe wandered round, Astrid searched a fridge downstairs for a couple of lagers to go with the picnic. It had huge potential and was actually quite big. There were two bedrooms, one mostly full of a double bed and another, mostly full of a desk and a lot of papers. Apart from that there was a largish room overlooking the street that had a sofa and an armchair in it and a tiny kitchen and bathroom.

'Do you need me to clear my stuff out of the second bedroom?' Astrid asked, handing Zoe an open bottle of Beck's.

Zoe could take a hint. 'Of course not. One bedroom is perfect.'

'And I know there isn't much in the way of home comforts but I've got a telly at my house I'll bring over and the bed and duvet etc. are new. Anything else you'd like?'

Zoe looked around. 'I just need a table for my laptop.'

'The kitchen is pretty damn bijou, ditto the bathroom, and they're both cold as charity, but we'll get it sorted before the winter,' Astrid went on.

The thought of winter made Zoe shiver, not just because of the potential cold but because she couldn't imagine how life would be in winter or if she'd still be here. And would she be over Gideon by then? Or would he still haunt her thoughts? Still, she'd spent quite a long part of the morning – ten minutes at least – without thinking about him at all. That was progress!

The days passed quickly although the hours were long. Zoe found herself doing anything from decorating to checking deliveries (trying not to wonder if the olive oil had come courtesy of Gideon's company) to helping Astrid with her press release.

'They always have a big new opening party in those television programmes,' Astrid announced.

'I know. My mother is addicted to those "rescuing a scuzzie hotel from being closed down by the health authorities" programmes,' said Zoe, dunking a ginger-nut in her tea. They were having a break from shelf-filling, perched on paint-splattered chairs, using an upturned box as a table.

'I'm addicted to them too! All those sort of makeover things – I love the one when Ruth Watson is really rude to all those aristos and they come round to her way of thinking like lambs. Mostly.' Astrid paused. 'We'll open first, in a quiet way, when we're ready and all the health-and-safety stuff is signed off, then we'll invite everyone we can think of to a massive party.' She paused again. 'I'd love you to do the catering for that, if you want to that is . . .'

Astrid had by now discovered the breadth of Zoe's talents when it came to food. She'd heard how she'd had to make canapés and cupcakes at the same time. She'd also heard quite a bit about Gideon. Having suffered her share of wrong-man syndrome she approved of Zoe's zero-tolerance policy when it came to contact.

'OK, we just need to know how many people it's for.' Zoe pulled a battered notebook from her back pocket and got out an old Ikea pencil. 'Would you want hot and cold canapés? And pudding ones?'

'Yes to everything. And . . .' Astrid eyed Zoe speculatively. '. . . what would be really good to put in the window is a croquembouche.'

Zoe sighed. 'I shouldn't have told you about that! But I have pretty much got the hang of them now I think.'

'It would be so eye-catching. And stylish,' she said wistfully.

Zoe was a cook: window displays hadn't played any part in her life up to now. 'If you say so.'

'I do! And my mate, who has a kitchen shop in a little town near Birmingham, has got a mould she'd lend me. I'm seeing her at the weekend. I'll pick it up.'

'We wouldn't be able to fill the choux buns with anything but I reckon I could make it look good. And you're right, it will draw people in.' She tapped the notebook with the pencil. 'So, how many?'

Astrid looked worried. 'They never tell you how they come up with the guest list on those programmes. We'll have to start with the local telephone directory.'

'And the local paper?'

Astrid nodded. Zoe wrote it all down.

Finally they were ready. Health and Safety had given their seal of approval (an official document they had to pin up on the wall), the paint was now dry and the shelves stocked. Zoe felt a certain amount of pride and satisfaction to think how much time and energy she had put in. If only it were her very own deli. Still, this was a good second best. Astrid had been the perfect boss and apart from the weekend she went to Birmingham and the nights spent alone in the flat above the shop Zoe really hadn't had that much time to think about Gideon. A production line of ready meals she'd got together in Astrid's kitchen also helped keep her focus on food and not love. And with free accommodation and a modest wage, Zoe knew she could survive working here for as long as Astrid needed her. With luck her heart would have mended by then.

The actual opening, as opposed to the launch, was

disappointingly low key. Astrid opened the front door of the shop and turned the sign to 'Open' and that was that.

However, they were both thrilled with how the shop looked. The long display shelf was lovely. It also provided storage for some random items Astrid couldn't think what else to do with. There was a huge Majolica-ware pot, attractive if badly chipped, that she'd fallen in love with at a junk shop. Lots of tins of olive oil as well as jars of olives and one of pickled lemons were punctuated by decorative plates, many of them donated by Astrid's mother.

'I'm so glad we decided to do that shelf,' said Astrid admiringly. 'It looks fab!'

'It was all your idea,' said Zoe.

'Yes, but you arranged the plates and things. Not doing ladders is a terrible disadvantage for a shopkeeper.'

Zoe chuckled. 'I had the other shelves as extra support. Anyway, it's done now. We can get a feather duster with a very long handle to keep it clean.'

Astrid instantly made a note. 'Excellent!'

Apart from their beloved shelf for decoration only the other shelves were loaded with the rare, the useful and the simply delicious. There was a small freezer filled with Zoe-made ready meals so the second-homers could rush in and buy something quick and easy when they'd foolishly invited friends for dinner. There was a section where ingredients were grouped together with a recipe sheet for people who wanted to cook but needed inspiration. There were organic vegetables sourced from local farms as well as a select range of 'Strictly Local' cheese and charcuterie.

Zoe was pleased to provide another outlet for some of the people she'd used during the competition. There was milk and cream from a source so local and so special it practically named the cow who had produced the milk on the carton. There was also a tray of bread pudding. The recipe had come from an old lady Astrid had run across and Zoe had made it. She and Astrid had eaten nearly the entire first batch, it was so delicious, but they had sworn not to eat any more until they'd actually sold some. 'The mark-up is so brilliant!' said Astrid. 'We always have day-old bread to use up so it costs almost nothing!'

Zoe thought fleetingly of what the other contestants might be up to. She wondered if Cher was right now being signed up as a glamorous TV presenter – she wouldn't put it past her. She also wondered if Gideon had contacted Fenella and Rupert at all and then dismissed the thought. It was no good worrying away at it like a dog with a sore leg.

As they weren't exactly rushed off their feet to begin with, Zoe was able to plan the food for the launch when Astrid was on duty, and Astrid tweaked her guest list and press release while Zoe served.

They often ate together in the evenings, most often in Astrid's little cottage, which had a tiny courtyard garden with a table that was, Astrid declared, just about big enough for two plates and two glasses and a bottle.

'I've got all the local press, the free papers and *Cotswold Life* lined up,' said Astrid, 'and a new foodie mag that's based locally. Should be good!'

'Should be excellent but how many people do I cater for?'

'Fifty,' said Astrid firmly.

'You just took that figure out of the air, didn't you?'

Astrid nodded. 'It's as good a way as any to decide! We can sell the leftovers.'

'I don't think so!' said Zoe. 'But we could eat them.'

*

A few days later Astrid was writing an order and Zoe was behind the counter, retweaking the display of Bach flower remedies, when she heard the bell. She turned round with a welcoming smile on her face but when she saw who it was she ducked down, out of view. It was Rupert's parents.

Fortunately for her, they were talking loudly to each other and weren't paying attention.

'How do we get any service? The first proper shop in the town for ages and there are no staff!'

Astrid turned round. Zoe had been there only seconds before. But not now. 'Can I help?' she asked.

'Ah! Good! Glad to see there's someone here. M'wife wants a snoop around, don't you, m'dear?'

Behind the counter, Zoe's desire to giggle increased.

She could hear Lord and Lady Gainsborough wandering round the shop, picking things up, making faintly disgusted noises and moving on. 'What in merry hell is this! Look like dried brains!'

Those must be the fantastically expensive dried wild mushrooms, thought Zoe.

'And baked beans? In a shop like this? What's that fancy label for? Where are the ones we always have? Perfectly good.'

Hmm, thought Zoe. Was the whole town full of people not prepared to pay over the odds for the special beans from America made from a traditional recipe involving black molasses?

'Algy!' said Lady Gainsborough. 'They've got that vile fish paste you like!'

That will be the Gentleman's Relish, thought Zoe, who was now developing cramp in her legs.

'Thank God there's something edible.'

Zoe wished they'd hurry up and decide whether they

wanted to buy something or not before she fell over. She also wished she'd just served them.

While she heard Rupert's father stride over to the fridge she decided that wanting no contact from Gideon had made her paranoid. He'd hardly have applied to Lord and Lady Gainsborough for details of her whereabouts. She sat down. She could hardly pop up from behind the counter now.

'Gold!' Rupert's father boomed. 'I've found gold!'

Rupert's mother rushed over. 'What in God's name have you found that's made you so excited?'

'Bread pudding!' declared Lord Gainsborough. 'I never thought I'd eat it again!'

Astrid laughed when Zoe appeared from behind the counter once she knew the coast was clear, stretching and rubbing her legs. 'That's where you were! Gotta love those wrinklies. They bought all the bread pudding. That's a tenner in the till with hardly any outlay. Apart from your skill in the kitchen,' she added hastily.

Zoe just smiled. The thought of the indignation Lord and Lady Gainsborough would have felt at being described as wrinklies was worth the cramp.

Chapter Twenty-Eight

❧

Astrid and Zoe had decided that the launch of the deli should be held in the gastro-pub two doors down from them as there just wasn't room in the shop to entertain everyone. But of course the shop would be open and people would be encouraged to amble down with their special money-saving vouchers in their hands. The very pretty daughter of a friend of Astrid's had been bribed to stand behind the counter and serve the Pimm's-fuelled punters as they arrived.

Astrid and Zoe took a last look round the room at the pub. The trays of canapés were set out along with pitchers of Pimm's and wine, beer and soft drinks.

'The trouble is,' said Astrid, obviously not quite happy with the arrangement even though they had no choice, 'it doesn't look like us. It could be any old do down the pub.'

'It's a posh pub,' said Zoe. 'But I see what you mean. We're launching the shop and the shop is sort of absent from the party.'

'Those catering trays with the canapés don't help,' said Astrid.

'I know! I'll go and get those old plates from the shop, they're huge. We'll put the food on them. It'll make it much more Mediterranean and special.'

'But they're on that high shelf,' Astrid objected. 'And Tilly won't be there for another half an hour.'

'But I don't mind ladders. I put them up there, I can get 'em down.'

Zoe had it all planned. She placed the ladder so she could pass the plates down into a basket that she had hung on it, and not have to climb down the ladder with precious china in her hands. Astrid had insisted she put her mobile in her bra so she could call for help if she got into difficulties. Only the imminent arrival of her guests stopped her going with Zoe to make sure nothing bad happened.

Zoe had carefully laid two platters in the basket and was reaching for the third, a little further away, when she heard a familiar voice call her name from the door.

Panic made her move up instead of down and she found herself off the ladder, standing on a lower shelf and clinging to the top one. 'I don't want to see you, Gideon!' she said. She was hardly able to speak her mouth was so dry.

He heard him chuckle below her. 'I don't think you have much choice.'

Zoe shut her eyes, thinking it was safer if she couldn't see him. Part of her had wondered, just for a second, if he had been conjured up by her fraught imagination. She'd been thinking of him just as she reached for the second plate, a thought prompted by the olive oil can she now knew *had* been imported by his firm.

She heard him move so he could face her but she kept her eyes tightly closed.

'Zoe, please listen to me. Let me explain. I've been trying to get in touch with you for weeks. No one would tell me where you were.'

'Good.' At least her friends and family had done what she'd asked. 'So how did you find me then?' While she couldn't see him she felt safe to ask him questions.

329

'I was staying with friends. He's a food writer and got the press release. I saw the croquembouche on it and knew it had to be you. I rushed straight down here.'

Her eyes still shut, she sighed deeply. How romantic it would have been if they actually had a chance of a relationship. What did he think he could achieve by coming to see her now? He was married! It strengthened her resolve to be firm.

'Zoe, could you come down from there? It's hard to talk to your back and your white knuckles.'

'You can't see my white knuckles! And anyway, they're not. I don't mind heights at all.' She didn't mind heights but she was getting a bit stressed by having to cling on to a couple of shelves while she dealt with Gideon. It would have helped if part of her hadn't been secretly pleased he was here. She knew she shouldn't be, but her stomach was fluttering with excitement and confusion. Her heart and her body were determined to betray her.

'Please?'

That sounded quite polite for someone more used to giving orders than asking permission or making requests.

'No.' She longed to say yes, longed to get down from her lofty situation – the high ground in every way – but she had to be strong.

She couldn't see him but she heard him sigh. 'I'm sorry to be domineering, but I think I need to take control.'

Zoe suddenly felt herself clutched around her knees and pulled backwards. She clung on to the shelves for balance and he turned round so he was facing her. The next second she was hanging over his shoulder.

'Gideon!' she said as firmly as she could. 'Put me down!' She tried not to sound hysterical but her breathing was restricted. She just hoped no one chose to come in at that moment. It was so undignified. And how dare he manhandle her like this?

'What's going on?'

Zoe spotted Astrid's gold-spangled FitFlops. 'Help! I'm being kidnapped.'

'Yes but, darling, have you seen who by?' She sounded like a bad impression of Leslie Phillips. Why wasn't she helping her out here? Gideon had obviously had time to get her on his side.

'Yes! Gideon! Put me down! We have a party to organise. I'm working!'

'I'm giving you the day off,' said Astrid, the traitor.

'Has he bribed you?' demanded Zoe. 'How will you cope? It's ridiculous!'

No one paid any attention to her. She found herself being carried out of the shop into the street. She was already red in the face so she couldn't blush any more. She'd given up struggling. It would only make her look even more ridiculous.

Fortunately, Gideon's car was parked right outside. She heard him unlock the door with his fob. Then he tipped her on to the back seat. She sat herself upright.

'Do up your seatbelt,' he said. 'Please.'

Zoe sighed deeply. The car smelt wonderfully familiar. She did up her belt.

'Where are you taking me?' she said crossly.

'Somewhere we can talk.'

She sighed again and settled back into the worn leather. What could he possibly have to say to her that would make it all better?

She thought about asking him to stop so she could sit in front next to him; she felt a bit weird on her own in the back. But then she decided that being near him was not

331

a good idea. If she got too close she might not be able to resist if he tried to seduce her again. She mustn't give in. She'd taken some small steps towards getting over him. If she tumbled into his arms at the first opportunity she'd be worse off than before. But what if he'd come to tell her he was sorry, he'd enjoyed their time together but it was over and he hoped she didn't feel bad about it? It would be gentlemanly of him to come and tell her in person but she wished he hadn't.

After about fifteen minutes of silent driving, Gideon pulled into a clearing by the side of a wood. There was a ford and a seat visible a little way up the track. The trees came down almost to the water and a patch of sunlight tinged the area with gold. It looked impossibly romantic. How ironic, thought Zoe.

'Here we are.' He opened her door and let her out of the car.

Zoe's resolve to be strong wavered and then strengthened. In the silence of the car she had decided the best way to handle the situation was to keep it light. She wouldn't let him know the effect he had on her, or how much he'd hurt her.

'This is where you produce a bottle of champagne or a picnic basket full of starched napery and quails' eggs,' she said, aiming for flippantly but not quite making it.

He shook his head. 'Sorry. I haven't got anything up my sleeve or in the boot. I didn't know if I was going to see you and when I saw the flier, well . . .' He paused and smiled. 'I flew.' He seemed nervous all of a sudden, as if unsure of himself or her. Zoe was gratified to see this at least.

Then his familiar quirky smile sent her stomach into free fall and her emotions into the sky. The combination made her feel slightly sick and weak at the knees with longing and confusion.

'Let's walk,' he suggested. 'I like your dress,' he added.

The compliment threw her rather. She was wearing a simple scoop-necked sleeveless number designed to look good under a pinny. It wasn't anything special. She suspected him of trying to make up to her. 'Do you?'

'Yes!' He held a hand out to her which she studiously ignored, shrugged and then said, 'Come on.'

'I can't go far. These shoes aren't suitable for mud.' She sounded like a petulant child, but that's how she felt. She had a deli to help launch. She didn't have time for walks in the woods.

'The path is good and we'll stop when we get to the seat. I've got so much to tell you.'

'I should be helping Astrid. There's a lot still to do. I can't just run off.'

'I'm sure Astrid will cope and you didn't run – you were carried.'

Zoe could do this. She'd hear him out. She was getting used to being with him again and her sense of humour was coming back. 'That's true and she did see it happen.'

'She seemed positively encouraging!'

'I know! She's such a romantic.' Zoe shook her head. 'She just let me be carried away like a Sabine woman.'

He paused as if remembering. 'I'm not sure it was quite like that. According to *Seven Brides for Seven Brothers* the Sabine Women were carried off in bulk.'

'Well, you know what I mean.'

He stopped and looked down at her, his eyes narrowed as if trying to read the small print of her mind. 'What I can't quite work out is whether or not there was any sort of willingness on your part when I abducted you.'

Zoe caught her breath, hoping he didn't realise that

despite her resolve, she was as utterly and hopelessly in love with him as she had always been – and she was his for the taking, if only he were free. She mustn't let him know that. Somehow she must prevent him from touching her. But there was a diffidence about him that made her hope. She wasn't even sure what she hoped for: that he'd leave her alone for ever? Or that he'd somehow stopped being married – in love – with his childhood sweetheart?

'I don't know what to say.' She didn't know what to think or how she felt either, and she certainly didn't want to admit to anything.

'Things are in rather a muddle,' he said.

'That's one way of saying you're married,' she murmured.

They'd reached the bench and although in some ways Zoe would have liked to go on walking her shoes were getting muddy and it was too late to tell him she didn't care about them.

'Let's sit down,' he said, pulling her gently down next to him.

They both gazed at the river. It was so wide and shallow it could almost be forded without wellies. Swallows skimmed the surface catching flies and wagtails went about their business reminding Zoe of a poem she'd learnt in childhood. From deeper in the woodland a bird sang. Zoe would have loved being here if she weren't so full of confusion and anxiety. He had come to find her, but why? Even if he told her he loved her it would do no good.

'I was married, but I am about to be single,' he said, breaking the silence. 'My divorce comes through next month.'

Zoe sighed deeply in reply. The couple she had seen at the wrap party didn't look on the verge of divorce. They had looked like a couple who still loved each other.

'I knew you'd find it hard to believe,' he went on. 'Because, as you threw at me before storming off, it's what every married man cheating on his wife says: "We're married in name only," or "She doesn't understand me."' He paused. 'But it's true. You rushed off without giving me any time to explain.'

Zoe felt a tiny flicker of hope. Did he really mean it? He sounded sincere but sophisticated, but wasn't this what sexy men always did when they were trying to paint themselves in a good light and get what they wanted? She shifted a little further away from him. It was agony sitting so close.

'Zoe, what's the matter? You seem terribly nervous.'

'I am!'

'Why? Are you frightened of me?' He sounded horrified.

'Of course not! Not of you exactly . . .'

'Of what then?' It was a whisper. The concern and tenderness in his voice almost made her cry.

She shut her eyes and tipped her head back, trying to focus on the birdsong. 'I've spent every second of every minute of every day since we last saw each other trying to forget you.'

'But I don't want you to. I want us to be together.'

Zoe turned on him in frustration. 'But you're *married*, and despite what you say about your divorce you looked on very good terms with your wife!'

'We are on good terms. She's a very tactile person—' He stopped, realising that he was probably making things worse. 'What I'm trying to say – in a very clumsy way, I know – is that we've always had a very easy relationship but there is absolutely nothing between us now, hasn't been for ages. She's been living in the States for years now. What can I say to make you believe me?'

'Why did she come over to see you?' Zoe said.

'She wanted me to go to America to front a cookery competition. She's a TV producer over there. Remember when I went to New York in the middle of the competition? That was to talk things through with her and the team over there. She came over here to see if—'

Zoe broke in before he could finish. 'So why didn't you go?'

He bit his lip. 'I wanted to see if there was a job for you as well. There wasn't. It took a little while to find that out. I tried really hard. But if you couldn't go I didn't want to either. Rosalind came back to try and persuade me to go anyway. She said I was throwing away the chance of a lifetime, but I just couldn't leave you.'

'Oh.' Zoe closed her eyes, trying to will back the tears threatening to seep through her eyelids and down her cheeks.

'You might not have wanted to go anyway but I had to know.'

Zoe still didn't dare look at him. Everything he was saying was giving her more and more hope but she had to be sure. 'Why didn't you get divorced before now? I mean when you realised you weren't happy in your marriage?'

Gideon sighed. 'I need to tell you everything really. We were very young. We met at university – in fact we were almost the first people we met when we got there. We fell into it really. It was companionship and lust and at the time it felt like love.'

'Isn't that what love is?'

Gideon looked at her intently. 'I don't think so. Love is when you can't contemplate life without that person, when you think about them obsessively, when you'd happily, without even thinking too hard about it, cut off your arm if it would benefit them in any way.' He made a sound, half laughter, half desperation. 'Pretty much how I feel about you really.' He picked up her hand and kissed her wrist as if he didn't know he was doing it. She didn't pull it away.

In her heart Zoe recognised every word as true. That is how it is! That is exactly how I feel about you! she wanted to say. But she couldn't afford to let him know how she felt until she'd heard everything. He still hadn't explained why they'd stayed married for so long. 'But why did you get married if you didn't feel . . . weren't truly in love?'

He shook his head. 'We talked about this recently, and decided it was a combination of family pressure, the fact that we got on so well, and that we were both very ambitious. She had the offer of an amazing job. We knew we couldn't go to America together unless we were married. Let's just say it seemed like a good idea at the time.' He paused. 'And then time passed and we went our separate ways. But we stayed friends, and we sort of forgot about getting a divorce. It never mattered before. In fact – and I am being honest here although it doesn't reflect well on me at all – it was sometimes useful to be able to say I was married.'

Zoe shuddered to think how many hearts had been dashed on the rocks of his indifference.

'But now . . .' Gideon paused.

'But now what?'

'Now it matters because I've met you. So when I went to America I told Rosalind I wanted to start divorce proceedings. And that was one of the other things she came over to tell me: that we'd both soon be single.'

Zoe's heart had begun to sing, but then it jolted again. 'Someone I met – Sylvie, you probably don't remember her – Sylvie said she thought you were really in love with someone else, someone in your past.'

'I do remember Sylvie. I'm not that much of a Casanova. But she was wrong about the lost-love thing. I was just always looking for the one.' He looked at her, and Zoe noticed that uncharacteristic hint of diffidence again. 'Does that make me sound like a teenage girl?'

Zoe smiled, biting her lip. 'It does a bit.'

'Sorry. Not good for my image.'

'Your image is fine.'

'Well, that's something. But I want everything else to be fine too. In particular, I want you to trust me again.' He grinned suddenly. 'And if you still fancy me – well, we can go from there.'

Zoe found she was smiling too and the smile went from a twitch at the corner of her mouth to a full beam in seconds. She flung herself into his arms and a second later they were hugging and kissing and laughing. And then he gripped her so tightly she couldn't breathe.

'I've missed you so much! I would have found you much earlier if I hadn't felt I had to get everything settled between Rosalind and me before I looked for you.'

'Where would you have looked?' she said to his shirt, which now had a couple of buttons undone.

'I'd already tried Somerby, your house—'

'I made them promise not to tell you where I was.'

'And they didn't! Your mother was really sweet.'

'You charmed her?' she said accusingly.

'I did but she still wouldn't tell me. Took her out to lunch and everything.' He paused, laughing at her sideways. 'I checked her out. If you end up looking like she does you're a good long-term prospect.'

'Oh, am I? And have you a father I should check out?'

'I certainly have! And he's got almost all his hair so you're on to a good thing.'

She nestled into his chest and sighed happily.

'What are you thinking?' he asked her after a few moments.

'I'm wondering if I'd still love you if you were bald,' she said.

'Monkey! Of course you would!'

It took them a little while to settle the argument but as they walked back to the car, arms entwined, he said, 'Oh, and I got some other little bit of unfinished business sorted out.'

'Oh? What?'

'Cher and the photographs.'

Zoe felt a flutter of anxiety. Those wretched photographs, she'd hoped to never hear them mentioned again.

'I can't imagine she gave them up easily. I've been worrying about them, on and off.' She didn't want to say, even now, that her thoughts had been so full of him that Cher's attempts at blackmail seemed almost unimportant.

'It was quite easy actually. I took her for a drink. She was very happy to accept the invitation. And then I put it to her if she did anything with the photos the television show wouldn't be aired and her big break would be lost for ever.'

'So did she delete the photos there and then?'

'Yup. And from her laptop too.'

'But she might have backed them up?'

'I'm afraid I was very underhand. I found out that she isn't remotely techie. So it's possible, but unlikely. And even if she has, I think the threat of not starring on a primetime cookery show will keep her quiet.'

'Thank God. I do regret throwing the competition but

339

at the time it felt as though I didn't have any choice – for both our sakes.'

'I know you were thinking about my career – that was one of the things I was angry about. But, actually, the show has been shown to a few select people and you come across very well. I'm sure someone will back you to open a deli if that's what you still want.'

'It is. I've had such fun with Astrid. And talking of which, I must go back.'

He kissed the top of her head. 'And I'll go back and bring my friend to the launch. He edits a very upmarket food magazine and will be a good contact for Astrid. And then I'm going to book the most luxurious hotel bedroom in the Cotswolds to take you to after the launch. And there I will tell you and show you exactly how much I love you . . .'

'And let me count the ways?' She giggled.

'You're shocking! Do you think of nothing but sex?'

'But that was poetry! And sometimes I think about cooking.'

'I'm glad to hear it. And I'm happy to attest that you're very good at both.'